Embers of Analon

THE EMBERBORN · BOOK ONE

PAUL MICHAEL WINTERS

MAELSTROM PRESS

A Maelstrom Press publication
maelstrompress.com

EMBERS OF ANALON

Ebook ISBN: 978-1-965643-04-4
Paperback ISBN: 978-1-965643-05-1
Hardcover ISBN: 978-1-965643-02-0

Cover Illustration by Cynthia Sheppard
Cover Design by Valerie Gomez

First edition 2026

Content Warnings:
This novel contains depictions of violence, imprisonment, and persecution, including state-sanctioned abuse. It includes themes of grief, trauma, betrayal, and familial separation. There are scenes involving sexual content between consenting adults, references to parental murder, rodents, and harm to enslaved individuals. This story also portrays emotional distress, panic reactions, claustrophobia, and moral injury. Reader discretion advised.

To Mom, who read *The Hobbit* to me as a child. Your unforgettable Gollum impression sparked my lifelong love of fantasy.

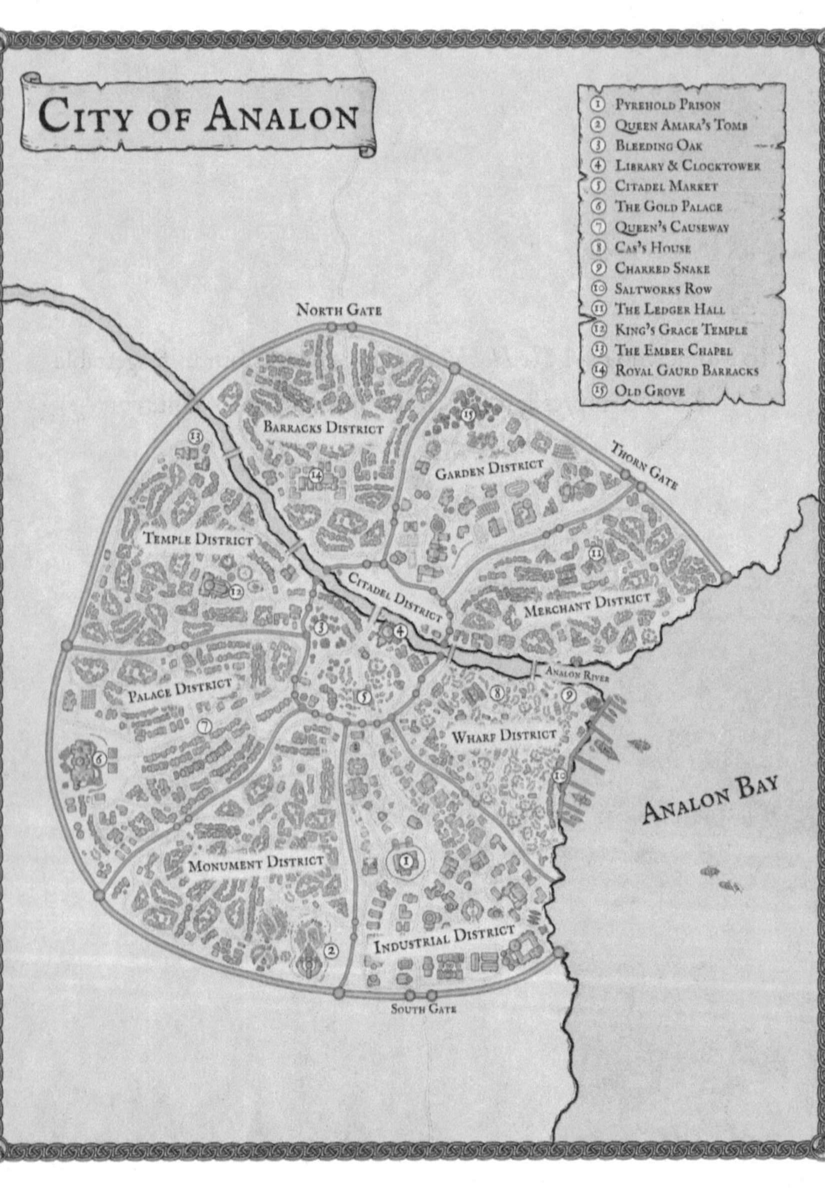
City of Analon
1 Pyrehold Prison
2 Queen Amara's Tomb
3 Bleeding Oak
4 Library & Clocktower
5 Citadel Market
6 The Gold Palace
7 Queen's Causeway
8 Cas's House
9 Charred Snake
10 Saltworks Row
11 The Ledger Hall
12 King's Grace Temple
13 The Ember Chapel
14 Royal Gaurd Barracks
15 Old Grove
North Gate
Thorn Gate
South Gate
Barracks District
Garden District
Temple District
Citadel District
Merchant District
Palace District
Wharf District
Monument District
Industrial District
Analon River
Analon Bay

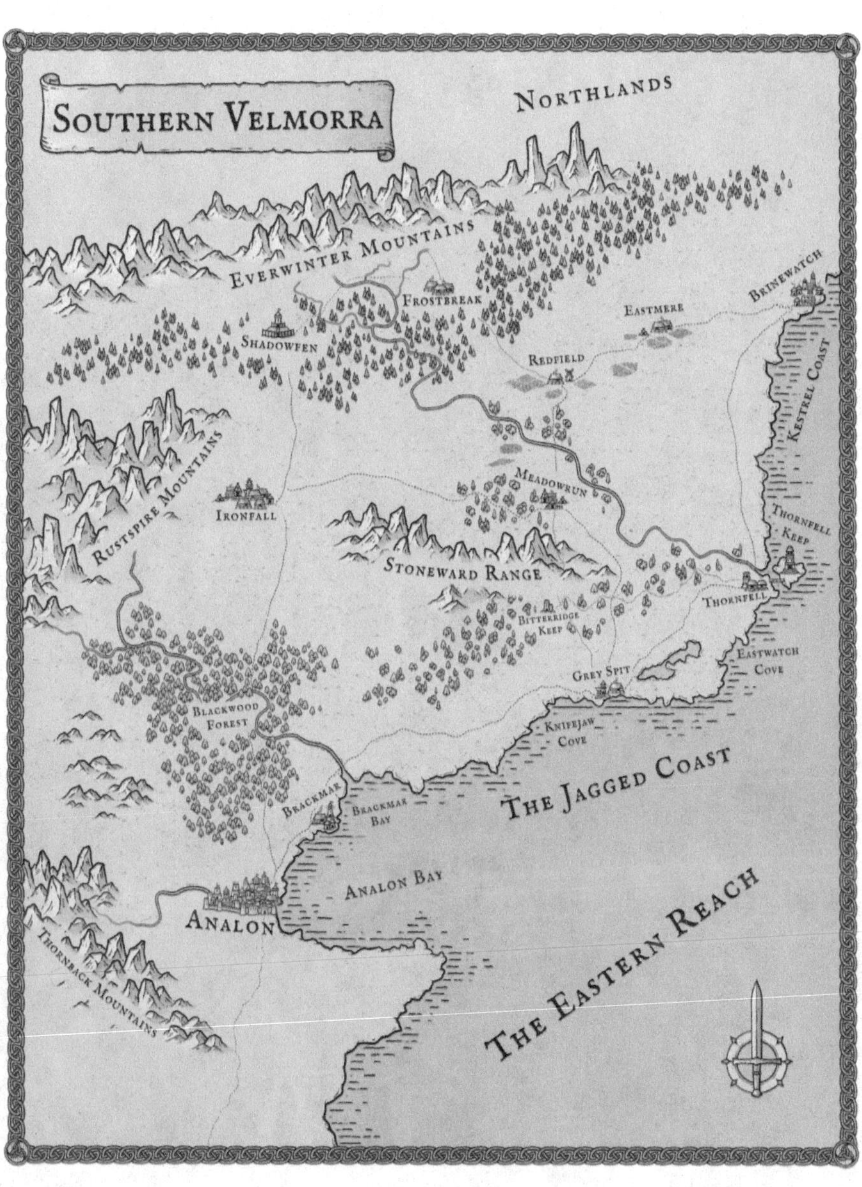

Southern Velmorra
Northlands
Everwinter Mountains
Frostbreak
Shadowfen
Eastmere
Brinewatch
Redfield
Kestrel Coast
Rustspire Mountains
Ironfall
Meadowrun
Thornfell Keep
Stoneward Range
Thornfell
Bitterridge Keep
Eastwatch Cove
Grey Spit
Blackwood Forest
Knifejaw Cove
The Jagged Coast
Brackmar
Brackmar Bay
Analon Bay
Analon
The Eastern Reach
Thornback Mountains

Part One

Chapter One

On a Knife's Edge

Every night I went out looking for coin, but also for calm. Picking locks made my mind go truly quiet, the only time I felt in control. Precision was my anchor. Danger reminded me I was still alive.

As I walked down the darkened alley, my fingers instinctively went to the locket around my neck, the metal worn smooth where I had rubbed it a thousand times, all to find a little peace.

From the outside, the Charred Snake seemed similar to countless other taverns in the sprawling Wharf District of Analon: siding in desperate need of repair, cracked windows, and the stink of booze, bile, and piss wafting through the air. A typical rowdy tavern bustling with life. Teon, a large man with a bushy brown beard and a steely demeanor, guarded the door. As I approached, he waved me in.

"Garrick's expecting you," he said in a gravelly voice, gesturing toward the door in the back of the tavern.

I nodded with a tight smile, then entered.

Sailors and fishermen with mugs of ale, cider, and other spirits were everywhere, sitting at long tables in front of a roaring fire in various stages of drunkenness. Despite it being early summer, the night air still had a chill.

Several women and men catcalled as I wove through the crowd. Something about my slender build, dark hair, and sun-warmed skin seemed to invite it. But I ignored them all and continued on my way. I wasn't immune to flattery, but I wanted a man who did more than sit around in a tavern getting drunk.

"Little fun for a silver?" one man slurred while reaching for my crotch.

I swatted his hand away as I passed. "Fresh out of coin."

"No," the man said with a drunken smile, chin resting on his mug of ale. "I mean I'll give *you* a silver."

I held back a laugh. At least he was close to my age, and he wasn't half bad-looking—he had pretty eyes, anyway. Losing myself to temptation had an appeal, but it might loosen what held me steady, and I wasn't sure I could regain my control.

"Another time," I said.

He made an exaggerated frown fueled by too much ale, but his disappointment melted away when a man set a new tankard in front of him.

I pushed through the crowd, ignoring the rest of their lewd remarks. At the back door, I knocked three times in quick succession, followed by two slower knocks. A booming voice came from inside. "Come in!"

The small back room had few furnishings except for a large wooden desk in the middle, where my friend Garrick sat in a chair that creaked under the weight of his substantial frame.

"Ah, Cassian!" he said with a grin that pulled at the scar on his cheek, pale against his dark skin. "How's my best man? Ready to celebrate, I see!"

I sighed. "Do you have a job for me or not?"

He laughed. "Cas," he scolded playfully, "if you don't get drunk and sack up with some lad on your twenty-first birthday, then when in all the hells will you?"

I shook my head and waved him off. "Let's get on with it."

"Very well," Garrick grumbled as he rooted through the papers on his desk. "You'll like this one. Nasty bloke. Practically begging to be separated from his coin."

"Nastier the better." Of course, I took the jobs for the coin, but a large part of the appeal was exacting vengeance on those who had earned it. And if I had a personal connection to them, so much the better.

Garrick smiled as he found what he was looking for. "Aha! Thank dust." He handed me a parchment with a rough sketch of a floor plan and some notes scrawled in the margins. "Here's what we got from the kitchen maid."

I scanned the map and the notes, locking them in my memory. The home was three stories tall and obnoxiously large, but straightforward paths led to the safe from various windows. "And you're sure this is accurate?"

"The maid has no love for this family, that's for damn sure. They threw her out on the streets last month for slapping The Butcher across the face when he tried to get under her skirt," he said.

The Butcher. The name hit me like a punch. This connection was almost *too* personal.

Garrick continued, "Poor lass barely escaped with her life. But I would have paid gold to see the look on Orlik's face!"

Orlik "The Butcher" Leonom was the king's top lieutenant, well known throughout the land for carrying out the Crown's cruel edicts with ruthless efficiency. And I had personal experience with that.

"That man is a bastard all around," I said, my voice dripping with contempt.

Garrick looked up with concern in his eyes. "Stay focused, Cas. Remember the job."

"I will," I said, shoving my rage down deep. But if I were to run into The Butcher, it might take all my effort not to go out in a blaze of bloody vengeance. I fumbled for the locket around my neck as my sister Elena flashed in my mind. There was more than just myself to consider.

I breathed deeply. My heart rate slowed. A calm descended over me.

I dropped the map on Garrick's desk, spun around, and headed for the door. "Be back soon."

"You don't want the map?" Garrick asked.

"Don't need it," I replied without looking back.

Elaborate homes with ornate facades flickered in the torchlight. The cobbled path was pristine, not a stone missing or a single piece of trash strewn about. Even the damn alleyways of the Garden District were better maintained than the major roads of the Wharf District. The rich and privileged demanded it.

Slipping around shadowed corners, I made my way down the alley. Anything less than utter silence was a failure. A single misstep, and a dog would bark. A moment too long in the torchlight, and the guards would sound the alarm. At best, I'd ruin the job. The worst case was a trip to the Pyrehold prison—almost worse than death, if the rumors were to be believed.

I scanned the buildings for the family crest of my latest mark. I soon spotted it: two torches danced in the gentle evening breeze, illuminating the profile of a lion's head engraved on the stone wall, gilded in gold—a symbol of respect and fear in the city of Analon. To me, it evoked only disgust and fury. So much rot hidden behind such a pristine exterior was hard to fathom. I closed my eyes and fought down the rage that threatened to spill out. Tonight it would only serve to distract me.

Refocused, I scanned the back of the building. Most of the windows were too exposed, but a third-story window with a generous ledge was shrouded in shadows. The climb would be easy, no more than thirty feet, but it would leave me vulnerable to prying eyes. Speed was critical.

To most, the wall looked sheer and flawless, but the minor imperfections in the mortar would serve as my toeholds, and the subtle cracks in the stone blocks were all my fingers needed to find purchase. In five beats of my heart and two kicks, I was on the ledge.

I paused in the shadows. No barking dogs, no rush of footsteps, no shouts of alarm.

I gave the window's handle a quick tug and—locked, of course. But a lock was only a suggestion, and one I chose to ignore. I pulled a thin metal tool from my pouch and slid it into the gap between the windows. With a snap of my wrist, the latch disengaged, and I slipped inside the house without a sound.

Everything was exactly as the map had specified. As I crept down a passage in the darkness, I couldn't help but wonder which of the doors led to the personal chambers of Orlik Leonom. It could be over so quickly with a simple slash to his throat—a fitting end, given my parents' deaths. The memory flashed in my mind, an image so horrible that it had left a permanent stain, discoloring everything. I clutched my locket so tightly that it nearly drew blood.

The faint echo of footsteps down the hallway brought me back to the present. I choked down my rage and slipped into a shadowed alcove, taking deep breaths, slowing my heart.

But mixed in with the clatter of boots on stone was another sound: the soft pads and clacking nails of a beast on four legs. This complicated things.

The clacking grew louder. I felt it in the soles of my feet before I heard the sniff. Hiding from humans was easy, but a dog?

I thumbed through the vials on my belt, slipping one out. A quick twist of the vial's cap revealed a light purple liquid—a concoction of my own making. A single drop would be enough to cover my scent, even from a canine's superior sense of smell. With the slightest flick of my wrist, a splash of liquid dropped onto the stone at my feet, followed by a fleeting puff of smoke.

I waited in the shadows, melting into the stone wall behind me, as the figures approached. An enormous man dressed in a guard's uniform appeared from the far end of the hall, carrying a flickering candle. Nearly as broad as he was tall and carrying a sword at his hip, he walked alongside a gigantic beast that looked to be half dog and half wolf, with massive jaws that could rip me apart in a heartbeat. I held my breath.

The pair walked past the alcove. Just beyond it, the wolf-dog paused, stopping to sniff. My heart pounded so loudly in my head that it was hard to believe they couldn't hear it.

"What is it, boy?" the man whispered to the dog while peering into the darkness feet from where I stood.

The dog whimpered, raising its snout and sniffing some more. Wound up like a spring, I got ready to sprint for my life. Escaping would take all of my speed and skill.

The dog huffed, almost a sigh, and sniffed again. Then he padded away, apparently satisfied, tugging his master along.

Only when they turned the far corner of the hallway did I dare to breathe. I uncoiled, releasing the tension in my limbs. Dust, that was close.

Now fully focused on the job and a half step more cautious than before, I descended two flights of stairs and navigated the first floor until I found the grand study. Embers in the giant stone hearth cast a dim golden glow throughout the room, but shadows still lurked in every corner. The char of smoke permeated everything. Rich woven carpets lined the floor, and padded chairs upholstered in elegant fabrics surrounded the fire, all stinking of opulence.

On the far side of the room, a painting of a beautiful young lady hung on the wall next to an ornately carved wooden desk, just as the map had shown.

I lifted the portrait to reveal a small locked iron door. I pulled the lockpicks from my pouch. My mind focused as the tumblers fell into place. With a barely perceptible click, the lock disengaged.

I gently pulled on the door, testing the iron hinges. They groaned at even the slightest tug, impossibly loud in the silent room. A drop of salve from a vial in my belt was all it took to silence them.

Beyond the small iron door, a velvet bag of gold coins rested on a leather-bound book. All my risks had paid off. I couldn't hold back my smile.

The book had the word *Emberborn* embossed on the spine—the name of an extinct race of people who supposedly had magical abilities. To me, they were no different from fairy-tale creatures like dragons or imps.

But under King Tarnasau's rule, even uttering the word *Emberborn* was a death sentence. So why would the top lieutenant of the king have a book about them locked up in a safe?

As I reached for the gold, the hairs on the back of my neck stood on end. A charged energy flowed through the room, that subtle shift that occurred when another presence was near. The sharp, metallic scent of ozone mixed with bright citrus assaulted my nose. Where in all the hells had that scent come from?

With the bag of gold in hand, I spun on my heel and surveyed the room. In the opposite corner, cloaked in shadows, were two glimmering eyes. I might not have spotted them if I hadn't been looking, but they were undeniably there.

This was no normal person who stared back at me, no servant or lord of the house. This was a fellow thief.

When two thieves attempted to claim the same prize, we followed a protocol—a parley, if you will. Just above a whisper, I uttered the code: "When two coins are in dispute..."

I waited with a hand on the hilt of my dagger. If this thief adhered to the code, all would be well. If not...well, I'd worry about that when the time came.

A gentle voice whispered back, "...each will take one, or both will get none."

I let out my breath as a cloaked man left the shadows. Shimmering golden eyes flashed in the dim light, but the rest of his face was covered by a mask. Those eyes—they were almost glowing.

"I stake no claim to the coin." The voice was as soft as a gentle breeze, almost melodic. "Just the book. Those are my terms."

"Agreed," I said without a moment's hesitation. I almost laughed at my luck, but then, as my brain caught up with my tongue, my mistake became obvious. "Wait," I said. "Why is the book so valuable?"

Before I could react, he was behind me, and a blade was at my throat. I'd never encountered such a fast and silent opponent, never met someone faster than me. I didn't even see him move. The very idea made me flinch.

"You're in no position to negotiate." The melodic voice turned as sharp as the blade. "Those are my terms. Accept them or die." With each word, his breath tickled my neck.

"I accept your terms gladly." The words tumbled out of my mouth, as I very much did not wish to die that night. An opponent had never bested me—not once—so this was very intriguing.

The clomping of boots echoed in the hallway. We both froze, the blade still at my throat, as the sound grew steadily louder.

The footsteps approached the door, paused, then continued down the hallway. Only then did I realize the blade was no longer at my throat. I spun around. The only door in the room was shut, and the curtains drawn over the window were undisturbed, but the thief and the book were gone. The smell of ozone mixed with citrus hung in the air again, like sucking on a lemon at the start of a storm.

On top of my bag of gold sat a small piece of parchment that hadn't been there a moment ago. It was entirely blank. Along with the familiar woody scent of papyrus were the aromas of chamomile and ginger, ingredients suitable for two purposes: making excellent tea, and—along with a few other specialty items—writing hidden messages. This golden-eyed thief was becoming more interesting by the moment.

I tucked the note into my breast pocket, stowed the gold in my pack, and then headed for the exit.

I retraced my steps to the window and sped up the stairs as fast as silence would allow. Just as I reached the third floor and turned down the hall, a loud ruckus came from below. Horns blared. Barking, shouting, and the sound of boots on stone echoed up the staircase.

"They went this way!" a man yelled from below as clomping feet grew steadily louder.

Now that stealth was no longer the priority, I broke into a sprint, lifting my mask to cover my face. I raced toward the room with the shadowed window as my heart beat against my chest.

I barreled into the room and smacked directly into something hard and unforgiving. My vision swam with stars as I fell back, landing hard on the floor with a grunt. Standing directly above me was a guard dressed in studded leather armor, smelling of ale and stale bread. Solid man—felt like a damn wall.

"Well, what do we have here?" the guard said with a sardonic grin as he reached for his sword. "Looks like I found a rat."

Chapter Two

No Clean Exit

The first trick to besting an opponent who outmatches you is to avoid them completely. With that option off the table, I relied on my reflexes, fighting through the panic clawing at my chest.

The guard reached for his sword, shifting just off balance. I swept my leg in a broad arc, smacking his legs and knocking him down. He hit the ground hard with a grunt and a clatter of studded armor that echoed off the walls.

With a moment's advantage, I jumped to my feet and leapt over him, heading for the window. The bastard was faster than his oaf-like appearance suggested, and he swiftly pulled out his dagger. There was a sharp sting in my calf as his blade sliced my skin, but I gritted my teeth and continued.

In seconds, I was outside the window, leaving a trail of blood behind.

Perched on the ledge, I sized up my options. The guard inside was racing toward the window, and three guards patrolled the alley below. One of them pointed upward. "There he is!"

So much for an easy escape.

As guards yelled and dogs barked, I climbed to the roof in half a heartbeat. Slate tiles slick with evening dew made every step treacherous and potentially my last. I skittered gingerly to the peak and tiptoed along the narrow top ridge. As I raced toward the end of the building, guards poured out of dormer windows on either side. It was an impossibly far jump to the next roof. Why did rich people's alleyways have to be so damn wide?

Guards scrambled up the slope, slipping on the tiles and reaching for my feet as I danced above them.

One guard leapt, grasping my ankle as he fell forward. "Gotcha, ya little runt!"

I frantically shook my leg, trying to keep my balance. His grip slipped on my blood-soaked ankle. Despite the pain, I laughed at my bad luck turned good.

With guards closing in all around me, I had only a moment to decide my fate. The jump to the next rooftop was too far. The drop to the ground was too long. I'd never survive.

Across the street and one story down, a wooden balcony jutted out, perhaps just close enough for me to reach. Running as fast as I could along the ridge, I kicked off the edge of the roof with every ounce of strength I had, and leapt into the unknown, hoping for the best.

I stretched out my hands, grabbing for the railing. My body slammed against the balcony, knocking the breath from my lungs and making me retch. Cracking sounds rang out as the planks beneath my fingers splintered. The world tilted. The entire structure collapsed under my weight, and I dropped to the ground, tumbling into a hay trough amidst a shower of broken wood.

The trough broke my fall—barely. My head slammed back against the hard surface, and stars burst behind my eyes. Splinters of the balcony rained down as darkness threatened to overtake me, and the fingers of unconsciousness tickled my senses, tempting me to succumb to the darkness. Only the hollering guards dragged me back from the edge. I jumped out of the trough, fighting my nausea, the pain in my ankle, and my swimming head as I raced down the alley.

“He went this way!” a voice called out over the barking of dogs.

My breathing was heavy, and my limbs felt weighed down with lead. The guards were closing in fast, and outrunning them would be next to impossible. I could think of only one way to escape, and I wasn’t happy about it. At the next side alley, I jump-kicked off the edge of a building to keep up my momentum.

At the end of the alley was a hole barely big enough to slip through that led deep underground.

The storm drains of the city of Analon were famous throughout Velmorra, a modern marvel built to prevent floods during the torrential spring rains. They had the bonus of being a convenient—albeit claustrophobic—escape route. As I ran toward the hole, I took off my pack and held it over my head. It would be a tight fit, and I needed to be as narrow as possible.

The guards chased behind me as I leapt toward the hole feetfirst. Direct hit. I slid down the pipe, which was barely large enough to fit my slender frame, and prayed that it didn’t narrow too much on the way down. Getting wedged in a drainpipe was the stuff of nightmares.

What I hadn’t anticipated was how an open gash on my leg would feel against the rough stone as I slid down. Maybe this wasn’t the best idea. I screamed out in pain.

After what felt like an eternity but was probably only a handful of seconds, I dropped into a massive tunnel made of stone. My feet splashed into a sluggish and musty stream of water.

No sound came from the hole above. None of the guards could fit through it, even if they wanted to follow me, and the stale air covered my scent from the dogs. I was safe for the moment.

A rodent scurried along the edge of the stream, pausing long enough to look up and sniff, wriggling its nose at me.

“Well, you don’t smell great either,” I said. The rat scurried away without a sound.

I could have left the drains at the nearest exit, but I continued southward toward the Wharf District and the Charred Snake. Better to stay down here a little longer than go topside too early and get my head chopped off. Plus, I needed time to think.

I'd never had such a narrow escape. I still didn't know how the guards had discovered me. My mind drifted to the thief with the golden eyes. A few details were gnawing at my thoughts.

First, I had never met a soul who could best me in the shadow arts, and yet this thief had run circles around me. Very intriguing. Very worrying.

Second, those golden eyes of his had almost seemed to glow. The image stuck in my mind. And why did the smell of ozone and citrus follow him around?

Oddest of all, he hadn't cared about the gold. He had wanted only the book, which meant he traded in information.

I rubbed the edge of the parchment he'd left me, still safe in my breast pocket. At home, I'd have the ingredients, the fire, and the quiet calm I needed to decipher it. I was eager to learn its secrets, but first I had a few stops to make.

When I finally emerged from the sewers, I found myself at the edge of the Merchant District, right near the Wharf District. Blood still flowed from the wound in my leg. I wouldn't get far without attracting attention. I could use a good scrub anyway, so I looked for a place to clean up.

Analon was famous for its luxurious baths, and one of them was only a short walk away. Though they were exclusively for the high-born, one could usually gain admittance with the proper form of persuasion. As I approached the marble-arched entrance, the attendant at the front eyed me suspiciously, but he quickly looked the other way after a few coins made their way from my bag to his hand.

The air was thick with steam, obscuring me from prying eyes. Vague shapes moved through the mist hanging over the vast marble pools. I stripped off my clothes and headed for the nearest bath.

My skin tingled as I stepped into the piping-hot water. Once submerged, I scrubbed as best I could, taking particular care to clean the gash on my calf. It was only skin deep, but it still stung like all the hells of the world combined.

One vial in my belt contained an excellent antiseptic and cauterizer, something my father had taught me to craft when I was younger. He'd been a brilliant man and our town's local physician. But the local townsfolk had leered when he'd set a broken leg or used a salve on a wound, whispering "wizard" under their breath. They were gullible fools.

That was all a long time ago. I fought back the waves of grief that inevitably welled up anytime my mind drifted to my father. Fingering my locket to quell the memories, I focused on the task at hand.

The pain was fast and fierce as the healing liquid seeped into my cut. White foam formed around the gash. I bared my teeth, hissing in a quick breath. The cauterizing felt far worse than the wound itself, but it was nothing compared to the pain of an amputated leg lost to the ravages of infection. I had witnessed many gruesome things under my father's tutelage.

After disinfecting my wound and cleaning up with the bath salts provided in glass jars along the pool's edge, I waded out and dried by the fire.

Now that I was more or less presentable, I continued on my way.

When I arrived at the Charred Snake, it was far later than expected, and the typical din of the tavern had fallen silent. Teon sat just outside the front door, snoring loudly, lost to the world. My eyes widened when I saw a mark written in charcoal next to the door. It had not been there earlier that night. Two snakes intertwined, forming an *o* and an *e* casting a shadow in the shape of a flame. I knew this mark well: the Order of Emberlight. These tags appeared all over town, and though their purpose wasn't clear, it made me worry that something had happened. I rushed inside.

My knocks on Garrick's door went unanswered, which made me fear the worst. I carefully cracked open the door and spotted Garrick face down on his desk, and my pulse shot up. "Garrick!"

He stirred with a loud snort, blinking—only asleep, thank dust.

"There you are, Cas. I tried to stay up. What took you so long?" he said, rubbing the sleep out of his eyes.

"Long story."

"Care to elaborate?"

I didn't particularly. My eyelids were heavy, and I wasn't exactly proud of what had happened, so I deflected. "First tell me why the Order of Emberlight tagged your wall."

"Bloody hells!" Garrick said, jumping up. "What in the dust do they want with me?"

He dashed out of the tavern with me on his heels. Garrick took a quick glance at Teon, asleep on the job, and sighed. "Useless." He rubbed away the charcoal with the edge of his shirt until the image was just a dark smudge.

The Order of Emberlight intrigued me, and a pang of regret hit, which Garrick picked up on the moment he looked my way. "Cas, they're nothing more than a band of vigilantes and rebels who will all end up dead."

"Isn't that what I am, too?"

"The jobs you do are only a flea on a dog. The Order of Emberlight is trying to kill the damn dog. And it's a dog with very sharp teeth."

Garrick's dismissal of my work was like a slap in the face. Half the reason I did what I did was to mete out justice in the only way I could.

"That's the point," I said. "I *want* to do more."

Garrick gave me a measured look. "Not at the expense of your life," he said, and the look on his face said the rest: *Don't leave Elena to fend for herself.*

He was right, of course, but that didn't make it easier. From the moment I'd heard of the Order of Emberlight, I'd wanted nothing more than to join them. But I had also promised my mother I'd keep my sister safe—her dying wish. That was my *real* job.

"C'mon," Garrick said, ushering me back to his office. "Let's finish our business. Seriously, though, what took you so long? It's not like you. In fact, I'm not sure you've *ever* been late."

All the problems of tonight came rushing back. Garrick continued to stare. He wouldn't let this drop without some explanation. But I didn't want to mention the other thief, at least not until I knew what I was dealing with. First I'd decipher the parchment, and then I'd decide what to tell Garrick.

So I simply said, "Guard problems."

His eyes opened wide. "Were you seen?"

"I had my mask on." Technically the golden-eyed thief had seen me, but I didn't want Garrick to worry—or scold me—about that.

"Thank Queen Amara." He sat back down at his desk and let out a long breath of relief. "Did you get the gold?"

I removed the sack of coins from my bag and handed it to him. It was hard to hold back a smile.

"Excellent." Garrick emptied the heap of gold onto his desk and split it into three piles of varying sizes. "This is for the kitchen maid," he said, pointing, "and this is my twenty percent commission." Finally he tapped the largest pile. "And this is for you, Cas. Good work tonight. Not a bad haul."

Garrick took a decent cut, but he was fair. He helped to find me targets and provided intel. He knew my preference was to hit only targets who were truly bad people or had done my family harm. He was the middleman and my only point of contact. It was best to minimize the number of people I interacted with.

I scooped up my share of the gold and stashed it in my pack.

"I'll be back tomorrow night," I said.

Garrick's brow crinkled. "Cas, considering what happened tonight, maybe we should let things cool down for a bit."

Annoyance tinged with grief built in the pit of my stomach. I took a deep breath. "I need this."

Garrick's expression softened, and he spoke in a whisper. "This won't bring them back, you know."

"I know that!" I shouted, surprising even myself with the anger that sprang up like wildfire. But he didn't have to drag my parents into this. My face heated, and I worked to regain control. Garrick looked at me with pity, which made me even angrier, so I turned away before I said something I would regret.

After a few deep breaths, my pulse slowed, and I whispered, "I didn't mean to shout."

"I may have overstepped," Garrick said in a soft tone. "Come back in three days. I'll have another job for you by then."

"Thank you."

He put a hand on my shoulder, and it was all I could do not to flinch. "Let me know if you ever need to talk."

His expression was earnest. He was a good friend, but I had no desire to go into any of this with him. I nodded and then left the office without another word.

As I walked toward the tavern door, my thoughts were a maelstrom: Garrick's words, the night's harrowing events, and the golden-eyed thief. My mind spiraled from one thought to the next. I knew this feeling, and if I didn't get hold of myself soon, there was no telling how deep down the hole I would fall.

I needed a distraction.

The reasonably cute guy who'd propositioned me earlier that evening was face down on a table, breathing deeply. It took only a couple of shakes before he blinked his eyes open.

"I paid m' bill," he slurred in a dreamy stupor, but then his eyes focused on me, and he smiled. "You're back."

"You still interested?" I asked, heading for the door.

He grinned. "Been waiting all night."

"You sure?"

"Very sure," he said, then raced after me.

Chapter Three

Marked

THE MOMENT WE WERE behind the tavern and out of sight of prying eyes, he dropped to his knees, smiling widely. He hastily unbuttoned my trousers and pulled them down, and the rest was a flurry of heat and haze. It was just what I needed to quell my racing mind.

After, we both took ragged breaths, letting our hearts slow. He sat back against the alley wall, smiling. "You seemed to enjoy that."

"You seem to know what you're doing."

"I've had a bit of practice," he said, laughing, then yawned.

He leaned his head back and let his eyes shut. Before I could even pull my trousers up, his breathing was rhythmic and deep, his sleep aided by endorphins and a bit too much ale.

"Fuck," I said to no one in particular, at least no one who could hear me.

In a way, I envied him, lying there in quiet contentment, whereas I could already feel the dark clouds in my head returning.

Suddenly the night felt cold. The tavern looked even shabbier than before. The reek of the alley assaulted my nose, and this sorry bloke was lost to the world. I couldn't just leave him passed out here. I leaned over and gave him a shake, to which he responded with unintelligible mumbling. Gods, I didn't know he was this far gone.

"Hey...um." Dust, I didn't even know this guy's name. But maybe that was the point. "Hey, friend. Let me take you home."

"Mmm..."

It took him a bit to stand. He leaned on me as we lurched down the road. Luckily, not a single soul was out to witness this sorry sight.

"Where's home?" I asked.

He gestured in a nondescript direction without even looking. I cursed under my breath. I had only myself to blame for this.

We hobbled up to a building with a sign reading LARK INN in white lettering. Below, in flaking paint, was a picture of the bird in question. The front door wouldn't budge, so I knocked three times. After a few moments of silence, I knocked again, hard enough to make the door shake. Soon a ruckus came from the other side.

The door opened a crack, revealing a sliver of a wrinkled face, a hooked nose, and a sour expression. "We're closed!" a man snapped.

I held up three silver. "Are you still closed?"

The door opened wide. "This isn't a brothel," said an ancient man wearing a disheveled robe and a frown so deep, the corners of his mouth nearly touched his jaw.

"I just need a bed for my friend here, who partook of a bit too much ale."

"*Five* silver," the man said.

"I'm sure the place across the street has some rooms." I started to turn away.

"Very well," the man grumbled as he snatched the coins from my hand.

Within moments, my *friend* was in a bed, sleeping soundly with thunderous snores, and I was on my way home. But I had one stop to make along the way.

After a short walk, I approached a small cottage with darkened windows. I pressed my ear to the door, but no sound came from within, save for the slight crackle of a dying fire. I placed several coins in a small pouch, then flattened it and shoved it under the door.

Few had cared about the fortunes of the homeless and starving eleven-year-old boy and four-year-old girl, but Mrs. Yarrow had taken us in when no one else would. A bag of gold from time to time was the least I could do.

My knuckles hovered inches from the door, but I pulled them back, like I did every time. Dust knew Elena would love to see her again. But that had been another time. My life now was hard and dangerous, not suited for such a gentle soul like Mrs. Yarrow. Maybe someday, but not tonight.

With my errand done, I headed home. Our dwelling was humble—half of a stable and a small loft belonging to a friendly couple who lived next door and took pity on us. The pungent smell of horses permeated everything. Embers flickered in our hearth, casting the room in a golden glow. I walked like a mouse through our main room so as not to disturb my sleeping sister. Her soft breaths came from the doorway to a small nook where she slept.

I paused at her door and peered inside. Her chest moved in a steady rhythm, gently illuminated by the firelight that spilled across the room. She looked so much like our father, with her strong build and hair as bright as the sun. Every time I saw her, I couldn't help but think of him—a bittersweet memory. I absently fiddled with the locket around my neck. Dust, how I loved her. I would do anything to protect her.

This was why I did what I did—why I closed myself off and did what needed to be done, even when it was killing me piece by piece.

Tiptoeing to the fire, I threw a log onto the coals. I'd need the light and the heat to solve the riddle of the hidden message. That parchment had occupied much of my thoughts since the moment the thief with the golden eyes had left it, then disappeared into thin air.

Parked in the corner of our home was our herb cart, stuffed with all the herbs and reagents I'd need. I pulled out several glass bottles. Herb merchant was my daytime profession, giving me access to supplies to make enough smoke bombs, fireballs, and noisemakers for a small army. I was also teaching Elena the skills of our family; the skills our father would have taught her. The skills he *should* have been able to teach her.

I filled a small iron pot with water, then set it over the fire. As wisps of steam formed on the water's surface, I sprinkled in a few key ingredients and stirred. When an earthy herbaceous smell filled the room, I dipped the parchment into the pot and quickly removed it. Before my eyes, lines formed on its surface. Slowly at first, then suddenly, crisp black markings appeared.

For the briefest moment, I nearly threw the parchment into the fire. I felt as if I were on the precipice of something. Maybe it was better to burn it up and be done with it. Maybe it was better not to know what lay over the next hill. But in the end, I climbed over it.

On the parchment was a drawing of a fence surrounding a great oak tree—a familiar image. The Amara Tree—known by its more infamous name, the Bleeding Oak—grew deep in the Citadel Gardens, protected by guards. All could view the tree, but none could approach it under penalty of death.

Within the top boughs of the tree, a few marks were drawn with a different pigment—slightly lighter, with the faintest hint of red. It shimmered in the flickering firelight until the lines solidified into two marks crossing each other. What in the dust was this? A treasure map? Did X mark the spot? I laughed under my breath at the audacity.

When I turned the parchment over, my eyes grew wide and my heart sped up. Printed on the back were two twisting letters and a flame—the same mark that had been on the door of the Charred Snake.

Everyone in the Underworld knew of the Emberlight Trials—a gauntlet to join the Order of Emberlight. But not just anyone could join.

You had to be invited.

This hidden message was just such an invitation.

Chapter Four

The Bleeding Oak

Elena and I were walking through a forest. But she was impossibly small—no older than three or four. She ran down the trail, tripped, skinned her knee, jumped back up, and continued on as if nothing had happened.

Father was there, guiding us to our favorite spot: the wishing well in the middle of the forest. A cool summer breeze made the trees sway, creating dancing shadows on the forest floor.

"Be careful, children," he said as we ran up to the well to give our offering of seashells. Elena squeezed her eyes tight, then threw her shell in. A soft splash echoed up.

"Don't ask me what I wished for," Elena said to me with a stern look, "or it won't come true."

"I know that, silly fox," I said, rubbing her hair. "Who do you think told you?"

I closed my eyes and wished that the boy at the farm next to ours would kiss me. Bren was his name. So far, it seemed like he had barely noticed me. My shell banged against the side of the well on the way down, making a sharp crack.

I thought I heard a mocking laugh, but when I looked up, Father and Elena were talking to each other softly. I spun around, looking for the source of the laugh.

"Did you hear it, too?" Father said, noticing my confusion.

"Where did it come from?"

"You can hear the whisperhawks, like me. See it?" He pointed up at a golden-and-brown hawk perched in a tree, looking down at us. "It's your special gift. But you must keep it a secret. Tell no one."

"I promise," I said, though I longed to tell Bren. He was sure to be impressed.

The hawk stared at me with golden eyes, blazing like the sun. It tilted its head. There was something in its gaze. Not judgment exactly—more like it could peer into my soul.

Everything in the world darkened around me except for those two golden eyes. They moved toward me, getting closer and brighter. Soon I could make out the shape of a dark figure framing the eyes. The shape was familiar. I let out a gasp as it resolved into the golden-eyed thief. He was within reach, his features still obscured by the mask. I longed to rip it off.

"Who are you?" I said, but it came out as a choked gasp.

The figure opened its mouth to speak.

"Cas, it's time to get up," said four-year-old Elena, who had appeared next to me.

"We'll be late," her voice called again, more insistently, but this time from the edges of my perception, stirring me from my slumber.

A fucking dream. This golden-eyed thief had worked his way into my subconscious.

The sunlight was warm and bright on the backs of my eyelids, and I dragged the blanket over my head and buried my face in the pillow. The smell of hay mixed with burlap flooded my nose, comforting and familiar.

After discovering the secret message last night, I'd lain awake for a long time. How could I possibly sneak up to the top of that tree, which was heavily guarded and sequestered in the far reaches of the Citadel Gardens? Perhaps a scouting visit was called for...but maybe after a bit more sleep. I longed to return to the golden-eyed thief.

"Get down here, Cas!" my sister yelled from the room below. For a sweet girl of fourteen, her voice rivaled those of some of the best merchant barkers in the city, which came in handy when trying to sell wares but was less desirable when I was trying to sleep.

I blinked several times, shielding my eyes from the rays of sunshine streaking through gaps in the ceiling. Dust motes floated lazily through the beams of light, carried by a slight breeze that blew through the loft.

"If we don't leave soon, we won't get a good spot," Elena pleaded.

"Coming," I said, my voice raspy with phlegm. I cleared my throat, then lazily dragged myself out of bed. "What time is it, anyway?"

"Almost second bell."

Shite. I really *had* slept in. The best spots were always gone by second bell, with all the merchants eager to take advantage of the heavy foot traffic in the morning. After throwing on clothes, I opened the hatch to the loft and slid down the ladder, a thing I'd done so often that the wood had smoothed to a fine polish.

"He's alive!" Elena quipped in a far-too-precocious tone.

I mumbled an unintelligible response.

Of the two of us, Elena was clearly our father's daughter. She had his sharp wit and was already nearly as tall as I, with bright green eyes that gleamed above her heavily freckled nose. Dust, that dream about Father had been so vivid. I had forgotten just how much like him she was. Something inside me tightened, sharp and brief, like a plucked string.

Most who inspected Elena and me side by side wouldn't suspect that we came from the same parents. I took after our mother, inheriting her dark features, slight build, and nimble fingers. But Elena and I were bound by more than blood. Every hardship, every scar, had helped forge the bond we shared.

"I made some breakfast," Elena said, handing me a bowl of scrambled eggs from the hens we kept in a coop on our small patch of land outside the barn.

"Thanks." I took the bowl and scooped up the eggs with the wooden spoon.

A slight smirk on her face hid the unasked question: *What were you up to so late last night?* She never asked, but Elena was far wiser than a typical fourteen-year-old. She knew of my talents and my rage. Perhaps not the depth of it, but we had the same history, the same wounds. Those lies of omission weighed on me, but they were the price I paid to preserve her innocence for just a bit longer.

"We'd better get going soon," she said. "Second bell will be any moment."

I scarfed down the remaining eggs. "Let's go."

The Citadel Market wasn't far, but the herb cart's wheels kept catching on the broken cobblestones of the Wharf District. Unlike the *fucking pristine* roads of the Garden District.

I cursed as the wheels caught in a rut for the fifth time. "This fucking road!"

"Language, Cas!" Elena scolded, but she was smiling. "You'll taint my delicate ears."

"You already curse like a tavern drunk," I quipped back.

"The hells I do!"

We locked eyes, trying to look serious, then burst into laughter and traded insults the rest of the way.

When we reached the Citadel District, it was like we had entered a different city. Trees and gardens lined the streets, and elaborate banners hung from poles, each adorned with a serpent wrapped around a sword—the emblem of the Tarnasau Dynasty. The homes had intricate stone facades. The people on the streets in their luxurious clothes scurried around like mice, all undoubtedly heading to very important engagements. Stationed at every corner were members of the Royal Guard, eyeing us with our ragtag cart, worn shoes, and peasant clothes.

The Citadel District was at the center of Analon, so this was the ideal spot for vendors to sell their wares. The kingdom knew this, of course, so the tax was atrocious. As we walked into the large central square that housed the Citadel Market, an imposing guard wearing gilded gold armor put out an arm to stop us.

"Six coins," he said flatly, holding out his hand.

It had been five coins last week, but I bit my tongue and fought down the rage. Arguing with a guard was like yelling at a brick wall. A wall that would likely fall on you if you yelled too loudly.

I handed the guard six coins from my purse.

"Move along," he said without a second glance. When I peeked back, I caught him putting five coins into a chest and slipping the sixth into his pocket. I held back the urge to punch him.

The market was already bustling, with countless carts and tables lined up under canopies and customers buzzing between them like bees. Merchants from across the kingdom sold everything imaginable: fish caught this morning, hand-painted pots, fruits and vegetables freshly picked from local farms.

As we pulled the cart, the booming sound of the second bell rang out. The mechanical clock tower rose high above the Citadel Library. People miles away could hear the bells.

"We're late," Elena groaned.

Most merchants had already set up their carts. We claimed a less-than-ideal spot and folded down the side doors of our cart, turning them into long tables on which to display our wares. Inside the cart were dozens of small drawers filled with dried plants, herbs, minerals, and a hundred other items that could be used for everything from formulating medicines to flavoring stews.

It was a slow morning for business. One young woman needed lavender to scent a candle she was making. I let Elena handle the sale as I watched, but I had nothing to worry about. She answered the woman's questions with ease and haggled a price that was fair but still fetched us a decent profit. My heart swelled at the young woman she was becoming.

This was why I took the risks I did—to make a better life for us. If I could save enough to buy a farm of our own, we could escape the city's corruption and live in peace. Maybe just one more year of stashing away coins. Perhaps two.

As the morning wore on and the drought of customers continued, I rested my head on my arms and daydreamed about the Bleeding Oak and how I might scale it. The Citadel Gardens were not far away.

It took only a bit of convincing to persuade Elena to watch the cart by herself for a while.

"Only if you're off to woo some handsome man," she said.

I rolled my eyes. "I'll be back soon."

It was a short walk from the market to the Citadel Gardens. The city's laws restricted most amenities in the Citadel Districts to highborn residents only. My kind was explicitly forbidden from the library, theater, and eateries, among other things. But the gardens were open to all. However, that didn't prevent the Royal Guards from giving me long, suspicious looks as I walked by.

The entrance to the gardens was a towering arch more than twenty feet high that spanned the road, mounds of purple wisteria weaving through its wrought-iron filigree. Beyond the arch was a wonderland of trees, bushes, and flowers, exploding with color. The fragrant scent of honeysuckle wafted on the gentle morning breeze. The gardens were silent, save for the buzzing of honeybees and the gravel crunching under my feet as I walked down the path.

After weaving through mazelike trails bordered with box hedges and maple trees, I came to the center of the garden: the site of the Bleeding Oak. The tree towered over the surrounding landscape. Its massive trunk had many branches that lifted to the sky. True to its name, there was a gash across its trunk where sap flowed out continuously and pooled beneath it.

An expansive circular lawn spread out around its trunk, bordered by a tall and imposing wrought-iron fence topped with razor-sharp spikes. Guards orbited the fence, looking as though they'd rather be anywhere else.

There was something about this place that I couldn't quite put into words; it was as if an energy were spilling from the gash in the trunk and leaking into the surrounding landscape. It wasn't a bad feeling, but it wasn't particularly pleasant either.

As I approached the stately old oak, I stayed out of sight. I had every right to be here, but there was no need to raise suspicions. So I stood quietly in the shadows a stone's throw away, observing the guards and their patterns. One guard with a bushy mustache never quite finished his circuit, leaving a sizable gap unmonitored. Sneaking past him should not be hard.

Getting over the spiked fence was simply a matter of having the correct equipment. I'd be back this evening with my thieving tools in tow. This seemed like too easy a task for the Emberlight Trials. There had to be a catch. I supposed I'd find out tonight.

I finished my reconnaissance and was heading toward the exit when something caught my attention—a man around my age, maybe a few years older, twenty-four or twenty-five. He was on the other side of the courtyard, peering my way. The sun streamed through his sandy-brown curls. He was taller and more muscular than the beanpole that was me. His trousers and shirt were common, but they fit his body nicely and were clean and well constructed, so he was likely a merchant's son or a downstairs servant in a noble house.

He smiled as our eyes met. For a moment, the world narrowed, and he was my singular focus. Why had this strikingly handsome man chosen to direct his attention at me? As he continued to stare, my cheeks grew hot. Dust, was I actually blushing?

That direct stare was too much, so I looked away. But from the corner of my eye, I could see that he was still looking toward me. A guard noticed his very obvious staring and squinted in my direction. I backed into the shadows quickly. This ridiculous man was blowing my cover.

I was hit with a strong familiar scent—ozone and citrus.

"I'm watching," a melodic and familiar voice whispered right behind me, and I felt breath hot against my neck. I spun around, looking for the golden-eyed thief, but no one was there. What in all the hells?

I scanned the courtyard, but nothing was amiss. The handsome man still watched me from across the square, scratching his neck and smiling. If he had seen the golden-eyed thief, he gave no indication. Was I losing my mind?

A crowd crossed between the man and me—scholars dressed in robes of simple black and white, each adorned with a silver crest of a snowy owl. These were students of the Citadel Academy. An older man with deep wrinkles, dressed in purple robes and an elaborate pointed hat, led them toward the tree. He gestured around the square, speaking in lofty tones, droning on about how a woodsman had gone mad and attacked the tree with his ax and the brave Royal Guards had struck him down when he'd begun to attack innocent bystanders.

Lies.

My mother had told me a very different story. The king had ordered the woodsman's wife executed, so he'd fought back in the only way he knew how, with the blade of his ax against the bark. He hadn't hurt a soul, but the cost had been death.

The procession continued past the tree and out the entrance on the other side. I searched for the handsome man again, but the place where he'd stood was now vacant. I glanced around, but the courtyard was empty, save for the guards and a lone bird flying from limb to limb, chirping in the sunlight.

At least I didn't have to worry about him being way too obvious and attracting the guards' attention to me anymore.

Even so, my heart sank in a way that surprised me—a feeling I'd not had in a long time. It was absurd to feel this way about a stranger, but the space he'd left behind felt unusually empty.

Chapter Five

X Marks the Spot

Our swords clashed, the clang of metal echoing through the yard outside our home. Elena mounted an aggressive attack, as she always did. She had natural strength and enough quickness to get herself out of overcommitments...most of the time.

This time, she lunged so hard that she lost her balance, and I found an opening, smacking my blade against her straw-padded chest.

"Ouch!" she cried. Dull blade or not, a rod of steel never feels good.

"You overcommitted," I said. "Let's go again."

Elena grunted and reset, a scowl on her face. She didn't like to lose.

I'd been training her to duel since she could pick up a wooden training sword. If she ever found herself cornered and alone in the city, I wanted her to stand a chance. Lately she had gotten quite good. She'd nearly powered out of that last jam with sheer strength alone. It was the nuances she still needed to learn.

We clashed swords again. This time, she held back and didn't overcommit, but her eyes were on my sword and not on *me*—another of her typical weaknesses. So I feinted left, and when she moved in that direction, I swung my sword for the killing shot, and—

Somehow she parried my strike, following up with a quick counterstrike, her sword smacking my shoulder.

"How in the dust did you do that?" I asked in utter shock.

Elena smiled widely, enjoying herself way too much. "First of all, I know that trick you do when you think I'm watching your sword. I saw it coming."

"So you *faked* watching my sword as a diversionary tactic?"

"Yep," she said, her wide smile somehow getting wider, perhaps a little evil.

"Elena, that's amazing!"

"*I* thought so."

"You said 'first of all.' What's the second thing?"

"You had that *look.*"

"And what look is that?" I asked.

"The one you get when you're thinking about a man you fancy."

Did I? I supposed she was probably right. Since that afternoon, my mind had been a jumble of thoughts, including ones regarding how I'd get to the Bleeding Oak. But the infuriatingly handsome stranger had indeed occupied much of my attention, not to mention the ghost of the golden-eyed thief. I was up to my neck in men. Anyway, it was a good enough deflection to keep her from asking more probing questions.

"Guilty as charged," I said with a laugh.

"So you really were wooing some man this afternoon," Elena said, looking a little disappointed. "And here I thought you were off on some grand adventure."

"Sorry to disappoint." If she only knew. But of course I couldn't tell her.

We finished her lesson with little more conversation.

Later, we had a simple dinner of cured meat, cheese, and freshly baked bread from the local bakery. After we cleaned up, I gathered my supplies, ready to head to the Bleeding Oak.

As I snuck toward the door, Elena looked up from the book she was reading by the fire. "Where are you off to, Cas?"

"Off to run some errands," I said, not meeting her gaze. I didn't like lying, but it was for her safety. If the Royal Guard were ever to catch me, I didn't want them coming after her, so the less she knew, the better.

"Very well. Have fun. And I'm not the least bit curious about the mysterious things you do wearing your all-black clothes and carrying your little bag of tools." She gave me a knowing smile, then waved me off. "Go on. I'll be fine on my own."

I sighed. "Based on how smart you seem to be, I don't doubt that you'll be fine. Good night, Elena."

"Good night, Cas. Don't let thoughts of men distract you too much during your *errands*," she said, the last word dripping with sarcasm thick as honey.

Sometimes Elena's keen observations were downright infuriating. When had this girl turned into a young woman, and a clever one at that?

I shook my head, then snuck off into the night, sinking into the shadows.

The last rays of sunlight licked the edges of the sky, casting the clouds in a golden hue. By the time I arrived at the center of the Citadel Garden, the Bleeding Oak formed a stark silhouette against the deep-purple sky.

The guard I had scouted earlier was still on duty, still displaying the same weakness. Beyond him, the wrought-iron fence topped with razor-sharp spikes barred entry to the tree. From my pack, I took out a glove coated in Wildwood sap and a piece of Vanara silk, which rivaled chain mail in puncture resistance.

I waited for my moment to strike. The guard turned early, not completing his entire circuit, just as he had done this afternoon. I raced out of the shadows and ran for the fence, my boots barely whispering against the stone.

With a leap and one grab of my sticky glove, I scaled the slick iron fence. In a single motion, I threw the Vanara silk over the spikes on top and slipped over them unscathed, dropping to the grass without a sound. But as I grabbed for the silk, the edge caught on a sharp spike. No matter how I pulled and wriggled the silk, it wouldn't come free.

There was no time to climb up and free it. The guard was turning around, and I had only a moment to act before he saw me.

Reaching into the pocket on my belt, I grabbed a small pebble and lobbed it over the fence, and it landed on the pathway in the opposite direction. The guard spun around. "Who's there?"

With only a moment to act, I climbed the fence, snapped my wrist to free the silk from the spike, then raced for the cover of the tree. A half breath later, I was crouched in the shadows of the Bleeding Oak as the guard continued on his rounds.

My pulse hammered in my ears. That had been too close. Maybe this whole thing was foolish. Was the risk worth it? After all, getting caught here meant more than a beating or a night in the stocks. It might mean death or a life sentence in the Pyrehold prison. It meant leaving Elena alone.

For a moment, I considered simply climbing back over the fence and forgetting this whole thing. But I had made it this far, and quitting now would mean I'd taken all these risks for nothing. I owed it to myself to at least see this trial to the end. So I started to climb to see where fate would take me.

The tree's generous boughs made navigating up the spine of the stately old oak as easy as climbing a ladder. Still, the bark bit into my palms, and sap stuck to my fingers. On more than one occasion, I froze as the guard walked by on patrol.

A splash of red caught my eye. In the middle of a hefty branch was an X carved in the same flowing script as the writing on the parchment. The thrill of discovery, that rush of endorphins, rippled through me, and I knew that this was something only a select few had ever seen.

I inspected the mark, analyzing the shape of the broad red strokes. The two slashes were not perfectly balanced. The upper-right point of the X was more pronounced than the others, its end tapering to an arrow that pointed directly up the branch. I followed it. Ten feet up, there was a hole bored into the limb.

I reached into the hole, expecting a note or some kind of clue, but it was empty. Had a previous recruit taken the clue and not replaced it?

Frustrated, I sat down on the limb. I couldn't climb down empty-handed. There had to be more here.

A knot in the limb dug into my rump. As I shifted to avoid it, a splash of moonlight shone through the hole, which I could now see went all the way through the limb. I pressed my face to the bark, the smell of sap sharp in my nose. For a moment, only a circle of black was visible. Then light filtered through and framed an image so perfectly centered that it couldn't be anything but intentional. The Royal Crypt stood atop the lone hill in the Kingsrest Cemetery—the final resting place of Queen Amara, the Bleeding Oak's namesake.

The hole didn't contain a clue. It pointed to the *next* clue.

A laugh nearly escaped my throat, half wonder, half dread. Was this what the Trials were all about? Upping the stakes and seeing how far I would go to chase this foolish dream?

Entering the tomb would make climbing this tree seem like a task for a child. Going in directly was out of the question. The Royal Guards surrounding the perimeter would cut me down in seconds flat, and there would be far too many on patrol to sneak past.

But there was another way in that only members of the Underworld knew of and few would dare attempt—the mazelike catacombs that stretched for miles below the city. Every thief in Analon knew of the voracious bone rats that could swarm you and strip you of all your flesh in no time. And while most of the tales were probably exaggerations, one fact was indisputable: few who went far into the catacombs came back out alive.

I wondered yet again if that was a risk worth taking.

Chapter Six

Hunted

"You want *what*?" Garrick's voice boomed, filling the small office.

"A map of the Citadel Catacombs?" Garrick's glare made me turn my statement into a question at the last moment. The words sounded ridiculous as they exited my mouth.

"I certainly hope you want it out of morbid curiosity, because going in there is pure madness. Have you gone mad, boy?"

"No." I looked down at my feet. "But I still want it."

"But why?"

"I hoped perhaps you could do this for me, no questions asked." I peeked up to gauge his reaction. "After all we've done for each other, consider it a favor."

Garrick's stare was unwavering. "I personally know people who went into the catacombs and didn't return."

"Which is why I need your help."

Garrick let out a long sigh, running his hand through his beard. "Please don't get yourself killed. You're my best thief, and..." He paused for a long moment and then looked down at the ground. "I like you too much."

"Thank you, Garrick," I said, giving the words the weight they deserved. This was a big favor. "And for the record, staying alive is always top of mind."

Garrick huffed out a sad laugh. "Let me see what I can scrounge up."

He headed to the back door of his office and gestured for me to follow.

The door opened onto a narrow room, the opposite of the Spartan office in nearly every way. Shelves and cabinets lined every square inch of the walls; there was barely room to navigate. Books, scrolls, and etched tablets covered every horizontal surface.

In all my years working for Garrick, I had only caught glimpses of this room, but today he led me right in without hesitation. I paused in the doorway. Entering felt like an invasion of privacy.

"Come along, Cas. It's time you see how my brain works." Garrick raised his hands, gesturing to the endless piles. "But don't touch anything. I've organized everything exactly as I want it."

That was hard to believe, since everything seemed entirely haphazard, as if a strong wind had stirred it all up. Nonetheless, I followed him, taking each step with care, being sure not to disturb a thing.

Garrick approached a long row of cabinets with countless drawers, each with a small label embedded in a frame, arranged alphabetically. He ran his finger along the drawers, stopping at the letter *c*. He opened a drawer filled with parchments and scrolls, carefully leafed through the contents, and pulled out a yellowed parchment covered with dark lines—a map of the Citadel Catacombs. There were hundreds of passageways crisscrossing the page. It was literally a maze.

"This is both valuable and fragile. Be very careful with it," Garrick said with a stern look.

"I only need to look at it for a moment," I said as I gently set it on a small table in the middle of the room. Despite the frayed edges and darkened surface, the parchment was surprisingly sturdy.

I scanned the document and imprinted it on my memory. My head buzzed with the myriad of lines and angles. The entrance to the catacombs from the Underworld Market was just where I remembered it being on my previous visits when I was a child.

With my eyes closed, I could literally see the lines of the crypt forming in my mind as the passageways etched themselves into my memory. I could visit each dead end and pass every crossroad.

"Got it," I said, rolling up the parchment and handing it back to Garrick.

"I'll never understand how you do that," Garrick said, shaking his head.

"It's like an artist draws a picture in my mind."

"And you don't believe in magic." Garrick laughed. "But you're sure you don't need to keep it for a while? Sometimes memory can falter under pressure."

"I'm good," I said. "Thank you again, Garrick. I should get going."

"One last thing," Garrick said. "Let's sit at my desk."

I flinched. Good things rarely came from a *sit at my desk* talk. I followed him back into the office, feeling like a child about to be punished.

He peered at me over his desk. "Earlier this evening, two Royal Guards came into the bar, asking questions about the Leonom break-in. They were with a Sentinel."

A Sentinel—one of King Tarnasau's elite enforcers. That word chilled me to the bone. Nothing good came from them. Sentinels didn't patrol. They hunted.

"Why in all the hells was a Sentinel here?" I asked.

"I don't know. The guards were roughing people up, trying to get answers. I heard they visited several other taverns after ours, so I don't think they were targeting us specifically. But you're sure no one recognized you last night, right?"

"Yes, I'm sure," I said.

Garrick's eyes narrowed as he considered my answer for an uncomfortably long time.

Guilt batted at my insides. I had lied about the golden-eyed thief, and that lie was coming back to bite Garrick. And now I was doing it again. But revealing my invitation to the Emberlight Trials would likely disqualify me from the organization. If there was one thing people knew about the Order of Emberlight, it was that they valued secrecy above all else.

But I couldn't stand the guilt. I opened my mouth to tell Garrick what had *really* happened that night, but he nodded before I could get a word out.

"Very well. Even so, it's best for you to keep a low profile. Let's wait a bit before your next job. Maybe stay clear of the tavern for a couple of weeks until things cool down?"

I nearly blurted out *no*. I needed these jobs, both for the money and for my sanity. But I could hardly justify arguing when I wasn't being entirely truthful with him. So instead I nodded and turned for the exit before I could say something I regretted.

"Be safe, Cas," Garrick said.

I looked back one last time. His expression was caring and earnest.

"I'll try my best," I replied as I walked through the door.

While I ached to discover the next link in the Order of Emberlight's chain of riddles, it was too late to enter the twisting labyrinth of the Citadel Catacombs tonight. I was tired and a little upset about Garrick's rebuke, and the first hints of dawn would color the sky in just a few scant hours.

As I walked the back alleyways of the Wharf District, my head was a jumble of thoughts. What were Sentinels doing tracking down the thief of a single bag of gold? Surely they were searching for the book instead. So what made it so valuable?

Maybe it was paranoia and my overactive mind, but I had an overwhelming sense of being followed as I walked. Nothing concrete, just a slight shift in the air—some subtle cue that was barely perceptible but undeniably there. I gritted my teeth, trying not to overreact. The first rule when you suspect you're being followed is not to let your potential pursuer know you're aware of them. Without turning my head, I scanned the dark corners of the street with my peripheral vision.

A shape in the shadows was darker than the surrounding area.

And then that shape moved.

I forced my breath to remain steady. The road turned just a few feet ahead. I kept my pace even, revealing nothing. The delicate sound of footfalls echoed behind me, maybe twenty paces away. My senses sharpened, letting my instinct guide me.

The moment I turned the corner and was out of sight, I broke into a sprint, hoping the slight advantage would be enough. The light footfalls behind me turned into the loud clomping of boots on stone, all stealth abandoned. Up ahead, the narrow alley opened into a courtyard. A waist-high fountain dominated the center, its stone rim slick with spray. Five roads radiated outward like spokes on a wheel.

I reached for the smoke vial on my belt and slipped it out with the ease of a task done a hundred times. As I entered the courtyard, I threw the vial behind me, smashing it on the cobblestones, sending up a massive cloud of smoke in my wake.

With only a moment to act, I scanned the roads radiating out from the center of the courtyard. Some were dark and narrow, offering ample opportunities to hide. The road directly across the courtyard was the major thoroughfare, wide and bright. Only a fool would choose that direction. It was the perfect way to go.

I sprinted for the central fountain and leapt off the rim, landing on the other side. In fewer than two beats of my pounding heart, I was racing down the main road. Without a moment to spare, I dove behind a barrel. It was scant protection. If my pursuer chose this road, they would see me immediately.

Racing footfalls echoed through the courtyard and then stopped, followed by deep breaths and a noise resembling the snarl of a wild beast. I froze, every muscle locked. I held my breath, hoping my gamble paid off.

Heavy breathing and clomping feet headed in my direction. Whatever it was, it was close—too close. Goose bumps prickled along my arms as coldness descended around me. This was no natural cold. It permeated my core, sending ripples of chill radiating outward.

The urge to peek over the barrel was nearly overwhelming.

Then a familiar scent hit me: ozone mixed with sharp citrus. It was the same scent the golden-eyed thief had left behind when he'd disappeared into thin air. But the feeling tonight was different—colder and harsher. Unforgiving. Wild.

Footfalls echoed through the courtyard, getting louder. My breath puffed out in fleeting mists as the temperature turned bitterly cold. I clenched my teeth to keep them from chattering. Whatever was in the courtyard let out a long breath, like the snort of a hooved beast. It was nearly upon me.

A crashing sound and the wail of a cat came from the courtyard. The footfalls stopped, then raced away toward the noise. The relief from the cold was instant, and my galloping heart slowed. As the footfalls faded away, I peeked over the barrel. A tall figure wrapped in a black cloak with an inhuman fluidity disappeared into the leftmost dark alley—my second choice for escape.

I let out a long stuttering breath.

Only when it had been silent for several moments did I dare move again. Even then, I took each step with care, keeping to the shadows. I turned down the first alley, then turned twice more, weaving through the back streets, putting more distance between myself and...whatever that creature was. Only then did I scale a drainpipe and make my way along the rooftops of Analon. The night was clear, and starlight shone off the buildings of the Wharf District and Analon Bay beyond. A gust of air carried the briny scent of the sea.

I perched on the top of a tall roof to clear my mind. No human moved like that figure had. And the smell—it was the same scent I'd detected in the study and at the Bleeding Oak, but it couldn't have felt more different. Was all of this connected to the book? What a colossal mistake it had been to let it go without knowing what I was giving up.

But regret solved nothing. My only path forward was to solve the Order of Emberlight's chain of riddles and hope that it would end with answers. Tomorrow night, the Underworld Market and the Citadel Catacombs awaited.

With the plan fixed in my mind, I sprang up and danced across the rooftops, hopping from building to building until I neared my home. Even though I was certain I wasn't being followed anymore, I still approached the barn with care. I paused at the crossroads near it; all was quiet. No beast or human stirred in the early morning darkness.

But when I made my way to the front door, my heart lurched.

There, drawn in black charcoal next to the entrance, were two twisted snakes forming an *o* and an *e*.

Chapter Seven

A Familiar Face

SLEEP DIDN'T COME EASILY.

So when Elena woke me up early the next day to get a good spot at the market, I was a bit out of sorts. The entire walk there, my mind jumped from one thought to the next. I had rubbed the Order of Emberlight's mark from the door with the edge of my shirt and had mentioned nothing to Elena. These symbols showed up all over town, and most likely this was simply some random graffiti. And yet I couldn't shake the unsettled feeling in my gut.

"Everything okay, Cas?" Elena asked with a creased brow as we walked along the cobbled road. "You're quiet today. You haven't insulted me once."

"Sorry, just lost in my head," I replied. Elena was getting better at reading my moods. It was harder to hide things from her. "Umm...you smell like wolf's breath."

"Do not!" Elena exclaimed, sniffing her shoulder. "You're the one who stinks. Even your insults are half-hearted."

We continued to the market, trading insults, and some of mine were even good ones. Elena had taken my mind off my troubles, at least for a while.

Our spot at the market was much better than yesterday's. We were busy enough that day that we both had to attend to customers. I assisted a portly gentleman who needed an indigestion tonic as Elena helped another customer with a deep but youthful voice. Something about it was captivating.

I waited for a brief lull in my conversation and stole a glance at Elena's customer.

My jaw dropped.

It *couldn't* be. And yet it was.

The same man I had seen in the Citadel Gardens yesterday stood an arm's length away. Remembering the way he'd smiled made my chest flutter in a way I didn't expect.

His eyes met mine, and he smiled slightly. I adjusted my assessment of him. He wasn't just handsome. He was stunning—infuriatingly so. I'd known men like this before, and they were inevitably trouble.

The sun dappled his wavy sandy brown hair, his beautiful face, and bright smile. Time stopped for a moment as I watched this gorgeous man.

The customer I was helping cleared his throat, his brow furrowed. "Excuse me."

"S-sorry," I stuttered as I rubbed the back of my neck. "I—uh—I thought I saw somebody I knew."

As I continued helping my customer with his tonic, I stole glances at the other man out of the corner of my eye. What in all the hells was he doing here?

When I finally finished, I turned to face him. He was staring directly at me with his emerald-green eyes, a crooked smile tugging at his mouth. Our eyes locked for longer than any two strangers might consider normal.

Elena looked back and forth between us with a crinkled brow. "Do you two know each other?"

I said, “No,” just as he said, “Yes.”

“We met at the Bleeding Oak yesterday,” he added.

Met was a bit of an overstatement, since all we’d done was exchange a look from a distance, yet he remembered the moment as clearly as I did. That made my pulse quicken, despite all my attempts to suppress my emotions.

“Are you following me?” I asked, perhaps a bit more pointedly than I intended.

“No,” he said. “I mean, maybe a little? When I saw you here, I remembered you from yesterday. I needed some herbs anyway, so I...um...just came over.” He was beaming as he spoke, his rosy cheeks reddening further. I couldn’t remember the last time a beautiful man had seemed so enamored with me. It was unsettling. I didn’t have time for this.

And yet I couldn’t help feeling the tiniest bit flattered.

“And so you stood in my sister’s line?” I quipped.

“Well...I mean...you looked busy.”

Elena gawked at us like we were a circus act. “I’ll let you finish helping him,” she said, handing me a parchment list of no fewer than twenty items, a few of which had check marks next to them.

“This is pretty extensive,” I said, running my finger down the list. “What are you making?”

“I really can’t say.”

“Of course, sorry. I shouldn’t have asked,” I said. “I’m Cassian, by the way. But people call me Cas.”

His face lit up. “Pleasure to meet you, Cas. I’m Darion. No one calls me Dar.”

We both laughed, continuing to stare at each other until a light breeze ruffled the parchment I was holding, snapping me back to the matter at hand. I glanced down at the list and tried to focus on anything other than Darion’s handsome face.

“We have most of this,” I said, “but we just sold out of goldvein root.”

"That's too bad," Darion said, looking crestfallen. "I need all this today. Guess I can try another vendor."

"Cas is going foraging today," Elena cut in. "Isn't that right, Cas?"

I glared at her, and she looked back at me with the most innocent smile. Sure, I had planned to go foraging *soon*, but not necessarily today. What was she doing?

Elena continued, "I bet we could have it for you by half past third bell."

Darion looked between Elena and me. "That's a very kind offer, but I'd hate to impose on you like that."

"Honestly, it's fine," Elena said, still wearing the smile of an angel.

Darion looked directly at me. "Are *you* sure it's okay?"

Elena had backed me into a corner. If I said no, I'd look like a tremendous lout. But a walk wouldn't kill me. I *supposed* it wouldn't be the worst thing to see Darion again later today. But I was still going to kill Elena.

"It's fine," I said, although I should have said no. "I know a spot where I can get some goldvein root. I can go during my midday meal." Darion still looked a bit skeptical, so I finished with, "I insist."

"Well, if you insist," he said. "Thank you."

He smiled so brightly that I felt a flush in my neck and cheeks. This was ridiculous. Everything about him felt like a magnet, pulling me closer. Why did this man have this much of an impact on me? I didn't like losing control. It was dangerous.

I quickly filled the rest of his order and sent him on his way, watching him as he headed off. When he was nearly out of sight, he turned and looked in my direction, sending me one more smile. I ignored it.

After he disappeared, I glared at Elena.

"What?" she asked.

"What the dust was that?"

"I don't know what you're talking about," she said, the picture of innocence. "We need more goldvein root."

I headed north, weaving through the crowds of customers and merchants until I reached the edge of the Citadel Market. Soon I crossed from the Citadel District into the Barracks District. This part of Analon housed many of the Royal Guard as well as various other soldiers and mercenaries. It was packed to the gills with the three *b*'s: brothels, barracks, and bars.

A woman dressed in not much at all catcalled me from an open window. "Hey, sweetie! Aren't you cute! You looking for some fun?"

I avoided her gaze and moved on, but in the process, I nearly smacked into two Royal Guards who were walking like they owned the road. "Watch it, punk!"

I hated this neighborhood.

But this was the most direct way to get to the city's North Gate, and beyond that was the Blackwood Forest, which had some of the best foraging spots. So I hurried through the district, keeping my eyes on the ground, avoiding eye contact with everyone. Soon I approached the city's imposing north wall.

Of all the city's gates, the North Gate was the most impressive. The walls towered a hundred feet in the air, casting a long shadow across the nearby homes. The gate itself was thirty feet high, made of massive timbers reinforced with iron, and a large metal portcullis with deadly spikes pointed downward, threatening everyone who entered.

Carts, horses, and peasants pushed through the entrance, jostling in both directions. I kept my head down as I passed through the gate, ignoring the questioning looks of the guards. The best strategy when dealing with them was to go unnoticed. I used my thieving instincts to the fullest, hiding behind carts, horses, and peasants, making myself smaller, quieter, not worth noticing.

Soon I was out of the city, heading along the North Road toward the Blackwood Forest.

The third bell rang out from the Citadel Clock, easily audible beyond the city's walls. With just half a bell to forage for the goldvein root, I doubled my pace.

Thatched-roof homes and farms dotted the landscape outside the city walls, but they grew less frequent the closer I got to the forest. Even the traffic on the road died down, and I soon found myself alone, imposing trees looming ahead.

As I entered the woods, the temperature cooled dramatically. The evergreens and stately oaks closed in on either side of me, seeming to suck the heat out of the air. I couldn't see very far in any direction.

The shadows here felt wrong. Despite being alone, the strange sensation of another presence batted at my senses. My skin prickled as my stealth instincts buzzed. I darted my eyes from side to side but saw nothing out of place. My hand didn't stray far from the hilt of my dagger.

The light snap of a twig came from behind me, and I spun on my heel, brandishing my blade. There was a flash of movement in the forest. Like a lightning bolt, I sprinted toward it. Whoever it was wouldn't expect the speed of my approach.

I ran around the tree where I had seen the movement. Sure enough, a dark figure pressed against the trunk. They spun around as I closed the distance, and I held my blade up to their throat.

Then my brain caught up with my hand. Emerald eyes. Sandy brown hair. That ridiculous smile.

"Darion?"

Chapter Eight

Foraging and Waterfalls

"Hello, Cas," Darion said in a shaky voice as he stared down at the blade at his throat. "Um...sorry for sneaking up on you like that."

I pulled the blade away but kept it unsheathed at my side. Why the dust was he following me? My mind instantly went to negative places. Maybe he was a competing herbalist, trying to find my foraging spots. Or worse, maybe he'd followed me out here to steal my coin purse, waiting until we were alone to strike.

"Explain," I said with an edge to my voice as sharp as my blade.

"I wanted to surprise you," Darion said with a sheepish grin. "I could tell you didn't want to forage today, and I felt bad about you missing your midday meal, so I...uh...I brought it to you."

He started opening the bag at his side. I held up my blade and barked, "Slowly!"

Slower now, he opened his bag and showed me the contents. Inside were a few pieces of fruit, a loaf of bread, and some cured meats and cheeses. He really had brought me food.

Well, now I felt like an idiot.

Still, why had he followed me this far out of the city? The food could easily have been a cover story. I decided to let my guard down a little while still keeping my eyes open. "You shouldn't sneak up on people like that," I said. "You might get yourself killed."

"Noted. For the record, you are wicked fast. You were on me before I could even react."

"One of my talents," I said dryly.

Darion raised a single eyebrow and gave a half smile. His expression plainly said, *I'd love to see some of your other talents*. My face burned. One of *his* talents was clearly flirting savagely without even speaking. It was infuriating how easily he got past my defenses.

We stared at each other for way too long. This wasn't me. I didn't let people in. I couldn't. I'd made the mistake of trusting people before. Letting them get too close. Telling them secrets. And it had backfired in the worst possible way.

Darion finally broke the silence. "Should we find a place to eat?"

This was spiraling out of control. Now we were going to eat together, like a picnic?

I felt trapped. I couldn't just turn him away after he'd gotten that food and come all the way out here. But this was not what I had planned for my afternoon.

I sighed. "We're close to my foraging spot. There's a place we can sit."

I wasn't excited about revealing where I got my goldvein root, but I was already in deep, and my current assessment was that Darion posed no threat. Either that or he was a very competent liar.

After a short walk farther down the path, I spotted the boulder at the trail's edge that marked where to turn. I quickly found the primitive trail I always took to the foraging spot.

"Where are you taking me, exactly?" Darion asked after a few minutes of walking.

"Almost there. It's worth the hike."

Soon, the forest opened onto a clearing filled with tall grasses and brilliant wildflowers in orange, purple, and red, their perfume floating on a gentle breeze. On the left side of the clearing was a small waterfall about ten feet high, splashing into a glimmering pool.

Darion's eyes sparkled as he took in the scene. "You weren't kidding about it being worth it. This place is beautiful."

I pointed at a smattering of plants growing near the pond. "It's a perfect place for goldvein root. With morning sun, afternoon shade, and plentiful water, this place was practically designed for it."

Darion nodded in appreciation. "Should we forage first or eat first?"

At the mention of eating, my treacherous stomach let out an audible growl.

He laughed. "I guess that's my answer. Good thing I brought food."

I still couldn't shake the feeling that this whole thing was a little...odd? What was his angle? What was he getting out of this? He couldn't have come all this way just for my company. That sort of thing didn't happen to me—I never let it, unless my meddling sister got involved.

For now, I'd play along. I'd see where this was going and try to uncover his *real* motivations.

We found a flat spot near the pond, dappled with shade from the nearby trees. Darion laid out a small blanket he had packed, then sat down on it and tapped the spot next to him. "Come join me."

I did as he said while he unpacked the food. He made little sandwiches from the bread, meat, and cheese as I popped a grape into my mouth. The whole thing felt ridiculous.

When he handed me one of the sandwiches, I couldn't take it anymore. "Can I ask why you're doing this?"

"Does no one in your life do nice things for you just because?"

"Not generally."

"Well, if you need a reason," Darion said, "then it's because you're nice to take the time to do this. Just paying you back. Plus the company isn't bad."

He smiled. Still, for a moment, I could swear there was something else behind his eyes. Was it excitement? Fear? *Deception?*

Once my stomach was full, I tried my hardest to relax. We chatted about the weather, the state of the streets in Analon, and other inconsequential things. Darion mentioned nothing personal, and neither did I. In my line of work, it was smart to keep things close to your chest. I'd never liked deciding what to reveal and what to hide, so avoiding everything suited me just fine.

One thing Darion *did* reveal was that he was wickedly funny. Nearly all of his comments were laced with a dry wit, but his observations were never mean.

When we finished eating, he got up from the blanket and stretched. "We should get to foraging."

We spent the next twenty minutes on our hands and knees, digging up goldvein root and stuffing it in our packs. The afternoon sun was hot, and soon dirt mixed with sweat covered us in a muddy mess.

Darion stood up and tried to shake himself clean, but the mud clung to him like glue. "I'm filthy."

"You are. You've got some mud on your face."

"Where?"

"Right there." With my index finger, also covered in mud, I tried to point to the smudge of dirt on his face. But a chunk of mud dislodged from my finger and smacked him right on the cheek.

His eyes went wide, and he barked out a laugh. "Why, you little—"

"It was an accident! I'm sorry!"

"I'll show you an accident." He smeared the entire palm of his muddy hand across my face.

My jaw dropped. I smeared my hand across his face in return. Then he reached down, grabbed a handful of mud from the bank of the pond, and flung it at my vest.

I looked down in shock at the mud stuck to me. "You didn't just do that."

Darion smirked. "Don't start a mud fight if you don't want to get muddy."

An all-out battle started, and both of us grabbed piles of mud from the pond's edge and hurled them at each other. Our laughter grew louder, punctuated by the occasional gasp when a handful struck home. An unfamiliar emotion flowed through me. I never let loose like this...but I didn't want it to end. Being with Darion was intoxicating. And yet I couldn't help my reflexive thought: *I should stop before this becomes something I don't know how to stop.*

I rested my hands on my knees and yelled, "Truce!"

"Agreed. Truce." He held out a muddy hand, and we shook on it.

I looked down at my clothing. "How am I going to get clean now?"

"Like this," Darion said, pushing me backward into the pond.

I pinwheeled my arms to stop the momentum, but it was no use.

Utter shock. Then cold—very, very cold—water enveloped me like icicles against my skin. Maybe I should have been upset with him for pushing me, but there wasn't an ounce of anger inside me.

Then he jumped in next to me.

When Darion surfaced, he cried out, "Wow! That's cold."

My eyes were daggers, but my voice was teasing. "Yeah, I know. Thanks for that."

He shrugged and smiled. "We need to get clean somehow."

Then he pulled off his shirt. His strong shoulders and the top of his chest peeked above the surface. It wasn't a big deal, right? Plenty of guys swam together—this was just two new friends cooling down in a pond on a hot summer day.

That was when Darion pulled off his boots, threw them onto the shore, and then took off his pants. The water hid everything, but I felt my cheeks go instantly hot.

He saw me gawking and laughed a little. "You going to get clean too or just watch the show?"

Without waiting for an answer, he swam over to the waterfall with his clothes in his hands. With a strange mix of relief and disappointment, I noticed he still had on his drawers. I sorted through my conflicting emotions as I watched his lean muscles work to propel him through the water. I couldn't recall ever being so attracted to a man so quickly. This was bad.

He rinsed his clothes under the cascading spray of the waterfall.

As I pulled off my shirt, I felt my locket bat against my chest. Letting him see the locket felt too personal, so I hurriedly took it off and stashed it in my buttoned trouser pocket for safekeeping. It hurt a little in a way I didn't expect—an ache in my chest. I looked back at Darion's smiling face, which took the sharp edge off.

I finished stripping to my drawers, then swam over to join him. When I approached, he smiled. "The water feels warmer once you're used to it."

"Speak for yourself," I said, teeth chattering. "You've got more meat on your bones."

Darion made a sad face. "Sorry. Once you're done washing, we can get warm in the sun."

When everything was as clean as it would get, we swam to the shore. Darion lifted himself out of the pond, water cascading down his beautiful body, glimmering in the noonday sun. His drawers clung to his backside in a way that left little to the imagination.

When he turned around, I nearly gasped. The front side left even less to the imagination, and it was pretty clear that this wasn't just "two guys going for a swim."

Despite the cold water, I could feel blood running south.

Darion seemed entirely unfazed by his own arousal. "You coming out of the water?"

"Yeah, just a moment. I missed a bit of dirt." I was spotless, but I didn't dare leave the water in my current state. Darion shrugged and then headed for some large smooth boulders baking in the sun.

The first trick was turning away so Darion's body and general sexiness stopped turning me on. I made a show of washing my armpits, all the while trying to occupy my mind with unsexy things, such as recounting every herb and reagent in *The Guide to Potions and Tonics*, first alphabetically, then by toxicity, then both in reverse.

That did the trick.

I turned around to see Darion lounging on a boulder, basking in the sun and gazing up at the sky. Trying hard not to look too closely for fear of having to start this entire process over again, I made it safely to the boulder next to him without any mishaps. Then I stole a glance at him as I was getting situated and noticed he was entirely naked, all his clothes drying on the boulder next to him. This man had no inhibitions.

I hesitated. Not because I didn't want to join him or because I was particularly shy. I had been naked around plenty of men. But this felt different, more vulnerable. Then again, I was wet, the sun was warm, and he wasn't looking my way. So I shut off that part of my brain, stripped naked, spread out on the rocks, and thought of shoveling horse manure to help quell any stray urges.

We both looked up in quiet reflection at the puffy white clouds floating in the sky.

"You're different out here," Darion said softly. "Less...sharp."

"Look, I'm sorry about the knife to the throat."

Darion laughed. "I didn't mean it like that. I meant it as a compliment. I like this version of you."

I didn't know what to say to that, so I said nothing.

After a while, Darion asked, "You ever want to drop everything and just run away? Leave it all behind?"

"All the time. Except in my dream, I run away to a farm and take my family with me." I shouldn't have said it. That dream wasn't for other people. I had told no one about the farm I imagined. Darion was the first.

"That sounds wonderful." Darion paused to think. Then he said, so softly I almost didn't hear it, "Except maybe the family part."

I looked over at him in shock. "You don't like your family?"

"Not really."

"Why not?"

Darion turned away and looked out at the trees, his jaw tightening. "It's complicated. My parents are...my parents are gone."

I felt a tightness in my chest. I knew his pain.

"I lost my parents too," I said. "What happened to yours?"

For a moment, it felt like there was something he wanted to say. But then he swallowed and smiled. "A story for another time. Speaking of time, your sister is probably wondering what happened to you."

"Oh no, Elena! We've got to go. She'll be worried sick." I scolded myself for letting my guard down, losing track of time, and oversharing. I scolded myself for this *entire thing.* I couldn't let myself be distracted like this. It had happened with Bren, the boy next door, back at the farm when I was eleven. And look what it had cost me. Never again, I had vowed.

I reached for my locket, only to find that it wasn't around my neck. A splash of panic hit me, and I fumbled for my buttoned trouser pocket. The locket was safely tucked away. I quickly put it around my neck.

On the way back, Darion and I chatted about nonsense. We told off-color jokes and made fun of the Royal Guards. Like me, he had no love for the kingdom. Agreement on that subject was important—a deal-breaker, in fact—so I was happy when he joked about the king and his noblemen.

I talked a bit about Elena, but I didn't mention my evening profession, my early childhood, or anything else unpleasant. I didn't meet new people too often—especially handsome men whom I liked—and was struck by how much of my life I needed to keep secret.

But Darion didn't complain when I steered around a subject. It seemed he had topics he wanted to avoid as much as I did. He never talked about his family or his profession, and I didn't press the issue.

Overall, the whole afternoon was...nice. And although many of my alarm bells were ringing, beneath them, a part of me wondered if a simple life could be enough. Maybe I didn't need to do the Trials. They were enormously dangerous and risky. Maybe it would be enough to have this simple happiness.

As we entered the Citadel Market, the fourth bell began to ring. I approached the cart, watching Elena's reaction like a hawk. At first, when she caught sight of me, she looked purely annoyed, standing with her arms crossed and a scowl on her face. But when her eyes drifted to Darion beside me, that scowl transformed into a smirk.

"It's about damn time. I was worried sick," Elena chided as I walked up. "But when this guy"—she gestured to Darion—"didn't show at the time he said he would, I figured something was up."

"Sorry, that was my fault," Darion said, raising a hand. "I ambushed him on the way to the forest."

"And by that, he means he brought me food." I paused for a moment. "And shoved me into a pond."

Darion playfully scowled at me. After all, I'd left out the detail that I'd started the mud fight and had it coming.

Elena's eyes widened as she watched us chat, a smile on her face. "I'm glad you two had a wonderful afternoon swimming while I stayed here and worked."

"I'm sorry, Elena," I said. "I'll make it up to you."

"You will." She smiled slyly. "You can count on it."

Now that we were fully stocked with goldvein, we filled the rest of Darion's order. After quickly double-checking to be sure I hadn't missed anything, I handed him the supplies, and in return, he gave me a small stack of coins.

"I didn't charge you for the goldvein, of course," I said. "Thanks for helping."

We said our goodbyes, and Darion walked off into the crowd. The moment he was gone, I realized I had no way to contact him. And perhaps that was for the best.

I shouldn't have hoped he would come back. Hope was dangerous. It could get you killed. I knew that from experience. But I hoped anyway.

With Darion gone, Elena turned toward me. "Details! Tell me everything."

Chapter Nine

The Lantern Mile

Elena interrogated me as we pushed the cart home along the shoddy cobbled roads of the Wharf District. I recounted my lunch with Darion, foraging, and our dip in the pond. I left out the part about us taking off our clothes, swimming, and then lying naked in the sun. There were details she just didn't need to know.

Besides, I felt a little ashamed of letting my guard down so much. What was Darion after? Was he really interested in me? I'd been so lost in my thoughts that I hadn't even considered my plans for entering the catacombs that night. Typically I went over scenarios a hundred times in my mind, considering every threat, every contingency.

Elena, on the other hand, was beside herself. She was a bit of a romantic and loved the idea of me finding a man.

I was so busy deflecting all her questions that I barely noticed the crowd that had formed in the public square ahead of us. I hadn't even been scanning the alleyways and rooftops for threats like I always did, which was particularly bad since I had been followed just last night. Something about the gathering didn't sit right with me, and we'd just stumbled directly into it.

The crowd was cheering on a man in common merchant's clothing who stood on a raised platform with his fist in the air.

"And that's why the bastard in the throne room must be stopped!" the man shouted to scattered cheers. The majority of people shared worried expressions and spoke in hushed tones. I froze. This was treasonous talk and could only lead to trouble.

"Even the rumor of Emberborn blood is enough for King Tarnasau to steal our children!" the man yelled, almost pleading.

My blood went cold at that forbidden word. *Emberborn.* Many in the crowd called out in shock. Elena looked my way, her demeanor serious. She knew the penalties as well as anyone else in the city.

"They took my little Katie," the man cried out, his voice filled with desperation. "Do you want them to steal your children?"

Many people shouted "No!" But a few were starting to back away, their faces revealing worry or even outright fear. I started glancing around, planning our escape route in case things got ugly. But this damn cart would make a quick exit difficult.

"We must march to the Gold Palace!" the father yelled over the cheering crowd. "Demand our children back!"

There was movement on the rooftops around the square, where several figures stood watching. They wore flowing black robes and silver masks covering their faces. Sentinels: King Tarnasau's elite enforcers, feared throughout the realm. Stationed next to them, Royal Guards stood at the ready, wielding crossbows and swords. This would get ugly fast.

"Elena, we need to go," I hissed, turning the cart around.

"But I want to hear what he has to say," Elena pleaded.

"Please, just do this for me, okay?" I said.

The seriousness of my tone got her attention, and she started helping with the cart. We pushed it back the way we had come, but the crowd was all around us now, and we continually bumped into people who shot dirty looks and curses our way.

A low thrumming came from the rooftops—from the Sentinels—almost like a chant. It started low and slowly grew in volume and pitch.

"Grab your swords, your hammers!" the father yelled behind us as the thrumming grew louder. "Whatever you c—"

A sharp whizzing sound ripped through the air, followed by a thud. He broke off mid-word. I glanced back to see a crossbow bolt embedded in his chest.

The crowd gasped collectively. Then the entire square went deathly silent. Even the Sentinels' chanting ceased.

Blood spurted from the man's wound and from his mouth as he coughed, trying to breathe. For a moment, it seemed as if the entire world had stopped to focus on his agony. Then, quite suddenly, the chanting from above resumed, morphing into high-pitched wailing. The crowd broke into screams and shouts.

"What's happening?" Elena asked. Luckily, she was in front of the cart, and we were far enough down the road that she was spared from seeing the ghastly sight.

"They murdered that man," I said, trying hard to hold back my rage. "We have to keep going, quickly!"

Elena's face was pinched, but there was no panic there. Just a grim acknowledgment of the horror of the moment.

As we hurried away, I looked back to see a woman with skin so pale it was nearly white, dressed entirely in black, jump onto the platform. She wore a tight-fitting vest gilded with golden thread forming the pattern of lions' heads on her chest. I would've recognized that symbol anywhere: the Leonom family's house crest. The sight of The Butcher's emblem sent a simmering rage coursing through my veins.

The woman in black came up behind the dying man, slashed his throat as casually as if she were cutting a loaf of bread, then pushed him off the platform. It was almost mechanical, inhuman. The crowd recoiled, letting the man land face-first on the cobblestones. The woman in black never even looked at the crowd.

An older middle-aged man walked up behind her, wearing the lavender robes of a noble over studded leather armor.

No. Not him.

It couldn't be.

He was more wrinkled and worn than he'd been on that fateful day more than nine years ago—the worst day of my life. But I would never forget that face. This was undoubtedly Orlik "The Butcher" Leonom, the man responsible for shattering our family. The man whose house I had broken into just the other night.

The chaos around me faded away as I stared into the soul of that wretched man. I considered throwing my knife. I could hit him. It wasn't impossible.

"This is the price of treason!" Orlik yelled over the Sentinels' shrieking. "Go now, or share this man's fate."

With that, the entire crowd ran away from the platform. My tunnel vision broke as the first waves of panicked citizens hit us, all trying to avoid the same fate as that poor man. It was all Elena and I could do to keep the cart from toppling over.

When we finally cleared the crowd and the chanting faded, Elena ran to me with tears streaking down her cheeks and buried her face in my chest. She was strong, wise beyond her years, and we had shared a lot of trauma, which meant that sometimes I forgot she was still a child and wasn't as hardened as I was to the cruelty of the world. I rubbed her shoulder to calm her, holding back my fury.

Usually Elena and I lived day to day, happy to have what we had, and I thought our life might be good enough. Maybe we could make do. But seeing that innocent man cut down by the very people who had destroyed our family made me realize that any peace we had was an illusion that could shatter at any moment.

Yes, the Trials were dangerous. Perhaps the most dangerous thing I would ever do. But doing nothing meant simply waiting for fate to catch up with us rather than setting our own course. So that evening, I gathered my supplies and headed out, more determined than ever to see the Emberlight Trials through to the end.

There were many entrances to the Underworld, but given the circumstances of the last few days, a more obscure route felt safest. I knew the perfect one, rarely traveled and easily forgotten. I'd discovered it as a child while at Mrs. Yarrow's home for wayward children. Going to the Underworld had been a common dare among the kids, and the obscure entrance was the best way to avoid the prying eyes of those who might object to a gang of wildlings running amok.

As I approached the abandoned city bath in the Wharf District, memories of my childhood flashed through my mind—my first boyfriend and first kiss. Gideon had been brave and handsome, and I'd been hopelessly obsessed with him. My heart ached at how that had ended. Not all love was requited, and not all boys were kindhearted.

I tucked that memory away.

Long ago, someone had boarded up the entrance to the baths, but I knew the way past the barrier. A hidden latch held an entire section of boards in place. With a simple flick of my finger, the wall swung open, and I slipped inside without a sound.

Each of my footsteps on the bath's glazed clay tiles echoed through the vacant hall. Vast pools surrounded by archways stood empty and crumbling. Where throngs of people had once gathered, now there was only dust and disrepair.

Past the main pools, I entered a room with much smaller basins for hotter baths. In one such basin, smashed tiles formed a human-size opening. Just below the lip, a ladder was hidden in the shadows—nearly impossible to see if you didn't know where to look.

I scampered down it, descending thirty feet into darkness. Only after my eyes adjusted did shapes emerge in the shadows. I was in the front room of an abandoned storefront that was nearly ready to collapse from rot and disrepair. Boarded-up windows lined the far wall on either side of a door, beyond which lay a hidden world.

I cracked open the shop door, revealing an alley-like corridor. Although I was deep underground, it was like any street you might find in the upper city. A long row of storefronts with hanging wooden signs lined the alley. Phosphorescent moss grew on the ceiling high above, casting the space in an eerie blue glow with pinpricks of light resembling a starry sky. Most of the businesses in this part of the Underworld were dark and shuttered.

I was always amazed by this alternate world, built from the ashes of a great fire hundreds of years ago. The audacity of constructing an entirely new city atop ruins rather than starting from scratch perfectly encapsulated how Analon worked. And of course, thieves, mercenaries, and rebels had claimed the discarded world for themselves.

After a few twists and turns through deserted back alleys, the passageway opened up onto the primary thoroughfare of the Underground Market, known as the Lantern Mile. True to its name, dozens of lanterns created a kaleidoscope of flickering light, forming jagged dancing shadows. Despite the late hour, the street was bustling with activity, resembling many merchant districts in the upper city but with a decidedly more questionable crowd. Ruffians, thieves, and mercenaries headed in and out of taverns, gambling dens, and shops selling contraband.

I slunk down the path, making myself small, avoiding sudden movements and staying out of view when I could. No one paid any mind to an unassuming thief. Attention was not something you wanted along the Lantern Mile.

A barely noticeable storefront with a windowless black door sat between a bustling tavern and a weapons shop. A sign hung above it bearing the image of a mortar and pestle with a serpent tangled around the handle. I cracked the door and slipped inside.

Shelves and display cases lined the cramped room, filled with jars and boxes of countless reagents, plants, and minerals. Despite the sheer number of items for sale, everything was orderly.

I had been here a thousand times. My father had taught me the fundamentals of potions, but Mrs. Crowe had helped me hone my craft. She stood behind the counter now, her knitted brow only adding to the deep-set wrinkles in her pale skin, as she poured a brown liquid from a vial into a flask. Her ironclad concentration broke only the slightest bit as I entered the shop. I stayed quiet, knowing better than to disturb the master at work.

She measured out each ingredient, pausing occasionally to swirl the flask, mouthing numbers in a silent countdown, then continuing on to the next step in her delicate work. After several minutes, she stopped, corked the flask, and placed it on a tall shelf out of reach, letting out a quick breath. Only then did her eyes meet mine through wisps of her long, stringy gray hair.

"Cassian," she said matter-of-factly in her gravelly voice. "Thank you for not interrupting. I'm rather fond of this shop...and my limbs staying attached to my body, for that matter."

I let out a stuttering laugh, but Mrs. Crowe's expression remained stony.

"I'm rather fond of my limbs as well. Always enjoy watching you work. I learn something new every time."

She raised a skeptical eyebrow. "And what did you learn this time?"

"That you alternate between mixing clockwise and counterclockwise."

She cracked the slightest smile. "What brings you to my shop at this late hour?"

"I need a few...specialty ingredients," I said, handing her a list. Seeing it reminded me of my adventure with Darion earlier that day.

Her eyes narrowed to slits, and her lips pursed. "I've never seen your eyes do that."

"Do what?" I asked.

"Twinkle." Her expression was sour as ever as she looked me over as if trying to solve a puzzle.

This effect Darion had on me was infuriating. Could people so easily read it on my face? This was exactly why I avoided entanglements like these. They made me sloppy. I didn't need this distraction banging around in my mind. I made every attempt to keep my face neutral.

"*Oh*," she said, nodding, her question apparently answered. "Men. Waste of time, them. I hope he's handsome, at least."

"Can we just get to the list?" I asked, trying desperately to change the subject.

Without another word, Mrs. Crowe took my list with a huff and rummaged around her shop, adding ingredients to a small pouch. In short order, I tucked everything safely into my bag, my purse a few coins lighter.

"Thank you, Mrs. Crowe," I said, heading for the door. She replied with a grunt.

Just as I reached for the doorknob, I paused. "Mrs. Crowe. Can I ask you a question?"

Her eyes flicked to my coin purse, and then she sighed. "As long as it has nothing to do with whatever made your eyes twinkle."

"Definitely not!"

"Very well. Go ahead."

"What kind of potion would smell of ozone mixed with citrus?"

Her eyes widened for only a moment. "Why do you ask?"

"I smelled it during some..." I didn't want to get into specifics, but my curiosity got the better of me. "During some unusual activity. I thought maybe it came from a potion?"

"Did this unusual activity involve a person?"

"Yes." My encounters with the golden-eyed thief and the beast-like stranger flashed in my mind.

Mrs. Crowe beckoned me over. I complied, standing only a few inches away. She smelled of a hundred different potion ingredients, an eclectic potpourri. Her voice was barely a whisper. "What do you know of the Emberborn?"

"Emberborn? You mean the extinct race of magical beings?" I asked.

She shushed me and got even closer. "Not so loud," she said, almost in a panic. "Yes, Emberborn. And they're not extinct, just rare. And they do have...special abilities."

It was a shock to hear this from someone I considered rational and level-headed. It was just a bunch of superstitious nonsense.

"What do they have to do with ozone and citrus?" I asked.

She leaned in even more. "Some people have the ability to sense Emberborn."

Before I could respond, the door opened, and in walked an elderly man with expensive-looking dark robes and a fat coin purse. Mrs. Crowe transformed back into her typical stony self in an instant. "Evening, sir."

She didn't give me a second glance. Our conversation was over, apparently, so I slunk out of the shop even more confused than I'd been before.

CHAPTER TEN

The Last Lantern

AS I CONTINUED DOWN the Lantern Mile, the bustle of the street died down. The crowds thinned, and the open shops grew sparse, many of them closed or fully boarded up. This was the darker part of the Underworld, and the entrance to the catacombs was near.

No light shone from any of the shops, save for a lone tavern where the golden glow of a dying fire flickered, casting dancing shadows on the cobbled path. A half-rotten sign above the door read THE LAST LANTERN in faded paint. Old ale casks served as makeshift tables out front. A handful of surly-looking types sipped their drinks, whispering in each other's ears, shooting me suspicious looks as I passed. I tried to melt into the darkness.

Then something caught my eye.

It wasn't possible.

That mop of curly brown hair and emerald eyes.

Darion.

He sat alone, frowning, eyes cast downward toward the mug in his hands. How could he be here? Another in an ever-growing string of coincidences.

I didn't like coincidences.

I stopped to watch him, but nothing was more obvious than someone standing still in the street, staring. I should have continued on my way. This was not a distraction I needed. But as I moved, he looked up from his mug, and his face transformed from glum to jolly as he shot me a glowing smile.

"Cas! What are you doing here?" His voice echoed through the quiet street.

I cringed as the other patrons looked up; so much for stealth. Resigned to my fate, I approached, trying my best not to smile, but the involuntary curve of my mouth betrayed me. "I could ask the same of you. Are you following me again?"

Darion laughed. "That would be some talented following, since I was here first."

"Maybe you were following me very quickly?"

Darion snorted. "Are you drunk?"

"You're the one with a mug of ale."

"Ale?" Darion shook his head. "No, this is cider. Almost no alcohol."

"Almost." I smiled. "But seriously. What brings you to the edge of the Lantern Mile?"

"I come here when I need to get away from people. When I don't want anyone to find me." His eyes sparkled. "Well, people *usually* can't find me. But I'm happy about my failure to hide this time. What about you? Why are you here in this place where only thieves and misanthropes dare to tread?"

"I was buying some special herbs from a potion merchant," I said, pointing to my pack.

"That makes sense, except..." Darion tapped his chin. "All the potion merchants are back that way." He pointed in the direction from which I had just come. "What brings you to the very edge of the Lantern Mile?"

My mind went blank. I hadn't expected to meet anyone I knew here and had no cover story planned. "I'm headed to the catacombs," I blurted.

"What?" Darion nearly spat out his cider. "Are you serious? Whatever for?"

That was where my honesty ended. "A scavenger hunt," I lied. It was a weak lie, but it was the best I could come up with, given the circumstances.

"Bloody serious scavenger hunt." Darion's smile broadened, a mischievous glint in his eyes. "Can I join you?"

Yeah, it was a terrible lie. Now what was I supposed to say? I couldn't very well drag Darion into the catacombs.

"Well, today I'm just scouting. The scavenger hunt isn't until...later." I almost rolled my eyes at myself. This lie was getting worse by the minute. But maybe scouting the catacombs wasn't the worst idea. It might be a prudent thing to do, and tomorrow I could come back without Darion in tow.

"I'd still like to join you, if you don't mind," Darion said with sad eyes that were hard to resist, looking up at me through thick lashes. "It would be very nostalgic. I used to explore them when I was a teen."

"You did?" I raised my eyebrows. Exploring the catacombs was not for the meek. Many people died or went missing there each year.

"Well, I never went in too far. It was all to impress a boy I had a crush on." Darion's cheeks turned the slightest bit rosy, and there was a hint of vulnerability in his expression. It was infuriatingly adorable.

I had assumed that his tastes leaned toward men, what with the way he flirted openly with me, but this was the first indisputable confirmation, and it made my heart flutter unexpectedly. Everything about Darion was unexpected. And annoying.

"That sounds remarkably similar to my own experiences," I said.

"The exploring part?" Darion paused. "Or the impressing a boy part?"

"Both," I said—my own indisputable confirmation.

Without another word, I turned and started down the street. If he followed me, so be it. He was a grown man. I could hardly stop him.

I peeked back. He was still sitting at the table, looking like a stray cat hoping for a handout. I let out a long breath. Then I flicked my head in the direction I was headed. With a ridiculous smile, he hopped up from his seat, chugged his cider, tossed a silver onto the table, and raced after me.

We were already near the end of the Lantern Mile, approaching the edge of the Underground, so it didn't take long before the storefronts and dwellings grew sparse. The few remaining structures were in serious disrepair; several were still just burnt husks from the fires many years ago. The light of the final lantern was now out of sight, so we had only the phosphorescent glow of the moss on the ceiling to guide us. Darion's handsome face looked almost angelic in the subtle blue light.

This man was an enigma. I knew practically nothing about him, and yet he captivated me in a way I couldn't explain. It was like an invisible string connected us, attached to my chest, and he kept tugging on it.

"So, who are you exactly?" I said, the words coming out a little more accusatory than intended.

"Darion Thorne, at your service." He performed a silly bow with a flourish of his hands. "Potion-maker and jack-of-all-trades."

"Potion-maker. What potion did you need that long list of ingredients for?"

Darion zipped his lips. "Client confidentiality. And what about you, Cas? Who are *you*?"

"My sister, Elena, and I just sell herbs, trying to make a life for ourselves. And I'm a bit of a jack-of-all-trades, too." Which was my way of saying I was a thief. "Cassian Nightbrook's my full name."

"Well, Cassian Nightbrook, it's a pleasure to know you," Darion said with an easy smile.

"Likewise, Darion Thorne."

As we continued, the storefronts and dwellings gave way to stone walls, some naturally occurring, some cut into the bedrock. Even the moss's glow dimmed as we continued.

I reached for a vial from the belt strapped across my chest, and after several vigorous shakes, it emitted a green glow, lighting our path. I tucked it back into its slot.

"Impressive," Darion said. "Did you make that?"

"Yep."

"I guess you're not only an herb merchant but a bit of a potion-maker yourself."

"It's just simple chemistry," I said.

"No magic, then?"

"Magic is a word people use when they don't understand how things work."

Darion looked my way, fighting a smile.

"What's so funny?" I asked.

"Not funny. Interesting."

"I'm not sure interesting is better."

"I just wouldn't have taken you for a skeptic of magic," Darion said, still smiling, almost laughing. "You know, since you sell herbs to people who use them to make *magic* potions."

"I'm not saying their potions do nothing. Just that there are logical explanations that don't involve magic," I said. "I don't trust most of the fantastical legends I hear. I need proof before I'll believe something."

"Wise beyond your years," Darion said without a hint of sarcasm. "Who taught you to think like that?"

Images of my father instructing me on the finer points of potion-craft flashed through my mind—his infinite patience, deep wisdom, and loving tenderness. His absence was palpable, a dark stain on my heart. The buoyed feeling I got from being around Darion deflated slightly.

I instinctively reached for my locket but then quickly moved my hand away. I had no desire to talk about my parents or dredge up old memories, so I simply shrugged.

Darion nodded with tight lips, seeming to sense my hesitancy, and said nothing more. Our unspoken pact of respecting each other's secrets remained in effect.

The cobbled path gave way to dirt and gravel. What had once been an alley became decidedly more twisted and cave-like. The crunching of our footsteps echoed off the walls.

"We're getting close," I said. "Keep your eyes open for the entrance."

"And watch out for bone rats," Darion added. He seemed to read the skepticism on my face. "Don't tell me you don't believe in bone rats either."

"Oh, I believe in them, just not that they are telepathic or can walk through walls," I said.

"All you need to believe is that a swarm of them can kill you in seconds."

"*That* I believe."

A moment later, Darion pointed ahead of us. "There. There's the rupture."

The "entrance" to the catacombs was a long jagged crack in the stone wall, barely wide enough for an average-size person to slip through. It was likely the result of an underground tremor many years ago. The catacombs were never meant to be accessible to the public, but the wardens of the Royal Tombs either didn't know about the rupture or didn't deem it a risk, since it was on the opposite end of miles of twisting, mazelike tunnels.

Anyone foolish enough to attempt the trek will be food for the bone rats, the wardens likely thought.

Darion and I stood shoulder to shoulder, peering into the crack and the inky blackness beyond. A shiver ran from my core to my extremities, which I wanted to think was because of the tunnel's coldness, not the sinking feeling coming over me.

"How much *scouting* do you plan on doing?" Darion asked. "Are we going in?"

With Darion in tow, I had only imagined getting to the entrance, then turning around. But now it seemed foolish to have come all this way without even going *into* the catacombs. I was reasonably certain it had nothing to do with trying to impress Darion.

"It couldn't hurt to go in," I said, sounding even more uncertain than I felt.

"After you," Darion said, gesturing toward the entrance.

The crack was narrow enough that I had to go in sideways, and it sloped, so I had to arch backward to fit. I removed my pack and shimmied through, the jagged edges of the rock rubbing against my back.

Halfway through, it occurred to me what a compromised position I was in. What did I really know about Darion? A simple dagger to my side would finish me, and I wouldn't be able to defend myself. My heart rate kicked up, and I fought back a wave of panic. How could I have been so stupid? Why did I think I could trust him?

I stepped up my pace and pushed my way through, but in my haste, I scraped my arm on the jagged rock. Red lines formed along my skin. When I was free of the crack, I squared my shoulders with my hand on the hilt of my dagger, preparing for whatever came next.

But Darion simply followed me in, much more gracefully than I had managed. When he was through, he smiled. I felt foolish for my bout of panic and mistrust. The longer I spent around him, the more I questioned my judgment.

He looked at my scratched arm and cringed. "You okay?"

"Yeah, just scraped it against the rock." There were about twenty small scrapes with tiny dots of red beading up. Dust, what a pain.

We had entered a long, narrow hallway cut directly into the bedrock. Along each wall was a series of stone shelves absolutely packed with human remains. Piles of skulls, rib cages, femurs, and every other kind of bone stretched on as far as the eye could see. As I moved from side to side, my glowing vial cast ghoulish bone shadows that danced along the walls.

Far in the distance, I heard a clamor like a group of people celebrating. Had a group of thieves decided to throw some kind of macabre party in the catacombs?

"What *is* that racket?" I asked.

"I don't hear anything," Darion said flatly as he bent over to inspect some loose bones scattered about.

"Seriously?" I asked. How could he not hear it? It sounded like a whole crowd of people yelling in the distance, and it was getting louder.

Darion picked up a bone fragment with jagged scrape marks along it as if it had been chewed.

"Bone rats have been here," he said, then pointed to my arm. "They can smell blood from a mile away. You'd better do something about that."

The stupid bone rats again. Overblown nonsense.

Still, my arm *was* a mess. A hundred pinpricks of blood had bubbled up, and now it was trickling down my fingers and dripping onto the floor. I ran my hand over it, streaking the blood across my arm and making quite a gory sight.

"Okay, now I *do* hear something," Darion said.

"Finally!" I said. "So you hear the voices?"

"Sounds more like squeals and chittering."

Huh. I heard the squeals, too, but they were mere background noise compared to the voices that were now shouting outright.

My father's voice echoed in my mind. *You can hear them, too. It's your special gift.*

A horrifying realization flowed through me. The voices weren't coming from the tunnels. They were in my head, and they were all chanting a single word over and over:

Blood. Blood. Blood. Blood. Blood. Blood.

Chapter Eleven

The Catacombs

THEY CAME IN WAVES. Hundreds of them, covering every square inch of the floor, climbing over each other, headed directly toward us—a writhing mass of tangled brown hair, sharp teeth, and glowing red eyes. Some were nearly two feet long. The stench of them hit me like a sledgehammer. The chanting in my head was nearly unbearable.

Darion and I shared a glance, both knowing that getting back through the crack would take more time than we had.

"Run!" I shouted as we turned away from the swarm and raced in the other direction.

A few of the faster rats near the front of the pack were just steps away, snapping their teeth and chittering just behind us. One leapt toward my bloody arm.

Blood. Blood. Blood.

Darion drew his short sword, and after one quick strike, the rat hit the ground with a red gash across its body. I gave him a thankful nod, then took a vial from my belt and tossed it behind us.

"Watch out!" I yelled.

An inferno of orange-and-yellow flames erupted through the corridor, sending a blast of heat rippling over my skin. The chorus of squeals was both deafening and sickening.

"Whoa, that's hot!" Darion yelled. "Nice job!"

"That won't stop them for long."

I'd been sure of the layout of the catacombs when we'd entered, but the army of bloodthirsty rodents on our tail jumbled my memory. Ahead of us, the corridor forked left and right. The wrong choice could lead us to a dead end, *dead* being the operative word.

Garrick's voice echoed in my mind: *Sometimes memory can falter under pressure.* I could almost hear him gloating.

As the intersection approached, I went with my gut.

"Left!" I yelled. Without a moment's hesitation, Darion followed me down the corridor. It wasn't a dead end, so that was something.

With the immediate pressure off, I dug deep and retreated into my mind. I was finally able to block out the wretched noises and the screaming in my head. I had only a moment of clarity, but that was all I needed for the map to come into focus, and I charted the twists and turns to the queen's tomb.

"Right!" I yelled at the next intersection.

"You really know your way around down here," Darion panted.

"I studied a map," I said.

"You *memorized* the whole thing?"

I shrugged. If he only knew how close I'd been to forgetting everything I'd learned, he might not have been quite so impressed.

We twisted and turned through the tunnels for what felt like an eternity. An occasional rat appeared in front of us, and Darion skillfully slayed them all. He was a wonder with a sword. Twice, the rats advanced on us from behind, close enough that we could smell their stench. Each time, I threw a fireball vial at them.

"That's my last one!" I yelled as the inferno blazed behind us. It would take only a few moments for them to overtake us again. This was not the way I'd imagined my end.

"How far can you jump?" Darion yelled over the squeals.

"Pretty far."

"Left at the next intersection," he said.

That was odd. Did he actually know where we were? Apparently he knew these catacombs better than he had let on. I had planned on turning right, the most direct path to the queen's tomb. I did some shuffling in my mind. We could still get there if we went left, but that path would take us well out of the way.

Darion said, "Trust me."

Trust. I almost laughed. People who told me to trust them usually deserved the opposite. I barely knew him, but somehow I had allowed my judgment to become clouded, and now my life was at risk. Then again, what was the alternative? Let the rats overtake us and hope we could fight them off? I had no choice but to put my faith in this near-stranger.

I nodded, and we raced to the left, my fate in his hands.

It wasn't long before the narrow corridor opened up into a large room resembling a chapel with rows of seats hewn from huge slabs of rock, all facing a large dais. On it was a massive stone tomb, its cracked top half open, with large chunks of stone surrounding it. At the far end of the room, the corridor continued.

I desperately hoped Darion knew what he was doing by leading us here.

We raced down the center aisle, Darion first. The rats entered the chapel behind us, spreading out, their claws scraping against the stone. The sheer number of them was hard to fathom; they fought each other, crammed down the aisle, and climbed over the rows of benches, spreading like a virus.

Darion leapt over the tomb with the grace of an acrobat. Dust, he was beautiful to watch. As I followed him, I stole a glance into the stone casket. A shriveled corpse dressed in rusted chain mail stared at me with empty eye sockets.

"Get ready to sprint, then jump," Darion yelled as we cleared the dais and approached the end of the room.

In an instant, I understood. A wide and jagged chasm had opened in the ground, taking a good section of the chapel with it. The exit was on the other side. This would require quite a leap.

My lungs burned, but I stepped up my pace to a near sprint. Darion and I ran side by side until we reached the edge. I kicked off and leapt, sailing through the air as the ground disappeared, my legs pinwheeling to take advantage of every bit of momentum. The chasm extended into darkness below me, farther than the light from my vial could reach.

My feet hit solid ground.

No problem.

Easy, even.

Darion's jump was not as successful. Only half of his front foot made it past the edge. His boot slipped on the rock, and his leg fell downward as his hands extended forward, grasping at thin air.

I reached out.

Our hands clasped.

I pulled with all my might. My feet slipped on the stone, and both of us headed toward the chasm. Just inches from the edge, my heel gained traction against the smallest bit of uneven rock. It was *just* enough to dig in and pull Darion back from certain death.

I landed hard on the stone, and Darion fell directly on top of me with a grunt, our bodies smashing together, legs a tangled mess. His face—his lips—were just inches from my own. I gulped.

"Thanks," he whispered. His breath tickled my eyelashes, smelling of mint and cider.

"You're welcome," I said, the only thing my brain would let me say at that moment. His emerald eyes stared into mine with a ferocious intensity, but there was vulnerability there, too. I wanted nothing more than to lift my head a few inches and kiss those lips. The pull was overwhelming.

The scrape of dozens of claws on stone and loud shrieks came from the other side of the chasm. Darion rolled off me, the moment lost. It was for the best.

Side by side, we watched in horror as the rats on the opposite edge scraped and clawed to stop their momentum. A few attempted to jump the chasm, but all fell well short. And the whole time, I could still hear their chanting in my mind.

For years, everything before that horrible day at the farm had felt like a dream. There had always been a before and an after. But now those childhood memories of my father showing me the whisperhawks sharpened into focus.

Darion couldn't hear the rats speaking, so either I was losing it or they were somehow projecting their thoughts into my mind. I wasn't sure which option I liked better.

"That's going to smell pretty bad in a few hours," Darion said flatly, watching the carnage.

"Hard to imagine them smelling worse than they already do," I replied. We shared a glance, then burst out laughing, mostly at the absurdity but also to release the tension of our narrow escape.

Darion sprang to his feet and put out a hand to help me up.

"Thank you again," he said earnestly. "I wouldn't have made that jump without your help. You didn't even hesitate."

"Thank *you* for leading me this way. You saved us both," I said as he pulled me up. The only question lingering in my mind was *how* he knew to come this way.

"You should clean up that wound," Darion said, pointing to the streaks of red running down my arm. "Otherwise we'll just attract them again."

"Good idea," I said, reaching for a vial of antiseptic that I kept on my belt. As I tended to my arm, I asked, "How did you know about this room?"

"I memorized a lot of the routes down here when I was a kid. My crush was a powerful motivator," Darion said with a laugh.

"Impressive memory," I said. "Especially since it was so long ago." I didn't mean to sound accusatory, but it seemed odd.

"Hey, not *that* long ago," Darion laughed. "Also, this is coming from the guy who memorized the whole map."

I shrugged. "Just my own bit of magic, I guess. I remember everything I see."

"That's some pretty potent magic," Darion said. "So, Mr. Memory, which way now?"

I paused for a moment to think.

"I don't think we can go back the way we came," I said, watching the rats continue to fall into the chasm, though the tide had slowed considerably. "We'll just run into the rats again. We should give this area a wide berth and make our way back to the entrance."

Since we'd come this far already, I picked a path that led us past the tomb of Queen Amara. I could complete my next Order of Emberlight trial with Darion none the wiser.

"Lead on," Darion said, gesturing toward the corridor.

We walked in silence as the din of the rats died down, both externally and in my head. Soon it was deathly quiet, with only the sounds of our steady breathing and our boots on stone. The silence pressed in, thick, ancient, and heavy. The corridors ahead felt like a different world.

Darion's face flickered in the light, his brow furrowed in concentration, which only made his chiseled features more handsome. A pang of guilt hit me.

"I'm sorry I got you mixed up in all this," I said.

Darion waved me off. "I knew the risks. You have nothing to be sorry about. Besides, this is a lot more fun than sitting in a tavern, sulking."

"Why *were* you sulking?" I asked.

He looked away. "Story for another time."

Who *was* this mysterious man? Given the way he handled his sword, it was clear he'd had formal training. People with sword skills like that tended to be the sort trying to stop me from robbing someone. I reminded myself that the less we knew about each other, the better. I had found him at a tavern on the Lantern Mile, after all, and most people there had something to hide.

I guided us out of the older sections of the catacombs and toward the newer and more traveled ones. The farther we went, the more elaborate the corridors became. Rough-hewn stone turned to polished granite. Haphazard skeletons lying bare on shelves were replaced by sealed crypts with ornate carvings.

We entered a large and elaborate antechamber with a row of granite tombs in the middle, each with a marble statue behind it. The statues were of descendants of the royal line, all in regal poses, holding staffs or swords, each with a crown atop their head. Just past the tombs was a large doorway lined with grand columns through which moonlight streamed, forming a pale blue rectangle on the ground. Queen Amara's crypt was in the very next room.

Darion inspected one of the golden placards affixed to the front of the tombs, and his eyes went wide. "These are the past kings and queens of Velmorra. We're in the Royal Crypt."

"This way," I said, gesturing for him to follow as I headed toward the door to the next room.

"Grave robbers are common here, so guards patrol this part of the tomb. If they find us, they'll kill us on the spot," Darion said with a nervous glance over his shoulder.

"Well, let's not let them spot us, then."

If the room we left was dramatic, the next room was breathtaking. The ceiling soared above our heads, at least five stories high. A row of windows looked out onto the city of Analon and the starry sky, which bathed the entire room in a soft glow. A massive tomb lay in the center with a statue of Queen Amara behind it that nearly reached the ceiling. Marble robes cascaded over her shoulders and pooled around her feet. She had one hand resting on her heart and the other raised, palm out, in the universal symbol for peace and love. Atop her head was an actual golden crown studded with diamonds and gems. The amount of money that crown would fetch could likely feed an entire village for a lifetime. Beside her stood an enormous feline beast that came up to her waist—a mythical creature known as a shadowlynx. Its massive fangs were the size of daggers, and its claws left deep gouges in the marble.

At the base of the statue was a plaque with the engraving:

Here lies Queen Amara, the last of the royal Emberborn.

Emberborn? How was that possible? I'd never heard even the smallest mention of it. I thought back to the Emberborn book that had started this whole quest. Maybe it was related.

I paused near the center of the room, looking for any sign of what my next clue might be. I had hoped that when I entered the tomb, the solution would present itself, but there was nothing obvious.

"What are you looking for?" Darion asked. "Is it related to that scavenger hunt you mentioned?"

"I just need a moment," I said. I hadn't counted on Darion being here. I thought I'd have as much time as I needed to search for clues, but every minute we stayed increased the danger I was putting him in.

Faint footsteps echoed several chambers over.

"Someone's coming," Darion said in a hushed but urgent tone. "We need to go!"

That was the moment I saw it: a faint red X right above the window opposite Queen Amara's tomb, etched into the stone above the middle window, high above the ground. It looked the same as the X from the Order of Emberlight invitation. Without a word to Darion, I climbed the wall.

"Are you half spider?" Darion whispered with a soft laugh, watching me climb. "Well, whatever the dust you're doing, do it fast. We're going to have company soon."

I ignored him as I climbed to the top of the window. My goal was so close; I couldn't back out now. Carved directly into the granite, the X was embedded with a red gemstone that shimmered in the faint moonlight. Much fainter was an inscription extending to either side of the X, so faint that only someone right next to it could possibly read it.

May her wisdom eXtend beyond the hands of time's embrace.

The top right part of the X pointed to a hole bored into the stone. Inside the hole was a rolled-up piece of parchment similar to the original Order of Emberlight invitation. But this one was covered in strange glyphs I didn't recognize—some kind of foreign language or code, most likely. I committed the entire thing to memory and tucked the parchment into my breast pocket. Then I peered through the hole.

Framed directly in the middle was the clock tower of the Citadel Library. In a hundred years, that bell had never failed to ring, and it was never a moment late—the ultimate symbol of control and accuracy for the Tarnasau Dynasty.

Apparently the clock tower was my next target. Getting in there would make this task seem like a stroll through the Citadel Gardens. Legend spoke of the tenders, trained warriors who would defend the tower with their lives.

"Hurry!" Darion insisted from below.

This was not the time to consider how I'd get into the clock tower. I scampered down the wall and landed next to Darion.

"Did you find what you were looking for?" he asked.

"I think so."

The door we had entered a moment before opened, and a group of Royal Guards walked in. They looked startled to see us.

Darion glanced at the guards, then back at me. “I hope it was worth it.”

Chapter Twelve

River of Souls

Five Royal Guards dressed in full armor and wielding massive swords approached us, less than a stone's throw away. The tallest one in the middle drew his sword. "Die, thieves!"

An instant later, two of the guards unsheathed their daggers and threw them our way, the blades spinning as they flew.

Darion drew his short sword with the fluidity of a practiced swordsman and sent one dagger clattering harmlessly to the ground. His speed and accuracy were impressive.

I ducked, and the second dagger flew over me, the edge of the hilt barely glancing off my shoulder. I drew a vial from my belt and threw it directly in front of the guards, sending a massive cloud of smoke billowing throughout the crypt. Coughs and the clash of armor on stone rang out.

I ran for the exit on the far side of the room, Darion on my heels. No matter how tonight ended, one thing was clear: we worked well together, coordinating without even speaking like two pieces of a well-oiled machine. Despite the chaos, I couldn't help but marvel at the fluidity of his movements, the confidence of every decision.

As we raced through the corridor, horns blared in a staccato rhythm behind us, echoing through the catacombs.

"Dust," I said. "They've raised the alarm."

"This whole crypt will be crawling with Royal Guards in no time. We can't go back the way we came."

Darion was right. Any moment now, the guards would overtake us. But there was another option—one I would consider only in the direst of circumstances, but this situation fit the bill.

"There *is* another way out of the catacombs," I said. "But it won't be easy."

"The River of Souls," Darion said grimly.

I nodded. "It might be our only option."

The River of Souls was fed by an underground spring and ran under the catacombs, where priests used it to cleanse bodies as part of the burial ritual. Fortunately, the preparation chamber and entrance to the river were not far away. But the river was dangerous, verging on deadly, with a strong current. Some of the tunnels were entirely full of water, and there were jagged rocks ready to tear our flesh to tatters.

"I'd rather face a raging river than a hundred blades," Darion said. "Lead the way."

"We're already halfway there," I said as I navigated us from room to room.

With the sound of blaring horns and marching boots behind us, we passed through several antechambers filled with the tombs of lesser royals, bishops, and wealthy merchants. Soon we came to a room with several waist-high tables, each with a channel running along the perimeter, emptying into a trough that ran between them. The stone was stained the faded brown-red of old blood, and the scent of incense was stale in the air. We had entered the body preparation room.

Along the far wall were six nondescript wooden doors.

"Where now?" Darion asked, with utter faith in my memory.

I had no idea. The map I had memorized hadn't specified. With his fate in my hands, I simply guessed. "Third door from the left."

We passed through the door, shutting it just as the sound of clomping boots grew louder outside. The footsteps paused for a moment, and then a deep voice barked, "Check them all!"

The room we had entered was small with just a rectangular hole in the ground, slightly larger than a typical man. A strong current of water rushed past just a few feet below the lip of the hole. A wooden pallet hung from a pulley mechanism above the hole, presumably to lower the bodies and bathe them in the sacred water.

"We found it. Thank dust for your memory," Darion said, gesturing toward the entrance to the River of Souls. I didn't dare tell him that I had guessed. Sometimes it was better to be lucky than smart.

The sound of splintering wood came from just outside. Our door could open at any moment.

I looked at Darion, whose face was steely and resolute, full of bravery and determination. How had I led this beautiful man to such a horrible fate? Would I ever see him again?

"No time to think this through," I said, grabbing hold of his hand. "Let's try to stick together."

Darion cupped the back of my neck and pressed our mouths together in a hasty, sloppy kiss. I was so shocked that I scarcely knew how to react. His lips were soft and welcoming, and his stubble scraped against my cheek. For a brief moment, the tumult of the world around us drifted away, and it was only the two of us.

I didn't want this. And yet it was also everything I wanted.

We separated, and the world came crashing back.

"For luck," Darion said.

"For luck," I echoed, half dazed, touching my hand to my lips. Then I snapped back to reality. "Let's go!"

Below us was churning white water and darkness. We jumped together, hand in hand, plunging into the torrent.

The first sensation was one of bitter cold as the icy water instantly filled every crack and crevice on my body, including my nose and ears. The only warmth was that of Darion's hand, which gripped mine like a vise. Rushing water pushed us swiftly down a narrow tunnel, barely illuminated by my vial. I fought to keep my head above the surface, gulping precious air at every opportunity. The tunnel twisted and turned. The ceiling of the cave undulated over us, towering far above us one moment, plunging the next so that we had only just enough room to breathe.

The current picked up. Darion shouted something, but the splashing water was far too loud for me to make out what he said. Just ahead, the ceiling of the tunnel dropped below the water's surface. I had just enough time to take a deep breath, then pulled my hand away from Darion just in time to push against the top of the cave and duck below the surface.

Under the swirling water, avoiding the rocks took every bit of concentration, the vial's glow providing barely enough light to keep me from crashing into them. I kept my hands out in front of me, feeling for craggy edges, dodging each time a rock threatened to bash my head in. A sharp edge scraped my leg, most likely drawing blood.

My lungs burned, hungry for air, and I desperately wished the tunnel would end. But it continued, and the pain in my chest consumed my every thought. Panic wrapped its fingers around me as if trying to squeeze the last bit of air out of my lungs. Had I drawn my last breath? Was this to be my watery grave?

An unexpected warmth flowed through my body like the golden glow of the sun. My mind calmed. My heart rate slowed. The burning in my lungs diminished. For a moment, I wondered if I had died and this was the afterlife. But if this wasn't death, perhaps I could last a little longer. Maybe a few more seconds. Maybe enough to live.

The tunnel forked again, the left channel pulling at me with a ferocious energy. I had no choice but to submit, and the current sucked me through, plunging downward faster than ever.

I was at the end of my endurance. I needed a breath. A gasp of water would end everything.

And then it was over. The river leveled out, and the shiny luster of water against air appeared above me. My head burst through the surface, and I gasped for air, lungs sucking in oxygen as if they'd never tasted its sweetness before.

I'd made it. I was alive.

"Darion!" I called, coughing up water as I yelled.

Only echoes replied.

The river still moved swiftly, but it had slowed enough that the surface was calm. I treaded water and looked around as I floated through a wide, tall tunnel that grew larger as it went. Just ahead, a large opening revealed a sky full of stars glimmering off Analon Bay.

"Darion, where are you?" I cried.

He would surface any moment. He had to. He must be right behind me.

But with every moment that passed, the panic I'd felt in the throes of the tunnel increased tenfold. Had he met the fate I had narrowly escaped? And if so, could I live with myself? My heart shouldn't have hurt this much for a man I'd just met.

I had made it through alive, but Darion was nowhere to be found.

Chapter Thirteen

Spiral

"You were out late last night," Elena said as I descended into the kitchen, bleary-eyed.

"Mmmm" was my reply. I had gotten home only a few hours earlier. My head pounded from lack of sleep, and red scratches ran up my arms and legs from the rough ride in the River of Souls. My entire body ached down to my bones.

I had floated into Analon Bay, then swum to shore and searched for any sign of Darion. But after only a few minutes, a contingent of Royal Guards began to scout the beach, no doubt looking for us. I watched from the shadows. After nearly an hour of searching, the guards finally left. Only then did I make my way home, wracked with guilt that I might have been responsible for Darion's death. He had gone into the catacombs because of me, and he had only entered Queen Amara's tomb because I'd led him there, all under false pretenses.

My last memory of him was our kiss. I couldn't bear it if that was my *final* memory of him. It would shred me to pieces.

And all for this stupid parchment that didn't even make sense. I was sorely tempted to throw it in the fire and be done with the whole thing.

When I moved into the sunlight, Elena's jaw dropped. "You look like shite," she said. "What in the dust happened to you?"

"None of your damn business," I snapped. I didn't mean to be so harsh, but I was in a foul mood.

Elena's face crumpled, and then she lashed back. "Look, I don't care if you were out messing around with Darion and it got a little rough."

My jaw dropped. I must have really riled her up, and I needed to defuse the situation before it got out of hand.

"Hey, I didn't mean to shout," I said. "I'm sorry. It was a terrible night, and it's complicated."

"But you're not going to tell me what happened," she said. It wasn't a question.

My only reply was a sigh.

"You *were* out with Darion, weren't you?"

"No..." I said, then shook my head. "I mean, yes. He was there. Just not in the way you think."

"Did you kiss him?"

"Kind of. But it was just a peck."

"So what happened?" she said, her face softening. "You know I'm not a kid anymore. I understand more than you think."

"You're right," I said. "You're not a kid. He and I got separated. And I'm not sure what happened to him after that."

"Separated in the catacombs."

"How in the dust—" I blurted.

"You sometimes talk in your sleep," she said with a shrug. When I stood there, speechless, she continued, "I know you have your secrets and that you think it's important to keep them from me. I've learned to live with that, but I want you to know that when you're ready to share them, I'm ready to hear them."

Elena was growing up faster than I ever could have predicted. Maybe she *was* ready to hear more. But I didn't know how to start. There were just too many secrets, and once I started, I wasn't sure how I'd stop. And what if she didn't understand my motives or disagreed with what I was doing? My primary goal had always been to protect her and make a safe home for us outside the city, and I couldn't let anything jeopardize that.

I just couldn't handle being honest at that moment. I wasn't ready.

"We don't want to be late for the market," I said.

Elena shook her head, her lips pressed tightly together, and walked away.

The entire day, I searched the crowd for that mop of curly brown hair and those emerald eyes. That coy smile—slightly sarcastic but friendly—was sure to sneak up on me when I least expected it. But each time I thought I saw him, it was somebody else.

He didn't show up, not that day or the next.

With each day that passed, I felt worse, sure that his blood was on my hands.

Every time the bell rang, I stared up at the massive Citadel Clock, knowing that it was the next destination in the Emberlight Trials. But what would that knowledge cost me? Was Darion's life the price?

I felt unmoored. Between being banned from Garrick's tavern, my concern over Darion's fate, and the uncertainty that I was even worthy of joining the Order of Emberlight, I felt like my whole life was caving in on me.

Each day, I walked by the Bleeding Oak on the off chance that I might see Darion. Each night, I headed down to the Lantern Mile and stopped by the Last Lantern, where I had bumped into him on that fateful night. But each time I came up empty.

I also stopped by Mrs. Crowe's potion shop each night to ask her more about the ozone-and-citrus smell and what it had to do with Emberborn.

But each time, her shop was shut up tight with no lights on and no sounds coming from within.

On the third day after the catacombs, Elena confronted me. "Cas, I'm worried about you. I want to help."

"I don't think there's much you can do. There's not much *anyone* can do."

Elena frowned. "Well, just promise me you won't do anything stupid. Okay?"

"I'll try, Elena."

That night, I was too distraught to sit at home. The image of Darion's bloated body washing up on some beach consumed my thoughts. I tried to banish the image by remembering his warm, bright smile. But every time I pictured it, the smile morphed into a grimace plastered on his dead, rotting corpse.

I wasn't typically the type to drown my sorrows in ale, but tonight nothing was stopping me from getting drunk, so I made my way down to the Last Lantern once more.

Just before I entered, I swore I saw movement across the street out of the corner of my eye. I spun around and scanned the shadows. Absolute stillness. Apparently I was just chasing ghosts.

The clientele at the Last Lantern was a rough bunch. When I walked in, I attracted more than one long stare from the patrons, who looked like they might just as soon slit my throat as say hello. While I didn't exactly look like a topsider who had accidentally wandered into the wrong part of the Underworld, perhaps my lean physique and short stature made me look like an easy mark. I ignored the looks and strode up to the bar.

The bartender, a surly older man with a shaved head and more scars than I could count, looked up and grunted.

"Ale," I said.

I sat in the corner with my back to the wall, gulping my ale, surveying the room, alert and vigilant. At least I was alert to start. After the third drink, the room got fuzzy, and I tipped to one side. But the ale was doing its job—I had only thought of Darion once in the last five minutes.

Out the window, I saw something move in the darkness again. Or maybe it was just my imagination.

I was staring into my fourth mug when a shadow fell over me, blocking the golden lantern light. I looked up to see a very tall, very thick man looking down at me. He had a long scar across his face and a grin that didn't look friendly.

"Oi, you," he bellowed in a gravelly thick accent from the southern regions. "What's a precious thing like you doing drinking alone in a place like this? You're liable to get mugged...or worse."

I didn't particularly care for his characterization of me. *Precious thing?*

"I can take care of myself," I said. It came out shakier than I had hoped, likely because of the many pints I had just consumed.

"You sure about that?" the man asked just as two others joined him on either side. They nearly looked identical but for the first man's scar. My pulse kicked up a notch. One oafish idiot was easy to dodge. But three?

"Look, gentlemen, I don't want any trouble," I said.

"Funny you should say," the scarred man replied. "See, we was about to offer you a chance to avoid just that. I reckon that if you give us your coin purse, we'll make sure you make it out of this tavern alive."

Well, that had gotten nasty quickly.

Fortunately, I had a plan for dealing with opponents who outmatched me. I acted fast, tossing my ale in their faces with one hand and reaching for a smoke vial with the other, all while ducking under the table.

At least that's what I tried to do. In my drunken state, what I actually did was slip on the ale I knocked on the floor and land hard on my back, missing my smoke vial completely.

I lay on the ground under the table in a puddle of ale, gasping for air. The man with the scar threw the table across the room as if it were a toy.

As he reached for me, I squirmed away. I finally got a grip on my smoke vial and tossed it right at their feet.

Clouds billowed throughout the room. That was enough of a distraction for me to crawl past them, but as I did, a hand reached through the smoke and grabbed my tunic. I pulled out my dagger and dragged it across his hand, drawing blood.

"You little prick!" a voice yelled out.

I got to my feet, a little wobbly, steadied myself, and dashed for the door. I was only feet away when hands grabbed the back of my cloak, lifted me, and smashed me against the wall face-first, the entire body attached to them pressing against me. The force of the impact sent my dagger clattering to the floor.

"You're going to regret that," a deep man's voice whispered into my ear. His breath smelled of rot and nearly made me gag.

I shoved my elbow into his torso. He didn't flinch. The metallic sound of a blade being unsheathed rang out behind me. Perhaps this was the end.

The man's hand moved. I gritted my teeth, waiting to feel the cold steel and hot pain of a blade in my back.

Instead, there was a loud thump behind me, and my captor fell to the ground. A hand reached out through the smoke and grabbed mine.

"Let's go!" a familiar voice called.

Chapter Fourteen

Under the Night Willow

I couldn't believe my eyes. Was I drunk enough to hallucinate?

Darion and I ran out of the Last Lantern with smoke billowing behind us. There were bruises on his face, but he wore a smile that said he couldn't be happier to see me.

"How?" was all I could say.

"Later."

"But...you're alive. How did you find me?" I asked as we ran along. "Was that you watching me from outside the bar?"

"Later."

He dragged me into the first alleyway, and we weaved through the maze of streets—left, then right, then left again. Boots clomped behind us, but with each turn, they got fainter.

"Down here," Darion said, descending a flight of stairs that ended at a closed front door. It appeared to be the entrance to a basement dwelling, but it looked as if it had been years since the door had been opened.

Darion put his index finger to his mouth, and we waited in silence. Minutes passed. The road above was quiet.

Even with adrenaline coursing through me, my brain was still fuzzy from ale. I put my hand to his face. I meant to do it gently, but it turned out to be more of a slap.

"Ouch!" Darion whisper-shouted. "Right on my bruise."

"Sorry!" I said. "A bit tipsy."

Darion pulled a vial from his belt. "Here. Drink this. Brightleaf potion. It'll clear your head."

I swigged it down in one gulp. My mind immediately sharpened—almost *too* much. A torrent of thoughts rushed through my head, all the things I had tried to forget. I'd been sure Darion was dead and that I was the cause. And now, days later, here he was, somehow both finding and rescuing me. A strange mix of relief, anger, and desire swirled through me.

"Where *were* you?" I pleaded. "What happened to your face?"

"It's a long story. But the short version is, I ran into some guards."

"What?" I nearly shouted. "Did they capture you?"

"In a manner of speaking."

A barking dog and a loud thud came from behind the door we stood at. I supposed it wasn't as abandoned as I'd thought.

"Let's go," Darion said with a cringe. We hurried up the stairs and ran down the street.

Once we were clear of the house, I turned to Darion. "Can you please tell me the rest of what happened?"

"Yeah, but not here," he said, smiling. "I want to show you something."

"That's mysterious. I'm not sure I can handle mysterious right now."

"I think you'll like this."

Darion led me through various alleyways, and we soon entered a part of the Underworld I'd never been to. This was the second time I had trusted him to guide me. I was on high alert despite the fact that he'd just rescued me and *I* was the one who'd nearly gotten *him* killed. I couldn't control my suspicions any more than I could stop breathing. And yet I desperately wanted to trust him.

Darion guided us to a narrow cave-like opening and then down into a tunnel covered with the blue phosphorescent moss that lit much of the Underworld. It clung to every surface, denser than I'd seen anywhere else, casting us in an eerie blue glow brighter than a full moon on a cloudless summer eve. Darion's smiling face shone in the light.

"Where are you taking me?" I asked.

"Almost there."

The passage opened up onto a massive cavern with a moss-dotted ceiling that soared high above our heads. Large mounds of the same glowing moss covered the ground, creating the illusion that we were standing on a grassy hillside under the starry sky. Farther into the cavern, a small tree sprang from the moss. A twisting trunk led to boughs full of pale oval-shaped leaves. Next to the tree was a shallow pond of the clearest water I'd ever seen.

"How is there a tree here?" I asked.

"It's a night willow," he said. "They're very rare and only grow in the light produced by the moss. Its roots drink from this pond."

"It's beautiful." I couldn't hold back my smile. The leaves were soft as silk. When I touched one, it broke free from the branch. I snatched it up and held it out to Darion. "Have you felt these?"

He took the leaf, rubbed it between his fingers, and smiled. "You know what giving a night willow leaf to someone signifies?"

"No idea."

"It means you like that person. I'm keeping this." He pocketed the leaf with such tenderness and care, and with it a tiny piece of my heart.

He sat down beneath the tree and patted the ground beside him. When I sat, the ground had a give to it, almost like I was sprawled on a large feather pillow.

Darion looked me right in the eye. Dust, those eyes were beautiful.

"So, I owe you an explanation," he said.

"I want to know what happened, of course," I said, "but you don't *owe* me anything."

"I think I *do* owe you," he said with a grave look. "After we were separated, I must have ended up in a different part of the river. I floated into a long cave that had a shoreline, so I climbed out. I waited for a long while but never saw you. I even tried to swim upstream to see if I could find you, but the current was too strong. I found a way back into the catacombs, but I ran into a band of guards there."

"You were captured?" I asked.

"Yeah. But luckily, one of the guards simply needed the right kind of persuasion to let me go." Darion mimed rubbing two coins together with his fingers.

"I was worried you had died," I said, unable to hold back the anguish in my voice. "I thought I was responsible for your death."

"I'm sorry I put you through that," Darion said, taking my hand in his. The contact sent warmth radiating through me. "Honestly, until I saw you walk into the tavern, I thought *you* had died."

"So that *was* you watching me," I said.

He nodded.

"Why did you hide?"

"Honestly? I was afraid."

"Afraid of what?"

"Cas, there are things..." Darion paused for a moment, then sighed. "There are things about me that I'm not proud of. Things I can't really share."

This didn't surprise me in the least, and to be honest, I was relieved. There were things about me that I couldn't tell him, too, and since we both had secrets, maybe we could cobble together some kind of half-broken relationship. Or maybe I was getting way ahead of myself. Maybe he didn't want the same things I did.

"You don't have to tell me everything," I said. "Maybe it's even better that way."

Darion's expression was complex, perhaps a little sad. "Maybe."

"But there is one thing I need to know," I said.

"What's that?"

"In the catacombs, when you kissed me..." My throat dried up, and the words stuck in my mouth.

"Yes," Darion said with certainty. "I meant it. And I want to do it again."

He cupped my cheek.

"Slower this time," I said. "And less water."

Darion laughed quietly, then pressed his smile against my lips. We kissed tenderly, deliberately, savoring the moment. His lips were soft and receptive. The air he exhaled through his nose tickled my cheek, sending a tingle through my entire body, all the way to my fingers and toes.

His tongue explored my lips, and I welcomed him in. Our tongues met, but we continued gently, in no hurry, neither of us feeling the need to turn up the heat too much. And yet it was the most passionate kiss I'd ever experienced.

We leaned back, resting on the soft moss, letting our hands explore each other. He caressed the small of my back in broad strokes, just barely dipping his fingers under the waistband of my trousers. I ran my hand down his neck, across his strong shoulders, feeling the strength in his arms. I grazed his armpit, and he giggled into my mouth.

"Sorry," I said.

"No, I like it."

"You do, huh?" With that encouragement, I raised his arm by the wrist, then pressed my nose into the tender skin under the shoulder. Darion gasped, a mix of surprise and pleasure. And wow, that sound he made flipped a switch in me. Suddenly all I could think about was ripping his clothes off. The image of him in his wet drawers at the pond flashed in my mind.

Somewhere deep in the cavern, a rock shifted. We both sat up, instantly alert. We were, after all, in a cave in the Underworld. Obscure as it was, it wasn't exactly a private space.

I wasn't sure how to broach the subject of what came next. We couldn't go back to my place with Elena there, and I didn't even know where Darion lived.

I looked into his eyes. "So…"

"So," he echoed.

But the mood had shifted. I could sense it.

"Can I come by your cart tomorrow?" Darion asked. "I thought maybe I could bring us lunch and we could have another picnic. But maybe one with more kissing."

"More kissing sounds great," I said. "And maybe more than just kissing."

The longing in Darion's eyes nearly bored holes into my chest and straight through my heart. "*Much* more than kissing," he said.

Chapter Fifteen

Rotten Apples

I HAD SLEPT SOME. Maybe not enough. But knowing Darion was alive and safe had lifted such a weight off of me that even with yesterday's whiplash of emotions, I still felt like I was floating on air.

"You look much better today," was the first thing Elena said when she saw me coming down from the loft. Then her eyes went wide. "You found Darion, didn't you?"

"I did." I could almost cry, seeing the relief in her eyes.

She hugged me. "I'm so glad."

"So am I. You have no idea."

"What happened to him?"

"He had a run-in with the Royal Guards. He didn't really tell me much more than that."

"Why do men think they need to keep all these secrets?" she asked nobody in particular. "When will you see him again?"

"He's stopping by the cart around midday."

Elena rolled her eyes. "Yes, I'll watch the cart again."

I kissed her cheek.

As I helped patrons throughout the morning, my mind drifted to Darion again and again. Why had this man, of all the men in Analon, captured my interest? What was so special about him? The answer to my question presented itself quickly when Darion walked up to me with a blazing smile that made the last three days of dread melt away like snow in the hot sun.

He didn't say a word. He simply came up, wrapped his arms around me, and kissed me without a care for what anybody else thought. Even with my jubilant mood, I was still taken aback by his public affection.

Still holding me in his arms, he said, "Hello."

"I like how you say hello," I said with a smile.

Elena watched all of this with an incredulous expression, her eyebrows high and her mouth a crooked smile.

When we separated, Darion held up a sack. "I brought food, as promised."

"I also like how you keep feeding me," I said, taking the sack and inspecting the contents. "Thank you."

"My pleasure," Darion said. "And I brought some food for you, too, Elena. It's nice of you to keep watching the cart."

Elena beamed. "He's a keeper."

"So, are you ready to—" Darion broke off as his gaze fell on something past my shoulder, and his eyes widened. Something he saw behind me made the blood drain from his face. I'd never seen him look so shocked.

"Sorry," he said, then spun around and raced away, disappearing into the crowd.

Stunned, I gawked in his direction with his sack of food still in my hands. I turned to see what had scared him off. Right where Darion had been staring were two figures walking briskly in our direction. The crowd parted around them like lambs who'd spotted a wolf. The woman in front scanned the surrounding crowd with all the prowess of a well-trained bodyguard. Her hand never ventured far from the hilt of her sword. Her clothes were all black with a gold lion embroidered on her vest.

Oh no.

The woman who'd slashed the throat of the man in the square the other day was walking toward us.

Close behind was none other than Orlik Leonom, his burgundy robes spilling over his chain mail armor. His nose was turned up and scrunched as if the act of walking among the market-goers was a disgusting ordeal.

I had to choke back my rage at the sight of him. My hands shook. I steadied them on the hilt of my dagger.

They barely acknowledged our existence as they approached. Elena's focus was on me, so she didn't see them marching right toward us.

"Watch out!" I called.

Elena spun around at the last moment, brushing against Orlik's robes. She barely touched the fabric, but he reeled back as if she had struck him.

"Out of my way!" he shouted, shoving Elena aside, sending her crashing into our cart, knocking over half our display. She cried out as she smashed her knee.

"Elena!" I called out as I rushed between her and Orlik, rage coursing through me like molten iron. "Keep your hands off her!"

My mind flashed to the dagger hidden in my tunic. I could rid the world of this foul man in less than a second.

The bodyguard ran forward, sword drawn. Her face was steady, her eyes neutral, almost vacant. The flat of her sword smacked against my vest. "Do you want to die today?"

I coiled up like a spring. My focus sharpened. The hilt of my dagger was cold against my fingers. The din of the crowd faded into the background. The bodyguard was fast, but I could be faster. If she moved her sword even the slightest bit, she'd hit the ground before she even saw me move.

"Stop!" Elena pleaded, racing to my side.

Her voice snapped me out of my tunnel vision. My one task in life was keeping Elena safe, and I was seconds away from putting her in the greatest danger of her life.

The ruckus had drawn a crowd, everyone eager for some bloody entertainment to break up the monotony of the day. The bodyguard and I stood still as oak trees, eyes piercing each other, in a deadly standoff.

Then an apple flew from the back of the throng of revelers. It struck Orlik squarely on the side of his head, sending chunks of rotten brown fruit flying in all directions. He jumped back, howling in pain.

The crowd that had formed around us gasped.

A second apple followed the first and glanced off the bodyguard's shoulder. I caught a glimpse of curly brown hair and green eyes near the back of the crowd.

"After him, Syra!" Orlik commanded the bodyguard, who immediately chased after the perpetrator.

The Butcher glared at us. "Elena, is it?" he spat, pointing a crooked finger at my sister and me. "I'll be back to deal with you two. I never forget a face."

"Neither do I," I said, my voice as cold as death itself. I had a brief window of opportunity, a singular moment. It could be over so quickly. With a simple slash of his throat, I could avenge my parents' deaths.

I felt Elena's warm hand on my arm. It anchored me, reminding me of the cost of vengeance, bringing me back from the edge.

Orlik sneered, then raced off, following his bodyguard into the crowd, and the moment was gone.

I spun around to face Elena. "Are you okay?"

"I may have a bruise on my knee, but it's not too bad." She rubbed the spot. "Thanks for coming to my rescue."

"Listen." I held Elena by her shoulders. "Pack up the cart as fast as you can and go home. Don't stop for anything, and don't open the door if anybody knocks."

Her eyes narrowed. "What's going on?"

"Those were wicked people. They were the ones who killed that man in the square. We shouldn't be here if they come back."

"But where are you going?" she asked. "Are you chasing after Darion?"

"I have to see if I can help. But please, go home now!"

She nodded with steely resolve. "Okay. Be careful."

Oh, dust, did I love her. I took one more look at her, then chased after Orlik.

Darion and his two pursuers were shoving through the crowd in the distance. I'd never catch them by pushing through the throngs of people, so instead I ducked into the nearest alleyway and scaled a three-story building like a cat climbing a tree. From that perspective, I spotted three moving dots in the vast central courtyard where the marketplace sprawled, filled with dozens of stalls and hundreds of market-goers. Darion was in the lead, heading for the market's perimeter, with Orlik and Syra in pursuit.

Dancing along the rooftops under the cover of night was easy. In the middle of the day with a large crowd below me, however, I had to take great care to avoid wandering eyes. A bystander could easily dismiss a flash of movement on the rooftops as a bird or another city-dwelling animal, but only if I was fast enough.

Darion was nearing an alleyway at the edge of the courtyard, so I picked up my pace, breathing rapidly. The rooftops were slick; a single misstep would send me tumbling thirty feet to the cobblestones below.

Just as I caught up, Darion ducked into the alleyway below me with Orlik and Syra only a few dozen steps behind. Orlik pulled up, panting hard and clutching his side.

"Go after him!" he commanded, pointing down the alleyway.

Syra gave a quick nod and raced off in pursuit.

From my vantage point, I had a perfect view. Darion darted left at the first intersection, and Syra followed, even faster now that she didn't have Orlik to worry about. This game of cat and mouse continued through the twisting, narrow streets with me following from above, jumping from rooftop to rooftop.

I leapt to the top of an ancient temple, barely making the jump. The weathered stone crumbled under my feet, sending debris down. I steadied myself and continued.

Perched on the edge of the temple roof was a series of stone gargoyles, weathered and cracked with age. One looked like it might fall in a strong breeze. Darion had just raced past in the alley below, Syra close behind. I shoved the gargoyle with all my might. It gave way easily and tumbled to the ground far below, crashing into a cloud of dust and rubble just in front of Syra, who dove to avoid it.

Syra looked up, and our eyes locked for only a moment before I ducked behind the roof's edge. Darion glanced back only long enough to see the damage, which he quickly used to his advantage, racing off faster than before. I continued my pursuit from above.

After several minutes of twisting and turning through the mazelike alleyways, Darion stopped when he hit a dead end. He was breathing hard, hands on his hips. He paused and glanced back at the alleyway behind him as if contemplating what to do.

I leapt down the side of the building, bouncing off ledges and awnings until I stood just feet away from him.

Darion's eyes lit up. "You really are an impressive climber. The gargoyle was your doing, I take it?"

"Figured I owed you for the apples."

"Thanks," he said with a smile. "We should go in case they come this way. Don't want to get stuck in this dead end."

But something was bothering me. "How do you know Orlik Leonom?"

Darion let out a humorless laugh. "Who *doesn't* know The Butcher? Carrying out thousands of death sentences can make you pretty infamous."

My throat felt thick as my parents' fate at the hands of that wicked man flashed in my mind. But I swallowed my grief and refocused. "But why is he after *you*?"

"It may have something to do with some errant fruit thrown in his direction," he said with a wry smile.

I shook my head. "I saw the look in your eyes before you ran away. You were afraid. I've never seen you look that way before."

He drew in a long breath. "He's always hated and hunted my kind."

My head spun. His *kind*?

"He went this way!" a voice yelled down the alleyway, followed by the sound of stomping boots getting louder.

"Dust!" I said, looking around the dead end, seeing no chance of escape. The walls were tall and smooth with few handholds. I could make it out with some fancy climbing, but a typical person couldn't. Darion would be stuck alone. I pulled out my dagger, ready to face our enemy.

"Can you climb out?" Darion asked.

"Yes, but I'm not leaving you," I said. My tone left no room for debate.

Down the alleyway, Syra and two guards were running in our direction. She looked our way, then stopped, signaling the guards to do the same. She took a deep breath. A shimmering light surrounded her, almost as if the air had caught fire. I blinked and shook my head. "What in all the hells?"

A coldness gripped me. Her hands and feet transformed into hooves. The sound of bones snapping echoed through the alleyway. Twisting, razor-sharp horns emerged from her head, and her nose turned into a snout. She was half woman, half beast.

"Darion, are you seeing this? I can't believe—"

"You need to go," Darion insisted. "Climb out. I can take care of myself."

"I already told you, I'm not leaving," I said, squaring my shoulders.

"I'm sorry, Cas. I didn't want you to find out this way."

"Find out what?" I asked, looking toward him.

A glimmer radiated from his body. He looked directly at me with sad eyes, their deep emerald color transforming into a golden hue.

One moment, Darion was standing next to me, and the next moment, he had vanished. And in his wake was the smell of ozone and citrus.

Part Two

Chapter Sixteen

The Emberborn

I STRUGGLED TO GRASP what was happening before me. For an instant, time was broken. There was no other way to describe it—the world simply stopped around me. Syra's mouth was open, frozen in mid-snarl. A bead of sweat that had flown from my head was hanging in midair. Only Darion was moving, running down the alley. I was barely able to even turn my head.

Then time came rushing back like a torrential river, and Darion was gone.

The woman-beast Syra and the guards flew back like they'd been hit with cannonballs, careening halfway across the alley and crashing to the ground.

With no time to rationalize what had happened, I scaled the wall, pausing for only a moment at the top to look back. The beast peered up at me with black eyes like a predator hunting its prey. I raced away.

As I made my way across the rooftops of Analon, shouts came from below but quickly faded as I jumped from building to building. My mind was a jumble. Maintaining my concentration took everything I had.

The events in the alley were starting to sink in.

Darion was the golden-eyed thief.

The truth landed like a blow.

And he'd hidden it from me. *That* was his secret. And last night, when he'd pulled away from our kiss, I hadn't questioned it. This was how it always went: I let someone in, and then they vanished. Something deep within me cracked the slightest bit, subtle but fundamental. My hands shook so badly I nearly missed the next jump.

I paused on a rooftop and sank down next to a chimney to try to stop spiraling. But my brain wouldn't slow down. Darion could vanish into thin air, leaving behind the scent of ozone and citrus. And he could...what, manipulate time? And Syra had transformed before my eyes—she must have been the one who had stalked me outside the Charred Snake.

Some people have the ability to sense Emberborn, Mrs. Crowe had said. Did that mean that *I* could sense Emberborn, that Darion and Syra *were* Emberborn? The implications made my head spin.

I kept making connections and slotting truths into place that I had previously refused to accept. It was Darion who had left me the invitation to the Emberlight Trials. That was plain now. Had he been following me from the start? Spying on me from the moment I first saw him at the Bleeding Oak? Was this part of the Emberlight Trials? Did all recruits to the Emberlight Trials have someone to watch over them, as Darion had done for me?

Crouched on a rooftop, I replayed every moment, every interaction, everything he'd said to me. Were the things he'd said sincere, or was it all just part of the Trials?

And what of our kisses? I had leaned into them. I had wanted them to mean something. My heart ached at the possibility that it was all a deception, part of an elaborate ruse. He couldn't care for me, not really. What a fool I had been. I didn't even know how to find him again.

But there was one person who might have some answers. If I really *wanted* answers, that is. If I wasn't afraid of what I'd find.

I jumped up before I could lose my nerve.

Mrs. Crowe's shop in the Underworld was as dark as it had been the last few days. My gentle knocks went unanswered, and the shades over the windows concealed everything within.

"Mrs. Crowe," I called, first quietly, then louder. The tavern next door was noisy, but even so, a few people standing outside glanced my way. When there was still no answer, I banged hard on the door and shouted, "Mrs. Crowe, it's important!"

Finally the door creaked open until just a sliver of her face was visible.

"Are you insane?" she hissed.

"Mrs. Crowe, please let me in," I pleaded.

She scowled and shut the door. I was about to bang on it again when the sound of chains rattling came from the other side.

When the door creaked open all the way, she waved me in. "Come, quickly!"

The moment I was inside, she shut the door and locked it.

"Thank you," I said. "I have to ask you about Ember—"

She cut me off with a shush and a sharp gesture, then waved me into the back room, past a curtain. Countless metal and glass devices filled every horizontal surface. The two of us had spent many hours in here as I had refined my craft.

She cranked the handle of a large centrifuge, which emitted a loud whirring sound.

She leaned in close. "Tarnasau's spies are everywhere. This should keep them from hearing us," she said.

How any spies could hear us when we were locked deep in her house was beyond my comprehension. I hoped she wasn't getting irrationally paranoid in her older years.

"Last time I was here, you said that some people could detect Emberborn. Can you tell me more about that?" I took a deep breath. "Because I think I might be one of those people."

Despite the noise, she still cringed when I said the word *Emberborn*. "You ask too much of me."

"Please, Mrs. Crowe," I pleaded. "I need to understand what's happening."

She let out a long breath, as deep a scowl on her face as I'd ever seen. "I'm taking a perilous risk even talking to you. But I'll be leaving soon anyway."

"Leaving? Where are you going?"

"Thornfell."

My jaw dropped. "Why would you go to that horrible place?"

Thornfell was a secluded town far to the east at the end of the Jagged Coast. Its only purpose was to serve Thornfell Keep, the king's private citadel, where it was rumored that he conducted nightmarish medical experiments.

"I have...unfinished business there," Mrs. Crowe said. "I'll talk to you, but I have two conditions."

"Name them."

"First," she said, "what I tell you must never be traced back to me."

"Of course," I said. "And the second?"

"You must never seek me out again."

My mouth dropped open in shock. I had known Mrs. Crowe for years, and the thought of never seeing her again made my stomach churn.

Seeing my expression, she added, "Or you can leave now, and that second condition will still hold."

"Guess I have no choice. Agreed."

She studied my expression, then nodded. "How much do you know about the history of the Emberborn?"

"Not much."

"Not surprising, given your age," she said. "Emberborn used to be common. Although they were not as numerous as non-Emberborn, thousands lived in Analon alone. Emberborn and humans lived peacefully side by side. Then, twenty years ago, King Tarnasau declared Emberborn a threat to the kingdom. He was afraid of their power. He and his Sentinels and Royal Guard began to hunt them down. The Butcher was the master architect of it all."

At the mention of Orlik's nickname, I flinched.

She continued, "Emberborn were either killed or conscripted into King Tarnasau's army. The ones who escaped fled the country or went into hiding. Even mentioning Emberborn became a capital offense. The king's lackeys scrubbed the libraries, removed them from the history texts, and destroyed their artwork. He literally wiped Emberborn from existence."

How does an entire race get wiped out such that only a few remain? The thought made me sick to my stomach.

"And I can detect them," I said. "At least when they use their abilities, that is."

Mrs. Crowe turned the centrifuge's crank to increase the whirring sound. "Emberborn call their abilities Embers. What you've described is Veilsense: the ability to detect when Emberborn draw on their Embers."

"And how did I get this Veilsense?"

Mrs. Crowe looked me directly in the eye. "Veilsense is itself an Ember."

It took me a moment to absorb the implications of what she'd said.

"But...only Emberborn have Embers."

She nodded. "Now you understand."

I couldn't accept it. It wasn't possible.

I was Emberborn?

"But...but I've seen what these Embers can do—make people disappear or turn into beasts. I can't do anything like that."

Mrs. Crowe's gaze looked like it could cut glass. "Turn into beasts? You've seen this?"

"With my own two eyes. Orlik's bodyguard Syra."

Mrs. Crowe looked visibly pained. She let out a long breath and continued. "Each Emberborn's Ember is as distinct as their appearance or personality. Some Embers are innate and passive, like Veilsense. Others are more active and take great energy to perform and great skill to master."

I still didn't want to believe I had a "magical" power, but a growing feeling told me it was the truth. Perhaps a part of me had always known.

"Why didn't my parents tell me?" I asked, not expecting an answer.

"Emberborn were hunted and murdered because of their Embers. Would you trust a child with that secret?"

My father had trusted me. *You can hear whisperhawks, like me. It's your special gift. But you must keep it a secret. Tell no one.*

I had told someone. And it had cost me dearly.

It was hard not to feel betrayed. I'd been Emberborn all along, and my parents had chosen to hide that from me. Maybe if I had known what it meant—how dangerous it was—things might have been different.

"But how did I not figure it out?" I asked, more to myself than to Mrs. Crowe.

"Most people don't develop Embers until their teen years. And Veilsense is innate, so it's not that surprising that you didn't even know."

Until their teen years.

Oh no, Elena!

In all the commotion, I had forgotten about her. The last time I'd seen her was at the Citadel Market, when I'd told her to go home. Only now did I realize how critical that advice had been. If Elena hadn't heeded my warning and had stayed in the market, it was possible that Orlik could have found her. And if she had some kind of latent Ember that Sentinels could detect...

"I have to go home and check on Elena!" I said.

"Just as well," Mrs. Crowe said. "I've told you too much already." She grabbed my shoulder with a bony hand. "You must know this: Veilsense is a rare Ember, and one coveted by King Tarnasau. All of his Sentinels have it."

At the word *Sentinels*, a chill ran down my back. That I had something in common with them disgusted me.

Mrs. Crowe continued, "If he finds out you have Veilsense, he'll do everything in his power to capture you and add you to the Sentinels' ranks. That's how he hunts down Emberborn. Be vigilant."

The idea of Sentinels hunting Emberborn, hunting Elena and me, was horrifying. My mother's dying request that I protect my sister took on a whole new dimension. Now I was doubly worried about her. "I have to go!"

Mrs. Crowe walked me to her door, undid the locks, and turned to me, her face drawn into a deep frown. "Remember, I'm leaving for Thornfell. Don't ever seek me out again."

I gave her a grim nod, knowing a significant part of my life had come to a close. "Goodbye, Mrs. Crowe."

Chapter Seventeen

Long Overdue

"Elena, where are you?" I yelled, bursting through the door to our home. The herb cart was parked in the corner where it always was, but there was no sign of my sister. I checked every room and climbed the ladder to the loft, calling her name. Only silence greeted me. My heart was already pounding from my sprint home, but now it felt like it might burst through my rib cage.

I was on the cusp of panic and doing a terrible job of suppressing it. I imagined Orlik and Syra tying Elena up and stealing her away. I had failed at the one job my mother had given me, all because I'd let Darion distract me. Just like what had happened with Bren back at the farm when I was eleven.

I fumbled for the locket around my neck. *Deep breaths.* My mind quieted as the only option I had became clear: I would confront Orlik directly. I began to gather my thieving supplies and stock my belt with new potions. I was stashing my throwing daggers under my tunic when a voice called out from behind me.

"Where are you off to *this* time?"

I raced to the front door and hugged my sister like I'd never let her go. "Thank the heavens you're safe."

"Of course I'm safe," she said. "Ouch! Not so tight. Your dumb potions are digging into my chest, and you're smashing our dinner."

I pulled away and took a moment to inspect her. Everything looked normal except for the crushed loaf of bread sticking out of the sack of food she held.

"What in the dust has gotten into you?" she said with genuine concern in her eyes. "Is this about those bastards at the market? I can take care of myself, you know."

I had spent my entire life looking out for my little sister, so it was tough not to protect her from everything. But by hiding things from her, I was, in a way, making her *less* safe. I had to tell her what I had discovered today. She had to understand the danger we were in.

"Elena, sit down. We need to talk."

I told her everything, starting with my thieving and my grand plan to escape to a farm, which all felt quite naïve as I spoke it aloud. The idea of the farm touched Elena, but she was more than a little annoyed that I had kept it from her, once again reminding me that she wasn't a child. She had guessed on her own that I was a thief, but I filled in the gaps.

An unexpected thing happened as I told Elena all the things I'd been keeping secret: I felt better. A massive weight was being lifted, one I hadn't even realized I was carrying.

Next I recounted the Emberlight Trials and everything I'd done with Darion (except a few intimate details). Elena listened with rapt attention, as if my story were one of the plays at the local theater she loved. She particularly enjoyed the race through the catacombs with the bone rats on our heels.

"Were there really hundreds of them?" she asked.

"I didn't really have time to count, but you couldn't even see the floor."

She grimaced and giggled at once, wiggling her body. Elena was fond of the macabre.

Finally, I told her about my conversation with Mrs. Crowe, though I didn't mention her by name, per her conditions. When I told Elena that we were Emberborn and that some Emberborn had special abilities, she didn't seem as surprised as I anticipated.

"I kinda suspected that," she said.

"What?" I was genuinely shocked.

"You've always seemed special to me," she said. "Your memory, the way you can climb, all of that. And sometimes it's like I can feel an energy flowing through me, especially when I'm doing physical things like sword fighting."

"Let me try something," I said. I closed my eyes and cleared my mind. Only the crackling of the fire broke the silence. And then I felt it. Without all the background noise, I could very subtly feel Elena's Ember flowing through her, detecting just the faintest hint of ozone and citrus.

"Dust, I can sense it!" I said.

"Sense what?"

"That energy you mentioned. It's called Ember."

"And you can sense it in me?"

"Yeah. There's a glow and an odd smell. It's called Veilsense, and it's *my* Ember. Sentinels have Veilsense, too. It's how they hunt Emberborn down."

Elena looked scared, and I was glad. She needed to be.

"You mean Sentinels are Emberborn who hunt their own kind?" Elena asked. "That's horrible."

"It is."

"Well, what are we going to do now?"

"I really don't know," I said. "We can't sell our herbs in the market anymore. Not for a while, anyway. I'm worried about The Butcher spotting us. I'm not sure I should do the Emberlight Trials anymore, either. The whole thing feels like a fantasy now, and to be honest, I'm upset with Darion for keeping this from me."

"What?!" Elena nearly screamed. "You have to keep doing the Trials! You've already come so far, and if there's anything we can do to stop The Butcher, it's that."

Hearing her say those words with such certainty was a surprise and a shot of confidence. She was right. I had to keep going, and having her support made the decision much easier. All this time, I'd been so worried about keeping her from knowing too much, but in doing so, I'd ignored what keeping these secrets was doing to *me*. That profound sense of relief at revealing the truth continued to flood through me. I'd had no idea just how much this burden weighed until I had someone else to confide in who could help carry the load.

"Okay," I said. "You're right. I have to keep doing it."

"Of course I'm right," she said with a sly smile. "I always am. The sooner you realize that, the better off we'll be."

For the rest of the day and well into the night, I was lost in thought, planning how I might infiltrate both the Citadel Library and the Citadel Clock Tower. Entering the library seemed doable, but I knew next to nothing about how to get into the tower. What I really needed to do was visit Garrick again. He'd said I had to wait since he was worried about attention from the Sentinels. But what if nobody saw me enter the tavern?

Late in the evening, as I was preparing potions that could help with stealth, I reached into my pocket and discovered something flat and soft. I pulled out an oval-shaped pale green leaf.

My breath hitched. This was the very leaf I had given to Darion when we'd kissed under the night willow. Markings had been scratched into the flesh: six hash marks and a bell.

Sixth bell, under the night willow?

I had no idea how Darion had slipped it into my pocket, nor was I sure if I had interpreted the message correctly, but either way, sixth bell was not far off. I shouted to Elena that I'd be back later and headed into the night.

[illegible]

Chapter Eighteen

A Second Chance

I rushed as fast as I could. Six bells signaling the middle of the night gonged steadily, barely audible in the Underworld but making its way through air vents and cracked foundations. I quickened my pace.

Conflicting thoughts banged around in my mind. I was desperate to see Darion but also angry and hurt by his deceptions. Had any of his affection been real, or had he simply been manipulating me?

As I ran along the tunnel leading to the massive cavern, chest heaving, I was sure he wouldn't be there, certain that I had misinterpreted the message on the leaf.

But those worries evaporated when I spotted a figure sitting under the tree, patiently waiting.

Darion stood as I approached. I wanted to run up and shove him, force him to explain himself. I had so many questions that needed answering and too many swirling emotions. I didn't plan on hugging him. And yet I ran right into his warm embrace, feeling an instant torrent of relief and comfort.

"I'm so sorry, Cas," he whispered softly in my ear. "And I'm so happy you're safe."

"I'm happy you're safe, too," I said, clutching him tight. I wanted to stay that way forever and ignore the pricklier feelings building in me. But then hurt and anger punched their way through, and I pulled away from the hug.

"That day at the pond. And in the catacombs. And here under the willow." I swallowed. "Was that just...part of the Trials? Was any of it real?"

"Yes," Darion insisted, reaching for my shoulders. "It was all real, and it still is."

"You were the thief in Orlik's study," I said, a statement rather than a question. Darion nodded, and the confirmation made me flinch.

"Why did you hide so much from me?" I asked.

"It's complicated. I'm oath-bound by the Order of Emberlight. I'll explain what I can, but first I have to ask *you* a question. Do you still want to complete the Emberlight Trials?"

"Yes," I said emphatically. "I have to, now more than ever."

"Good," Darion said. "I wanted to be sure that hadn't changed. I can tell you more when you finish the Trials. I've been bending the rules for you."

"Why?"

He hung his head, eyes on the ground. "I couldn't help myself."

"What do you mean?"

"I thought that might be obvious," Darion said. He looked up, his expression deadly serious. "I'm mad about you, Cas. I have been since the moment I saw you in that study."

My pulse sped up as I looked into Darion's eyes, which were filled with longing. I wanted so badly to kiss him again, but I wasn't ready to forgive him yet. I cleared my mind of those thoughts and focused on things I needed to know.

"About that night in the study...what was so important about that book?"

Darion paused and looked around, then spoke in a soft tone. "The book has a list of known Emberborn and Orlik's plans to capture and corrupt them."

"*Corrupt* them?"

He looked around again. "We shouldn't be talking about this out in the open. Would you be okay with going to my place? It's not far."

I was *very* interested in seeing where he lived. So much about him was a mystery. But I also didn't want him to deflect what I wanted to know. "You promise you'll answer my questions?"

"I promise to tell you what I can."

That sounded like a half promise. But I understood the responsibilities that came with being honor-bound. How many lies had I told in the service of fulfilling my mother's dying wish that I protect my sister? I'd have to take what I could get.

"Let's go," I said.

Darion led me out of the cavern, and we twisted through the Underworld's back alleys. Soon we came to a staircase that led to the Merchant District. We reached an unassuming home, neither lavish nor run down, made from stone and mortar. His house was sparse, with only a few furnishings and little in the way of decorations. A lute sat on a stand next to a comfortable-looking chair by the fireplace, and various books were strewn about.

"It's not much, but it's home," Darion said. "Now, ask away. We should be safe to talk here."

"You said the book contained plans to corrupt the Emberborn. What does that mean?"

"Very few Emberborn have been convinced to turn on their own kind through normal means: torture, blackmail, coercion. So the Crown devised something more nefarious. Nobody knows exactly how it works, but it results in their minds being corrupted. Once it's done, they become subservient slaves."

"Dust, that's horrible."

"One of the Order of Emberlight's goals is to figure out how and where they do this corruption. We've wanted that book for a long time."

"How did you just *happen* to be in the study at the same time as me? That seems like a remarkable coincidence."

Darion looked down. "We knew you were robbing Orlik that night. The Order of Emberlight has eyes everywhere." Darion looked back at me with a pinched face, gauging my reaction.

"So you were trying to set me up to take the blame," I said, the words coming out hot. This confirmed one of my worst suspicions—that I was being manipulated.

"The Order wanted to deflect suspicion. I hated the plan, and I wouldn't have agreed to it if I thought you'd get caught. But it was still wrong, and for that I am deeply sorry. It's my biggest regret."

That stung. The only saving grace was that Darion had admitted to it. At least he was finally being forthright. But I wasn't sure I was ready to accept his apology. I'd have to think about it.

"How did you know I wouldn't get caught?" I asked.

"Are you kidding? The infamous Cas Nightbrook? You're practically a celebrity in the Underworld."

"I'm what?!"

Darion nodded. "Among thieves, you're a bit of a legend. Think of that night as your first Emberlight Trial."

"But it was a trial I didn't ask for. I try to remain unnoticed for the sake of my sister."

"And yet you chose to do the Trials," Darion said, speaking delicately. "And you still plan to."

That I couldn't dispute. He was right, of course. I couldn't claim I didn't want to join the Order of Emberlight while continuing to do the Trials.

"We knew from your reputation that you were the best and that you'd escape Orlik's house with a hefty sum," Darion said. "It was a golden opportunity to keep the Order of Emberlight above suspicion. It seemed like a scenario where everybody would win."

"Well, now Sentinels are showing up at the Charred Snake and chasing me through the streets of Analon," I said, anger still just under the surface. "And also the Order invited me to the Trials? How does that keep them above suspicion?"

Darion flushed. "Well, that wasn't exactly part of the plan. A bit of improvisation by me. I wanted to give you more than just a fighting chance. We protect our own. When I saw for myself what a skilled thief you were, I knew we had made the right choice. Honestly, I've never met a thief as talented as you." Darion paused as if contemplating his next words. "But something else happened that night that I *didn't* expect. The moment I saw you, I couldn't stand the thought of not seeing you again."

That caught me off guard. The look on his face was so genuine, almost pained. My anger softened a bit.

"So following a recruit around isn't a normal part of the Trials?" I quipped.

"Not at all. The most we usually do is watch them from afar. Some of the Emberlight Council hasn't been happy about how involved I've been, but I've never stepped over the line. I've let you interpret the clues and solve the problems on your own. But I need to be hands-off from now on." Darion paused, then smiled. "Hands-off as far as the Trials are concerned, that is."

"Let's not get ahead of ourselves," I said. I was still upset. "I have more questions."

Darion nodded, his smile fading. "I'll try my best to answer."

"How do you disappear?" I asked. "Is that your Ember?"

Darion raised his eyebrows. "I guess you know more about Emberborn than the typical Velmorrian."

"I've learned a lot recently."

"Apparently so. To answer your question, I have a connection to time. I can manipulate it," Darion said simply, like it was the most normal thing to have said.

"What?! What does that mean?"

"I can do different things, like slow down time for everyone around me while it's still normal for me. It's how I snuck in and out of the study without you seeing me. How I escaped the alley and knocked over those guards. How I left you those notes. It's called Chronothene."

"So doesn't that make *you* the best thief of all time?" I asked.

"It has limits. I can only do it for a very short time. Not long after using it, I'm exhausted and barely able to move for hours."

Slowing down time should have been hard to wrap my head around, and yet I could understand it because I had felt it. Part of me understood his Ember in a way I couldn't articulate.

"You don't seem that shocked," Darion said.

"It makes sense. I could feel it as you were doing it."

"No one can feel it," Darion said, eyes narrowing.

I paused. Knowing I was Emberborn was new to me, and revealing it should be a calculated decision. I didn't know how people would react. But since Darion was being truthful to me, I at least owed him the same.

"I have Veilsense. I'm Emberborn, too."

Darion's face went ashen, and his jaw dropped as he stared at me, stunned.

"You didn't know?" I asked.

"I had no idea."

"The first time I felt it was with you in Orlik's study, but I only just found out what it meant. That it's my Ember."

"I don't know how that's possible," Darion said, still stunned. "You're not on any of the ledgers. The Order of Emberlight has tracked the lineage of every Emberborn for the last twenty years."

"I guess your ledgers are incomplete. When you use your Ember, I can sense it. There's a smell, and I can even see it a bit. I can *feel* it. Same thing when Orlik's bodyguard used her Ember. I can even sense it a bit in my sister."

"Oh dust, your sister! Of course she's Emberborn, too. I can't believe the danger I've put you in," Darion said, his face drawing tight, etched with worry.

"You didn't put us in danger. We'd have to grapple with this with or without you," I said. "If anything, you've helped me to understand my ability faster than I might have otherwise."

Darion looked almost panicked. "But I've put a target on your back. If Tarnasau finds out you have Veilsense, he'll do everything in his power to capture you."

"Well, if I join the Order of Emberlight, I might finally be able to do something about it."

"No! Forget the damn Trials," Darion implored. "It's too dangerous. We need to get you out of the city, move you and your sister to safety."

Until that moment, I hadn't been certain of Darion's true intentions. Part of me thought he was still trying to recruit me, that he only wanted me to use my talents for the Order of Emberlight. But the fear in his eyes was genuine. That he would abandon his plan to protect my sister and me made me feel for him that much more.

That was the moment I truly knew I could trust him—the moment I started to forgive him for his deceptions, knowing that they came from a place of care.

"I'm not running from this," I said, voice unwavering, taking Darion's hand.

"Cas, don't!" Darion said, his voice rough. "If anything happened to you—" His voice grew unsteady, and he broke off.

"I've spent my whole life feeling powerless. For the first time, I can do something about it."

Darion's emerald eyes were damp with emotion. Dust, what a beautiful man. I put my hand on his cheek, and we touched our foreheads together. "You have to let me do this. You have to trust me to take my own risks."

Darion nodded slowly. "If anything goes wrong at the Citadel Library, I'm helping you, Order of Emberlight rules be damned."

"You'd come to my rescue?" I said, a slight tease in my tone.

"Of course."

"Like I'm a damsel in distress?"

"Stop teasing," Darion said, but a smile peeked through his gloomy expression.

"I'm sorry," I said with a playful frown.

"Cas, I'd tear down the whole damn Citadel Library to save you." His tone was so earnest, so raw, it took my breath away. He looked into my eyes with a tenderness that almost scared me. I'd known him for only a short time, and yet the peril we'd already faced together heightened every emotion.

"I care for you," Darion said. "You need to understand that."

"I understand," I said. "And I care for you, too."

I knew I might regret this, but we'd gone too far to turn back. We moved toward each other simultaneously, and our lips smashed together. Gone was the tenderness of our first kiss, and in its place was a hasty, burning desire.

I grabbed his hips and pulled our bodies together, Darion's stiffness pressing up against my own. He grabbed a fistful of my hair, trying to kiss me more deeply. His gentle moans against my lips turned me on even more.

Still locked in a kiss, we fumbled to rip each other's clothes off, pausing only to pull our shirts over our heads. I needed to feel his bare skin against mine as sure as I had to breathe.

As I pulled off my shirt, I fumbled for my locket and stashed it in my trouser pocket. He didn't seem to notice. I didn't want him to ask about it, just like that time at the waterfall; I wasn't ready to share that part of my life yet.

I grabbed him by the waist of his trousers, where a patch of hair extended from his belly button to areas I was very eager to explore, then dragged him toward the bedroom.

Once there, Darion pulled away, just like he had the other night under the willow. My heart nearly shattered then and there. Was this man *trying* to break me?

"Cas. I want to be sure you're really okay with this. I don't want to force this on you. Not if you're still angry or unsure."

We *were* moving fast. I should still have been angry. But I needed him *so badly* at that moment.

"Shush," I said, answering him with an overwhelming look of desire. There was no turning back now, and I jumped off that cliff with no hesitation.

We went back to kissing and furiously fussing with our buttons, then pulling our trousers down to our boots. Darion's cock glistened. I bent down and took him in my mouth, sucking him clean, then returning to our kiss. Darion took me in his hand and gently stroked, then swirled his thumb through my leaking wetness, running along the head, making me moan.

Enraptured by that sound, Darion grabbed my wrists and guided me down onto his bed, lying on top of me, pinning my arms above my head as we ground our bodies together. I wasn't used to losing control like this, and I was simultaneously intoxicated and terrified.

His mouth explored my neck, kissing and nibbling as he went, then along my shoulder, across my armpit, which made me wiggle with delight, to my nipple. He sucked deeply, forcing a startled gasp out of me, which only made him suck harder.

He released my wrists and moved downward, kissing my stomach, following the tuft of hair below my belly button, cruelly avoiding my throbbing cock, then rewarding me by sucking my inner thigh.

"Oh gods!" I moaned.

This was all moving so fast, and the emotion I felt was far deeper than I had expected. I only hoped I could survive when this was over.

He took my balls in his mouth and worked his tongue around them, making my eyes roll back in my head and my toes curl. While he sucked, his finger probed my ass, sending a shiver of pleasure through me.

Trying not to interrupt the seriously fucking fantastic job he was doing, I reached for my discarded belt of vials resting on the bed. I grabbed a particular vial that would help in this situation. Flicking the cap off with my thumb, I tapped his shoulder.

"Here," I said, showing him the vial. He held out his hand, and I dispensed some of the viscous salve into it. He wasted no time slathering his fingers, then inserting one inside me, which sent me into immediate ecstasy.

"Oh fuck!" I yelled. He responded by shoving his finger up to the knuckle, making me moan uncontrollably.

He inserted a second finger, which heightened everything. The look in his eyes as he pleasured me—the pure joy, almost awe—took my breath away. He continued to work his fingers, hooking them to hit *that spot,* which got a massive groan out of me.

With his other hand, he grabbed my cock, then took the entire length in his mouth, right down to the base. My body exploded with pleasure. For a moment, it was too much, and I nearly climaxed.

"Hold on," I said with hurried breaths.

He backed off instantly, smiling up at me.

"You were a second away from having a mouthful."

"Don't tempt me," he said with a gentle laugh.

"Okay, my turn," I said. "But first, let's get these damn boots off." We both sat up and kicked off our boots, then pulled our trousers the rest of the way off so that nothing would hinder us.

With our legs now free, I flipped Darion over onto his back, slathered my cock with salve, and hooked his knees over my shoulders. I rubbed his ass with the head of my cock, making him groan with pleasure. Gently, I pressed inward, teasingly, but not too far. Darion gasped, and I gave him a devilish smile.

"Fuck, I want your cock inside me," Darion begged.

"All in good time."

I continued to press into his ass, rubbing the spot between his ass and balls, and watched his cock throb with pleasure, leaking onto his stomach. I scooped up the liquid and mixed it with the salve in my hand, then grabbed both of our cocks, stroking them together. Mine was a bit longer, and his was a bit thicker, but they fit together nicely.

"Please," Darion cried. "Please fuck me."

"Well, since you asked so nicely," I said with a wicked smile, adding more salve to my fingers. I gently probed his ass, feeling the instinctive flex and then the relaxation.

I positioned my cock at his ass and pushed. The entire length slid in with little resistance until my stomach was pressed against his balls. I looked down at this beautiful man, who stared back up at me with piercing emerald eyes, both of us lost in bliss. With each stroke, he moaned, and I could think only of getting deeper inside him, the two of us together as one.

I could tell from his moans that he was getting close. Without a word, I pulled out of him. He smiled and nodded, understanding my plan without speaking.

I poured salve from my vial onto his cock, which I slathered evenly, then got on top, positioning my ass right over it. There was a moment of pressure, so I took a deep breath and relaxed. The rest came easily. As I sat on him, I stroked myself. The feeling was so intense, and the pleasure on Darion's face meant so much more than anything I'd ever done with anyone else.

Darion grabbed my hips and thrust upward, shoving himself in deeper. I was right on the edge of control, and the pulsing inside me told me Darion was right there as well.

"I'm going to try something unusual," Darion said. "Is that okay?"

"Sure," I said. At that point, I was willing to try anything with him.

We got back into our rhythm, and just as we both reached climax, a shimmer surrounded us, along with that familiar scent of ozone and citrus.

Time stopped.

It sped up the slightest bit, just as the first shot of cum left my cock, moving ever so slowly. It was utter bliss like I'd never felt, and it continued for longer than I could ever imagine. Darion pulsed inside me in a slow undulation—a sensation I didn't have words to describe. For what felt like an eon and an instant combined, we drowned in an unending pool of ecstasy.

Just when I couldn't take any more, time sped up. Shot after shot covered Darion's chest and neck, and the pulsing of him inside me was an explosion of pleasure.

As our breathing slowed and we came down from our high, my head spun. That had been the strangest and most wonderful thing I had ever felt. And Darion had chosen to share it with me. The sheer weight of the moment filled me with awe.

"Oh my gods," were the only words I could utter as I looked at him, stunned at what we had just experienced together.

Darion smiled coyly. "Did time slow for you, too?"

"Gods, yes," I said, still a bit out of it.

"I thought it might. Since you said you could feel it when I slowed time, I wanted to try."

"Well, that was quite an experiment. It fucking worked," I said, as I slid off and lay on top of him with my head on his chest, letting our lovemaking mingle between us. "And you've just ruined regular sex for me."

"Yeah, I can relate," Darion said with a laugh. "After I figured out I could do that when I pleasured myself, the regular thing just never felt as good. You're the first person I've been able to share that with."

The first? I glanced up at him with a questioning look.

He nodded yes. That filled me with overwhelming emotion, and I had to fight back tears.

"Did you enjoy it?" Darion asked.

"It's the best thing I've ever felt."

"Me too," he said, and that was both wonderful and terrifying.

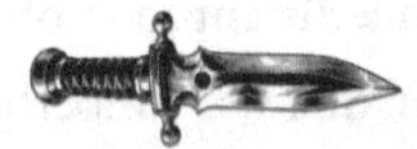

We lingered for a long while in each other's arms. With Darion by my side, I felt safe in a way I hadn't in a very long time.

He ran his hand through my hair, caressed my cheek, then stroked down to my shoulder. He leaned in and kissed me. The look in his eyes was almost one of wonder. I imagined my expression was similar. How had I been lucky enough to find a man this beautiful and caring? Did I deserve it? Could I risk it?

Up until now, I'd always shut myself off and driven people away. It was a defense mechanism that had kept me safe. And I had just blown it open.

I had closed myself off for as long as I could remember, maybe since I was a child, even before my parents died. Dust, why did it hurt so much every time my mind drifted to them? I reached for my locket, then remembered I had taken it off. Its absence amplified the loss. A tear leaked out of my eye.

"Hey, what's wrong?" Darion said, wiping the tear away as it streaked down my cheek.

"Just thinking about my parents. They died when I was young, and they never told me or my sister we were Emberborn. They never mentioned our Embers—not directly, anyway. I just don't understand why they kept that from me."

Darion had a look of deep empathy that I imagined came from true understanding. "A lot of parents did. They waited until their kids were older to tell them, since kids rarely start showing signs of their Embers until their teenage years. Keeping that secret was literally a matter of life and death."

"Is that what your parents did?" I asked.

"No," Darion said with a distant look of muted pain. "My mother died right after I was born. She was Emberborn, and my father didn't even know. *I* didn't know until my Ember started manifesting when I was fourteen. I lost my father shortly after that, so I dealt with it on my own."

"That must have been very hard for you."

"You have no idea," Darion said, looking away. His jaw was clenched, and he seemed to be trying hard to suppress a complex mix of emotions.

We lay there quietly for a moment, both lost in thought. I supposed that was another thing we shared: dead parents and painful family histories we didn't love talking about.

He let out a long breath, then turned back to me. "It must have been hard for you, too. How old were you when your parents died?"

"I was eleven, and Elena was four."

"Dust, I'm so sorry," Darion said, holding me tighter and kissing me.

I thought back to that worst day of all, when Orlik Leonom and his army of Sentinels had destroyed my family. As they'd approached the farm, my mother had taken me aside. *It's your job to protect your little sister. Elena is counting on you*. Then she'd told me to take Elena and hide. *Do as we practiced*, she had said.

Elena and I had run to the grain silo on the far side of our farm and hidden under a trapdoor at the bottom. But I couldn't just sit there and do nothing. After all, I assumed this was all my fault for trusting Bren, my next-door crush.

I told Elena to stay and ran back to the farm. Halfway there, I watched as my parents were murdered, their throats slashed. I was too far away to help. I ran as fast as I could, but by the time I got there, my father was dead, and my mother was dying, lying in a pool of blood. Orlik and his men had ridden off. My mother took me by the hand. She was clutching her locket, stained with her blood. She was only able to choke out two words, barely audible: *Protect Elena.*

Darion looked deep into my eyes as I relived those memories in my mind, as I'd done a thousand times before.

"You okay?" he asked.

"Yeah," I said, although my eyes likely betrayed me.

"If you want to talk about it, I'll listen."

"I do," I said. "But another time."

Chapter Nineteen

A Slice of Normal

IF I WAS GOING to sneak into the Citadel Library, I'd need some help. Since Darion could no longer get involved, I turned to the only other person I knew who might have some ideas.

I knew of no fewer than three ways to get into the Charred Snake without being seen. Today I sneaked in through the back window of the kitchen. Hiding in the shadows, I threw a snap-flare across the room into the smoldering hearth. As everyone in the main hall turned to watch the fire erupt in an explosion of sparks, I slipped into Garrick's office quietly.

Garrick looked up from his desk, his face tinged with annoyance. "Cas, I told you to wait before coming back."

"I was discreet."

"And yet I still don't have a job for you, so you wasted a trip."

"I'm not here for a job," I said.

Garrick lifted his eyebrows. "Why do I get the sense that I'm not going to like this?"

"Did you know?" I asked.

Garrick gave me a look that said, *I'm not falling for that one. You'll have to tell me what you're talking about.*

The din of the room outside hid our voices from prying ears, but I still approached him and spoke in a hushed tone. "Did you know that I'm Emberborn?"

Garrick's eyes opened slightly, but any trace of surprise was gone in a heartbeat. "I didn't *know*. I suspected."

"You *suspected*?"

"Your uncanny memory, your speed and stealth, and your ability to climb up a damn wall without so much as a crack...when I was a much younger man, I knew Emberborn who could do similar things, but never all of them. And then there was your parents' death. It all added up."

"Why didn't you tell me?"

"Because that's not the kind of thing you speculate about openly. It often has the nasty side effect of getting you killed," Garrick said dryly. "How did *you* find out?"

"It's complicated."

"I have time," Garrick said. "And as long as we're telling truths, maybe you can tell me what really happened the night you broke into Orlik's house. I'm guessing it's related?"

As usual, Garrick was sharp as a whip. I suspected that this conversation might lead to that question. After opening up to Elena, I was learning to appreciate the benefits of not keeping secrets from people I trusted. And yet I still hesitated. I closed my eyes, let out a long breath, then let the words flow.

"I ran into another thief when I was stealing the gold. I could sense that he was Emberborn," I said. "Which I recently found out is an Emberborn ability."

"Dust, Cas, you have Veilsense?"

"Yes. Same as the Sentinels, as much as that sickens me."

Garrick's face looked as sour as I'd ever seen it. "What happened to the thief?"

"He was after a book in the safe. We did the thief's parlay. He took the book, and I took the gold."

Garrick nodded. "That explains why the Sentinels showed up here. What was in the book?"

"It was about Emberborn and how the Crown corrupts them."

"And why did you choose not to tell me about all this?" Garrick asked, and his tone didn't sound too accusatory. He seemed genuinely curious. We'd been partners for years and rarely kept secrets without good reason.

I considered for a moment how much to tell him, but I owed him an explanation, especially since this involved him now. The only thing I wasn't ready to reveal was any personal details about Darion and me.

"The thief is a member of the Order of Emberlight. He invited me to the Emberlight Trials. I was worried that telling you would disqualify me."

"Ah," Garrick said, nodding. "This is starting to make sense. That explains why you needed the catacombs map."

I nodded.

Garrick sat back and let out a long sigh. "You really are in deep, aren't you, Cas?"

"So it would seem."

"I know you're an adult, and I'm not here to lecture you, but the Emberlight Trials? Isn't that dangerous? Those are designed to weed people out, not let them in. What about your sister?"

"Elena's showing signs of being Emberborn," I said. "I could sense her Ember, and that means the Sentinels will be able to sense her too if her Ember ever manifests."

"Oh." Garrick frowned. "Well, that *does* complicate things."

"Just the other day, we saw the Sentinels murder a man simply because his Emberborn daughter was taken away and he spoke up about it." Saying that out loud made me unexpectedly emotional, and my throat constricted. I had to choke back tears. "I can't lie low anymore."

"I understand," Garrick said. "So what do you need from me?"

"A way to get into the Citadel Clock Tower."

Garrick laughed, then stopped when I stayed silent. "Oh, you're not joking."

"I'm afraid not."

Garrick stroked his beard. "Cas, you're my best man, but this is putting me at tremendous risk."

He paused, and for a moment, I imagined he was figuring out how to let me down gently.

But then he said, "I have a friend who owes me a favor. He works at the Citadel Library. I'll need to contact him. For now, go home. I'll let you know when he responds." Garrick paused again and looked me right in the eye. "*Don't* come back here."

The first night came and went with no word from Garrick.

I was anxious and jumpy cooped up in our barn. We couldn't sell herbs during the day, and I didn't have my usual jobs at night to keep my mind from wandering to dark places.

Thinking of my night with Darion helped. He had such a calming effect on me, and I longed to see him again. But when we'd parted, we hadn't made arrangements to meet again. We at least knew where each other lived now, since Darion had walked me home after our night together. But I had no idea when he'd be home, and I couldn't exactly loiter outside his house and wait for him to return.

So to keep my mind occupied, I spent time with Elena, which was something I meant to do more of anyway, but I had always been so busy. Since I had revealed my secret life as a thief to her, I was finally able to teach her the fine art of clandestine potioncraft. Now that everything was becoming more complicated, I owed it to her to give her every advantage. She took to the craft immediately and found it endlessly fascinating, asking questions and trying experiments with different ingredients.

Later in the evening, we practiced sparring with our dull-bladed rapiers in the spot next to the chicken coop outside our barn. We continued until dusk, when visibility began to fade. We finished with a particularly nasty exchange that ended when Elena, through brute force, knocked the sword out of my hand with a loud grunt.

"Ouch," I cried, shaking my hand, my fingers aching from the brutal impact. "I've taught you too well. You're getting too strong."

Light clapping came from behind us. In a flash, I spun around, hand on my dagger. "Who's there?"

Darion sat on a bale of hay with an infuriatingly amused look on his face. "It is I, your adoring fan. That was quite a show, Elena."

Elena smiled widely. "Not bad, huh?"

"It was masterful," he said.

It took me a moment for my heart rate to drop. I'd been on edge ever since we'd bumped into The Butcher in the marketplace, and I wasn't crazy about surprises, but I was happy about this one. Seeing Darion instantly made me feel safer.

I walked over to him, unable to hold back my smile. He stood up as I approached, and our eyes locked. The slightest rosy hue bloomed in his cheeks, which I found adorable. How I could make this grown man blush with a simple look was beyond me. But I enjoyed it.

"Don't let me stop you," he said, looking at my sword, which still lay on the ground.

"Oh no," I said, gesturing him over to the sword. "Be my guest. Show us how a master does it."

Darion shot me a coy smile and a shrug. He walked over, picked up the sword, and assumed a guard position, pointing it toward Elena.

"Elena, do you accept this challenge?" Darion asked with gravitas and just a hint of playfulness.

"Dust yes!" Elena said, launching immediately into an attack that Darion skillfully parried.

It soon became obvious that Darion was exceptionally skilled with a sword, so much so that he must have had some professional training. But it was also clear that he had infinite patience and restraint, as he never pressed his advantage, letting Elena set the pace. He was also a joy to watch, displaying a subtle grace I hadn't noticed in him before. Each motion was considered, and each step was well planned. A tide of emotion swept over me as I watched this beautiful man treating my sister with such respect.

A few times, Elena got an advantage, but Darion always fought back until they were even again. After the third time this happened, I realized he was intentionally making mistakes to give Elena openings, but he was subtle enough that Elena didn't pick up on it. This was his way of keeping her engaged. I imagined he could win the fight at any moment if he chose.

Only after Elena successfully got her first hit on Darion's left side did he start a more offensive attack. They continued back and forth, each getting the occasional hit. When dusk turned into night and I could barely see them anymore, they finally called a draw.

"That was excellent, Elena," Darion said, still panting from the exertion. "Your brother has taught you well."

"You're amazing!" Elena beamed. "Will you stay for dinner? We're making a stew!"

Darion looked my way, and my smile told him everything he needed to know.

"I'd love to," he said.

During dinner, Elena asked Darion a barrage of sword-fighting questions, which he gracefully answered. He had done an apprenticeship under a sword-master and had won a few tournaments when he was younger.

"Why did you stop?" Elena asked when Darion mentioned that he no longer competed.

"There comes a time in life when you assess your priorities and decide what's really important," he said. "And sword tournaments are decidedly not important."

I smiled at this, understanding that the Order of Emberlight had become his top priority. And maybe other things.

Elena nodded with a slightly disappointed look. "Well, I think you would win every tournament you entered."

"Elena, I think it's probably time for you to head to bed," I said. It was well past her usual time, and I also wanted some time alone with Darion.

Elena rolled her eyes but didn't complain too much. After she said good night, Darion and I were alone in the flickering firelight.

"You were amazing with her," I said to him. "Thanks for putting up with all her questions."

"Not at all. I enjoy talking to someone with a passion for sword fighting. And she is quite good. You really have taught her well."

"Perhaps you and I should try a sword fight sometime," I said, realizing the innuendo halfway through and closing my eyes in embarrassment, letting out a quiet laugh.

Darion laughed, too. "I'd like that."

I opened my eyes to see him watching me with that smile still on his face.

"You don't ever talk about what *you* want," he said softly.

"I do," I said, maybe a bit too fast. "I want Elena safe. I want a home for us."

Darion let out a gentle laugh. "That's not what I mean."

Oh. *This* talk. A tiny jolt of panic hit, but I covered it up.

"I don't...I don't do *this*," I said, waving my hand between us. "Not this way, anyhow. When people try to fit into my life, they usually find out they don't. And then they leave."

Darion leaned in, then paused, like he was choosing his words carefully.

"I can't promise everything will work out," he said quietly. "But I can promise that this means something to me, and I don't want to pretend it's nothing."

I felt like I was standing on the edge of something big, a line I was about to cross. My chest felt tight, like I was bracing for impact. But in the end, I crossed it.

"Then let's not pretend it's nothing," I said, my voice shaking.

Darion smiled, then closed the distance between us and gave me a gentle kiss. It was short and tender but felt monumental. After we separated, he looked into my eyes.

"Well..." I said.

"Well," he echoed.

"I'm sure you must be tired after all that sword fighting."

"Not too tired." Darion smiled. "In fact, I thought perhaps you might want to...I mean...if you're okay with leaving Elena here."

"Yes," I said, with enough insistence to put any doubt to rest.

We raced to his humble home, which felt impossibly far. The entire way there, I imagined the things I would do to him, and I wasn't disappointed in the least. We recreated the other night, adding even more variations to our repertoire. Gone were the uncertainty and expectations of the first time, and in their place was playful fun as we each discovered what gave the other pleasure.

The next day was much the same. Darion visited in the evening, helped Elena with her sword lessons, and joined us for dinner. Then Darion and I sneaked off for the night.

It was possibly the closest thing to a family that I could remember having since I was a child. But I knew it wouldn't last.

The next day, I began to wonder if Garrick had forgotten about me. His blunt warning about not coming back to the Charred Snake only worried me more.

Darion came over again, and we were preparing our evening meal when a note slipped under the door. I grabbed the note and then looked outside. The street was empty.

The note was lengthy, and to the untrained eye, it appeared to be a letter between friends. But I recognized Garrick's handwriting and the code we used. Every eighth word was a note within a note, starting with a pass phrase that only he and I knew—a safeguard that indicated the note's authenticity. Hidden within the note were instructions to meet at a location near the Analon wharf at sixth bell.

Darion watched me in anticipation as I read the note. When I was done, I nodded and mouthed the word *tonight.* Darion nodded back, his face stoic. A strange mix of feelings swirled within me. I was eager to continue my Trials, but I would miss this little slice of happiness we shared. At least it reinforced what I was fighting for.

That night, after Elena had gone to sleep and Darion had gone home, I snuck out of the house and made my way to the designated meeting place by the wharf. I stopped short to observe, to make sure no one was watching and that this wasn't an ambush. Soon a figure in a dark cloak walked up to the spot. That massive, hulking shape could only be Garrick. I'd know that silhouette anywhere.

I walked up beside him, and we shared a subtle nod.

"My contact can help you get into the Citadel Library tomorrow afternoon. But I'm warning you, you won't like what you'll have to do."

I laughed under my breath. "Sounds like a typical job."

"Nothing about this is typical," Garrick said with no humor in his voice. He handed me an envelope. "These are instructions on where to meet him and maps of the lower levels of the library, but I'm afraid you'll have to figure out how to get up to the clock tower on your own. Destroy these when you're done."

"I don't know how to thank you, Garrick."

He held up his index finger. "I have one condition."

I thought back to Mrs. Crowe's harsh terms. It seemed conditions were the norm when Emberborn were involved. "Name it."

"There's a job I've considered for a long time, but it was always too risky. But since you're going in already, I need you to steal something inside the library."

"What is it?" I asked.

"Not an *it*. A *her*."

Chapter Twenty

The Ascent

Garrick was right. I didn't like the plan.

The Citadel Library and its lofty bell tower were barely visible from where its steam exhaust pipes jutted out into the Analon River. The pipes vented from the massive steam engine that provided heat and power to the entire library—one of the many innovative marvels within its walls. The circular pipes came up to my shoulder—just barely tall enough to walk through without crawling, which was fortunate since they would burn bare skin on contact.

Fourth bell had rung, and the pipes were venting, shooting jets of deadly hot steam. The moment they stopped, I raced into one of them, taking great care to avoid the scalding sides. My burning leather soles gave off the smell of searing flesh, a grim reminder of the cost of slipping.

I had counted 358 and 342 seconds between the last two ventings. The slight fluctuation probably depended on how much steam power the library used. Either way, I figured I still had plenty of time as I ran the half mile between the pipe outlet and the maintenance hatch.

I had packed light, forgoing my backpack and nearly half my vials. I did, however, have the parchment I'd found in Queen Amara's tomb safely tucked in my breast pocket. Perhaps there was something in the tower that could help me decipher it.

The heat was thick and oppressive, and sweat poured down my face. More than once, I nearly tripped on the seams of the pipe as I raced along, narrowly avoiding the scalding sides.

I was also unhappy about relying on other people to get this job done. Other people were messy and unreliable. Other people made mistakes. Other people could betray you.

I had counted 260 seconds when I finally got to the maintenance hatch, which was barely an outline on the wall of the pipe. I knocked on the hatch with the hilt of my dagger in the rhythm Garrick had shown me.

No response.

A low rumbling came from farther down the pipe.

Dust! More than sixty seconds early. Why had I been in such a hurry to run into the pipes? I should have counted a few more times.

Vibrations ran up my legs. A hot wind blew past, buffeting my hair and clothing—a precursor to the deadly vapor that would follow.

I knocked on the hatch again and cursed under my breath. This was precisely why I never relied on others. There wasn't time to escape from the pipes. In moments, steam would envelop me and melt the skin off my bones. The heat was getting fierce, nearly scalding my skin. My eyes burned.

I knocked hard on the hatch once more, trying to keep my panic at bay. Halfway through the pattern, the hatch cracked open, flooding the pipe with cooler air.

"Quickly," a man hissed on the other side. He didn't have to tell me twice.

I leapt through the opening with steam lapping at my feet and rolled onto the stone floor of a small maintenance room. A man in dark robes tried to slam the hatch shut, but steam continued to escape through the edges. He was relatively young with a plump body, brown hair, and bangs cut straight across.

"Help me!" he yelled as he struggled with the latch on the door. "We'll be cooked alive!" Steam buffeted the door, trying to escape.

I hopped up and shoved the door with every bit of strength I could muster, trying to keep the deadly vapor from flooding the room. The extra force was just enough to allow the man to wedge the latch closed before the pressure of the steam blasted the door open.

We shared a glance of relief, panting hard. But my relief quickly turned to anger, and I scowled at the man. "That was cutting it fucking close."

"It couldn't be helped. The high scholar, Master Corvane, stopped me on the way," he said, shrinking back at my aggressive tone. "I was lucky to get here at all."

And I was lucky not to be a puddle of dead flesh, but there was no need to be gruesome, so I held my tongue. "Do you have something for me?"

"Ah, yes," the man said, pulling a bundle of dark brown fabric wrapped in twine out of his robes. "This will help you blend in."

I undid the twine and unfurled a robe very similar to the one he was wearing. The only difference was the silver ribbon sewn along the edges—his was lined in blue.

"These are the robes of an initiate, our lowest rank," the man said. "In these, you're less likely to raise suspicion when people see a new face. But I'd advise you to avoid people, lest they ask you questions you can't answer."

I nodded. "Thank you."

"I'll leave the room first. Count to one hundred before you exit."

"Okay."

As the man approached the door, he looked back. "I wish you luck, whatever your task. If you somehow live, tell Garrick I've paid my debt in full." He left the room without waiting for a response.

After slipping on my robe, I surveyed my surroundings. Metal pipes crisscrossed the walls and ceiling. A glowing glass ball illuminated the room. I had heard about the legendary flameless candles but had dismissed them as yet another exaggeration. But inside the ball, no flame flickered. Instead there was a solitary line of glowing light. I had no idea how it worked.

After sufficient time had passed, I left the room and entered a long stone chamber lined with the same glowing orbs. I passed countless rooms filled with wooden crates and barrels but encountered no one as I made my way along the curving passage. The lower chambers of the Citadel Library appeared to be largely untraveled, used mainly for storage and maintenance.

Soon I came to a narrow stairway twisting upward. I passed the entrances to four different floors, pausing each time to be sure no one was approaching. At the fifth floor, I ducked into the hallway, covering my head with the brown hood of my robes and keeping my face down.

My first stop was the aviary to complete Garrick's job. Based on the maps he had provided, it should be just ahead. I passed through the door and entered a massive circular room as tall as it was wide. A choir of chirps, squawks, and caws erupted the moment I entered. Countless cages lined the walls. In the center was a cage large enough for a sizable bird to spread its wings and fly. It rose many stories and had a wire mesh door in the roof that opened to the blue sky.

An elderly man looked up from a table where he was crafting a leather harness. Garrick had warned me that I might run into someone here. Luckily, this man was small and looked quite feeble, and I was prepared.

"May I help you, Initiate?" the man asked.

"Master Corvane sent you this note," I said, taking from my inner pocket a parchment that glistened with a powerful sedative.

"Why would Master Corvane send me a note?" he said, face scrunched in confusion. As he reached for it, I raced behind him, holding the parchment up to his mouth and nose. But he shoved it away with far more strength than I'd given him credit for.

"Help!" he cried out. Several birds squawked in reaction.

I drew my dagger quickly and knocked him over the head with the butt. That startled him enough for me to reposition the parchment. Before he could fight back again, his frail body collapsed into my arms.

I paused, holding my breath, listening for the inevitable sound of rushing footsteps after the ruckus. But the hallway remained quiet. I was lucky.

I hid the man's unconscious body under a table. He'd be out for at least half a bell. From that moment, the clock was working against me, so I had to act swiftly.

Each of the cages housed a different bird, ranging from the common swallow to more exotic species like a golden eagle and a multicolored bird with a large black beak that I didn't recognize. Below each cage was a note with the bird's name and species. Before long, I came to a cage with a note reading ZEPHYRA – WHISPERHAWK. Inside was a large bird whose feathers alternated between golden and brown. She had a hooked beak and powerful talons. Her keen black eyes peered back at me.

"Hello, Zephyra," I said. "So you're the girl Garrick is keen to set free."

Zephyra cocked her head. *Garrick sent?*

I nearly jumped at the voice inside my head. It wasn't so much that I heard those exact words, but the thought *behind* the words was suddenly present in my consciousness. It had been years since my father had taken me to the forest to listen to whisperhawks, and I had nearly forgotten what the feeling was like, or that it was even possible. My memory of it was like a dream, faded and distant. This would take some getting used to.

"Yes, Garrick sent me. I'm here to free you. My name is Cas," I said as I opened her cage.

Can Cas hear Zephyra?

Zephyra danced back and forth from foot to foot, ruffling her feathers.

"I can."

It's been years since anyone could hear Zephyra, little Cas.

"Little?"

Cas is much littler than Garrick.

"I can't argue with that."

Cut Zephyra's bonds, little Cas.

Zephyra pecked at the leather strap wrapped around her right leg. A chain attached to the strap looped around the cage, holding her captive. Her skin looked raw from rubbing against the leather.

"Hold very still." With my dagger, I cut the strap, taking great care to avoid her tender skin. The moment she was free, she jumped out of the cage and flapped around the aviary, finally settling on my shoulder.

Thank you, little Cas. That strap has bound Zephyra for years.

"I'm sorry for what they did to you."

It wasn't little Cas's fault.

"I can still have sympathy for you. Holding an intelligent animal such as yourself captive is nothing short of torture. But let's figure out how to get you *fully* free. Is there a way out of that flight cage?"

At the top, a locked hatch leads to the outside. But unless little Cas can fly, that won't do much good.

"I can't *fly*, but let me give it a try anyway. Where's the key?"

In Master Solcor's robes. Zephyra must admit, Zephyra took pleasure in seeing Master Solcor fall. Master Solcor isn't always kind.

I rooted through Master Solcor's robes until I found a ring of iron keys. It took me several tries, but I finally found the key that unlocked the entrance to the flight cage. The cage was easy to climb, and I was at the top in seconds. Zephyra flew beside me in ever higher circles.

Little Cas is like a bird without wings!

At the top of the cage was a hatch, which I unlocked using the same key. The hatch groaned as I pushed it upward. It had likely been a long time since it had been opened. I scampered through and onto the top of the cage, and Zephyra followed me out. I was standing on top of the aviary, which jutted out from the main library with the clock tower looming above me. The whole of Analon spread out below me in every direction.

Zephyra's wings flapped as she circled around me.

Oh, the wide-open air, and the wind! Zephyra forgot about the wind! And the sea air! Oh, how Zephyra longs to taste a fresh fish!

With that, Zephyra ascended, then flew directly toward the bay. Her joy in her newfound freedom hit me harder than expected with a mix of happiness and longing.

She was nearly out of sight when she looked back, her thoughts barely a whisper in my mind.

Thanks again. Zephyra is forever in little Cas's debt.

From the top of the aviary, I considered the clock tower before me, rising to the clouds. Its height was dizzying. It would be easy enough to climb, and I had hoped I could find a window, but in broad daylight, I would stand out starkly against the ivory-colored stones. A well-aimed arrow from a Royal Archer would end my ascent quite abruptly. I needed to find a way up from the inside. But according to my map, if any such path existed, it had been walled up long ago.

The clock tenders were legendary. Sequestered for life in the clock tower, their one job was to keep the clock running with perfect accuracy under penalty of death. No penalty had been administered in hundreds of years.

It stood to reason that if the clock tenders lived in the tower, there had to be ways for them to obtain supplies. The most obvious place to check was the kitchens, one set of which was positioned just under the tower. That would be my first target.

I weaved through the hallways, peering into rooms filled with books and lab equipment as I passed. I was tempted to stop in and see if I could uncover any secrets, but the danger was too great, and the clock was ticking. My time would be up when Master Solcor woke up or someone found him unconscious.

Several stories up, the rooms changed from labs and libraries to classrooms filled with initiates, all wearing silver-lined robes like mine. Standing at the front of each room was a master lecturing in a lofty tone. I walked swiftly past. On more than one occasion, I ducked into an empty room to avoid a passing group of robed figures.

When I ascended another story, the pleasing aroma of seared meat and grilled onions hit my nose. I approached a door from which steam and smoke billowed. Inside was a large room filled with open hearths and a smattering of worktables filled with cooking implements. Cages filled with chickens, ducks, and other small animals were lined up along the wall to my left. A half dozen people in robes adorned with yellow ribbon scurried around, tending to fires, stirring stews, and rotating meat on spits over coals. I snuck into the room, hid in the shadows, and observed.

On the far wall were three small waist-high openings. Several minutes passed as the servants continued their work. Eventually one of the Initiates approached the far left opening, placed a basket filled with food and other supplies inside, and rang a handheld bell. A moment later, a platform began to rise, and the basket disappeared out of sight. *That* was how supplies made their way to the tower.

And that was my key to getting in.

This wouldn't be as simple as sneaking into Garrick's office in a dark tavern full of drunk people. This room was bright and filled with stone-cold sober initiates who were likely trained in combat. I looked around the room to assess the situation, and the solution presented itself.

Slowly, quietly, I unlatched the cages of most of the animals, leaving each door open only a crack, then snuck around to the other side of the room.

Out of my pack, I pulled a paper tube smaller than my pinky finger. Of the many skills my father had taught me, pyrotechnics was by far the most entertaining. In the early weeks of every summer, we'd toil away making noisemakers, flash bombs, and exploding rockets to launch at the midsummer festival.

With a quick toss, the tube flew across the room toward the animal cages. The moment it struck the far wall, a loud pop rang out. The animals went crazy. In moments, several dozen chickens had knocked their doors open and were flapping wildly around the far side of the kitchen. The initiates all stopped their cooking duties and ran over to wrangle the loose chickens, yelling as they went.

With everyone distracted, I raced over to the rightmost opening and ducked inside. I was in a shaft about two shoulder widths apart. Above me, it rose into darkness. A wooden slab suspended by a rope kept me from falling. I wasn't sure what I would find, but I began my ascent up the shaft, hoping to reach the clock tower.

The shaft was constructed from stone blocks and mortar, making the ascent relatively easy, although my robe hung awkwardly, making everything more difficult. I stopped every few stories to rest my arms and legs, but I didn't pause for long—at any point, the platform might start rising. Soon the ruckus of chicken squawks and calls of alarm from below faded until all I could hear was the wind whistling up the shaft.

As I climbed, I considered what I might face when I reached the top. How would the clock tenders react to a thief in their supply shaft? If the rumors were true, the tenders were trained in combat, ready to defend the clock with their lives. And even if I made it past them, I wasn't even entirely sure what I was looking for.

After what felt like tens of stories, a faint light shone above. I quickened my pace, eager to be done with this climb, ready to face what was next, be it friend or foe.

Soon I reached an opening. Although the shaft continued upward, my arms and legs ached from the climb. I needed the rest and was eager to see where I stood. Garrick's maps of the lower library were thorough, but none existed for the tower. I was exploring blindly.

I hopped out of the shaft and into a small stone room with only a single door. I expected a fight and was ready for armed resistance, but to my surprise, the room was empty and quiet. The silence provided little comfort, as a surprise attack could come at any moment.

I approached the exit cautiously, taking each step with care. The door opened easily and had no visible lock. Outside, a stone corridor extended in either direction with beams of light pouring in through small slits in the outer walls, just wide enough for an archer to shoot arrows out of. Each slit revealed a streak of blue sky and a small slice of Analon far below the tower.

Down the corridor, a flickering light came through an open doorway. Inside was a large room lined with bookcases filled with books of varying shapes and sizes. Sturdy-looking tables and chairs occupied the middle of the room, all adorned with elaborate carvings depicting forest scenes with wolves, bears, and other woodland creatures. Hanging in the middle of the room was an iron chandelier with a dozen or more small tubes pointing upward, each containing a flickering candle-less flame.

I took a moment to inspect the books' spines. The library included such titles as *Emberborn History: The Middle Years, A Comprehensive Guide to Embers, Emberborn Royal House Lineage*, and many other books that appeared to relate to Emberborn lore. Mrs. Crowe had said that King Tarnasau had wiped out the entire history of Emberborn, but it appeared that a slice of their—*our* history was preserved in the clock tower. Despite the fact that I'd only understood my Emberborn roots for a short time, pride bloomed within me.

The sharp scent of ozone and citrus assaulted my nose. I was struck with the same sensation I'd felt in the alley when Darion had disappeared. Time broke, disjointed from reality, just like in the alley. Was Darion here? Surely not.

In a flash, an arm was around my chest and the cold, sharp steel of a blade was pressed against my neck. Soft but deadly, a woman's voice said, "Say the pass phrase or die."

CHAPTER TWENTY-ONE

The Clock Tower

THE BLADE CUT THROUGH the top layers of my skin. My dagger was within reach, but I knew I couldn't beat someone with this Ember, and even flinching could mean a slit throat. I considered mentioning the parchment I'd found in Queen Amara's tomb but decided against it until I knew more about what I was dealing with.

So I spoke the truth. "I know of no pass phrase. But I know you're Emberborn. I could sense when you used your Ember. I have a friend who can stop time like you."

The woman's blade quivered for a moment, taking another layer of skin. "You have Veilsense?" she asked, sounding shocked and impressed.

"I do."

"And you're here for the Emberlight Trials?"

"I am. I have a parchment that was stashed in the queen's tomb."

"Then you should know the pass phrase," she said. "You would have encountered it along your path."

I thought through each step of the Trials that had led me to the clock tower. I recalled the details of the Bleeding Oak, the Royal Catacombs, Queen Amara's tomb, and my journey through the Citadel Library.

Oh! The engraving on the queen's tomb. I pictured it in my mind: *Here lies Queen Amara, the last of the royal Emberborn race. May her wisdom extend beyond the hands of time's embrace.* Now it made sense. *Her wisdom* could mean this library, and *the hands of time's embrace* must mean the clock tower.

I repeated the phrase.

The woman withdrew her blade from my throat and stepped back.

I spun around, hand moving instinctively to the hilt of my dagger.

A middle-aged woman with dark skin and short, curly black hair speckled with gray stood before me wearing worn leather garments like those of a craftsperson. Her warm brown eyes spoke of a wisdom beyond her years.

She assessed my defensive stance. "No need for that. You said yourself that you're familiar with my Ember, so you should know that if I wanted you dead, you'd be dead already. You are my guest here."

She was right—I was powerless to stop her if she wanted to kill me. I moved my hand away from my dagger.

"And you have a note for me, I assume?" she said.

My instinct was not to trust her, but she could easily take it from me by force, so I retrieved it from my breast pocket and handed it to her.

She took the note and raised her arms. "Welcome to the Citadel Clock Tower, the spiritual heart of the Order of Emberlight. My name is Adela Fenn. What is your name, recruit?"

While she could kill me and take my possessions, she couldn't take my name. She clearly knew about the Order of Emberlight and the Trials, but that didn't guarantee that she was trustworthy.

Adela seemed to sense my hesitation. "You're right to be suspicious. That shows good instincts on your part. You're welcome to ask me any questions you have."

"You said this was the heart of the Order of Emberlight. How are you able to be here? Why does King Tarnasau allow it?"

Adela let out a sad laugh. "You're starting with *the* question. We play a delicate game with Tarnasau by exploiting his own ego and hubris. He *thinks* he's holding us captive here, forcing us to tend this clock against our will."

"Couldn't he just replace you with people he trusts?"

"Because of our special relationship with time, only we can keep the clock going with such precision. To him, the clock is a symbol of control and perfection for his kingdom, so he has 'walled us in' and 'forces us to maintain it.' In reality, we could leave at any time."

"And yet you choose to stay."

"We do. Generations of Emberborn have maintained not only this clock but Emberborn history and knowledge." Adela gestured toward the trove of books around the room. The sheer number filled me with awe, knowing they were all filled with Emberborn lore.

"Still, it must be hard being captive here," I said. The weariness in her eyes spoke volumes.

"It is. But it's our sworn duty. Since Tarnasau destroyed our history elsewhere, maintaining this secret cache of information is of critical importance. We would defend it with our lives. And we have also become the core of the resistance against his tyranny."

"You keep saying *we*. Where are the others?" I asked.

"It might be easier to show you," she said. "Follow me."

Adela ushered me out of the library. We walked side by side along the corridor past several other rooms filled with books, much like the one we had just left. Shadows danced in my peripheral vision, vague shapes roughly the size of people.

"So many books," I whispered.

"Indeed," Adela said, the pride plain on her face. "I am the fifteenth generation of Fenns who have maintained the clock and the library. Come and meet the fourteenth and sixteenth." She paused at the base of the next flight of steps. "You are my guest, but I'll remind you that I am extending you a measure of trust. I expect you to honor it."

"Of course."

With that, she led me up the steps and into a large common room dominated by a massive fireplace, surrounded by ornately carved and upholstered sofas. Behind it were several tables and chairs where a handful of men and women studied, ate, and talked, all dressed similarly to Adela. Several people looked up as we entered.

At one table sat an old man and a teenage boy, both with a familial similarity to Adela. Open books and pieces of parchment cluttered the table before them. They watched as we approached.

These were not at all the "warrior clock tenders" I'd expected to find here, although I was certain that Adela would defend this place to the death. This was a family—a family of Emberborn, in fact. Something Elena and I had had ripped away from us. The boy was no older than Elena, and Adela was likely the age my mother would have been if she were alive, making this both the most beautiful and melancholy sight I could imagine. I had to swallow hard to hold back my surging emotions.

"This is my father, Edric, and my son, Corin," Adela said, gesturing to each in turn. "And this is our newest Trials recruit. He is Emberborn. He has Veilsense."

The old man, Edric, turned his deeply wrinkled face toward me, eyebrows raised. "Veilsense. Impressive. What is your name, son?"

Adela looked as if she were about to speak, but I held up my hand. I had seen enough to extend some measure of trust to them.

"My name is Cassian Nightbrook," I said. "But people call me Cas."

"Nightbrook," Edric said, as if trying out the name for the first time, assessing how it felt on his tongue. "And both your parents were Emberborn?"

"Honestly, I don't even know. They died when I was young, and they never told me about my heritage."

Edric nodded with a sad frown. "I'm so sorry. All too common a story, I'm afraid. Do you know your real surname?"

"My *real* one?"

"Most Emberborn families on the run adopt new surnames, both to hide their identities and to sound less Emberborn."

"Nightbrook is the only name I've ever known," I said.

"We have extensive records of Emberborn lineage in our library. Keeping track was a necessary evil, I'm afraid," Edric said. "Corin, will you go fetch my book of lineages? The one ordered by aliases. Volume N."

"Yes, right away, Grandpa," Corin said, then ran off toward the library.

I watched him as he descended the stairs. I couldn't help thinking of Elena and what our family could have been like had it not been ripped away from us. "Has he lived here—"

"All his life, yes," Adela finished, with a distant look in her eyes. "He was born in the tower, and he'll likely die here, unless we bring an end to the reign of Tarnasau."

"And I want to help with that," I said. "Are my Trials over? Am I part of the Order of Emberlight now?"

A laugh came from deep within Edric's chest. "Not yet, my son. You have one more task to perform, and then you'll stand before the elders of the Emberlight Council. They will make the final decision."

"I'll do what I need to do."

"That I do not doubt," Edric said. "Getting as far as you have takes talent and perseverance. But it isn't always about what you want or even what you can do. The council decides."

"Speaking of which," Adela cut in, taking out the parchment I'd given her, "I need to decipher this message and send one back. Delivering a message to the council is your last task."

She left us just as Corin ran back up the stairs with a book nearly half as big as he was. On the spine was the letter *n*. He ran to the table and set the book down in front of his grandpa.

"Thank you, Corin," Edric said, and opened the book near the middle. "We assess the lineage of each new Emberborn recruit. But it's a deeply personal thing, and you may find out things you don't wish to know."

"I understand," I said quickly, instinctively, although I wasn't yet sure how I felt about it. My parents had kept so much from me, which made me feel unmoored. Even so, I wasn't sure I was ready to know everything about my past, since I was still coming to terms with what I had already learned.

Edric ran his finger down the ledger. The writing in the book was as immaculate as it was intricate, with many columns and rows covering the entire page. He scanned the first column, titled "Alias," flipped a few more pages, and finally settled on a page filled with surnames starting with *n-i*.

"Well, there are many more Nightbrooks than expected," Edric said. "Do you know your parents' given names?"

"My mother was Cora, and my father was Edwin," I said, choking back emotion as I recalled my father's kind smile and my mother's warm embrace. She'd always doled out affection generously.

"Edwin and Cora?" Edric said. "Interesting."

"What's interesting?" I asked.

"Those names feel familiar to me, but alas, I'm an old man and my memory is failing. Let's see what we can find in the ledger."

Edric continued to scan. After flipping several pages, he stopped, a frown on his face. "Well, that's disappointing. And unusual. Our records are thorough."

"So that's it? There's no record of my family?"

"This is quite unprecedented," Edric said as he closed the book. His forehead was deeply creased. "It's possible that they changed their surname more than once or that their alias was never recorded. I can look for records matching their given names, but that will require going through all the volumes, and that will take quite some time."

Adela rushed back into the room. Her footsteps were quick, and her face looked almost panicked, a sharp contrast to her earlier calm. "Cassian, I need to know—do you have a sister named Elena?"

"I do," I said, feeling my stomach drop. "Why?"

"You and your sister are in terrible danger!"

Chapter Twenty-Two

Out of Time

Adela's words hit me like a punch in the gut. *Elena is in terrible danger.*

"What kind of danger?" I pleaded.

"The note you delivered contained intelligence from our spy planted in Tarnasau's Royal Guard," she said between puffs of breath, still winded from her speedy entrance.

"What does it say?" I asked with a hint of impatience.

"It often contains names of people on the Royal Guard's target list, people they suspect are Emberborn. We look them up in our ledgers, then find them and warn them, potentially helping them escape the city. Today's note contains your name and your sister's."

"What?!" I choked out. "Is my sister in immediate danger?"

"Possibly. The note was vague. It mentioned only your given names."

"Can I see it?" I asked, holding out my hand.

Adela paused for a moment, looking uncertain, but then she nodded and handed the note over.

I scanned her translation and locked it in my memory. Since I had the glyphs in the original note memorized as well, I thought I might be able to find the pattern. That would be an exercise for another time.

The note contained the following passage:

Detain subjects for questioning. Given names: Cassian and Elena. Short dark hair, long red hair. Often seen selling in the Citadel Market. Possibly dangerous.

My blood turned to ice. "I have to get to my sister!" I was glad I'd told Elena to stay away from the market. If only I could shake the nagging feeling that she hadn't heeded my advice, which was often the case.

Adela sighed. "I'm afraid the earliest you can leave safely is tomorrow morning. We sneak people out at the change of shift for the kitchen staff."

"Tomorrow's not soon enough. I need to leave now."

Edric cut in. "I'm afraid that's not possible. It's too risky. And the risk is not just to you."

"If I have to, I'll scale the wall right now."

Edric scowled. "The archers will shoot you down before you make it halfway. And you'll bring Tarnasau's wrath down on us."

My stomach churned. I didn't want to put the clock tenders in peril, but sitting here when Elena might be in danger was simply impossible. I was at a loss for words, so I squeezed my eyes shut and tried to hold back the anger and sadness spilling out of me.

Adela gently placed a hand on her father's shoulder. "There is another way."

"Bah!" Edric spat. "It's too dangerous."

I snapped my eyes open. "But if the danger is only to me, I'll do it."

Adela looked grave. "This path is treacherous. It's through the clockworks. There's a decent chance you'll slip and fall to your death."

"I choose that path," I said without a hint of uncertainty.

"Very well," Adela said. "I need to write a note back to the council, and then we can leave right away."

Adela left to write her note. It was all I could do not to jump out of my skin. Edric remained silent with a frown on his face. I knew I was harming his impression of me, but my need to get to Elena was simply too great.

Soon Adela returned, and we left right away, heading down a long corridor. We reached a stone staircase that rose in a tight spiral. It twisted up for several stories with only the occasional arrow slit providing a thin sliver of light. By the time we reached the top, we were both breathing heavily.

We came to an imposing iron door adorned with metal rivets. Adela knocked on the door, which boomed with each strike. A small slit opened near the top, and a pair of eyes peered out.

"The willow weed is bountiful this year," a gruff male voice called out.

"But not as bountiful as the dew lilies," Adela replied.

The man nodded with a grunt, eyes focused on me. "Who is he?"

"A recruit. He needs a quick exit using the emergency protocol."

The slit closed, and moments later, a loud scrape of metal on stone echoed throughout the hallway. The door creaked open, the metal hinges protesting with a high-pitched squeal. An imposing man stood behind the door. He had a beard that extended halfway down his chest and muscles that bulged beneath the same craftsperson's leather outfit that seemed to be common among the clock tenders. He stood back and gestured us in, his eyes narrowed and never straying far from me.

Adela guided me into a massive room filled with a maze of metal cogs, springs, and pistons, all in constant motion. A steady ticking came from every direction, marking the never-ending passage of time. The smell of machine oil permeated everything. Sunlight filtered in through towering stained glass windows on all four sides of the room. Clock hands and tick marks cast shadows on the glass from the outside.

"Welcome to the clockworks," Adela said. "You are now among a select few who have ever seen this room. Follow me, and watch that you don't get caught up in any of the gears."

Adela guided me deep into the mechanics of the clock. Whirring sounds came from all around us. She took out a parchment that looked similar to the one I had given her earlier. "This contains information that is critical to the Emberlight Council and will also help you and your sister. Do you accept this mission?"

"I do."

She explained that I was to meet a contact who would guide me to the council at a specific tavern in the Underworld.

"Now, on to the hard part," she said as we approached a mechanism within the clockworks where a notched lever clicked along a ratchet wheel. Both were the size of full-grown men.

"Beyond these clockworks is a shaft that drains excess machine oil. It drops all the way to the sub-basement of the Citadel Library. Once you're there, you'll be able to leave the building without attracting attention as long as you wear your initiate robes. But as you can see, getting to the shaft while the clock is operating is impossible, since you'd have only one tick of the clock to get through without being crushed by the machinery."

"You're going to use your Chronothene Ember to slow time," I said.

"That's right," Adela said, sounding impressed. "We do this occasionally to perform maintenance on the clock. It's how we're able to tune or repair it without ever stopping it. But you won't be aware of the pause in time. I'll push you through, but from your perspective, one moment you'll be here and the next you'll be beside a shaft that drops hundreds of feet. Everything is slick with the oil we use to keep the gears in motion, so you'll have to be ready for it."

"I've found that I have some awareness of time pauses, likely because of my Veilsense. Maybe that'll only happen if you let me perceive it? I'm not exactly sure how it works."

"That's not possible," Adela said, her eyes narrowing. "Only another person with Chronothene can share in the time shift."

"I've done it before, and I assure you it is possible."

"Done it with whom?" she asked.

My mind immediately went back to those nights with Darion. Although my thoughts were consumed with concern for my sister, I still felt my face heat at the memory of that intimate moment.

"His name is Darion Thorne. He's the one who invited me to the Emberlight Trials."

A subtle shift occurred in Adela's eyes, barely perceptible but undeniably there. She said nothing, but her face was pinched.

"Do you know him?" I asked.

"We can't delay any longer," Adela said, almost too quickly. "Are you ready?"

Something felt off, but I didn't have the time to dig further with Elena in danger. "Let's do it."

"I'll attempt to extend my Chronothene Ember to you, but if it doesn't work, be ready to hold on for your life."

"I'm ready."

Adela concentrated on the pawl as it climbed up a tooth of the ratchet. As it crested the edge, the warmth of her Ember enveloped me. The scent of ozone and citrus collided with what had become a familiar feeling of time ceasing to abide by its usual rules. Though I'd seen it happen many times now, it was still spectacularly unreal. All the machinery froze, and a low-pitched hum replaced the whirring and ticking of the clockwork. I couldn't imagine ever getting used to this.

Adela looked perplexed. "You really can perceive this, can't you?"

I nodded.

"Remarkable. But we have no time to waste."

Adela barely fit between the gears. Machine oil streaked her sides, but it blended right into her worn leather garments as if this had happened a hundred times before. With my slight build and dexterity, I mostly avoided touching the machinery, but with time frozen, it felt like moving through molasses. We both had to stoop to avoid the cogs overhead. The ground was slick with oil.

"Watch your step," she warned as we approached a dark square hole in the ground. I had never been afraid of heights, but the sight of the tunnel dropping so many stories made my stomach flutter.

"That's a long way down," I said.

"No one would survive the fall," she said grimly. "Well, Cassian Nightbrook, this is where we part ways. I wish you the best of luck on your journey. And one last word of warning: Be careful who you trust."

No one could say that I wasn't skilled at climbing, but by the time I was halfway down the torturous ladder, I was ready for this descent to be over. Machine oil coated all surfaces, making every handhold a chore to grip and every rung of the ladder an opportunity to slip to my death. My hands were raw and slick with oil, and the bottoms of my feet ached.

The entire way down, my thoughts were consumed with the danger Elena might be in. Knowing that the Royal Guard knew not only our names but also that we were merchants in the Citadel Market meant that if Elena were to even leave our barn, she would be putting herself in great danger. I desperately wanted to get home quickly, but moving fast was next to impossible on this godsforsaken ladder.

When I finally reached the bottom of the shaft, I found myself in a small room illuminated by a flameless candle. A large vat was positioned directly below the shaft to collect the excess oil. With a long leap, I swung past the vat and avoided ending up in a bath of oil.

Exiting the Citadel Library was supposed to be much easier than entering. Adela had told me to walk out in my Initiate robes and hope for the best, but I didn't love that plan. I hated not being in control. One overzealous guard would be enough to ruin it. So I decided to shed my robes, which were glistening with oil from my climb down. An initiate dripping with machine oil would draw too many suspicious eyes. But I had a backup plan.

A section of the eastern outer wall bordered the Analon River. It was a long drop to the water, and it was still light out, so it wasn't without risk, but it was a chance I had to take for the sake of Elena.

This part of the Citadel Library was on Garrick's map, so I navigated the twisting tunnels with ease. Soon I reached a door that led to a parapet running along the top of the eastern outer wall, beside which the Analon River flowed. Next to the door was a guard station with a large window, where two guards were exchanging stories and roaring with laughter about last night's drunken escapades at a tavern, which had apparently included a brawl, being slapped by women, and winning at dice.

The guard station was the only obstacle to my escape. I considered a distraction—perhaps a smoke bomb?—but the guards were deep in their conversation. Sometimes doing nothing was the best strategy.

Sometimes not.

I pressed myself against the wall and slid under the guard station window, making it past without a sound as the guards continued their tales of conquest. When I passed through a door, I found myself outside on the parapet. I walked along, inspecting the railing, which had regular notches in the stonework for archers. They looked just big enough to slip through. I peeked through the first notch. At least five stories down, the river flowed past. A light breeze ruffled the leaves of the trees along the bank far below. My heart fluttered as I considered the jump.

It was too far. I'd never make it.

But farther along the parapet was a flight of stairs descending to a lower level, making it a much easier jump. I stepped back from the treacherous drop to head for the stairs just as the distinct creak of a bowstring stretching broke the silence. I spun around to see an archer, bow drawn and aimed directly at me, well within range for a killing shot.

Apparently my black clothing and general appearance were justification enough to shoot without warning. I cursed myself for shedding my robes too early. His hand snapped, releasing the arrow.

At the same instant, a shadow passed over the archer. The caw of a whisperhawk broke the silence, just enough distraction to spoil the archer's aim. The arrow whizzed past my left shoulder, the fletching of the bow grazing the fabric of my tunic.

Quickly, little Cas! Jump before it's too late! Zephyra's thoughts boomed in my mind just as her talons grabbed at the head of the archer in a blur of golden and brown feathers.

Without another thought, I leapt off the wall, dropping the impossible distance toward the rushing river like a stone, hoping I'd come out alive.

Chapter Twenty-Three

The Rescue

It was a long drop when I had time to think about how long a drop it was *while* I was dropping. The good news was that I didn't see any obvious rocks or shallow spots directly below me. The bad news was that I was falling too fast to be sure.

When I hit the water, my open mouth snapped shut, and I narrowly avoided biting off my tongue. The rushing current dragged me along below the surface. Trails of bubbles streaked down as arrows pierced the water. My lungs burned, but I let the river do the work to carry me away.

When I couldn't take it any longer, I surfaced. Loud bursts of horns came from the Citadel Library, sounding an alarm. I floated along until the river ran under a bridge, where I quietly pulled myself to shore. In a few short moments, I climbed to the top of the closest building and raced along the rooftops of Analon toward home, soaked with river water. The Royal Guards on the streets below were on high alert, stopping anyone who looked suspicious.

My mind was still reeling at the idea that Elena might be in danger, and I worried that much of this was my fault. My thieving activities and the Emberlight Trials had brought this pressure upon our family.

A shadow crossed my path from the sky above. Zephyra's caw cut through the din of city noise. I paused to look up. The moment I did, she landed softly on my shoulder.

"Thank you, Zephyra," I said, stroking her golden feathers. "I owe you one."

Returning the favor, little Cas.

"After I freed you, I thought you'd head straight back to Garrick."

Zephyra does like Garrick, but Garrick doesn't own Zephyra. Plus little Cas is better at understanding Zephyra.

"High praise indeed, but I need to go. I have to get to my sister."

What does sister look like?

"A bit shorter than me with long red hair."

Zephyra looks!

Zephyra flapped her wings and took to the sky, circling high above.

The closer I got to our barn, the more my worry grew. Wisps of smoke curled above the buildings near our home, and a murmur of deep voices carried up from the streets below. Using every ounce of self-control, I paused on a rooftop across from our home and peeked over the edge. My stomach dropped at the sight before me.

The barn we called home was charred and smoking. The chicken coop was open and empty, the crops in our side yard trampled. The remains of our herb cart were strewn about the street, now just a pile of wood, broken vials, and spilled reagents.

Royal Guards stationed outside the barn door stood with their swords drawn while other guards walked about, conversing with passersby, exuding an air of toughness and superiority.

Elena was nowhere to be seen.

Images of our burning farm and my parents' slashed throats flashed before my eyes, and my chest ached like my heart had been ripped out. I squeezed my locket so tight it cut into my palm.

And then I saw a face that made my heart drop. Barking orders at the guards was Syra, Orlik's bodyguard, the very same woman who'd run into us in the market and pursued Darion. I shuddered, remembering her ghastly transformation into a beast.

She had seen Elena in the market that day, and now she knew where we lived.

Fueled by rage and despair, I pulled out two daggers, ready to slash her throat and the throat of every other guard. I moved to stand, but Zephyra's thoughts burst into my mind as she circled in the sky above me. *Stop, little Cas! Sentinels!*

I paused and scanned the surrounding area. Sure enough, Sentinels perched on the rooftops surrounded our home, standing next to archers armed with crossbows. It was a minor miracle that no one had spotted me already. It still took all the willpower I had not to race down there and take out everyone before their bolts cut me down.

Girl with fire hair nearby, running with a man.

Fire hair! That *must* be Elena. She was alive! There was still a chance to rescue her.

"Can you take me to her?" I asked.

Yes, Zephyra will fly to them.

I slunk away from the roof's edge and headed in the direction Zephyra was flying. Once out of sight of the Sentinels, I broke into a sprint, heart pounding.

Zephyra guided me away from our smoldering home. Soon she soared upward and then dove into an alley. Looking down, I saw two people racing along the cobbled path below, both in dark cloaks, one with unmistakable red hair flowing out. The other was a man of large stature.

They were running so close together that I couldn't tell if the man was holding Elena against her will. He could easily have been pressing a knife against her side. They turned right at the next road, so I cut across the roof to make up for lost ground. I bounded down from my perch, jumping off balconies and awnings and dropping to the street right in front of them.

I pulled out my dagger and aimed it directly at the large robed figure. "Release her now!"

Zephyra landed on the balcony behind me. *Should Zephyra pluck out their eyes?*

"Cas, don't!" Elena cried.

The person beside Elena drew back their hood, revealing a familiar handsome face and green eyes. Darion smiled. I ran up and wrapped them both in a big hug.

"I'm so glad you're okay," I said to Elena. "I was so worried when I saw our home."

"It's all thanks to Darion," Elena said. "He got me out of the barn, although I'm still a little confused about how."

Darion nodded and smiled, but I could see the fatigue in his face. He must have used his Ember to get them out. He looked drained.

There was so much more I wanted to know. How had the Royal Guard found our house? How had Darion known Elena was in trouble? I opened my mouth to speak, but Darion cut me off.

"We'll have time for questions later," he said. "We have to get you two underground. The upper city is no longer safe for either of you."

The three of us raced along back alleys, ducking into the shadows several times to avoid passersby and once to avoid an entire group of Royal Guards who were moving along at a swift trot.

"We're nearly there," Darion said, ushering us along, his fatigue clearly evident. "Just a bit farther down this street."

That was the moment we crossed an intersection and spotted an entire company of guards—twenty at least—just a stone's throw away, marching in the other direction. We all froze. I held my breath, but my heart rate skyrocketed.

Darion gestured for us to move, and we all crept along, trying to get past the intersection without a sound. I could sense that Darion longed to use his Ember again but that he was too tired after rescuing Elena.

We were almost out of sight when one guard looked our way. His eyes went wide the moment he spotted us. “There they are!” he yelled.

The entire company spun around.

Without a moment’s hesitation, Elena ran toward the guards.

“Elena, don’t!” I cried as I ran after her. What in the dust was she doing?

The smell of ozone and citrus hit me so hard it was like a punch to the face. To my utter amazement, it wasn’t coming from Darion but Elena.

A wooden scaffolding ran along the building just in front of the guards. Elena grabbed a supporting leg and broke it free with one sweep of her arm, sending the entire structure toppling down in a mass of splintered wood that blocked the entire street. The shell-shocked guards pulled up just in time to avoid being buried in the rubble. They watched in amazement and horror.

Elena turned and shrugged. “I probably should have told you. I have a few secrets of my own.”

I yelped out a laugh of surprise, staring at my amazing and apparently powerful little sister. “I can’t believe what I just saw!”

She smiled, but her tired eyes betrayed the cost of using her Ember.

A loud shrieking sound came from all directions. The Sentinels must have detected that large burst of Ember from Elena. They’d be on us in no time.

“Let’s go!” Darion yelled as he raced down the road with us in fast pursuit.

We turned left at the next alley, and then Darion led us down a darkened staircase beside a nondescript building. We danced around rubble strewn along the stairs until a collapsed passageway barred further progress. Darion reached into a hole in the wall and turned his wrist.

Something behind the wall clicked, followed by a low rumble like the grinding of gears. The wall parted along a seam, revealing a passageway lined with flickering lanterns extending as far as the eye could see. We all hurried in, Darion glancing up the empty staircase one last time before ducking inside. He activated a switch on the other side, and the door slid shut.

We all took a moment to breathe, safe for now and relieved that we'd made it unscathed.

"Elena, that was incredible," I said. "So you have an Ember that makes you strong?"

She nodded. "To be honest, I didn't even know if I could pull the scaffolding down, but I had to try."

"How long have you known?"

"A couple of months," she said. "I've been practicing here and there, but once you warned me about the Sentinels, I stopped."

"You were right to stop, but thanks for saving us back there."

"Elena," Darion said. "Do you think you have a bit more strength left?"

"I think so. Why?" she asked.

"This entrance is compromised," he said. "If Sentinels find it, we can't let them get in. Can you destroy the gears of this door?"

"I can try."

And try she did. Elena reached into the machinery and bent inch-thick iron rods as if they were made of straw. The metal groaned and snapped. In moments, the mechanism looked broken beyond repair.

Darion grinned. "Impressive. Okay, let's get a little farther, and then we can rest for a bit and talk."

Elena smiled, but it melted away quickly, and she nearly collapsed. I raced to steady her.

"You okay?" I asked.

After a moment and a deep breath, she nodded. "Yeah, I'll be fine."

Darion guided us through the mazelike tunnels of the Underworld, turning confidently at each intersection as if he'd walked this route a hundred times before. He stopped in front of a large archway leading into darkness.

"We're safe enough now to pause for a moment," he said, then turned to me. "First things first." He wrapped me in a hug. I was still on high alert, so the intimacy caught me off guard, and I stiffened. But that didn't stop him.

"I'm so glad you're okay," Darion whispered in my ear. His gentle voice had a calming effect on me, and I melted into his embrace. He kissed me on my forehead, then nuzzled his nose against mine. "Watching you go through the Trials has been hell."

I smiled and let out a quick laugh. "It hasn't exactly been easy for me either."

Darion laughed as well. "When I heard the Citadel alarm, I feared the worst. I wasn't expecting you back until tomorrow morning at the earliest. What happened? Did you fail the third Trial?"

"No, I made it to the tower," I said. Darion noticeably relaxed, as if a heavy burden had been lifted.

I told them about everything—the tower, the note, the escape. The only thing I held back was that I could hear Zephyra's thoughts. Something about that felt dangerous; even the idea of saying it made my chest tighten. Trusting someone with that truth had once cost me dearly.

"Do you have the message Adela Fenn gave you?" Darion asked.

"I do." I pulled out the note and handed it to him.

He looked it over and let out a long breath. "Thank dust. This is your ticket to see the Emberlight Council. And since Elena's on the watch list, I can bring her along as well." He turned to her. "But we'll have to blindfold you, Elena. I'm sorry."

"I understand," Elena said, looking happy just to be included.

"How did *you* know Elena was in danger?" I asked Darion.

"I've been worried about the two of you ever since our run-in with Orlik in the market. I've been keeping an eye on your house."

My heart swelled. For much of my life, it had been only me caring for Elena, constantly worrying and bearing the burden of the promise I had made to my mother. Of course I would always honor that promise, and I loved Elena dearly, but the weight of that burden got a bit heavier each day. And now, for the first time, there was somebody to share it.

"Thank you for keeping my family safe," I said, voice cracking. I put a hand on his shoulder. "I don't know how I can ever repay you."

"Looking out for the people you care for isn't something that needs repaying," Darion said.

The three of us hugged again. I choked back the tears that were welling up.

"We should get going," Darion said.

"Where to now?" I asked.

"Now I'm taking you to the Emberlight Council."

Chapter Twenty-Four

The Order of Emberlight

The entrance to the Order of Emberlight headquarters was an unassuming opening in a stone wall running along a desolate passageway. On first inspection, it seemed unguarded, but as we approached, two men in studded leather armor emerged, one with a beard and the other clean-shaven, both with their hands on the hilts of their swords.

"Welcome, Darion Thorne. Who do we have here?" the bearded man asked in a deep and authoritative voice, eyeing Elena and me.

"Hello, Caldren. This is Cassian Nightbrook and his sister, Elena," Darion said, pulling out the note. "Cassian has completed the Trials, and his sister seeks refuge. Their home was destroyed, and she's on the Royal Guard's watch list."

"Welcome to the Order of Emberlight," Caldren said solemnly. "I'm sorry to hear about your home. As the head of the guard, I offer you refuge."

"Oh, and I should mention that the Starling entrance is compromised," Darion said. "We...um...disabled it. Permanently."

"Understood," Caldren said with a slightly quizzical look, then whispered to the clean-shaven man, who nodded and then ran off into the building.

"You may enter," Caldren said, and gestured toward the door.

Once inside, Darion said to Elena, "We can remove your blindfold now."

Elena ripped it off before either of us could help her. "I won't miss that."

Few could accuse the Order of Emberlight headquarters of being too opulent. Flickering torches adorned the rough stone walls, casting dancing shadows. The furniture consisted of simple wooden tables and chairs. The air had a bite to it, as was typical in the Underworld.

A few people we passed in the hallway shot us questioning glances, but Darion continued undeterred. Soon a man walked up to us with brisk strides. He was tall and strikingly handsome with blond hair and a light complexion. He carried himself with confidence, his chin held high.

"Darion, it's a joy to see you," the man said, extending his arm. "It's been too long."

"Hello, Kael. It *has* been too long." Darion clasped Kael's forearm, and they shared a quick embrace. Something about the way they looked at each other didn't sit right with me.

Kael turned to me. "I'm Kael Marrick. You must be Cassian Nightbrook, our latest recruit."

I nodded, trying hard to keep my face neutral. "That's right."

"I've heard a lot about you," Kael said with a smile that felt a little too polished. Then he turned to my sister. "And you are Elena, I take it. I was just informed about your home. I'm sorry to hear that, but you are safe with us."

"Thank you," Elena said with the slightest bit of hesitancy in her voice. I couldn't tell whether she felt something was off about Kael, too, or if she was just reading my feelings.

Kael turned to me. "Cassian, the Council is gathering and will see you as soon as possible. I sincerely hope they see what Darion sees in you."

I had to admit, he did seem sincere. "I'll do my best."

"In the meantime, we'll have someone show you to the rooms we keep ready for visitors and refugees. I'm afraid they're not exactly luxury accommodations."

"Well, we grew up in a barn, so we aren't too picky." I meant it as a joke, but there was a bit more of an edge to my voice than I intended.

Kael looked at me, unsmiling. "Indeed."

Caldren, the bearded man from the entrance, strode up to the group. "Kael and Darion, the high steward has requested a meeting. I can show our guests to their chambers."

Darion put his hands on Elena's and my shoulders. "You two will be in excellent hands with Caldren."

I tried to hide my disappointment. I had so much more to ask Darion, plus after all we'd been through, I simply wanted his company.

Darion seemed to sense my unease and placed his hands gently on my cheeks. "I'll be back soon. I promise." And then he kissed me, making my insides flutter like butterflies. For a moment, my worries melted away. I hadn't realized that was exactly what I needed until he did it. It was proof that he cared for me, that our time together meant something, and that he wasn't ashamed to show it, even in front of others.

I couldn't help but notice when Kael raised an eyebrow.

When Darion and I parted, he smiled warmly at me, and I smiled back. "We'll be fine," I said, and I hoped my voice was convincing.

Darion turned to Elena. "You're safe now. You needn't worry." Then he hugged her, and based on the look on Elena's face, it was exactly what she needed as well. Seeing her response, I wondered whether I had shown her enough affection over the years. I had always been so worried about protecting her and being the parent. Either way, it only made me more grateful for Darion and how wonderful he was to Elena.

Darion strode off, leaving us with Caldren, who guided us to our rooms. Despite being described as not very luxurious, they were far superior to our humble barn. Elena and I each got our own room, and both had beds bigger and softer than anything either of us had ever slept on, with cotton sheets and mattresses that most certainly weren't filled with rough straw. Each room had its own washbasin and fireplace.

Once we were settled, Caldren told us how to find the kitchens if we were hungry, then left us to ourselves, promising to stop by later to check on us.

I had been worried that Elena might not feel comfortable by herself, but she was more than eager for her own room. Nonetheless, after only a short while, as I lay on my bed deep in thought, there was a soft rap at the door.

"Come in," I said.

Elena creaked the door open and slipped into my room, her shoulders slumped. "I can't stop thinking about it."

I sat up in bed and patted the spot next to me. "Come here."

Elena sat next to me and leaned her head against my shoulder. I pulled her close.

"Our home is gone. It's all I've known for most of my life. Why would someone do that?" she asked in a sad, almost trancelike manner.

"There are evil people in this world."

Elena sighed.

I hadn't had time to process it myself. We'd been running purely on instinct. But the idea that our barn was gone struck a very tender spot. We'd been here before, and now it was happening all over again. All the memories we'd made there, all the things we'd done, were now just charred remains.

We sat like that in silence, supporting each other, for a long while.

Finally Elena spoke. "I keep replaying it in my head."

"Tell me what happened," I said. "If you're ready."

"I went to the market to get food," Elena said, then quickly added, "Not the Citadel Market, just the small one by our home. I did as you asked. But something felt off. There were people there who I didn't recognize, and they weren't shopping, just standing around."

"Did anyone say your name?" I asked.

"I...I don't remember. Maybe? Why?"

"The Royal Guards know our names," I said, and Elena's eyes went wide. "So what happened next?"

"After the market, I went directly home. They must have followed me. Darion got there just before the Royal Guards surrounded the house—I guess he'd been keeping an eye on me. Then I smelled the smoke. I was really scared, Cas. I thought I was braver than that."

I nodded, arm around her shoulder, and felt a pang of guilt for not being there to help her. "Elena, you are one of the bravest people I know."

"Darion was there, and that made me less scared. The next part is confusing. One second we were in the barn, and then we were outside."

"Darion used his Ember. He can pause time."

Elena's jaw dropped. "How?"

"I don't really know, exactly. There are many things I don't understand. Embers are something I didn't even believe in until recently."

"And all I can do is lift things," Elena said, a smile cracking her glum face.

"You seem to be pretty good at tearing things down, too."

We both laughed at that. It felt good to laugh. It meant we weren't broken beyond repair.

"You saved us from an entire company of Royal Guards," I said, giving her a playful shove. "That was amazing."

Elena smiled at me. "It was pretty good, wasn't it?"

"It was."

"I'm sorry I didn't tell you earlier about my strength," she said. "I wanted to, but when you told me about the Sentinels...I dunno, I was just afraid."

"Hey, I've kept a lot of things from you, too, so I understand. But that's all in the past. We can talk about anything now. Deal?"

Elena nodded. "Deal. But I still don't understand what we did to deserve losing our home."

"We are Emberborn. There are people who hate us just for that. But hopefully we can do something about it now."

"Because you're joining the Order of Emberlight," Elena said.

"That's right."

"But what if I lose you, too?" Elena said as a tear streaked down her cheek. She wiped it away quickly.

"I'm not going anywhere. I promise," I said, but I felt a pang of guilt at making a promise that I might not be able to keep.

Chapter Twenty-Five

A Moment of Peace

Using her Ember twice was taking its toll on Elena, and her eyes began to close right in front of me. That on top of the emotional weight of the day made her practically incoherent. She could barely walk, so I helped her back to her room. That left me alone with my thoughts, lying on my bed, staring up at the stone ceiling, absently counting its imperfections.

Our world had changed so completely in the last few hours that my mind felt like a ship in a storm, lost at sea. Where would we live? Where would we even be safe now that the Royal Guard was hunting us? Hopefully I could keep myself busy with the Order of Emberlight once I joined their ranks, but what would Elena do? As hard as things had been, she and I had carved out a life for ourselves, but now that life was gone. It was a lot to take in.

I must have dozed off at some point because I woke up to soft knocks on my door. Before I could respond, the door cracked open, and Darion peeked in.

"Did I wake you?" he asked.

"I just nodded off. Didn't even mean to."

"I can come back—"

"No!" I blurted. Then, softer, "No. Please stay."

Darion smiled—a big smile, like he couldn't believe his luck. Or maybe I was projecting. He slipped off his boots and lay on the bed next to me, taking my hand. It was the smallest expression of intimacy, but that was what was special about it. Not an overt gesture, just a simple *I'm glad to be here with you.*

"How are you doing?" Darion said in a gentle voice.

"Our home is gone. It's surreal. I'm worried about my sister."

Darion nodded, concern in his eyes.

"But I'm hopeful about the future, about Emberlight." I paused for a moment, then looked into his eyes. "And hopeful about us."

Darion smiled, squeezing my hand.

We lay there for a moment, not speaking, and my thoughts drifted to my sister once again. How could I let myself enjoy Darion when her life had completely fallen apart?

"I don't know what I'm going to do about Elena," I said. "We can never go back home, and I don't know where is safe anymore."

"She's safe here for now, and we can figure out the rest later. I know that's not the most comforting thing, but the Order of Emberlight has a lot of experience with Emberborn refugees."

"What happens to them?"

"They often start here, like Elena. Then we sneak them out of the city to the northern lands, past the Everwinter Mountains, where Tarnasau's influence is weaker. There are families there who take in displaced Emberborn."

The idea of Elena leaving the city hit me like a punch to the gut. How would I know she was safe? How could I possibly entrust her to strangers after the promise I'd made to my mother? And on top of everything else, I'd miss her dearly.

"Isn't there any way she could stay in the city?" I asked.

"She would be in constant danger. Being on the Royal Guard's watch list means she'd have to stay locked up like a caged animal. That's not much of a life."

"I don't think I could ever be comfortable if she wasn't near."

"You don't have to decide anything now," Darion said in a calm voice. "Let's wait until you see the Emberlight Council and hear what they have to say. Speaking of which, several council members are occupied and can't make it here until tomorrow morning."

"Will you stay with me tonight?" I asked. A mixture of emotions swirled inside me, but the one thing I knew was that I didn't want to be alone.

Darion smiled. "I was hoping you'd ask. I didn't want to press. Of course I'll stay with you."

Relief and happiness bloomed in me like a field of wildflowers in summer. Given how much had changed, having this one good thing was more stabilizing than I could imagine.

Darion's thumb traced circles on my palm, and for the first time since I'd left the clock tower, my body stopped shaking.

"Hang on," Darion said, hopping off the bed. "I'll be right back."

"Where are you going?" A bit of panic tugged at my insides. It annoyed me because it was irrational. This was a new feeling for me, or perhaps just something I'd been good at hiding from myself.

"It's a surprise," Darion said with a coy smile. "Don't worry. I'll be right back."

He left me sitting there with my thoughts, but his smile and promise to be back soon settled my nerves enough for me to relax the slightest bit.

In a few minutes, Darion returned, grinning broadly and carrying a glazed ceramic basin with steam rising from it.

"A bath?" I asked. The prospect of hot water on my skin made me shiver in anticipation.

"I didn't want to say anything," Darion said in a teasing voice, "but you really stink."

"Hey!" I protested, laughing because he wasn't wrong.

Darion pulled up a chair next to the basin. "Sit," he said.

I sat down and started to pull off my shirt, but Darion stopped me.

"Allow me," he said.

He slowly unlaced my tunic with such delicacy and tenderness that each time his hand touched my body, it felt like a caress. He lifted my arms and pulled the tunic off, exposing my upper body. I had been naked in front of Darion a dozen times before, but this felt different. More exposed. More intimate.

He reached over to the basin, squeezed out a cloth, then gently pressed it against my chest. The scent of lavender teased my nose, and the water was deliciously hot, sending chills rippling through my entire body. Darion smiled at this.

He scrubbed my entire torso, lifting each arm, cleaning every nook. I tried to hold back giggles as he ran the cloth along my armpits. Any time I tried to help, he lovingly scolded me. He was mostly gentle, but he scrubbed harder in a few particularly soiled spots. The care he took, the loving touches, the occasional glance to see how I was doing, was the most intimate thing I'd ever experienced. He treated me like a fragile thing that could break if he was too forceful. I fought back the tears that welled up from sheer emotion.

"Stand," Darion softly commanded after finishing my upper body.

I did. He unlaced my trousers, even more delicate and caring than before. Then he pulled them down, along with my undergarments. Thus far, everything had been so affectionate and chaste that arousal had been the last thing on my mind. But the moment he pressed the hot cloth against my lower abdomen, that changed.

He continued to scrub, not missing a spot. When he spread my legs and cleaned my inner thighs, I entirely lost the battle, becoming instantly hard. He just smiled with zero judgment as he cleaned around my privates.

He had cleaned me from head to toe with only one exception.

"Bend over," he said.

I raised my eyebrows at that. His gentle smile didn't change, but I couldn't help but notice his cock pushing up against his trousers and the wet spot that had soaked through. My throat bobbed at the sight.

Leaning against the chair, I bent over, exposing my backside. He nudged my legs farther apart. The hot cloth made me breathe in sharply. The more he cleaned, pressing against my most delicate parts, the harder I got. This was quickly turning from a tender, caring moment into something quite different, and I was shocked by just how much I ached for it. For the first time since I had entered the Citadel Library, I let myself want something purely for me.

The sound of the cloth splashing into the basin signaled the end of the bath and what I hoped was the start of something that would sate the desire building up in me. I was about to stand up when I felt Darion's hands on my back, holding me down—not forcefully, just enough to keep me where I was.

"This okay?" he asked.

"Gods yes," was my desperate reply.

What I got was even more than I expected. He spread my legs, and something hot, soft, and wet tickled my backside. The ripples of sudden intense sensation forced a startled gasp out of me.

"Oh dust!" I moaned. I had heard people describe this, but this was the first time I had ever felt it, and...um...*wow*.

But what startled me the most was sharing such an intimate thing and not feeling my usual instinct to pull away. That I was able to allow this to happen, to fully lose control, rocked me far more than any physical act.

He continued to work his tongue against me, eliciting involuntary moans, while at the same time reaching around to stroke me. The combined effect nearly sent me over the edge.

Darion sensed my nearing climax and slowed down.

"How'd you like that?" he said.

"All the gods in the sky, that was amazing!" I gasped. "I want you inside me. Now!"

"Yes, sir," he said with passion and a touch of playfulness.

I peeked back to see Darion slip out of his clothes. His naked body was a study in perfection, the beautiful curves in his hips pointing down in a V shape, framing his extremely hard cock.

"Please!" I begged.

He slathered some salve on his cock and stood behind me. Whatever magic he had performed with his tongue had relaxed me to the point that he was able to push his entire length inside me in one motion. We gasped in unison.

With each thrust, my mind exploded with pleasure, and he reached around again and stroked me, matching the rhythm. We both howled and grunted like feral animals as our pleasure neared a crescendo. Suddenly he stopped and pulled out. I didn't even mean to, but I actually whimpered.

"Why?" I said in desperation.

"I want you to feel it when you're inside me," he said.

I smiled, knowing just what he meant: his Chronothene.

He hopped onto the bed, lying on his back. I followed right behind.

He lifted his legs, holding them up with his arms. I positioned myself on top, looking down at his beautiful face. What we had just done had been raw, hot, and bordering on wild. But this—looking in his breathtaking emerald eyes, seeing every bit of joy and pleasure on his face—was immeasurably better. His expression told me that Darion felt the same comfort, the same connection that I did.

"Let me know if I go too fast," I said.

"You won't."

Despite that, I still went in slowly, a little at a time, going deeper with each push. I bent down to kiss him. Our mouths met, soft and gentle at first, but then with growing passion and intensity, mirroring my thrusts.

Darion wrapped his arms around me and pulled me close. We continued like that with soft pushes, moaning through our kisses. He ran his hands through my hair.

I'd been with many men, but I'd never felt such closeness, such intimacy, such vulnerability as I felt at that moment with Darion. The feeling was so intense that it made my heart race, the sheer weight of it almost scaring me. But I gave in and let the emotion sweep over me. It was at that moment that I realized that this man had cracked open something inside me that no one had ever accessed. I was raw, unrestricted, and exposed.

I savored that feeling for as long as I could, but the gradual building of pleasure was reaching a point of no return. I sat up, lifted his leg, and began to thrust faster as Darion stroked himself.

He stared deep into my eyes with a look I had never seen from him before. It seemed I may have cracked something open inside him, too.

Then, just as release flowed through me, Darion's golden shimmer surrounded us. Our eyes were locked, both with looks of utter vulnerability, like we had stepped off a cliff together. It might have lasted ten seconds or an hour. Time had no meaning, and the two of us were utterly lost together, with no idea where one of us ended and the other began.

Then time rushed back, and we both gasped at the enormity of what we had just shared.

I collapsed onto him. Other than our heaving chests, we didn't move, just held on to each other. We stayed together that way for a long time, letting our heart rates slow.

There were no words. No words to describe it. Words would just diminish the moment.

I pulled out, and we lay on our sides, pressed together, face-to-face, soaking each other in, exchanging soft touches and the occasional kiss. And for once, I didn't brace for when this would all be taken away from me.

I felt my eyelids drop, and I fell into the most blissful sleep I could recall.

When I woke, it was late at night, and the fire had turned to embers.

I was still curled up next to Darion, but he was awake, staring absently at the ceiling, forehead creased. It was the look I'd seen before when he was thinking hard about something.

"Hey," I said.

He turned to me and smiled. "Hi. You were really out. You slept through my whole Ember hangover."

"Well, you take a lot out of me," I said with a smile.

Darion smiled back. "I like taking a lot out of you. You're amazing, you know that?" He ran his hand through my hair.

"*You're* amazing."

Darion turned and looked at the ceiling again.

"What's on your mind?" I asked.

Darion sighed. "Cas, when you meet the council tomorrow morning, it's better if I'm not there. There may be some who disagree with how I've handled your Trials, and that might complicate matters."

"I understand," I said, although I would have preferred for him to be there. Then again, I didn't really know what to expect.

He turned his head to look at me. "When the council asks you questions, be sure to answer them truthfully and from your heart."

I nodded, then lay my head on his chest, gently caressing the bit of hair between his pecs. "Thank you for all you've done."

He kissed the top of my head in answer, and we both drifted off again.

I woke to the second bell ringing. Gauging time was no easy task in the Underground, but the clock tower bells still reverberated through the foundations. I reached for Darion, but in his place was an empty indentation in the bed. The sheets were cold. Very cold, as if he'd been gone for a while. Panic hit. I knew it was irrational, but it didn't stop the way I felt.

I hopped out of bed, cleaned up at the washbasin, and threw on some clothes. I wanted to check on Elena; I hadn't seen her since last night when I'd helped her to bed, and guilt hit me at the thought of her being alone.

The hallway outside my room was empty. I knocked on her door, but no one answered. After knocking again, I gently opened the door. "Elena?" Still no answer.

The room was deserted, and the bed had been carefully made. The panic I felt doubled. I raced out of her room, not sure where to go but determined to find some answers. In my haste, I nearly ran into Caldren, the head of the guard, whom we had met at the entrance yesterday.

"Cassian Nightbrook," he said in a booming voice, "the council has summoned you."

Chapter Twenty-Six

The Emberlight Council

Caldren silently guided me through the hallways, ignoring my questions about the whereabouts of Darion and my sister. There was little I could do besides follow him.

Soon we entered a room dominated by a large table with nine people sitting behind it, facing toward us with stony expressions. They were all strangers to me except for Kael, who had greeted us and seemed to know Darion well. I wasn't particularly happy to see that he was a member of the council. In the shadows along the edges of the room, dozens of figures watched. I scanned their faces, hoping to spot Darion or Elena, but I didn't really expect to see them, and the dim light made it impossible to see details.

The murmur of voices died down as we approached the middle of the room. Caldren bowed to the nine people in front of us and joined the crowd. This entire thing felt like a tribunal, which made me jittery. My skin itched under yesterday's clothes.

In the center of the table was a middle-aged woman with long dark hair and olive skin, more handsome than beautiful.

"Members of the Order of Emberlight," she said in a smooth but commanding voice. "Both Emberborn and Unkindled, I draw this council to order."

The remaining voices went silent.

The woman cast an assessing gaze toward me. "Welcome, Cassian Nightbrook. My name is Mireth Averin. I am the high steward of the Emberlight Council." She gestured to the people beside her. "Tell us why you are here."

"To join your ranks. To bring an end to Tarnasau's reign of terror," I said. Now that I was staring at their stoic faces, my words felt inadequate and hollow.

"And you have completed the Trials," she said as she pulled out the parchment Adela Fenn had given me back in the clock tower.

"I have."

"With or without Darion Thorne's help?" Kael said sharply, leaning forward with a predatory look in his eyes.

A few muted gasps came from the crowd. My instincts were right. This man didn't like me, and his gracious host guise was disappearing fast.

"*Kael,*" Mireth said in a warning tone, shooting him a disapproving look.

An older man with a gray beard who sat next to Mireth cleared his throat to speak. "Kael's question is valid. I would like to hear whether Cassian completed the Trials on his own merits."

Mireth sighed, looked at me, and nodded.

This really *did* feel like a tribunal. I projected my voice. "Darion Thorne accompanied me on my trip through the Royal Catacombs. At that point, I was unaware that he was a member of the Order of Emberlight. I cannot undo the past, nor do I know how his presence altered my path for good or ill." The weight of the council members' eyes was on me, but I continued. "If that disqualifies me, then I will withdraw my request with much regret."

More gasps came from the crowd.

Kael had a slight smirk on his face. "If that's the case, then I move for a summary judgment and accept his withdrawal."

Heated voices erupted throughout the room.

Mireth stood and banged her fist on the table. "Quiet!" she yelled with such authority that the room went entirely silent. Her eyes pierced mine. "I ask you again, Cassian Nightbrook. Tell us *why* you are here."

I closed my eyes, digging deep, truly considering her question. Darion's words from last night danced in my mind: *Be sure to answer them truthfully and from your heart.* Why *did* I want to join the Order of Emberlight? At first I'd been driven by my desire to avenge my parents' murder, but that was no longer the only reason. I thought of the many near misses Elena and I had had and how I could best keep her safe. I thought of the man we'd seen brutally murdered in the public square. I reached for my locket and felt its shape in my hand. Then I opened my eyes and let out a long breath.

"When I was eleven, Tarnasau's thugs slashed my parents' throats before my eyes. I held my mother's hand as she lay dying."

My throat tightened, and tears threatened to spill out. The image was still vivid, as if it had happened yesterday. I choked down the emotion that nearly overwhelmed me.

"My mother could barely speak, but on that day, she made me promise to protect my sister. Everything I have done since has been in service of that promise. But I want more for my sister than protection. I want her to live free of fear. I want that for all Emberborn. All Velmorrians. And I can't do that by myself. *That* is why I am here."

Mireth nodded with a smile, and the crowd exploded into cheers. Several of the other council members, including the old man sitting next to Mireth, said, "Hear, hear!" Kael's face was neutral, but his smug look was gone.

Mireth looked at the parchment I'd delivered. When she spoke, the crowd grew quiet again. "Adela Fenn spoke highly of you, although your time in the tower was short. She was impressed with your abilities. But there's a curious note here. She said her father, Edric, the master of ledgers, was unable to locate your lineage. This is a rare occurrence; the Emberborn kept meticulous records as Tarnasau's grip tightened."

"Edric said he would continue to search," I replied.

"Indeed. We await his results with great interest. And Adela made another curious note as well. I understand you have Veilsense?"

"That's right."

A few people in the shadows leaned forward, whispering urgently.

"That is a much sought-after Ember by the Crown. If Tarnasau is aware of this, it could explain why you are on the Royal Guard's watch list and seem to have garnered so much attention. That puts this council in a tricky position. Your Ember would be valuable to us, but it would also put us at greater risk."

"A revolution is a risky endeavor," I said. "I will do what I can to make the risk worth it."

Mireth nodded with a crooked smile. "Well said. And Darion Thorne has spoken highly of your skills as a thief. That, too, would be an asset. If you join the Order of Emberlight, we'll ask for your pledge of loyalty. You must never reveal the names of any of the members or anything you learn in our service. You will do everything in your power to help us topple the Tarnasau Dynasty. We will vote as a council, and if we vote in your favor, you must pledge your loyalty to the Order. Is that acceptable to you?"

When I had considered joining the Order of Emberlight before, I'd never worried that my pledge to the council might interfere with the promise I'd made to protect Elena.

"I have a question before I give you my answer," I said.

"Of course."

"What is to become of my sister?" I asked.

"She may stay here for a short while until the city has quieted down—your escape has stirred up quite a ruckus topside. After that, we will ensure that she is safely transported to the Northlands to go into hiding."

"I request to be part of the contingent that sees her to her destination," I said.

Mireth paused for the slightest moment, then nodded. "We can accommodate that."

Analon had become so dangerous that it might be safest for Elena to leave, despite the twisting in my gut at the prospect of being so far away from her. I knew in my heart that my sister would always come first, no matter what promise the council asked of me.

Be sure to answer them truthfully and from your heart.

I cleared my throat. "I must be honest—no pledge I make here will ever supersede the promise I made to my mother. My sister will always be my top priority."

Mireth smiled with a keen look in her eye. "If you had said anything else, it would have disqualified you immediately. A person who would break an oath to a dying parent has no honor and cannot be trusted."

"So that was a test?"

"It was. And you passed. If you are ready to proceed, we shall vote."

Until that moment, I hadn't been sure I could do the pledge. But the fact that the Order not only honored prior pledges but *expected* people to uphold them tipped the scales in their favor.

"I am ready," I said.

"Council, do you have any further questions?" Mireth asked.

The council members shook their heads and remained quiet. Kael's face was expressionless.

"You have your ballots in front of you. The vote must be unanimous."

The council members all marked the parchments in front of them, folded them in half, and passed them toward the middle of the table. Mireth opened them one by one.

"The council has spoken," Mireth said.

My heart dropped. Kael was still expressionless.

"Cassian Nightbrook, if the council votes in your favor, do you pledge your loyalty to the Order of Emberlight?"

I knew this would mean new responsibilities and new dangers. Gone were my little acts of vengeance in the form of nightly robberies. I was about to enter a different world, and I was ready for it. This was the only way to keep Elena truly safe.

"Yes. I pledge my loyalty," I said, and the weight of those words reverberated to my very core.

"The vote is nine votes yea, zero votes nay. Cassian Nightbrook, you are now a member of the Order of Emberlight."

The room exploded with cheers. The people in the shadows emerged, surrounding me, all smiles, patting my back and congratulating me. But they were all strangers. Darion and Elena were still nowhere to be seen.

I walked toward the council table to talk to Mireth, but on the way, Kael intercepted me. "Congratulations," he said, putting out a hand.

I considered him for a moment, not sure what to make of this gesture. He'd raised concerns, but ultimately he'd voted for me. He'd had the power to stop me, but he hadn't. I clasped his arm.

"Thank you," I said, but there was plenty of hesitancy in my voice. "And thank you for believing in me."

"I saw which way the wind was blowing," he said as he ran his hand through a lock of blond hair that had fallen into his face. "I just hope you're ready for what's ahead."

"Only time will tell," I said.

"You should know," Kael said with that sharp tone back in his voice, "that when you robbed The Butcher and you first met Darion, you were meant to take the fall. You were a misdirection."

I bristled at this. I still didn't know whether he was trying to warn me, manipulate me, or just get under my skin.

"Darion already explained that to me," I said curtly.

Kael raised an eyebrow. "Did he, now? Did he tell you it was *his* idea?"

Darion had said *we* when he'd told me about the plan to take the book, so he hadn't denied being involved. The more I talked to Kael, the less I trusted him, and I wouldn't have put it past him to stretch the truth to advance his agenda, whatever it was. And yet the idea that Darion had left out this detail nagged at me.

"Kael, I don't want to be your enemy. Have I offended you in some way?"

"I just want to be sure you are going into this with your eyes open."

"I appreciate your concern," I said with an edge, which ended our conversation. His eyes followed me as I walked away.

I continued toward Mireth, who was still sitting at the council table, speaking to the older man next to her.

"Cassian, congratulations," she said with a smile as I approached. "This is council member Darrow Elkwright."

"Congratulations, young man," Darrow said with a solemn nod. "We are pleased to have you in our ranks. Your energy and abilities are exactly what we need."

"Thank you both for your endorsement," I said, then turned to Mireth. "Forgive me, High Steward, but do you know where I might find my sister? She wasn't in her room when I woke up."

"Yes, Darion Thorne took her to the sparring room. I'll have someone escort you." She caught Caldren's eye through the throng of people and asked him to lead me to them.

I said my goodbyes and left the crowd, which suited me fine. I had never been one for large groups and much preferred the company of the people I knew and trusted. As we left the room, everyone was still boisterously celebrating, which I found amusing, since the person they were celebrating was heading out the door.

"Congratulations," Caldren said. "That was no small achievement."

"Thank you," I said. "I just hope everyone is happy for me to join."

Caldren laughed, gently. "Kael can be blunt, but he means well. I have known him for much of my life. He's a good man."

I nodded, knowing I'd still need to make my own determination.

We walked through several corridors until the sound of clashing metal echoed through the hallway. We entered a large room with racks of weapons lining the walls, leaving ample space in the center. There, Darion and Elena crossed swords in a heated battle, their attacks more intense than I'd ever seen from either of them. Caldren bid me adieu.

They moved back and forth across the floor several times, neither conceding much ground before claiming it back. I remained quiet on the sidelines, observing. For only an instant, Darion's attention strayed in my direction. That was all it took to break his concentration, and a moment later, Elena had him off balance, knocking the sword out of his hand with a reverberating thud.

"Ha!" she yelled, victorious. But then she followed Darion's eyes toward me. "Cas!"

They both ran over, and for the third time in the last day, we all shared an embrace. Tears inexplicably ran down my cheeks.

"I did it," I said. "I'm part of the Order of Emberlight."

"Congratulations," Darion said, beaming.

"I knew you could do it!" Elena exclaimed. "They'd be stupid not to let you in."

"I was worried for a while there. Kael doesn't seem to like me."

Darion sighed. "Don't take it personally. More than anybody on the council, Kael is a stickler for the rules. Plus, Kael and I have a complicated history, to put it mildly."

"Complicated how?" I asked.

"We've been friends for a long time. Not too long ago, he confessed his feelings for me. I didn't share those feelings."

Good, I thought to myself with a smugness that I felt a little bad about.

"Kael was the one with the most reservations about you, but I partly blame myself, since I couldn't seem to stay away from you," Darion said with a ridiculous grin. "But he's a good person at his core."

"So everyone keeps saying," I said. "Your advice about being truthful and speaking from the heart probably saved me."

"I'm glad to hear that. The council members are wise and easily spot deception or insincerity."

We paused for a moment, gazing at each other with soft smiles.

Then Elena began to fidget. "So, what happens next?"

My stomach clenched as I thought back to the council's decision that Elena would need to travel north. But that was a conversation for later.

"Well, I don't know about you two," I said, "but I haven't had a thing to eat since yesterday morning. I'm starving!"

Chapter Twenty-Seven

A Growing Darkness

It had been a few days since the Emberlight Council had voted me in, and Elena and I found ourselves with little to do. I was feeling restless. Doing nothing just wasn't in my nature. Rather than relaxing, it felt claustrophobic, as if a rope were slowly tightening around me.

To keep my mind and body busy, I spent much of my time in the sparring room with Elena, practicing our weapons techniques. I also explored the twisting hallways and chambers, most of which were deserted.

I found a small library of books, maps, and scrolls, some of which covered various Emberborn topics. It was nothing compared to the clock tower library but far more than I had ever seen anywhere else. I pored over maps ranging from the entire Velmorrian continent down to the drainage systems of Analon.

One book listed a few of the known Embers; they were so varied that no exhaustive catalog existed. I recognized Veilsense, Chronothene, Elena's strength, which was called Stryn, and the shifter power, which was called Marrowbound. There were many others I had never heard of, including Stillbind—the ability to prevent someone else from moving—and Windspirit—the ability to run very fast.

I borrowed a few of the books and read them at night to calm my storming mind.

Darion stopped by frequently to update us on matters of the Order and the news from topside. Apparently the Royal Guard had stepped up patrols all across the city and stationed Sentinels throughout every district. No one was sure why, but I worried it had to do with Elena and me. Perhaps they'd found out I had Veilsense. This made me even more anxious about Elena's imminent departure for the Northlands.

There had also been no communication from the Citadel Clock Tower about my lineage. Darion suspected it was because of the increased Royal Guard patrols. Since the day Edric had been unable to find information about my family, the thought had gnawed at me. For most of my life, I hadn't thought much about my origins, but now that I knew of our Emberborn heritage, I yearned to learn more.

On the third day after the meeting of the council, I was lying on my bed reading a book from the library when Darion knocked on the door. I smiled as he entered and approached the bed.

He smiled back. "Are you up for an adventure?"

"Dust yes!" I said, practically jumping off the bed. "I feel like a caged beast! Is it dangerous?"

He lifted a mischievous eyebrow. "Would you expect anything less from me?"

"Perfect!" I said, planting a kiss on his cheek, which soon turned into a proper kiss. Before things got too out of hand, I shoved him away playfully. "Let's go."

Darion guided me through the halls of the Order and out the entrance. We nodded to the guards as we passed.

When we were out of earshot, Darion turned to me. "I thought it might be good for you to know your way topside. Especially since we destroyed the door we came through on the way in. If there were ever an emergency and you and Elena had to escape, I'd want you to know how."

"I appreciate that. I've been feeling a little unmoored, not knowing how to get out," I said. "But is that the only thing we're doing?"

"You mean other than spending time together?" Darion asked.

"Yes, other than that."

"There *might* be one other thing."

"I thought so. Is that the dangerous part?" I asked.

"A bit. *Technically*, this is your first assignment from the Order."

"Is this how a person normally receives assignments?"

"Not exactly," Darion said. "Actually, this is more for me. There's something I want your take on, and I need your Veilsense."

"Where are we going? What do you need me to do?"

"Stop asking so many questions," Darion said with a laugh. "Come along and I'll show you."

He guided me through the maze of Underworld tunnels until we reached a ladder. As we ascended, beams of light streamed through cracks in the wall. Finally we reached a hatch at the top. Darion opened it, and a burst of sunlight flooded in, blinding me; my eyes had grown accustomed to the sunless Underworld over the last few days. I blinked several times as we climbed out onto a roof.

The first thing that struck me was the briny sea air of Analon Bay. Living in it day after day, I had grown nose-blind to that scent, but today it was like being in the middle of a fish market. The breeze buffeted my hair as I scanned the rooftops of Analon, which stretched out in every direction. To the north, the Citadel Clock Tower rose proudly above the city, and to the east, ship masts swayed in the ocean breeze. These things told me roughly where we had emerged.

"Never gets old, does it?" Darion asked, watching me admire the city—the city I both loved and despised.

"Quite a sight," I said. "So, what is this dangerous assignment?"

"This way."

We ran along rooftops, occasionally jumping over a narrow alley. We hadn't gotten far when a shadow crossed over us and the familiar caw of a whisperhawk pierced the sky. Zephyra swooped down and landed on my shoulder.

Hello, little Cas. It has been many days since Zephyra saw you.

My stomach tightened. Being able to hear Zephyra was something I hadn't mentioned to Darion...or to *anyone.* I almost ignored her. But Zephyra hopped impatiently, talons pricking through the fabric of my tunic, and Darion was watching me. Once again, I was on the brink of doing something I couldn't take back.

I stroked Zephyra's cheek. "It's good to see you, Zephyra. How do you always find me so quickly?"

Darion's eyes narrowed slightly as he watched us.

Zephyra has much better eyes than blind humans. Zephyra hunts from above, seeing little rats scurrying around the city. Cas is little, yes, but not as little as rats. Cas is easy to see.

"Fair enough," I said with a smile. "Well, I'm sorry I haven't been up here in a while. Next time I'll bring you a treat. What would you like?"

Zephyra eats lots, but only disgusting rats. So dirty, and meat is tough. Zephyra would like something sweet.

"I'll see what I can do."

Thank you, little Cas. Now Zephyra must fly.

She flapped her wings and took to the air.

Darion stared at me, that questioning look still on his face. "You can...hear whisperhawks?"

Heat crept up my neck. "Yeah. I—I haven't really shared it with anyone."

Darion smiled, but there was something else there, too. He seemed thoughtful. Curious.

"Cas," he said quietly, "that's remarkable."

"It's just something I can do." I shrugged. "Let's go."

We ran along rooftops until we approached a notorious district of Analon. Smokestacks belched out black smoke, and the buildings shifted from the typical eclectic wood to harsh stone. The acrid smell of burning coal hit my nose, and the harsh sound of metal clanging against metal reverberated up to the rooftops. This was the Industrial District, home to many of the factories that were the backbone of industry for Analon.

But as with most things in this grand and terrible city, a duality existed. Along with the factories, this district contained the prisons required to house all the slave labor that kept the factories staffed.

"Why did you bring me to this horrible place?" I asked.

"I'm sorry. You'll see why soon," Darion said with a frown. "We're almost there. We'll need to be very quiet, as this place is crawling with Royal Guards and Sentinels."

A looming shadow appeared through the smog—the hulking shape of a building with a massive stone facade and only a handful of barred windows. It had been designed to be imposing and unforgiving.

This was the Pyrehold prison.

Darion crouched low to the ground and bade me do the same. "If you look carefully, you'll see Sentinels surrounding Pyrehold." Darion pointed off to the left. Sure enough, a Sentinel stood at attention, tucked into a shaded corner of a building.

"It's not that strange to have a *few* Sentinels guarding a prison," Darion said. "But by my count, there are twenty surrounding the building—a building famous for never letting a prisoner escape."

"They're trying to keep people out," I said.

Darion nodded. "I don't know how your Veilsense works," Darion said, "but do you feel anything unusual here?"

I paused for a moment to focus on my senses, but the air stank of soot, and the banging machinery rattled in my mind.

"I don't. When people use their Embers, I can smell it and see it a bit. Maybe there are just too many distractions."

Darion nodded. "Can you block them out?"

"I can try." I closed my eyes and imagined pleasant things, like the farm I had always wanted for Elena and me. Gradually, the acrid smell and harsh sounds faded into the background, and a warmth grew in my core.

Slowly at first, then with increasing intensity, a thrumming surrounded me. It wasn't a sound or a vibration, but something beyond my five senses.

The faintest scent tickled my nose: ozone. But underneath it was something different. An astringent sensation burned my nostrils—not exactly citrus, but close, like fruit left too long in the sun. This was unlike anything I'd ever sensed. Usually the scent of Embers was sharp and acute, but this had a muted, pervasive quality. And there was something else. It was dark. Festering. Evil.

My instincts told me to pull back. But I felt like I was on the cusp of understanding what was happening, so I kept exploring with my mind. I could almost *feel* each of the Sentinels. Maybe if I just pushed a little bit harder...

The darkness grew quite suddenly; it almost felt like it was reaching back out to me, as if it could sense me back. Panic flooded my mind. I tried to escape, but I was powerless to stop it. I wanted to open my eyes, but I could barely even feel them. The darkness wrapped its cold, bleak hands around my body, constricting my lungs like the tentacles of a giant sea monster.

My body convulsed, and a sharp pain seared across my cheek. That was enough to break my trance, and I opened my eyes to see Darion shaking me with a wild look of panic on his pale face.

A sickeningly high-pitched wail resounded off the nearby buildings—the Sentinels' signal of alert.

"Thank dust you're okay," Darion whispered. "We have to run."

I started out a bit wobbly, as the fog hadn't fully lifted from my brain, but getting even a few steps away from that dreaded building helped. Once I had my equilibrium, we moved as fast as stealth would allow, racing along the rooftops. Gradually the Sentinels' alarm faded, then stopped altogether.

When we were nearly back at the Underworld entrance, Darion stopped. He rested a gentle hand on my shoulder. "What happened back there?"

I shook my head. "I don't really know. When I closed my eyes and concentrated, I could smell the Ember, but it was faint and unlike anything I've ever experienced. And then I felt a darkness. It grew stronger, and then...I don't know. It seemed to sense me. Then it came after me."

"Dust! I'm sorry, Cas. If I had known that would happen, I never would have asked—"

"You don't need to apologize. I knew the risks when I joined the Order. And besides, we learned some things. Things we should report."

Darion nodded, eyes on the ground.

My heart swelled for this beautiful man. I'd spent my entire life caring for others, and for the first time, somebody was caring for me. But underneath that pleasant feeling was an undercurrent of worry. Part of it was because of what I just experienced. But another part was because I didn't know how long I'd get to keep this happiness.

And because now I had something to lose.

Chapter Twenty-Eight

A Simple Job

The day after my adventure with Darion, Elena and I were eating our midday meal, consisting of flatbread, honey, cured meats, and cheeses. We had befriended the cook, Tobias, who watched our expressions as we ate, smiling each time we voiced our approval. This may have been because Tobias—who could be no more than sixteen—seemed to have taken a liking to Elena and was making clumsy attempts to flirt. As her big brother, I kept a close eye on them to be sure Tobias never went too far.

He was serving us a dessert of sweet whipped cream and strawberries when a member of the Order entered the kitchens and approached us.

"Cassian Nightbrook, High Steward Averin requests your presence. Please follow me."

I had not heard from Mireth Averin since the day she'd pronounced me a member of the Order. I was anxious to speak with her and learn more about the plans for relocating Elena, so I followed eagerly.

As I walked toward the exit, I told my sister, "I should be back soon. Stay out of trouble," then turned to Tobias and said in my most threatening tone, "And I've got my eye on you."

Tobias blanched. Elena glared at me as I left the room. Maybe I was overreacting, but the world felt so dangerous now, and Elena was one of the few bright things left in it.

Mireth Averin's office was better furnished than most of the Order of Emberlight headquarters, which was to say that it approximated a normal room. She sat behind a desk that was meticulously tidy. Dozens of neatly ordered books sat on bookcases right behind her. Rugs warmed the cold stone floors, and upholstered chairs surrounded a roaring fire.

As I approached, she looked up. "Cassian Nightbrook, thank you for coming. Please take a seat." She gestured to the chair in front of her desk.

"You can call me Cas, Madam High Steward," I said.

"And you can call me Mireth, if we're being informal," she said with a coy smile. "Darion told us about your experience yesterday. I trust you've fully recovered?"

"I have," I said, although I shuddered at the memory. "Do you know what happened?"

"Our people are researching it. You've provided us with invaluable information. I wanted to thank you personally."

I nodded. "Is that why you called me here?"

"That, yes, and two other things. First, I imagine you're eager to talk about your sister's future."

"Very much so."

"We'd hoped to move her soon, but the Royal Guard has stepped up its patrols. However, we'll have an opportunity in a week. A caravan of traveling merchants is leaving the city, heading for the Northlands, which will give you excellent cover as you travel north. We'll keep the team small—you, your sister, and two of our finest fighters from the Order. She should be well protected. I'll go over more details with you in the next few days. Does that meet with your approval?"

"It does. I look forward to it," I said. "What is the other thing?"

She opened her desk drawer and pulled out a parchment. "I think it's high time we utilized those thieving skills I've heard so much about. How do you feel about stealing from a particularly nasty man?"

I nearly jumped out of my skin. It'd been weeks since I'd done a simple heist, and I desperately missed it. I missed the challenge. I missed the chance to use my skills. Mostly I missed the feeling of *doing* something—making progress toward a goal, even if that goal seemed unattainable.

"I'd like that very much," I said. "The nastier the better."

"Oh, he's plenty nasty. A corrupt merchant who helps fund Tarnasau's war machine in exchange for looking the other way as people constantly die in his factories, which earn him exorbitant profits. Hopefully this will be the first step in bringing him to justice."

She laid the parchment on her desk, and we pored over it. This job was as simple as it got. Get in, open the safe, steal a document, and get out. Almost *too* easy.

"If you come across any coin or other loot while you're in there, that'll be yours to keep. We prefer that you take some, actually, as it deflects suspicion. Looks more like a simple robbery rather than espionage."

"I think I can manage that," I said with a wry smile. This job sounded better by the moment.

"Very good. Oh, and have you met Sprocket?"

"Sprocket?" I asked, eyebrows raised.

"Our guild quartermaster. He will outfit you with everything you need."

"The Gearhouse" was in the depths of the Order's headquarters. I'd thought Elena and I had explored every room, but I was wrong. The entrance was in the very library I had borrowed the books from, behind a bookcase that slid away to reveal a winding staircase. One hundred twenty-six stairs later, I found myself in a large room filled from floor to ceiling with supplies, weapons, alchemists' tools, a blacksmith's forge, and countless other items that could've supplied a small army.

A grizzled man in dirty overalls—Sprocket, I assumed—was deep in concentration, sitting at a table and working on a mechanical contraption. He probed inside a mass of gears and levers with two delicate-looking instruments, his elbows poking out to the sides. This, combined with his haphazard hair and the magnifying glass attached to his spectacles, made him look like some exotic insect.

I stood quietly, letting him concentrate. Besides picking locks, I hadn't tinkered much with mechanical things, mostly because I had none around, and the intricacy fascinated me.

The man sighed. "Would you please stop looking at me so loudly?"

I looked around to see if there was someone else in the room. When I came up empty, I realized he must have been referring to me.

"Beg your pardon?" I asked.

"You're practically screaming at me with those eyes."

"You can hear my...eyes?"

"Yes, they are very loud," he said, then let out a sigh as he set down his tools and looked my way.

"I didn't mean to interrupt you," I said. "I can come back later."

"No need. After all that racket, I've lost my concentration," he said, not angrily or dismissively, just like he was stating a fact. "People call me Sprocket. From the look of you, I'd guess you are our new recruit. Cas, right?"

"That's right," I said.

"Rumor has it that you are quite the potion-maker."

"Oh? Who did you hear that from?"

"Darion Thorne speaks very highly of you."

I felt my cheeks flush. "Is that so?"

"Really likes you, that one," Sprocket said. "Never thought I'd see him that happy again after…" His eyes grew wide. Then he blinked and turned back to his device.

"After what?" I asked.

He said nothing, just continued to work. I was about to ask again when he said, "Feel free to use any of the herbs and reagents you need. Let me know if you need any help."

It seemed that conversation was over, but Sprocket had successfully planted a seed of worry in my mind, as if I didn't have enough to obsess about. What had happened in Darion's past to make him so unhappy? It got me thinking about how I knew very little about Darion's life before we met. He rarely brought it up, and he'd mentioned his family only once. Maybe now that I'd joined the Order, he might start opening up more. Time would tell.

I set to work, crafting a myriad of potions—smoke bombs, flash-bangs, scent cancelers, and other equipment essential for a typical job. Halfway through, Sprocket came over, observing my work and occasionally interjecting with a question or comment. He was a little odd, but he was smart, and I liked his enthusiasm. He even gave me a tip or two about how to improve the efficacy of several of my potions.

But he never brought up Darion again, and I decided not to press him.

Once I had a full load and a few potions to spare, I said my goodbyes to Sprocket, headed upstairs, and prepared to leave. It felt a little odd doing a job without Garrick.

The Royal Guard and the Sentinels were everywhere. The good news was that after my encounter with them yesterday, I knew that if I made my mind quiet enough, I could tune in to the thrumming they seemed to emit. Because of this, I could map their positions and avoid them. But I was also very careful not to overextend myself. If the slightest tickle of that horrible darkness licked at my senses, I could quickly detach.

The job was as easy as advertised, almost laughably so. The home was in a less dense part of the Garden District near the Old Grove—the last untouched bit of forest in Analon—and had its own yard and trees. There were so many doors and windows, a thief could get dizzy from all the options. Guards monitored the grounds so predictably that I could set a clock to it. I was in within seconds.

The only person inside was a portly man so drunk that even if he saw me, he'd likely think I was a symptom of too much ale. The safe was inside his bedroom, hidden behind the dresser. The only challenge was opening it, as it was so old that the hinges were nearly rusted shut. But it was nothing that a bit of oil from one of my vials couldn't fix. Within the safe were the documents the Order had requested, along with a pile of gold and jewels. I swiped them and made a quick escape.

Despite the Royal Guard's increased patrols, I still made my donation to Mrs. Yarrow's orphanage. Since it had been so long, I left ten times the normal amount. But as I was sliding the envelope under the door, it opened a crack.

Standing before me was the closest thing I'd had to a mother after mine had been ripped away. It had been six years since I'd left Mrs. Yarrow's home with Elena, worried about the risk I posed to her, and I hadn't seen her since. Those years washed away in an instant. She was a bit grayer and had deeper wrinkles, but she was the same person I loved.

"Cassian, what a beautiful man you've turned into," she said with a sad smile. "Thank you for all the gold you've left. I couldn't have made it without you."

"So you knew it was me?" I said, my voice breaking.

"Of course. No one else would have such a big heart. I've been wanting to thank you, but I also wanted to respect your wishes. I know why you've felt the need to keep away."

A mix of happy and sad emotions welled up in me, and I reached for my locket. "Why now?" I asked.

"I need to give you something. Something I've held onto for a long time. But you have to make me a promise."

Why did all the people in my life need me to make promises? Things had gotten so complicated. I longed for the simple days when my sister and I played in the forest and our only responsibility was getting home before sunset.

"What promise?"

"You can't risk coming here anymore. It's not safe for you or for me. Not until all of this is over."

This wasn't entirely unexpected, but my heart broke a little anyway. I nodded.

She reached into her skirt, pulled out an envelope that had yellowed with age, and handed it to me. "This is for you. I was to give it to you on your twenty-first birthday. Don't open it now. Go somewhere safe."

"Who is this from?"

"It's from your parents," she said tentatively, a tear streaking down her cheek.

That hit me like a punch in the gut. "You...you knew my parents?" I could barely get the words out as my throat constricted.

"Not personally. They arranged for me to take care of you and your sister in case something happened to them."

How many fundamental truths about my life could change before I couldn't take it anymore? I had never imagined I would receive a letter from beyond the grave.

"How..." I started to say, but I wasn't even sure what question to ask. I stood there, dumbfounded.

A dog barked, and shouts came from down the street. The Royal Guards were everywhere.

"Go!" Mrs. Yarrow whispered fiercely. "You have to go now!"

She gave me one last look that spoke of all the love she had for me, then shut the door. I wanted desperately to bang on it again and have her tell me so much more, but the barks were rapidly getting louder.

With my heart in tatters, I climbed to the rooftops and disappeared into the night.

Chapter Twenty-Nine

Letters and Lockets

Back at the Order, I called Elena to my room. Even though the letter had only my name on the outside, it affected Elena as much as it did me, so she deserved to be there when I opened it.

Elena had grown up a great deal recently, but although she was much stronger and braver than a typical fourteen-year-old, she still had a tender heart. She teared up as I recounted my meeting with Mrs. Yarrow.

"I miss her so much," Elena said with brimming eyes. "But how could she have kept a letter from our parents from us for so long?"

"I don't fully understand, but she said it was our parents' wish that she give it to me when I turned twenty-one," I said, placing a gentle hand on her shoulder. "Let's read it together and see if it answers any of our questions."

The parchment was dry and fragile, and I worried it would disintegrate if I opened it too hastily. So with delicate hands and my sharpest knife, I cut along the top and gingerly extracted the contents. The parchment inside was in better shape than the envelope but still brittle. Elena looked on, her face pinched with worry and anticipation.

With the letter in my hand, I paused, unable to digest the enormity of the moment. Then I opened each fold as though my very life depended on preserving this object. A sea of faded glyphs covered the page.

"It's just a bunch of scribbles," Elena said, crestfallen.

But I recognized the writing immediately. It was the code used by the clock tenders. Although a handful of symbols were foreign to me, I knew enough to guess their meaning.

As I deciphered the message, I read it out loud, and Elena looked on, amazed that I could make sense of it.

"Our dearest Cassian, if you are reading this letter, the worst has happened, and we are no longer with you. You may feel surprise, grief, and perhaps even anger upon learning that this letter was kept from you for so long, but please know that we made our plans from a place of love and necessity."

My voice cracked, and I fought back growing emotions. Tears streamed down Elena's face as I continued to read.

"There is much we need to tell both you and your sister about your place in this world, but we cannot risk putting it in this letter. You must return to Meadowrun, the farm where we raised you, and go to the special place. There, if you make a wish, you will find the answers."

Our place in the world? What mysteries might it unlock?

I continued. "We love you and your sister dearly. You are our entire world. Mother and Father." I gasped out the final words. Tears flowed as the ghosts of our parents' words hung in the air. And yet the letter raised more questions than it answered.

"The well in the forest by our old house, right?" Elena asked. "That's the special place where we made wishes. That has to be it."

"I think you're right," I said, surprised that she remembered the well so clearly. She had been only four years old the last time we'd been there.

"What did they mean about our place in the world?" she asked.

"I don't know," I said, although a bit of unease crept through me as I remembered how Edric had been unable to find anything about our lineage.

"Can we leave tomorrow?" she said.

I longed to do just that—pack our bags and head out immediately—but I knew it was too dangerous for us to go right away.

"It's only a few more days until we're supposed to leave," I said. "We can make a detour on the way to the Northlands."

She nodded, but she did so with downcast eyes and a frown.

"Hey Elena, remember when we were kids, we had a place we were supposed to meet in case anything bad happened?"

She nodded again, looking even more glum. "The grain silo."

"If we get separated on our journey, let's agree to meet at the wishing well. Okay?"

"Is something bad going to happen?" she asked.

"Nothing that I know of," I said. "But it's good to have a plan."

I tried my best to project confidence, but after this mysterious letter, I wondered if learning about our past was something we would eventually regret.

Later that night, I was alone in my room with my thoughts when Darion came to visit. He was in the habit of staying most nights, and I appreciated the company, the comfort, and the...other things. Tonight was no different.

After tender lovemaking, we lay wrapped in each other's arms. Between this blossoming affection and my parents' letter, I felt particularly open and vulnerable.

So I told him about the letter. After I recited it, he beamed. "Cas, that's amazing!"

"It stirred up a lot of memories," I said.

"I can't imagine getting a letter from my mother. I sometimes try to guess what she was like. I dream about her, although that's foolish because I never even knew her."

Hearing Darion mention his mother was genuinely surprising. This was only the second time he ever had.

"It's never foolish to dream of your mother."

Darion smiled at that. He traced his fingers along my shoulder, then across my chest, running them over the chain of my mother's locket. Up until then, I had taken it off every time we'd been together. I wasn't sure why, or why I'd chosen to leave it on this time. Perhaps I was finally ready to share that part of me.

"What's this?" he said, turning the locket over in his hand. It made me feel far more exposed than anything else we'd done together. But I let him do it because I wanted him to know all of me, the good and the bad.

"It belonged to my mother," I said.

Darion's eyebrows knitted with sadness. "I've never seen you wear it before."

"I know," I said, my voice cracking, barely holding back tears.

He could tell how important this was. The care in his expression was palpable. "Tell me."

"She gave it to me as she and my father lay dying, murdered because they were Emberborn. She told me to keep Elena safe, that it was my job to protect her now. I promised her I would."

Darion stared, letting the weight of my words sink in. Then he let out a long breath.

"I'm so sorry," he said as tears leaked down his face. "I've always known you loved your sister dearly and wanted to protect her above all else. But now I know the depth of it, why it's such an important part of you."

I laughed with no humor, my lips trembling as I spoke. "It's a pretty big thing for an eleven-year-old to absorb."

Darion looked pained. "No child should have to live with that burden. No adult should have to carry it alone. *I'll* help you carry it. I'll help protect Elena. I'll help you find who did this and make them pay."

"But I already know who did it," I said.

"You do?" Darion said.

"I saw him with my own two eyes. It was Orlik Leonom."

Darion's eyes burned with a rage I'd never seen before. But there was something else behind the rage. Something deeper.

He looked directly at me. "I promise you this, Cassian Nightbrook: I won't rest until you get justice."

Chapter Thirty

The Plan

EARLY THE NEXT DAY, I was summoned to Mireth's office. Kael and Darion were by her side, discussing something in hushed tones. They looked my way as I approached.

A strange twist of irritation batted at my insides, seeing Kael and Darion next to each other. Not exactly jealousy, but a reminder that Kael knew parts of Darion's life that I didn't. I wasn't used to that feeling, and I didn't like it in the least. It clung to me like sap.

"Cassian," Mireth said. "I mean, Cas. Thank you for joining us. We have an important matter to discuss. Please have a seat."

She took out a familiar leather-bound book, the one from The Butcher's study many weeks ago—the first time I saw Darion, and the moment my life took on a new trajectory.

"You recognize this book, I assume," she said.

"Hard to forget."

"And you've heard about how Tarnasau is corrupting Emberborn? How he turns them into Sentinels?"

"I've heard rumors," I said. "It's still hard to fathom."

"I agree," Mireth said gravely. "This book contains detailed information about how that corruption happens. The Kingdom created a serum that alters the mind. We think we can reverse it, but we're missing one key ingredient. We need a compound called Emberbane to make an antidote, but it is only available in two locations that we know of. We need you to sneak into one of them and steal it."

"And where exactly are these locations?" I asked, not sure I wanted the answer.

"The first is the king's private citadel at Thornfell Keep, but that's next to impossible to enter, so it's off the table," Mireth said.

"What's the other option?" I asked.

"The alchemist laboratories at Pyrehold."

I felt the blood drain from my face, remembering the place where I'd encountered that horrible darkness.

"That's the *easy* option?" I said flatly.

"This is no easy task," Kael said, clearly missing my sarcasm. "Pyrehold is where the kingdom locks up its worst offenders. Its defenses are substantial. Those laboratories conduct experiments on the prisoners, second only to Thornfell Keep in sheer horror. We've long suspected that this was how they learned to corrupt the Emberborn."

"Why would you send me?" I asked. "Surely you could send someone with a powerful Ember like Chronothene. They could just stop time and walk in and out."

Mireth looked directly at me. "What I'm about to tell you doesn't leave this room. Understood?"

"Understood."

"Recently we've noticed a disturbing phenomenon. It appears to be related to what you experienced during your visit to Pyrehold with Darion. A passage in this book has shed some light on the situation." She tapped the book's spine. "Some of our Emberborn members have found it harder to draw on their Embers in certain places. Sometimes they can't at all. This book discusses an experiment—a serum that enables Sentinels not only to detect Embers but to nullify them. They drain the energy in the Embersphere so Emberborn can't draw on it. They call it a null field."

"And you believe that experiment was successful," I said.

Mireth nodded. "You noticed all the Sentinels surrounding Pyrehold, correct? We believe those Sentinels are creating a null field. We believe that's what you encountered when you reached out with your Veilsense."

The memory sent a shudder through me—the darkness that seemed to embrace me still lingered in my mind. I let out a humorless laugh. "So you need a good old-fashioned thief."

"Exactly," Mireth said. She looked deadly serious. "This is of the highest importance. If Tarnasau perfects this, the Order will fall without a single sword drawn. We'll be defenseless."

It also meant Elena would be trapped here without her Ember to protect her, and Darion would be powerless.

"I understand," I said, with all the weight that the moment required.

Was this what had tipped the scales in my favor with the council? Had Kael voted for me to join the Order despite his objection because he knew they needed my skills? Was I simply a lamb being sent to the slaughter?

"The security inside must be rock solid," I said. "I assume there's a plan?"

Kael cleared his throat. "I have a contact at the prison. He's a spy for the Order and has agreed to help once you are both inside."

"Both?" I said.

"They won't let you just walk through the door," Mireth said. "That's where Darion comes in."

My stomach dropped as I turned toward Darion. The look on his face was complex—a combination of *I'm sorry I got you into this* and *We can do this together.*

"I've got a plan for how to get us in," Darion said. "And Sprocket has a plan for getting us out."

"I don't like it," I said to Darion after he'd walked me back to my chambers. "So much could go wrong."

"There are a lot of risks, but we've been over everything, and this is the only plan that might really work."

I couldn't argue with either of those statements. But I still didn't like it.

"I don't trust Kael," I said.

"Kael is an old friend," Darion said. "I know he's not always the easiest person to like, but he means well, and there are few people in the Order whom I trust more than him."

"But does he trust you? He almost didn't vote me into the Order even though it was you who invited me."

"You absolutely deserved to be voted in. But Kael may have had a point—I was too close to you. He was right to question it. And in the end, you convinced him you belong here."

I wanted to argue my point further. I wanted to explain that there was something about Kael that bothered me and that thus far he'd done little to earn my trust. But I didn't think saying that would accomplish anything.

Plus, Kael wasn't my only worry. I was simultaneously happy and concerned about Darion helping me on this mission. I knew from experience that he and I worked well together, and that was comforting, but I loathed the idea of putting him in peril.

Even now that I knew the details, there was little about this mission that I liked. Breaking into that hulking beast of a prison, especially one guarded by a null field and a small army of Sentinels, seemed like a terrible idea. It also meant I'd have to trust Kael's contact once we got inside. I never enjoyed depending on other people, and what with my lingering concerns about Kael, I was more than a little on edge.

So later that day, I did what I always did: I prepared.

I stopped by the kitchens and grabbed a handful of bright red cliff-berries, then headed topside. After only a few moments on the rooftops, the sound of flapping wings came from above.

"Hello, Zephyra," I said as she landed on my shoulder.

What is that smell, little Cas?

"Here you go, girl," I said, holding my hand out. Zephyra delicately but efficiently nibbled at the marble-size berries.

Thank you! This helps Zephyra forget the taste of filthy rats.

"It's the least I can do," I said, feeding her more berries. "Hey, Zephyra, how do you feel about a secret mission?"

Zephyra chirped.

Zephyra loves secret missions. Tell Zephyra! Tell Zephyra!

"I need you to fly to Garrick. I need all the information I can get on Pyrehold. Tell him to meet me tonight at our normal meeting place."

Pyrehold is bad. Why would little Cas want to know about it?

"It's very important for me to know this information. It could end up saving my life."

Zephyra is not happy about this. But Zephyra likes little Cas very much, and little Cas brings Zephyra berries, and Zephyra would hate to see little Cas harmed, so Zephyra will do this.

"Thank you," I said, stroking her head one last time before she took to the sky.

That night, at the stroke of sixth bell, Garrick and I met at our designated spot.

"So my secret is out," he said in a gruff voice. "That I can hear animals."

"Zephyra told me. But your secret is safe with me."

"That loud-mouthed bird," he said, but then he opened his arms and smiled. "Ah, bother. It's so great to see you, Cas."

"Likewise," I said, matching his smile and embracing him.

"What I'm not happy about is this nonsense about Pyrehold. Please, *please* tell me you're not considering breaking in."

The look on my face told him everything he needed to know.

"This feels familiar," Garrick said. "You looking for trouble, and me agreeing to help you for some reason. You'll send me to an early grave. Or yourself." He took a packet of papers out of his cloak and handed it to me. "Here's everything you'll need: a map, maintenance schedules, and prisoner transfer dates and times."

"I can't thank you enough, Garrick," I said, holding out a little brown pouch.

"Bah! Keep your damn coin. You've done far more for me than I could ever repay."

"I could say the same," I said, swallowing hard.

"We're getting soft in our old age," Garrick said with a laugh, and in the torchlight, I saw dampness at the corner of his eyes. "But just do me one favor."

"Name it," I said.

"Since the Royal Guard stepped up its patrols, there have been rumors swirling around that something big is about to happen. Watch out for yourself and your sister." He grabbed me by the shoulder and spoke in a tone so serious that it startled me. "And watch your back. Know who you can trust. Always have a backup plan."

"Is there something you're not telling me?" I asked.

"Nothing specific. Just trust your instincts and remember that there are bad people everywhere, even in the Order of Emberlight. Spies and double agents. People who would do you harm."

My stomach turned over as Garrick confirmed my suspicions.

"Have you ever heard of Kael Marrick?" I asked.

Garrick's eyes narrowed. "The name is familiar. Noble-born, if I remember correctly. Why?"

"Just trusting my instincts."

Chapter Thirty-One

Pyrehold

Darion and I stocked our packs with everything we'd need and headed topside just before sunset. The sky was aglow with a hundred hues of amber. Torchlight flickered across the city. A cool ocean breeze ruffled my hair, carrying the briny scent of the sea.

Typically, before a job, a sense of calm descended upon me. I felt in control, like my fate was in my hands. Not so today. Today felt unpredictable, like any outcome was possible. My stomach ached from worry.

"You okay?" Darion asked as we made our way across the rooftops.

"I'll just be happy when this is over."

He paused and turned toward me, his emerald eyes filled with care and understanding. That one brief moment was all it took to make failure feel less inevitable. I focused on the positive. We had a solid plan. Everything would be all right.

As we approached the North Gate, we climbed down to street level and found a dark alcove within sight of the guard booth.

"Do you feel anything?" Darion asked.

I closed my eyes and concentrated on my Veilsense. I felt nothing. None of the slow thrumming I'd picked up when Sentinels were actively projecting a null field.

"No, it's all clear."

"Good," Darion said. "In case things go south."

The plan was to catch a prison transport outside Analon. We'd exit the city without using Darion's Chronothene so he could save his energy for later. And despite the stepped-up patrols, it turned out that a simple bribe was enough to get us through the gate. I'd learned never to underestimate the power of a few coins on a greedy guard.

We made our way along the North Road until the dwellings dwindled to nothing and the road was less traveled, such that no wandering eyes were likely to see two dark figures waiting in the shadows. Hidden behind a boulder and a copse of trees, we pulled out Royal-issue prison garb and covered our clothing. Darion ate a brick of a honey concoction. It would help extend the amount of time he had before his Ember hangover hit, but when it did, he'd still be useless for hours.

"Now we wait," Darion said.

It wasn't long before clopping hooves and crunching gravel broke the silence. Almost exactly on time, an imposing-looking carriage with bars for windows, led by six massive workhorses, came around the bend in the road.

"That looks like our ride," Darion said.

"It does," I said. "And I don't feel any Sentinels."

Of course, I had left nothing to chance. Kael had provided the intel concerning the prison transfer carriage, but I had verified it against what Garrick had given me the previous night. Everything checked out so far.

"Okay, we have to act fast," Darion said. "Are you ready?"

"Just one thing," I said, and I kissed him with all the passion I had. Since I had joined the Order, we had felt more like colleagues than lovers, and I needed this moment. If things went badly, I wanted my last memory of him to be a good one.

Darion sank into the kiss. For a moment, it was just the two of us, and the rest of the world disappeared.

I pulled away. "Okay, now I'm ready."

Darion let out a gentle laugh and smiled. "You're insufferable."

"And you like it."

Darion's face got serious. "Okay, let's go."

Using all our stealth, we snuck up behind the carriage. Darion counted down with his fingers. Three. Two. One.

A shimmer, and the scent of ozone and citrus filled the air. I felt Darion extend his Ember around me.

Time broke.

The air thickened into a syrupy stillness.

This had happened enough times now that I was ready for it, but you could never *really* be ready for it. The world felt upside down, inside out, and backward all at the same time.

I had enough awareness in his Chronothene bubble to move around and do basic tasks, but I had no fine motor skills, so I let Darion do most of the work. He took the keys from the prison guard and unlocked the back door of the carriage. Then, while I was getting inside, he grabbed the prisoner manifest and hastily scribbled two additional names on the roster. The carriage was not too full but also not too empty. Exactly what we had expected.

Once I was inside, Darion hopped in behind me and swung the door shut, the click of the lock signaling that our last chance to abort the mission had passed. No going back now. We covered our heads with see-through hoods; Darion bound my hands and feet with the special breakaway shackles that Sprocket constructed. Then I helped him with his as best I could. We took our seats.

Darion gave me a thumbs-up, and I returned it.

A moment later, time rushed back like a torrent, cascading over me like an ocean wave.

We'd completed it all in twenty seconds, just as we had practiced. Darion would be tired but not spent. He'd be able to function long enough for us to carry out our mission. Everything was going according to plan.

Almost *too* well.

Even with the see-through hood, the darkness was disorienting, and the trip seemed to carry on forever as the carriage bobbed and weaved through the streets of Analon. The ride was rough, every missing cobble jarring my spine.

A feeling of unease sank into my bones. Soon I realized it was the null field around Pyrehold tickling at my senses. The closer we got, the stronger it felt until it was a constant thrum, a reminder of what I was up against.

Guards yelling and the clang of the portcullis being lifted announced that we had entered the belly of the beast. The outer doors crashed shut. We were now captives of Pyrehold.

The carriage door opened, and guards swarmed in. They brutally shoved and kicked us out, shouting that they would kill anyone who didn't comply. Once the prisoners were outside the carriage, they lined us all up with Darion directly to my right. They pulled off our hoods and forced us to our knees. I held back a shout as a stone dug into my skin. The one prisoner who cried out was rewarded with a kick to the back.

"Shut your fucking mouth!" the guard yelled.

Another guard went down the line of prisoners, frisking each one, looking for contraband. We hadn't been warned about this, and I held back a growing panic. I had vials and knives stashed all over my body. I had hidden them well, but I wasn't sure they'd be overlooked during a rigorous body search.

There were ten prisoners in total, and I was near the end of the line, but it would only be moments before the guard was upon me. Darion and I might have to fight for our lives.

The guard was frisking the prisoner directly next to me, and I wound my body up like a spring, ready to jump into action. I gave Darion the subtlest of nods, and he returned it. I counted five guards around us. With the element of surprise, we *might* be able to handle them, but it would be close. I hoped they couldn't hear the drumming of my heartbeat.

As the guard was reaching for me, a man walked briskly into the room, a cape billowing behind him. His uniform was meticulous, and he walked with the air of a leader. All the guards stood at attention as he approached.

"Prisoners, stand," he said, his tone leaving no question as to his authority. Darion and I quickly obeyed, along with most of the other prisoners. The few who didn't move fast enough were brutally dragged up by their hair.

The caped man walked down the line of prisoners, looking at each one. When he got to me, he paused. "This one with me," he said.

This had to be Verrin, our contact. He had sure cut it close.

Verrin turned. "Send the rest to the experimentation research holding cells."

I fought back panic. Leaving Darion behind was *also* not part of the plan.

But the guards shoved me forward before I could do anything. When I shot a quick glance at Darion, his face was expressionless. It wasn't like there was anything I could do anyway, so I sucked in my fear. Based on the maps Garrick had provided, I knew the location of the experimentation research holding cells, so I'd just have to let this play out and try to reunite with Darion soon.

I followed Verrin down a hallway with a guard at my side. His pace was quick, just below a jog. We hadn't gotten far before a gruff woman's voice called out from behind us. "Verrin, wait."

The woman walked up to Verrin.

My blood turned to ice.

It was Syra, Orlik's bodyguard. She wasn't facing me and hadn't looked my way, but the moment she did, I was sure she would immediately recognize me. And if she was here, it might mean Orlik was nearby, too.

She whispered into Verrin's ear, and he nodded occasionally. Then he whispered something back. Her eyes slid over me, unfocused, as if she was preoccupied.

This whole plan was a terrible idea. We'd been in this prison for only minutes, and already Darion and I were separated and had almost been caught twice.

But then, as quickly as she had arrived, Syra gave a final nod, then turned and walked down the hall away from us. I wasn't sure my nerves could take many more close calls like that.

Verrin continued at his relentless pace until we finally entered a small room with a desk. There was barely enough room for the three of us.

Verrin turned to the guard. "You are dismissed," he said with casual authority.

"Sir?" the guard questioned.

"Do you think I can't handle one scrawny, restrained prisoner?" Verrin spat out. "Obey, or I'll send you to the pit."

"Sir," the guard said, and marched out of the room.

The moment he was gone, something in Verrin's eyes shifted. He quickly shut the door.

"Okay, we have to act fast," he said, his demeanor changed from brutal officer to rebel spy in an instant.

"Why didn't you bring both of us?" I shot out.

"Both?" Verrin said, his brows scrunched. "I thought it was just you."

"The man to my right—he was with me."

"Well, it can't be helped right now," Verrin said, sounding impatient. "We have limited time. We'll clear this up once we're done."

"I'm not going anywhere until you fix this."

Verrin sighed. "Very well. What's his name? I'll have a guard bring him to meet us."

"He'll answer to Ravel," I said. That was Darion's alias.

Verrin opened the door and whispered something to one of the guards, then shut it again. "It's done. Do you need help with your shackles?"

"I've got it," I said. I triggered the secret unlocking mechanism, and the chains dropped to the ground.

"Good. Take that off," he said, pointing to my prison garb.

"That was a close call back there," I said. "We were five seconds away from a fight."

"It couldn't be helped," Verrin said. "You're lucky I made it at all. The schedules are all mixed up tonight. Something is happening within the prison that I haven't been made aware of."

"Will that interfere with the plan?" I asked.

"No," Verrin said as he took an alchemist's robe from a chest and threw it in my direction. "Put that on. Quickly!"

The two of us headed toward the alchemy labs as fast as we could without drawing suspicion. Guards patrolled the hallways, but with Verrin by my side, none of them even gave me a second look.

We twisted and turned through the corridors. I was happy to have memorized the maps Garrick had sent so I could anticipate each turn. I *hated* not knowing where I was going. Even so, I let Verrin guide me to our destination. He didn't need to know I had memorized the entire floor plan.

Verrin opened the door, and we walked into a room filled with a dozen alchemy stations, with many experiments underway. Smoke rose from vials, and cauldrons bubbled. Crystals, herbs, and reagents covered every surface.

"Excellent, there's no one here," Verrin said. "I'll stay by the door and distract anyone who tries to come in. You grab the vial of Emberbane."

The room was filled with hundreds of vials of various sizes, shapes, and colors.

"Do you know what it looks like?" I asked.

"In the very back, you'll find a rack with dozens of amber-colored vials. Only the vials that have a subtle shimmer to them are Emberbane. Take only one. Any more and they might notice."

"I'm on it," I said.

I wove my way to an alchemy station near the back, where I found the rack Verrin described. Of the dozens of vials, there were only a handful whose contents twisted and shimmered. I could sense the Ember within them.

Verrin watched from the front of the room. "Be very careful with that. It's extremely volatile. If you drop it on the ground, it will explode and take this entire room out with it."

"Good to know," I said flatly. I slid the vial into the belt under my robes.

As I approached, Verrin said, "Perhaps it's better for me to hold on to the vial in case someone gets suspicious. They might search you, but they would know better than to search me."

"I think I'll hold on to it myself," I said.

"Suit yourself," Verrin said with a frown that cut just a bit deeper than it should have.

A noise came from down the hall. "Quick! Someone is coming," Verrin whispered urgently. "We need to go!"

We hurried out of the lab and made it around a corner just before a group of alchemists spotted us.

As we continued through the prison, we encountered several more people heading in the opposite direction, all of whom appeared to be in quite a hurry. However, none gave us a second look. I gave Verrin a questioning glance, which he ignored.

Our destination was one of the body chutes. There were four of them in total: long, steep tunnels through which the prison disposed of its dead. The chutes emptied directly into incinerators. Tonight, three of the incinerators were running, and one lay dormant for cleaning. From there, we were to climb the ladder to the top of the smokestack, which towered high over the prison. And that was where the plan took a somewhat unusual turn, thanks to Sprocket's inventiveness.

"So my friend will meet us at the chute?" I asked.

"If he's not already there when we arrive, he should be there shortly," Verrin replied.

As we approached the chute, a gnawing worry built in my gut. Not only did the complication with Darion bother me, but Garrick had provided me with Pyrehold's incinerator maintenance schedule. Verrin was leading me toward one of the *active* incinerators. Perhaps it was an honest mistake. Perhaps Garrick's documents were incorrect or outdated. But just in case, I carefully slipped a smoke vial out of my belt and palmed it.

We turned into a room at the top of the body chute.

No Darion.

Then the overwhelming smell of rot hit me. Corpses lay in piles covered with stained white sheets. Flies buzzed around everywhere. I held back a retch at the gore. I'd seen death before—plenty of it. But something about the stacks of nameless bodies made my throat tighten.

The chute itself took up the entire far wall; the floor simply dropped away at a sharp angle. Most disturbing, however, was the smell of soot rising from it and the golden glow flickering far below. The incinerator was actively burning. My heart kicked into overdrive.

"Turn around slowly," Verrin said. He was suddenly holding a one-handed crossbow small enough to conceal beneath his cape. He pointed it directly at my heart. "Hand over the Emberbane, now."

Chapter Thirty-Two

Unmasked

I stood at one end of the room, near the chutes. Verrin had taken a step back, blocking the door.

"The thing I don't understand," I said, working hard to keep my voice calm, "is why this elaborate ruse? Why did you need me? If you wanted the Emberbane, why didn't you just take it yourself?"

"You really don't know?" Verrin scoffed, no longer hiding the contempt in his voice. "Only someone with Veilsense could see the shimmering of the vials. The other vials are all coated in poison. Even touching one would have meant instant death. I've heard the rumors about you. It was a risk, but those rumors turned out to be true."

It all made sense. Verrin wasn't working for the Crown any more than he was working for the Order—he was a ruthless free agent, doing only what served him personally.

I cursed myself for not trusting my instincts. I knew I couldn't rely on any contact that Kael supplied. Something had seemed off about Verrin from the moment I saw him. And yet I had walked right into his trap.

But I still had moves to make.

I pulled the Emberbane out of my belt, careful not to reveal the smoke vial in my other palm. As I did, I took a step back until I stood on the edge of the chute, holding the Emberbane at arm's length over it.

"You want the Emberbane?" I said. "Come and get it."

"The vial is of no use to you," Verrin said. "As we speak, Tarnasau's army is purging the Underworld and the Order of Emberlight with it. There won't be anyone left to give it to."

This must have been a bluff, some desperate attempt to convince me that hope was lost. It would take thousands of soldiers to invade the entire Underworld, and the Order would put up one hell of a fight.

"You expect me to believe that?" I snapped back.

"Why do you think I picked tonight for you to infiltrate Pyrehold? They're preparing for war in here. With all the chaos, nobody's going to miss one vial and one prisoner."

I refused to let him rattle me, keeping my voice level and smooth. "Well, you'll have to kill me to get it."

Verrin shook his head. "You truly are naïve, aren't you? I win either way. My *preference* is for you to hand over the Emberbane. I might even consider letting you live. But I guess I can just kill you instead."

"What good would that do you?" I asked. "I'll be dead, and the vial will be lost."

Verrin's mouth contorted into a cruel smile. "I could make a fortune with the Emberbane on the black market, which was my original plan. But given the price The Butcher has put on your head, I'll still make a tidy sum just by killing you."

Anger mixed with shock ripped through me like wildfire. Even the mention of The Butcher made my blood run hot. But a price on *my* head? Pieces were dropping into place in my mind: the encounter with The Butcher at the market; the way Tarnasau coveted Veilsense; the huge Royal Guard presence at our humble barn; Garrick's warnings about rumors. I had ignored it all, but it seemed I was part of something bigger than I could imagine.

Verrin's smile got even wider. "Oh, and consider this: If you die, there'll be nobody to protect your little wench of a sister. The price on *her* head is even more. Between the two of you, I'll make out fine, assuming the spies in the Order haven't already cashed in on her."

Blood pounded in my ears, and my vision tunneled until all I could see was this disgusting excuse for a man.

Nobody—*nobody*—threatened Elena.

I was done talking.

With a quick toss, I hurled the smoke vial in Verrin's direction. It exploded in a massive cloud, obscuring the entire room. At the same time, I hopped to the side. A crossbow bolt flew past, clanging off the stone wall behind me.

I pulled my dagger and threw it in Verrin's direction. A yelp of pain mixed with surprise filtered through the billowing smoke.

Verrin's hulking shape appeared through the clouds with my blood-soaked dagger in one hand and his crossbow in the other. He swung the blade, which I easily avoided. But as he tumbled to the ground, there was a sudden blunt pain in the side of my head as the butt of his crossbow smacked into my skull. I landed hard on the stone, stars swimming at the edges of my vision. The impact made me drop the vial of Emberbane.

We froze as it clattered along the stone floor, both of us waiting for the sickening sound of cracked glass and the subsequent explosion that would reduce us to ash. Instead the vial settled on the ground and rolled directly toward the chute.

Verrin scampered toward it on hands and knees. He scooped it up with a triumphant smile.

With all my might, I kicked Verrin in the rear. He and the vial tumbled into the chute.

"Don't fuck with my family!" I shouted, though I doubt he heard me over the sound of his own scream. It echoed off the walls before a massive explosion silenced him forever.

It wasn't so much a sound as a force when the shock wave of the explosion rushed toward me. I dropped to the ground, covering myself with the alchemist's robes as a firestorm flew up the chute and raged above me. I might have burned to a crisp but for the Salamander wool that alchemists' robes were made of, known for their fire-resistance. But the heat was still fierce. The moment the flames disappeared, I wriggled out of the smoldering robes.

The burning room was drenched in the sickeningly sweet smell of searing flesh, the air scorching hot against my skin. I raced out of the room before I also became fuel for the fire.

My mind reeled. If the Order was filled with spies, as Verrin claimed, then Elena was in *immediate* danger. I could rush to the inactive body chute and escape, but then this entire mission would be for naught, and that would also mean leaving Darion behind. I simply couldn't do that.

I knew what I had to do.

The corridors were deserted, which was surprising, since a massive explosion had just rocked the prison. But I still paused at every intersection to listen for footsteps.

My first stop was the alchemy lab, where other vials of Emberbane sat waiting. Thankfully, the labs were empty. In moments, I was headed toward Darion with two Emberbane vials tucked neatly into my belt. Only a few flights of stairs separated us.

I was nearing the staircase when I heard a rhythmic pounding ahead of me like the beat of a drum, soft at first but quickly building into what sounded like dozens of boots marching in unison, headed my way.

I ran to the first door I found: locked. In seconds, the tumblers clicked into place under the guidance of my picks.

I ducked into the room and waited. The marching continued. Relentless. Rhythmic. Unending.

When the sound of the boots passed, I risked a peek out the door. Down the hall, shoulder to shoulder in two rows, robed and masked figures marched with mechanical precision. Their uniforms were similar to those of the Sentinels but different enough that these people would not be mistaken for them. Each had a sword sheathed at their side.

These were Sentinel *soldiers*.

Verrin hadn't lied.

This was an army.

But as horrible as it was, it was nothing compared to what I saw when I turned into the room.

Hundreds of people were bound to wooden racks, naked, their eyes open but unfocused, their faces twisted into grotesque silent screams. Tubes ran in and out of them, carrying amber liquid shimmering with the glow of Ember. The racks continued deep into the room, as far as I could see.

My stomach lurched at the horror before me.

These people were Emberborn.

These were *my* people.

Enslaved.

I had to get out of there as fast as I could.

The only choice was to rescue Darion and get back to the Order, then escape with Elena and hope Darion would join us. The city wasn't safe anymore, not with Tarnasau building an army and spies in our midst. I would warn the Order, tell them about the prisoners here, and drop off the Emberbane, but we needed to leave as soon as that was done.

I dashed down the stairs as fast as stealth would allow, following the map in my mind. Soon I reached the entrance to the cells, which was unguarded. Luck was finally on my side.

The hallway I entered resembled a dungeon, with stone walls and a dirt floor. A long row of cells stretched along one side. The occasional flickering torch provided dim light, but there were plenty of shadows to hide in.

I made my way down the corridor, peeking into each cell. I recognized some of the prisoners from the transport, so I had made it to the correct place. But no Darion yet.

Finally, I reached a cell, and I knew before I even saw his face—it was Darion. He was sitting on the ground with his back to the wall, an arm draped over one bent knee. His eyelids drooped, a sign that the fatigue from using his Ember was starting to take hold. I'd have to get him out of here soon.

But there was something else—his face was bruised. Had the guards done that? White-hot anger flew through me, and all I wanted was to comfort him.

I was about to call his name when a clatter of footsteps came down the hallway. I let out a silent curse and ducked into the shadows.

I sized up the approaching group. There were four Royal Guards led by a man—a man in burgundy robes over chain mail.

It couldn't be.

But it was.

Orlik Leonom.

He wore a ring on his finger that seemed to be shimmering. Something about it felt wrong. There was a presence to it, something unseen. Like the Emberbane, Ember seemed to seep from it.

Orlik walked right past me and stopped at Darion's cell—my literal worst nightmare. My hands shook.

But this was also an opportunity. Five against one would be a stretch, but with a smoke vial, the element of surprise, and a lot of luck, I could have my vengeance and rescue Darion all in one go.

I drew a smoke vial from my belt.

This was it. No more waiting.

"Darion!" Orlik exclaimed. "I couldn't believe it when they said you were down here."

Something was terribly off. Orlik's tone was...jovial?

"Hello, Father. Yes, there seems to have been a mix-up."

Father? I must have heard that wrong.

"Look at that face. Caught up in a bar fight, I heard," Orlik laughed. He *laughed.* "Come along, son. I'm sure that's quite a story."

Son?

My head spun. Suddenly I was watching the scene unfold at the end of a long tunnel. My entire body went cold.

I couldn't have heard what I thought I just heard.

I barely registered what was happening. I was only vaguely aware of the guards opening the cell and Darion simply walking out, right up to Orlik. *Like they were family.*

But just as Darion passed, his eyes locked with mine. No one could possibly see me in the shadows, but somehow he did. His eyes widened with panic for only an instant, and then his expression smoothed over as if nothing had happened.

Orlik and Darion walked side by side down the corridor.

Then Orlik paused.

He tilted his head.

He started to turn in my direction. Like he sensed me.

"You think my face is bad?" Darion said. "You should see the other guy."

Orlik turned back toward Darion and barked out a laugh. "I knew all that combat training I paid for would come in handy, but not like this."

And with that, they continued down the corridor and out the door.

And I was alone.

I'd never been so alone as I was at that moment.

I was frozen in place.

And then I collapsed to the ground.

I couldn't breathe.

I started gasping for air. My lungs deflated. A wave of panic flooded me. I was suffocating, like that night on the River of Souls. Only that night, a warmth had saved me—a warmth I now realized had been created by Darion and his Ember. He had protected me. He had saved me. Tonight was the exact opposite.

Just when I thought I would black out, I finally managed to take a large gasp of air. I coughed, choking on my own spit. I pounded my fist against the floor.

How was it possible?

The Butcher was Darion's father.

My heart shattered.

Chapter Thirty-Three

Never Again

I SAT ON THE ground, unmoving, unable to think.

I might have just sat there and waited for the guards to find and kill me. That seemed preferable to living with the anguish in my heart.

But then my words to Elena echoed in my mind:

I'm not going anywhere. I promise.

I found the strength to stand. With my world crumbling around me, I ran.

I sprinted down the corridors, my lungs burning, not even bothering to hide from the few people who walked past. My heart was in tatters, but I actively blocked the thoughts banging around in my mind. If I let them through, I might simply collapse in a heap.

When I reached the body chute that was scheduled to be inactive, the absence of a burning scent was a small measure of relief. The chute was steep, but the slope was manageable enough to slide down, though with the Emberbane in my belt, I had to remind myself that the cost of slipping was a fiery death.

My feet landed in a thin layer of ash, but the incinerator was cool, and the piles of soot I had been worried about falling into had already been cleared. A narrow maintenance ladder led up to the smokestack. High above, I could make out a faint circle illuminated by a hint of moonlight.

I went up at a relentless pace. My fingers were raw and my muscles burned, but I ignored the pain and pressed on.

When I reached the top, I had to hold on tight as a blast of wind threatened to knock me to the ground. My stomach lurched with a touch of vertigo as I clung to the narrow rim of the smokestack, a ten-story fall facing me in every direction.

Visibility was a challenge at night, but I noticed that one of the other three smokestacks was belching massive clouds of black smoke, likely due to the earlier Emberbane explosion. I peered around, looking for Zephyra, but there was no sign of her.

After a short while, I pulled out one of my lamp vials and gave it a vigorous shake. A faint golden glow emerged from the vial. I waved it back and forth. The slight chance of being seen by unwanted eyes was worth the risk.

It didn't take long. Within moments, a flurry of flapping wings was all around me.

Little Cas, Zephyra is here.

Zephyra's beautiful form emerged from the shadows. I nearly cried from relief. In her talons, she carried the end of a rope that extended into the distance, and a V-shaped metal device with leather handles—Sprocket's creation. She flapped her wings, hovering next to me.

"Thank you, Zephyra!" I said with as much enthusiasm as I could muster.

So happy to see little Cas. When prison went boom, Zephyra was worried. But where is Darion?

"It's complicated."

So Darion is not coming?

I couldn't handle that conversation yet. I hadn't even had time to process it myself. "Not right now. Hand me that rope."

The rope was spun from Vanara silk, which made it both lighter and sturdier than traditional jute ropes. It was worth a small fortune. I wrapped the end of the rope around the smokestack until it was taut, then tied it off.

"Let's hope this works," I said to Zephyra, taking the metal device from her other foot. I positioned it over the rope so that the fabric fit snugly into the point of the V, then gripped the handles.

I slid down the rope, into the night.

At first, the descent was impossibly fast. I worried that when I got to the bottom, I'd smack right into whatever was at the other end and the Emberbane vials would take out half the city block, me included. But the farther I went, the shallower the slope became until I found myself cruising at a manageable speed.

Pyrehold passed below me. My stomach lurched at the sight of hundreds of Sentinel fighters marching out of the open courtyards and through the gates.

Verrin hadn't been lying.

This was the start of an invasion.

Soon I cruised over the outer walls and was on my way to freedom. Luckily, not a soul had a reason to look up, but even if they had, they likely wouldn't have seen a dark figure floating above them on this pitch-black night.

I raced across the rooftops, stealth and safety be damned. With the Sentinel army on the move, there was no time to waste. The clash of swords and screams drifted up from the streets, and plumes of smoke snaked up from the horizon in front of me. The soft thrumming of the null field in my head was an ever-present reminder of the Sentinels' power.

Zephyra flew just ahead.

"Zephyra, warn Garrick about the army!" I called out to her.

Zephyra will do this! she answered, then flew off.

As I sprinted along, the weight of everything I'd learned began to hit me. The look in Darion's eyes was forever etched in my mind. How could he not have told me? How could I ever forgive him? Was *he* the spy in the Order, distracting everyone while the king plotted our destruction? Had he been working with Kael all along? My heart couldn't take that possibility.

When I reached the ladder that descended to the Underworld, I paused to reach out with my Veilsense. No null field. I only hoped I had made it before it was too late. Before Elena was taken for the bounty. Before Kael found her.

I navigated back to the Order headquarters. When I arrived, the entrance was unguarded.

My gut twisted with worry. I had to find Elena.

Even as desolate as the Order headquarters often was, I typically ran into *somebody* on my way from one location to another. But now the halls were entirely deserted, and there were signs of a hurried exit. A meal sat half eaten at the guard station. A forgotten cloak lay on the floor.

On the way to Elena's chamber, I passed High Steward Mireth's office. Books and papers were strewn about as if she had left in a rush, taking only critical items. This didn't look good.

As I approached Elena's room, I paused, knowing that if she wasn't there, it would be the literal end of me. I pushed through the door, awaiting my fate.

The room was empty.

On the bed was a hastily written note, scrawled in Elena's handwriting.

Evacuating with Kael.

I dropped to the floor, the clatter echoing off the walls of the desolate room. The silence that followed was like a punch in the gut.

All around the room were signs of Elena's hasty departure: the books we'd found at the library, now discarded; her half-made bed; her cloak resting on it as if she were about to return. But she wouldn't return.

The training sword she'd used to practice forms in her room sat in the corner—forms Darion had helped her to perfect. He had given us such hope when he'd entered our lives.

The desperate note written in a panic sat crumpled in my hand.

Evacuating with Kael.

Pain gathered in my chest, and my limbs felt numb.

My mother's locket was like ice against my skin, mocking my failure.

I'd spent my whole life protecting Elena, and now, at her greatest moment of need, I had failed her. And I'd failed her because I had followed my heart. Because I'd tried to rescue Darion instead of the person I'd sworn to my dying mother that I'd keep safe. By choosing Darion, I had spat on that promise.

And now I was drowning in the despair of my own making.

This had happened before.

When I was eleven, I'd told Bren, the boy I had a crush on, that I could hear whisperhawks. I had only been trying to impress him. I hadn't known he would tell others. I hadn't known what the cost would be. A week later, Orlik had shown up and destroyed my family.

Never again, I had promised myself. I would stay strong, never let myself be distracted, never trust people with my secrets. These had been my guiding principles. They had kept us safe for all those years.

So why did I finally ignore what I knew would keep us safe?

Because I was a fool. Because I'd been caught up in some childish dream about happy endings. But that wasn't how life really worked. Life was cruel and took no prisoners.

I stayed there in the quiet until I thought it might envelop me. Maybe that was even what I hoped for.

And then...

Footsteps.

Part Three

Chapter Thirty-Four

What We Sacrifice

At first, I thought the footsteps were in my imagination. But then they grew steadily louder.

I hopped up and drew my dagger, then peered out the door.

Running down the hallway, out of breath, was Caldren, the man who had greeted us when we'd arrived at the Order and guided me to the council meeting. When he saw me, he looked as if a massive load had been lifted. "Thank dust! When you didn't return, we feared the worst!"

I did my best to regain my composure, but part of me just wanted to curl up in a ball.

"Where is everyone?" I asked.

"The entire Underworld is under attack," he said. "Scouts arrived with the news, and we evacuated. I'm to bring you and Darion to High Steward Mireth."

At the mention of Darion, I flinched.

Caldren looked around. "Where *is* Darion?"

"Darion didn't make it out," I said flatly, holding back the emotion trying to pour out of me. I couldn't bear to say what had really happened.

"Dust!" Caldren said. "I'm so sorry. I knew you cared for him."

"Have you seen my sister?" I asked, brushing off his concern.

"Yes," Caldren said. "Kael saw to her evacuation personally."

My chest tightened. The letter was true.

"Which way did they go?" I nearly shouted. "I have to get to her."

Caldren appeared taken aback. "She'll be quite safe with Kael. They left through the cellars, like everyone else. The city is locked down. All the normal routes are blocked."

"But did you actually *see* them leave through the cellars?" I asked.

"No," Caldren said, a quizzical look on his face. "I don't understand. Where else would they have gone?"

"I don't have time to explain," I said. "I need to find her."

Caldren shook his head. "My orders are to escort you to rendezvous with the high steward at Shadowfen. You have an item critical to the Order. I insist that you come with me."

I simply couldn't delay any longer, so I took the two vials of Emberbane from my belt and held them out to Caldren. "Here. Take the damn vials. But be careful. If you drop one, this whole room will be engulfed in fire."

Caldren looked at the vials as if they might bite him. But then he took one and added it to the satchel on his belt. "Very well. But you keep one. It's probably best that we split them up."

"I'm leaving," I said. If there was any chance they hadn't left through the cellars, I needed to get topside as fast as I could and have Zephyra track them.

"I still think you should exit through the cellars with me," Caldren said. "But if you want to leave through the front entrance, you'll need to hurry. The Sentinel army will be here any moment."

As if in confirmation, the thrumming of a null field hit me like a crashing wave, so strong that my teeth ached. It was much stronger than I'd ever felt it.

I cursed under my breath. "It's already too late," I said. "They're here."

With the front entrance cut off, the cellars were our only option. I ran with Caldren through an older part of the Order's headquarters that I had never been to. The walls looked worn from age and were in disrepair.

"When we get to the cellars, you'll have to follow me closely," Caldren said. "It's a maze of tunnels, and if we get separated, you're sure to get lost."

I had read about the cellars in a book on Analonian history—a series of natural caves that stretched for miles, a mazelike warren of passageways extending well past the city gates.

The null field continued to thrum. "They're getting close," I warned.

We reached a long corridor that ended at a narrow stone staircase twisting into darkness. As we took the first steps down, a group of masked Sentinel soldiers turned the corner at the far end of the hallway. Leading the charge was one of the last people I wanted to see. My blood turned to ice.

Syra, The Butcher's bodyguard, made eye contact with me, her face neutral as always. She started sprinting toward us, brandishing her sword.

"Fuck!" I yelled.

We flew down the stairs, two steps at a time.

"I can't use my Ember," Caldren said between breaths. "I tried to stop them, but all I felt was...emptiness."

"That's the null field," I said.

As we continued, the echo of boots was close. Too close. I snatched two vials from my belt and threw them behind us. Smoke billowed from one, and oil from the other coated the stone steps. In moments, shouts of surprise and the clatter of feet slipping on oil-slick stone reverberated from higher up the stairway.

"That'll buy us some time, but not much," I said.

After twisting down the stairs for what felt like forever, we came to a large room with stone arches in the ceiling. Countless casks of wine, most broken open and rotted with age, lined the walls. We continued through several similar rooms until we reached a massive timber door reinforced with iron bands. It was closed with three massive bolts that barred our exit.

"Here's where the caves start," Caldren said, grabbing the handle of one of the bolts. "Quickly, help me with these."

I joined in, tugging on the first bolt. It was wedged in tight, and it took quite an effort to get it opened. Two bolts left to go.

"How did they shut these from behind?" I asked as we pulled on the second bolt.

"I'm afraid that was me," Caldren said. "I saw the last people out and pounded the bolts shut with a hammer, hoping to give them more time. I never really expected to find you, honestly."

I felt a pang of emotion at Caldren's self-sacrifice and guilt at the way I had reacted to him. He hadn't expected to get out of here alive.

Down the corridor, the sounds of our pursuers echoed ever closer.

The second bolt came loose with a loud thud as the latch hit the stay.

As we tugged on the third bolt, Syra and a group of Sentinel warriors entered the room.

I hadn't brought much equipment into Pyrehold, so the only useful vial I had left was one lone firebomb. I flung it across the room. Fire exploded, but the room was so large that the fire barely even extended the width of it. That had likely bought us only a few moments.

Syra stared at me from the other side of the fire, her face inhumanly expressionless. As she paced back and forth, waiting for the flames to die down, her piercing gaze never left me. She tilted her head as a predator might when assessing its prey.

The final bolt finally gave way, and Caldren and I pulled on the iron ring, dragging the massive door open with all our might.

We had just gotten it open far enough to fit through when the whizzing sound of crossbow bolts zipped through the air. Most of them clattered against the stone wall or thudded into the wooden door. But Caldren cried out as one of the bolts hit its mark, embedding deep into his hip. He collapsed to the ground.

Quite suddenly, the thrumming of the null field stopped. Out of the corner of my eye, I saw a shimmer around Syra as she transformed.

"Caldren!" I yelled, reaching for his shoulders, dragging him toward the opening as two more bolts hit the door. "Help me get you to safety!"

"No time. And I'll slow you down," Caldren said through barred teeth. Blood was flowing freely from his wound.

Syra finished transforming and jumped through the fire, her beast form apparently impervious to flames.

A golden shimmer came from Caldren. He held out his hand toward Syra, and she froze, his Stillbind Ember in full force now that the null field was down.

"I can't hold her for long," Caldren said. "Rendezvous at Shadowfen to the north."

"I'm not leaving you!"

"Four left turns, three right, one straight, then one left. At the waterfall, go straight, then one more right," he said between labored breaths.

"No, you can make—"

"Go! They're reloading!" he yelled.

He pulled the Emberbane out of his pouch. His hands shook as he looked at me with the determination of a man who had just met his fate.

Several other crossbow bolts whizzed past us but missed their mark.

"Go now!" Caldren said as he hurled the vial of Emberbane in a broad arc toward the fire.

Chapter Thirty-Five

The Cellars

As a new round of crossbow bolts whizzed by, I slipped through the opening in the door. It was barely wide enough for me, and the buttons of my clothing caught on the frame.

As I dashed down a natural rock passageway, a massive explosion rocked the room I had just left. Small rocks and bits of debris rained down around me. Fire licked out of the doorway with a singeing heat, but I had made it far enough away to avoid the worst of it.

Once the firestorm died down, the cave grew dark. I shook one of my light vials, which emitted a dull green glow, just enough to guide me. The cave was rough and uneven, twisting through bedrock.

My chest ached. The raw finality of what Caldren had done threatened to crack me open. But grief was a luxury I didn't have time for. Not yet. I wouldn't let his death be for nothing. I needed to get out of this maze of tunnels alive.

I reached the first fork in the corridors, recalled Caldren's hastily relayed instructions, and turned left.

Far behind me, muted but still audible, Syra's voice called out in a bestial roar. "I will get you, Cassian Nightbrook! I will have your head on a stake!"

Apparently, in her shifted state, she had somehow survived the blast. I doubled my pace.

The caves were dank and cold. Water dripped from the ceiling, forming ankle-twisting divots in the ground that were hard to avoid. The smell of moss and earth permeated everything. I tried to move as fast as I could, but the uneven ground and slick rocks made the going much slower than I'd hoped.

I tried to build a mental map as I passed each intersection, following Caldren's instructions. But soon I approached a twisting knot of tunnels, followed immediately by another. Was this one intersection or two?

I guessed one. But just as I headed toward the tunnel, I felt something in my gut: the subtle clues of how the cave was formed, the way the air flowed. It had to be two.

"I'm coming for you!" Syra's voice echoed from deep in the tunnels, but closer this time. It was faint, but not faint enough.

I raced down the other path, hoping my instincts were correct.

The tunnel I'd chosen went on for a very long time, longer than any of the previous passages. If I was wrong and Syra caught up with me here, there'd be no place to run or hide. To make matters worse, this tunnel seemed to be heading downward. Before this, everything had sloped up. My gut twisted with worry. But I pressed on.

Finally, after what felt like half a mile or longer, I came to another intersection.

"Okay, left here," I said to myself. "If I don't pass a waterfall next, I'm fucked."

The new passage also went on for a long while, but this one slanted upward. I sucked in heavy breaths as my heart rate increased.

Soon the faint sound of water on stone reached my ears. I smiled, then broke into a run.

Moments later, I entered a large cavern illuminated by moonlight filtering through a hole in the cave's roof. Through it, water cascaded into a pristine pond in the middle.

I practically sprinted the rest of the way, completing the final turns. Ahead, I could make out the night sky framed at the end of the tunnel. It was all I could do not to burst out into the open. At the exit, I peeked my head out. A light wind ruffled my hair. The night air was crisp, free of the city's smog and pollution. All was quiet.

I left the cave and found myself in the northern foothills, well outside the city. They were dotted with dozens of caves, all exits from the infamous cellars. To the south, the lights of Analon gleamed against the night sky, and to the east, the edge of the Blackwood Forest loomed. Behind it, the sky was turning a dark purple as the first hints of dawn licked the horizon.

I had escaped. But I was still a captive of my mind.

Between Darion's lies, Elena's capture, and Caldren's sacrifice, I was a ship lost at sea. I closed my eyes tight. Before, decisions had come easily, but now my mind was a jumble of thoughts. So I grabbed at the one that floated to the surface first: I had to move before Syra tracked me down.

More out of instinct than anything, my feet took me toward Blackwood Forest. By the time I entered the shadow of the trees, the sky had changed from dark purples to warm oranges and reds.

I walked aimlessly, then suddenly looked up in surprise. I knew this place—it was the foraging spot where Darion and I had spent one of the best afternoons of my life. Had that really been only a few weeks ago? It felt like a lifetime. Gods, my heart ached.

It was a good enough spot for a few hours of rest. That was as far as I could reason.

Despite it being early summer, the morning was chilly. I curled up under a tree and used my cloak as a blanket. And moments later, despite the tumult in my mind, I fell into a fitful rest.

I woke with a start to a loud squawk.

I sat up and rubbed my eyes. A familiar whisperhawk came into focus, perched in the tree just above me. Zephyra was the first good thing I'd seen in hours.

Sleepy little Cas is awake, finally.

"It's good to see you, Zephyra," I said as she landed softly on my shoulder. "But I'm afraid I don't have any berries."

Zephyra finds her own berries in the hills. But that's not all Zephyra finds. Zephyra went to Garrick. Garrick told Zephyra to look for Elena.

"Did you find her?" I exclaimed.

Zephyra did!

If Garrick had been in front of me at that moment, I'd have kissed him.

"Is she headed north with a group of people?" I asked.

No. She's with a man with straw for hair. They are on the big road heading to the sunrise.

In an instant, my elation turned to dread. Elena, my Elena, was alone with Kael, not heading north to the rendezvous point but somewhere on the East Road.

Kael had captured her.

Chapter Thirty-Six

Wind Runner

"Can you lead me to them?" I pleaded.

Yes, Zephyra can do this. We go on an adventure!

Where could he be taking her?

Oh.

If we get separated on our journey, let's agree to meet at the wishing well.

Just before I'd left for Pyrehold, I had said those words to Elena. And the wishing well was near Meadowrun, which was east. For the briefest moment, I hoped that maybe everything was okay. Maybe there was nothing to worry about.

But then I remembered the terrible thing at the end of the East Road.

Thornfell Keep.

King Tarnasau's private citadel stood on the cliffs at the far end of the Jagged Coast. It was rumored to contain the king's private alchemy labs, where some of his worst experiments were carried out. If they had laboratories similar to the ones at Pyrehold... My mind flashed to the memory of the Emberborn strung up on racks, and I couldn't help seeing Elena among them.

For a moment, I considered the lone vial of Emberbane stored in my belt. The Order needed it. But it was Mireth herself who'd said that vows made to family were stronger than those made to the Order. And besides, who in the Order could I actually trust anymore?

So many of the things that had anchored me had come unmoored.

Which reminded me of Darion.

Up until then, I had successfully kept my mind off of him. That look in his eyes when he'd seen me hiding in the dark still haunted me.

He didn't give you up, though, the voice in my head reminded me, intrusive and nagging. *Orlik was about to spot you, and Darion distracted him. He saved you.*

No.

Darion's father had murdered my parents, and he'd kept that from me. That was all that mattered.

I put on my cloak, grabbed my bag, and headed toward the East Road. That was the only thing that I could do.

From the foraging spot, I headed south. Anytime I heard someone approach, I ducked into the woods until they passed.

When I reached the southern edge of the Blackwood Forest, I turned off the road and headed east, staying under the cover of trees, always keeping the perimeter within a stone's throw. The going was slow through the brambles, fallen trees, and dense spots in the woods. I spent hours navigating the obstacles. But the cover of the forest kept me safe from prying eyes.

Despite all my precautions, I couldn't shake the feeling that I was being tracked. Sometimes I saw a shadow out of the corner of my eye or heard a twig snap in the distance. I told myself that those things were to be expected in a forest teeming with life, but the unsettled feeling still lingered.

The sounds of Syra chasing me through the cellars haunted my memories. How had she lived through the Emberbane fireball? Her shifted form had to be nearly unstoppable.

Soon I reached the eastern edge of the Blackwood Forest and caught my first glimpse of the East Road and the Jagged Coast beyond. The briny scent of the sea filled the air.

Within moments of leaving the forest, Zephyra descended on me.

Little Cas! Elena and Straw Man are still on the big road. They keep walking, but humans are so slow. They passed the first people place right after I talked to little Cas.

"So they passed Brackmar this morning and are still moving east along the road?"

Yes, Zephyra said this.

Brackmar was still at least a few hours' walk away, and if they had passed it in the morning, that meant they were nearly a day ahead of me. That distance would be nearly impossible to make up...on foot.

Brackmar was a tiny coastal village east of Analon. I had done a few jobs for Garrick there and had made some contacts. If I could book passage on a ship headed east along the Jagged Coast, I might be able to leapfrog Elena and Kael and wait for them farther along the East Road.

That was the only plan my scattered brain could come up with, anyway. But I couldn't help but worry about all the ways in which it might go wrong.

As I walked toward Brackmar, I tried to keep my mind occupied with how I might rescue Elena, but thoughts of Darion kept intruding. Just a flash of his smile or his emerald eyes. It was never a full memory, but enough to feed the pain of his absence. I didn't let my mind linger long enough to consider where he might be or whether he was still with The Butcher. I banished such thoughts the moment they appeared.

By the time I saw the rooftops of the seaside hamlet, the shadows had grown long. Dusk was upon me. When I reached the village, night had fallen, and only the flickering torches guided my way.

Brackmar felt like the Wharf District in miniature, but without the grandeur of Analon. Shoddy buildings abounded, worn from the constant exposure to the sea air. Most buildings were made of wood and looked as if a strong wind would knock them down. The cries of gulls called. The crashing of waves rumbled like a never-ending background rhythm.

I headed straight for a sleepy tavern in an alley off a minor thoroughfare—the kind of place you'd go only if you were a local or a regular. Faded lettering above the door read BARNACLE & BARREL. The decor was nonexistent, just a bunch of haphazard tables and chairs and a bar at one end of the room. The tavern was mostly empty save for a handful of very crusty locals lost in their drinks.

I made my way to the bar and ordered a tankard of ale, mostly to keep up appearances. Then I whispered into the bartender's ear, "Tell Rook that Cas is here."

He gave me a subtle nod and walked through a doorway behind the bar.

I took my ale and sat in a dark corner where I wouldn't attract much attention, then scanned the room. There were three exits: the door I'd come in, the back door, and a window that would work in a pinch. The four patrons appeared to be too drunk to do anything. Only one carried a visible weapon. I allowed myself to relax the slightest bit and took a sip of my ale.

Every moment that passed made my chest tighten a bit more. Elena was out there somewhere, maybe in grave danger, and here I sat drinking piss-poor ale, not doing anything about it.

Soon the bartender returned, followed by a man with a shaved head and a dark complexion, wearing a tattered sailor's uniform. He had countless piercings, and his face spoke of a hundred battles fought. He walked up to my table.

"As I live and breathe. I never expected to see your ugly mug in here again, Cassian Nightbrook." His tone wasn't exactly hostile, but it wasn't friendly either.

I got up and stood face-to-face with him. "Considering the smell of this place and the fact that your ale tastes like piss, I never expected to be here again either."

We continued to stare at one another, our expressions stony. Then we both broke into smiles and laughter and shared a quick embrace.

"Good to see you, Rook," I said,

"Good to see you too, Cas," Rook said, slapping me on the back.

I sat back down and gestured for him to join me.

"So, I take it this isn't a social visit," Rook said.

"Straight to business, as always," I said. "I need to cash in on that favor you owe me."

Rook sighed. "I get the sense that there won't be any sleep for me tonight."

I shook my head. "I need to move east along the coast as quickly as I can. As far as Grey Spit, if possible."

"Most of my crew is either drunk or sacked up right now. But I get the impression that you want something small and fast anyway."

"The faster the better."

"The *Wind Runner*," Rook said. "Wicked-fast cutter, and easy to maneuver at night. Twenty gold."

"Fourteen."

Rook scowled. "In a hurry, but still got time to barter, eh? Fine. Dock six in a quarter bell. I'll at least need to track down my first mate."

"Make it in half that time, and I'll pay you sixteen."

"Deal," Rook said, and we shook hands.

Rook hurried off through the front door. Since I had some time to kill, I sipped my ale, but I didn't drink much. Best to keep my wits about me.

Rook was a friendly enough guy, and I could trust him as much as I could trust any smuggler. At the very least, we had a mutual interest in keeping our business secret and avoiding the Crown.

I took a few final sips before I headed out to make my way to dock six.

The *Wind Runner* was a fast-looking ship, around thirty feet long and ten feet wide, with a bow that tapered to a sharp point. Rook and a tough-looking woman with pale skin and short-cropped hair were on the deck, fussing with the riggings and raising the mainsail.

Rook looked up as we approached. "Kind sir, please come aboard. This is my esteemed colleague, Jask," he said with mock formality, twirling his wrist. Jask gave a tight nod and went back to her task.

"If you're really in that much of a hurry," Rook added, "you can untie the mooring lines while I help Jask hoist the mainsail."

"Will do," I said, and began to work on the lines. The ropes were slick with spray, and the algae-covered wooden dock made footing treacherous.

"Start with the fore and aft lines," Rook barked at me.

"Aye," I replied, mimicking the sailors I'd heard a thousand times while growing up in the Wharf District.

I had wriggled free the aft line and was working on the fore when a familiar and very uncomfortable feeling tickled my senses. Faint but growing steadily stronger was the thrumming of a null field.

I spun on my heel and looked down the dock, and my mind filled with dread.

At the far end were a handful of Sentinels and the unmistakable profile of Syra. They were still a good distance away but were running toward the ship. Syra was covering the distance quickly.

"Sentinels are here!" I yelled to Rook and Jask. "We have to go! Now!"

But then I saw the figure running ahead of them, which I hadn't noticed in the darkness. I could scarcely believe my eyes, and my heart dropped into my stomach.

It was Darion.

Chapter Thirty-Seven

Under Fire

"Cas, watch out!" Darion yelled. "Sentinels!"

I stood there, frozen, not knowing what to do. The man I had fallen for, the man who had lied to me so horribly, was running toward me, warning me of danger. But I couldn't trust him. How did I know this wasn't a trick?

"Of course it's bloody Sentinels!" Rook shouted. "I should have known it would be something bad with you, Cas."

Rook's voice snapped me out of my daze, and I struggled with the final line at midship. "Leave it!" Rook yelled. He drew his sword and sliced the rope.

Darion was about halfway to us with Syra just behind him. Several members of the Royal Guard loaded their crossbows as the Sentinels stood at attention, chanting. I didn't see how we could possibly escape. They were too close.

And then Syra made a hand signal and the chanting stopped.

The null field dropped.

A golden shimmer surrounded Syra as she started her transformation.

An instant later, a shimmer surrounded Darion. If he was a traitor and he used his Chronothene against us, we were finished. But instead of the betrayal I expected, Darion extended his Chronothene to me.

Time turned to molasses, and the world ground to a halt. I nearly spit up the few sips of ale in my stomach.

Darion turned and ran toward Syra, who was mid-transformation. He shoved her hard with everything he had. Suddenly I understood why he'd extended his Chronothene. Darion *wanted* me to see that he was helping us.

Time remained frozen as Darion walked up to me, a look of deep sadness in his eyes. I tightened my jaw and frowned. He had helped us, yes. But a rescue and a sad look weren't going to fix this.

Time snapped back.

Syra flew into the Royal Guard with the force of a cannon just as they were firing their crossbows. The bolts shot off in random directions, all missing their marks. In an instant, Syra was back on her feet, back in her human form, her transformation interrupted.

She signaled with her hand again, and the null field returned. In a rush, it hit me: when she'd dropped the null field, she hadn't expected Darion to use his Chronothene *against* her. She had thought Darion was on her side. But instead he'd protected us.

Jask raised her own crossbow, aiming it right at Darion; as far as she could tell, he was working with Syra and had just magically materialized next to me.

"No! Stop!" I shouted at her, standing in the path of fire. "He saved us."

Jask kept her crossbow aimed at Darion but didn't shoot.

"We'll sort this out later," Rook said. "Let's go! Give us a push, will you, Cas?"

Both Darion and I grabbed the ship's rail and pushed off the dock with all our might. The ship floated away from the shore with both of us holding on for dear life as the dock disappeared beneath our feet. The first crossbow bolts hit the hull just as we scampered up and over the bulwark.

The ship was already quite a ways from the dock as Syra approached the edge at full speed. Even in the moonlight and at a distance, I could see the relentless look on her face, like she was a machine without emotion and with only one purpose. I realized then that Syra wouldn't stop until her task was done or she was dead. And that realization sent a shudder through me.

She reached the edge of the dock and kicked off. I couldn't imagine that anyone could make that leap, but somehow she managed it, slamming into the edge of the hull, her arms draped over the railing. Her hair and eyebrows were entirely singed off, and blisters covered her face and arms. The sight was so horrific that it made my legs buckle. Part of me wanted to curl up and hide belowdecks.

Instead I steadied myself and drew my dagger, ready to slash at her fingers on the railing. But she moved with a frightening speed I hadn't anticipated, and in a blink, she was halfway over the bulwark, drawing her sword.

A twang came from behind me, and a bolt from Jask's crossbow buried itself in her shoulder. Syra let out a howl. For a split second, something in her face shifted. Gone was the mechanical, almost-blank look, replaced by...terror? Regret?

A second bolt hit her, and she recoiled, losing her balance, then falling over the edge with a large splash. I gave Jask a grateful nod as the adrenaline of the moment washed over me. But that look in Syra's eyes was stuck in my mind.

Rook finished hoisting the mainsail, and with a snap of canvas, the ship glided forward eagerly. In the distance, the Royal Guard stood at the dock, still firing their crossbows, but at this range, none of them came close to hitting their mark.

The *Wind Runner* cut through the water with ease and plunged into the darkness.

"Will somebody please tell me what in all the hells is going on?" Rook said. "Why are Sentinels after us, and who in all the hells is this?" He gestured to Darion, who sat on the deck with a wretched look on his face.

I stayed quiet, as interested as Rook to hear what Darion had to say. Probably more interested. The silence was deafening, with only the sound of the hull cutting through the waves.

"It's complicated," Darion finally offered, his eyes locked on mine.

Rook turned to me with a look of impatience. "Okay, your turn. Why shouldn't I throw this man overboard?"

"We'd be dead without Darion," I said simply.

"So you *know* him," Rook said.

"I thought I did," I said.

Rook looked between the two of us. "Okay, clearly there's *something* going on between you two. Which...fine. Whatever. But I still need to know why the blasted Crown is chasing us."

Darion sighed. "They're hunting Cas. And now I'm sure they're hunting me, too."

Now they were hunting him?

Rook shook his head and ran his hand through his scraggly beard. "You really are in deep, aren't you, Cas? Royal Guards? Sentinels? And who in all the hells was that hanging off my ship?"

"I never expected to bring all this to you," I said to Rook. "I had no idea I was being tracked so closely." I turned back to Darion. "How *am* I being tracked so closely?"

"The Crown has figured out how to amplify Veilsense. Sentinels can now sense innate Embers."

I shuddered. Sentinels could track me for just being myself? "And how long have you known this?" I snapped.

"Since yesterday," Darion said.

"Wait," Rook interjected. "They can track us? Are they tracking us right now?"

"Not this far out at sea," Darion said. "When we go to shore, yes. But I can show Cas how to suppress his Embers."

"That assumes they aren't already pursuing us," Rook said. "And Grey Spit is clearly off the table. The Royal Guard will be all over that dock."

"They aren't following us. Or at least, they aren't close," I said. As we had sailed away, the thrumming of the Sentinels had faded and hadn't come back.

"And how would you know that?" Rook asked with a critical look.

"I...I have a sense for these things."

Rook scoffed. "Well, that's a relief," he said, his words dripping in sarcasm. "Even if we escape, this ship is burned for smuggling without a complete refit. The last thing I need is *more* attention from the Crown."

"I'll make it up to you," I said.

"Damn right you will," Rook said.

"So where can we land besides Grey Spit?" I asked.

"We have options," Rook said. "But first we need to be sure we aren't being tracked. So *you*"—Rook pointed at me, then at Darion—"and you need to figure your shite out."

With Jask piloting the ship and Rook acting as lookout, Darion and I were suddenly alone for the first time since we'd entered the prison wagon.

It felt strange being this close to Darion, and I was filled with an odd mix of longing, sadness, and past memories, all tainted by his deception.

"I don't expect you to forgive me," he said. "But I hope at some point, you can at least understand."

"Why didn't you tell me?"

"I'd planned to. But it's hard. It's the part of myself I hate the most. And then you told me that Orlik had killed—" Darion choked on his words, and tears leaked out. "Gods, I'm so sorry, Cas!"

Seeing Darion break down sent a jolt of anguish through me, but I fought it back and kept my expression neutral.

"When I saw you in the cell talking to that...that monster..." I tried to keep my composure, but the memory was so painful, and it filled me with an ugly anger. "Watching you talk to him like he was a *normal person...* He was *laughing*. You have no idea what that did to me."

"Seeing you in the darkness, witnessing that, was one of the worst moments of my life," Darion said, despair on his face.

"So...is Orlik Emberborn?" I asked.

"No," Darion said. "He hates Emberborn. Only my mother was. And he still doesn't know that I am. It sickens me every time I have to talk to him. Every time I have to pretend."

"So you're...what? Like, a spy?" I asked.

"I've been providing information to the Order. And disinformation to Orlik, when I can."

"I don't understand how you can do it," I said. "I literally don't."

Darion opened his mouth to speak, but I put up my hand. "No," I said, forceful enough to make him stop. This was too much to hear at once, and I was swirling with conflicting emotions that I didn't know how to process. Hearing more from him now would only make things worse.

"I'm going to need some time," was all I was able to say.

Darion nodded slowly, a deep frown on his face. "Of course."

There was a long pause during which we both remained silent, looking out at the sea.

It was Darion who finally spoke. "Well, I guess Rook gave us a job."

"Huh?" I asked. "Oh, suppressing my Ember?"

"Yes. They can sense even the smallest bit of Ember within you."

"I didn't even think I was using Ember with my innate abilities."

"All Emberborn have some within them. I can feel it coursing through me all the time," Darion said. "But I've learned to suppress it. It takes some practice, but eventually it becomes second nature."

"And you're doing that now?" I asked.

"I am."

"I'm not sure I like the idea of turning off part of who I am," I said. "Do you think that if I shut it off, it will mute things like my memory and climbing ability?"

"Perhaps. But hopefully you can learn to control it enough that it gives you exactly what you need when you need it. Are you willing to give it a try?"

I didn't love the idea, but I didn't see an alternative, at least not while we were being actively hunted. "Yeah. Let's try it."

Darion talked me through the process. It involved reaching into my mind, isolating a part that felt like a warm, flowing river, and then damming it up. It was the opposite of reaching out with my abilities. After only a small amount of practice, I was able to at least *mute* the Ember flowing through me.

But I didn't enjoy it. It felt unnatural, and I had to concentrate every moment to keep it turned off. I hadn't realized just how intertwined with my very being it was until I knew what it felt not to have it. It felt no different from closing my eyes, or plugging my ears, or even holding my breath. It was stifling.

I hated having to turn off a part of myself.

"How did you learn to do this?" I asked.

Darion looked me in the eye. "Given where I grew up, it was learn to suppress my Ember or die."

Chapter Thirty-Eight

The Jagged Coast

We sailed deep into the night.

Sticking to the facts, I told Darion what had happened since we had been separated at Pyrehold. He was shocked and angry at Verrin's betrayal and surprised to hear that Kael had taken Elena on the East Road. He took my suspicions about Kael at face value and didn't argue or contradict me.

All this should have reassured me, but instead it tightened the knot in my chest. I could feel myself starting to trust him again. And I so wanted to. But that was the problem. Trusting him meant letting him in again, and the pain of what had happened at Pyrehold was still raw and exposed. I couldn't take that kind of pain again.

Soon Rook called us into the cabin to discuss strategy.

The space was cramped, just big enough for a handful of hammocks and the table we gathered around to pore over a map. An oil lantern hung from a hook, bobbing with each wave.

"So no Grey Spit," I said.

"They'll catch us before we even dock," Rook said.

"So where does that leave us?"

Rook pointed to a spot on the map. "There's a secluded inlet called Knifejaw Cove not too far west of Grey Spit where we can anchor. The entrance is treacherous, so few people know of it. Jask is one of the few pilots I trust to navigate us through it, especially at night."

"Sounds promising," I said, studying the map. "Can we get to land from there?"

"Yes. Jask will take you ashore in the rowboat. I'll stay and protect the ship. Once you're in Grey Spit, she'll bring another ship and crew so we can scrub the *Wind Runner.*"

"Solid plan," I said. "But I can't guarantee Jask's safety."

"Tough as nails, that one," Rook said. "She can take care of herself."

"Thank you," I said to Rook. "This means more than you know."

Rook just grunted.

With the plan in place, Darion and I went topside. It took a few moments for my eyes to adjust from the lamplight to the near pitch-blackness above. Darion walked over to the rail and looked out at the sea. I followed him.

"Cas, you are well within your rights to leave me behind," he said. "And if that's your decision, I'll respect it. But I would very much like to help you find Elena, if you'll allow me."

I knew this moment would come, and I still wasn't ready for it. "Don't you need to rendezvous with the Order?"

"Elena is very special to me, and if Kael turns out to be hostile, as you fear, you'll need all the help you can get."

Elena is very special to me. I knew that was true, and the weight of it pressed down on me. Here Darion was, choosing us over the Order, and letting him come with me meant I was choosing to take him back. I wasn't sure I was ready for that.

"You can come with me as far as Grey Spit. After that, I...I'll need to think about it."

Darion nodded. "I understand."

We had traveled all night, and not once was there any sign of our pursuers. The wind was in our favor the entire way, so we made good time. We slept in shifts, one person at the helm and one as the lookout while the other two tried to get some rest. Sleep did not come easily.

It was my turn to watch while Jask was at the helm, and I could barely make her out in the moonlight. She was chewing on a pipe, puffing out little clouds of smoke that dissipated in the ocean wind the moment they left her mouth, leaving only the lingering scent of tobacco.

"I'm amazed you can navigate at night," I said.

She smirked. "Been doing this so long, I could navigate this stretch with a blindfold on. All I need is my memory and my ears."

"Your ears?" I asked.

"Yep. I can hear every splash over rock, every current. Your eyes can trick you, but your ears never lie."

"That's impressive."

Jask shrugged, taking another puff from her pipe.

Just as the sky was brightening, we approached Knifejaw Cove. True to its name, the inlet looked like the maw of a giant beast with razor-sharp teeth. The waves crashed against the rocks, sending salty spray skyward in a constant rhythm. I understood why any sensible sailor would avoid this place and why smugglers would seek refuge here.

Jask took the helm while Rook kept a sharp eye out in front to be sure there were no surprises. Darion and I watched the coast as we approached, hoping no one would see us.

A few times on the way, Rook had barked orders, all of which Jask had executed flawlessly with the fluid ease of a master at her craft. I had noticed that most of the time when Rook called out that he'd spotted a rock, Jask was already in the process of avoiding it.

Jask tucked the ship into a nook where it wasn't visible from either the sea or the land. The rowboat ride from the ship to the shore was the most harrowing part of our entire trip; the tide was low but on its way in, exposing rocks and creating crashing waves all around us. But we made it without incident, thanks to Rook's expert guidance.

We landed on a rocky beach with a very narrow strip of sand. Jagged rocks surrounded us, not only out at sea but also on land, towering above us. Once we were on shore, Rook said a few private words to Jask, who nodded.

"I wish you luck," Rook said to us as he returned to the rowboat and began the treacherous trip back to the ship.

Jask took the lead, finding a path up from the beach and into the rough terrain. She was no-nonsense and a woman of few words, but she had a keen look in her eye and was always surveying for danger. In some ways, she reminded me of myself.

"How far do you think we are from Grey Spit?" I asked.

"A few hours," Jask said simply. "More if we avoid the East Road."

"That's probably for the best," I said.

The ascent was steep, and more than a few times we had to reach uncomfortably far for handholds and toeholds. I was still trying my best to suppress my Ember, and the difference in my climbing ability was stark. Where I would typically scamper up the rocks like they were nothing, now I found myself second-guessing every move, once even misjudging a handhold that gave way as I reached for it. Only when I didn't have it did I realize just how blind I felt without my Ember. Before, I could sense the cracks in the rocks like they were canyons. My fingers and toes clung to them easily. Now my limbs felt like hammers banging against solid rock.

So I worked on allowing a bit of my Ember to flow, just enough to be competent. I hated the feeling of being restricted.

"I don't understand how you can do this all the time," I said to Darion. "Turning off your Ember, I mean."

"It is tough," he agreed. "But every person is connected to their Ember differently. For me, when I let it flow, I have a greater awareness of and connection to time. You know how people say time flies, or that they wonder where the time went, or that some days seem to drag on?"

"Yes," I said. "That happens to me all the time."

"Well, it *never* used to happen to me. Time was constant and ever-present. I really didn't understand those expressions until I learned to mute my Ember, and then suddenly they made sense. But you, Cas...I've never met someone with so many Embers. They must flow through you like a massive river, and I can understand why it would be so hard for you to turn them off."

"Why am I different?" I asked, not really expecting an answer.

"I don't know. But maybe you can find the answers you're looking for when you get to your family's old farm."

That comment reminded me just how much of myself I had shared with Darion, how deeply I had trusted him, and how dangerous that trust had been. Putting faith in him now felt like standing on the edge of a steep drop, like the time with Bren when I was a child. Back then, I'd fallen so far that I'd barely made it out.

We soon got to the top of the cliffs. The Jagged Coast was a beautiful and treacherous sight to behold, with dramatic rock formations stretching in both directions. The ocean in front of us stretched to infinity, churning away at the hillside. Seagulls soared on the gusts of wind that blew past us.

Far off to the east, along the coast, the harbor of Grey Spit was just visible.

Predictably, Zephyra found us shortly after we ascended the cliff. She flew like the wind and dove dramatically, landing hard on my shoulder.

It took me a moment to remember to let my Ember flow so I could hear her thoughts.

Hurry, little Cas! Elena and the Straw Man are almost to the people place!

Chapter Thirty-Nine

Grey Spit

We set a relentless pace.

Having Jask along proved invaluable. This was not the first time she'd had to make an emergency stop at Knifejaw Cove. Because of its proximity to Grey Spit, smugglers often used it as an alternate docking location when the loot they were carrying was too hot or when local officials hadn't been adequately paid off and were cracking down.

"You guys doing good?" Jask asked a couple of hours into our march. We had paused only twice for water and a short rest.

Darion gave a thumbs-up.

"Doing fine," I said between labored breaths.

Getting to Grey Spit was all I could think about, and her punishing pace was exactly what I needed. Even without taking the East Road, we were making great time. The terrain was varied enough to provide natural cover, and what time we lost in navigating around the cliffs and boulders, we made up for in not having to worry about being seen.

It wasn't long before rooftops dotted the horizon. From a distance, Grey Spit appeared to be a typical coastal town, similar to Brackmar but a little smaller and more run down. Most of the buildings were one or two stories tall, with only a handful of larger stone structures in the center.

Zephyra had followed us the whole time, circling above and providing the occasional update. According to her, we had made it to Grey Spit just before Elena and Kael, so we took cover in a rocky glade that had a clear view of the road as it entered the town.

I turned to Jask. "I can't thank you enough for guiding us here," I said to her. "But this isn't your fight. Feel free to do whatever you need to help out Rook."

Jask smirked. "Rook was being dramatic back on the boat. We've moored there a hundred times, and he can wait a bit. I know Grey Spit better than either of you and like being where I can be the most helpful."

"We certainly welcome the help," I said. I liked Jask. I got the impression that she'd grown up on the streets like me. I recognized the ruthless pragmatism in her eyes—the way she was always watching the horizon, calculating, assessing.

"Okay," I said. "Here's the plan when we see Kael and Elena. If she's in immediate danger, we go right in. Otherwise, let's just watch. I'd rather not confront Kael right away. The situation is too unpredictable. Let's see what he does."

Jask nodded.

"Sounds good," Darion said, and for a moment, things between us felt normal. It was so easy to fall back into trusting him with my life. It unsettled me.

We sat there for what felt like forever. I grew impatient, worried that we had missed them somehow, but Zephyra flew overhead in tighter and tighter circles, presumably an indication of how close they were. Soon I made out two figures cresting a hill in the distance. Elena's fire-red hair was impossible to miss.

She didn't appear to be restrained or injured, a fact that Darion and I acknowledged with a relieved nod. In fact, if I didn't know better, they looked like any two people out for a stroll. And yet something about it felt wrong in my bones.

As they approached the town, they spoke to each other. Kael appeared to be pointing out landmarks in the distance. But they were moving very quickly, and as they got closer, I saw Kael glancing around, looking for danger.

I felt an irresistible urge to jump up and confront them and whisk Elena away. I'd missed her so much and had been so worried. She was literally right in front of me. As I fidgeted, Darion leaned closer.

"If you want to pull her now, just say the word," he said.

"We hold for now."

As they passed, Jask whispered, "If they decide to stop, there's really only one inn that's not a pleasure house. Hidden Reef Inn. Still pretty rough, though."

"Okay," I said. "Let's fan out. Jask, since they don't know you, you'll follow behind them. I'll walk one block to the left. Darion, you take one block right. If it looks like Elena is in danger, we'll converge. If they go into an inn or something, you follow them, Jask. If you need backup, give us a whistle."

They nodded.

As Kael and Elena passed the first buildings in the town, we began to follow. Walking a block away was nearly unbearable for me. Each time I lost sight of them behind a building, my pulse kicked up until they emerged on the other side. But from what I could see, Jask was a master of stealth, staying within a reasonable distance but never *looking* like she was.

Exactly as Jask had predicted, they approached a sea-worn but respectable-looking inn with the name HIDDEN REEF painted on a wooden sign, a mug of ale and a bed drawn below it. Elena and Kael entered together. After just enough time that it didn't look suspicious, Jask followed. Darion and I converged behind a stack of old ale barrels across the street.

"I *like* Jask," Darion said.

Despite the churning in my gut, that forced a smile from me. "Me too."

"Well, now we wait."

The waiting was *killing* me. I fidgeted with my hands and tapped the ground with my boot.

As we watched, several patrons entered and left. The inn appeared to cater to traveling merchants and locals of relatively high standing. I assumed the fishermen and dockworkers favored the inns closer to the wharf. I hoped Jask didn't stand out too much in her worn nautical attire.

Just as I was nearing the end of my patience, Jask stepped out the door as casually as she might if she were strolling home after a night on the town. Darion cupped his hands around his mouth and made a short series of chirps that sounded remarkably like a sparrow's call. Without even looking up, Jask pivoted and walked our way. She leaned against the barrels we hid behind, took out her pipe, and started fussing with a chunk of flint and a steel striker. As she did, she whispered while somehow barely moving her lips, "Kael's downstairs, meeting with a well-dressed man. Elena's upstairs, second room from the northwest corner."

"I'm going in," I said to Darion.

He nodded. "We'll keep watch."

Darion stayed put as Jask drifted back into the inn, and I orbited the building's perimeter. The inn had a small field in the back with a chicken coop and a few pigs and goats in a pen. There were stables attached to the building along the north side. Just above where the stables met the inn was a row of second-story windows.

I let the smallest bit of my Ember flow through me. Its absence felt very alien to me, and I welcomed the inner warmth. After scanning for anyone watching, I scaled the back side of the stables and crept up to the second window from the northwest corner. The wood creaked as I walked along the roof.

My heart leapt at the sight of Elena sitting at a small wooden table, tending to something in her bag. As quiet as a mouse, I pulled open the window and slid inside.

Elena spun on her heel, brandishing her short sword, eyes wide, a scowl on her face. But the moment she saw me, her scowl turned into a smile. "Cas!" she said, far too loudly, as she ran to hug me.

"Shh!"

She covered her mouth, then whispered, "Why did you shush me? And how did you find me? And why didn't you come in through the door like a normal person?"

"We have to go," I said. "Now."

Her brow crinkled in that same suspicious expression she'd had since she was a small child. "Kael is downstairs, trying to get us horses. We should go talk to him."

"*No,*" I said quietly, with as much gravitas as I could manage. "I can't explain right now. You have to trust me. Let's go."

"Through the window?" she said, still thoroughly confused.

A crashing sound came from downstairs.

"Oh my! Pardon me, sir!" Jask said loudly, her voice carrying up from the inn's main room.

"Watch where you're going," Kael's voice shot back.

"Now!" I said, holding out my hand.

Elena sheathed her sword, grabbed her pack, and followed me out the window.

We scampered along the stable roof, keeping low to avoid prying eyes. But as we did, a "Psst!" came from below.

I peeked over the edge to see Darion sitting astride a beautiful brown-and-black horse with a silver mane. In his hand was the bridle of a second horse, a bit smaller, mostly white with black spots and a black mane.

"You stole horses?" I asked.

"I left gold," Darion said. "You said I could travel with you as far as Grey Spit. If you don't want me along anymore, you can take one horse, and I'll take the other."

At that very moment, Jask was shoved out the front door of the inn. "Go down to the docks, you drunk fool!" a man shouted from inside. Jask staggered back, apparently playing the part of a drunk sailor. Then she turned and saw Darion on the horses and Elena and me on the roof just above them. It took her all of two seconds to size up the situation.

"Let's go!" she said, racing to the horses. "Kael will probably find out she's missing soon."

Darion sent me a questioning look.

"We stay together for now," I told him.

We climbed down from the roof, and Jask swung up onto the back of Darion's horse. I mounted the other horse with Elena riding behind me. But the moment we started to gallop away, a shout came from behind. I turned to see Kael racing out of the tavern. "Stop!"

When it was clear we weren't heeding him, he started to shimmer, and ozone and citrus hit me like a wave. Then he blinked out of view.

"Kael has Chronothene," I said urgently to Darion.

Before Darion could react, Kael appeared just ahead of us, holding out his hand. "I said stop!"

"Your call, Cas," Darion said.

"I don't trust him," I replied, and Darion nodded.

Suddenly Jask was on the horse alone. The ozone-and-citrus smell hit me harder than ever before. I realized that Darion had shared his Chronothene with me. But something about two Chronothenes joining together made the whole experience extremely disjointed. I was vaguely aware that Kael and Darion were having an all-out brawl with punching, kicking, and tackling. Darion looked almost solid, but Kael was just a shadow.

I wanted to get off the horse and help, but the clashing Chronothenes prevented me from moving. But I could still see bits of what looked like a brutal fight. Darion kicked Kael, who doubled over. Then he delivered a final hard blow, and Kael crumpled to the ground.

Time came rushing back like a torrent.

Kael lay unconscious on the ground in front of us, face bloodied and bruised, clothes torn and dirty.

Darion stood before me in almost equally bad shape, a cut across his eyelid and his clothes a mess.

Then Darion fell to the ground.

Chapter Forty

The Road North

I WAS ALREADY MOVING before I consciously decided to do so, hopping off the horse and running to Darion's side. Elena was right behind me.

He lay on the ground and looked up at me, eyes half lidded, awake but not fully there. At least he was conscious. He made an effort to stand, then fell hard on his rump.

"Hold up," I said, grabbing his shoulder.

Jask had run over to check on Kael. "He's breathing steadily, but he's out cold. That must have been one hell of a fight that I didn't even see."

Horns blared from far away, but not nearly far enough. The Royal Guard was on alert. The massive amount of Ember Darion and Kael had used must have been like a blinding beacon for any Sentinels in the area.

"We have to go!" Darion pleaded, finally able to speak.

Working together, we managed to get Darion onto my horse behind me. Jask hastily tied a rope around our waists. I wasn't entirely confident that if Darion lost consciousness and fell over, he wouldn't take me down along with him. But we made do with what we had.

As we galloped away, a few townsfolk gathered around Kael. It was a gamble leaving him, but we couldn't take him with us, and with the Royal Guard closing in, we couldn't risk staying around.

I watched for pursuers as we left the town, but as far as I could tell, no Sentinels or members of the Royal Guard had spotted our hasty getaway. Just a bit north of town, Jask guided us off the main road and onto a less-traveled trail with better tree cover. She explained that this was the remnant of an ancient road from a long-gone civilization. I could make out the occasional stone border wall amidst the overgrown grass. A worn marker sat by the side of the road, its carvings long eroded.

After a long while of hard riding, when it became clear no one was following us, we paused.

Elena spoke first. "Would somebody tell me what in all the hells is going on? What happened with Kael back there?"

"Kael's contact at Pyrehold betrayed me," I said. "And Garrick warned me there was a traitor in the Order. I fear he is a spy."

Darion had regained his wits enough to speak somewhat coherently. "And given what just happened—the way he tried to stop us, and the way he attacked me—it seems we might have confirmed it."

Elena scrunched up her face. "But he was so nice. I trusted him."

"How did you end up on the road alone with him?" I asked Elena, "And why the East Road?"

"Oh, that was probably my doing," Elena said. "When everybody started evacuating the Order, only Kael remembered me. He helped me escape. I told him that you and I had agreed to meet at our old farm, so he was helping me get there."

That was the only plausible explanation I could think of that *didn't* implicate Kael. If it had been his idea to take the East Road, it would have been very suspicious. I'd almost hoped he had so the issue would be settled, but instead I now had a seed of doubt in my mind.

On the other hand, Kael had attacked Darion, so maybe there was little left to discuss.

"You didn't tell Kael exactly where the farm was, did you?" I asked Elena. "Or mention anything else specific, like the wishing well?"

"No, just that our farm was near Meadowrun," she said. "That's it."

I breathed a sigh of relief. But even still, I feared the area might be swarming with Royal Guards if Kael had fed them that information.

Zephyra, who had been circling overhead, dove down and landed on my shoulder, and I let my Ember flow.

Little Cas, the people place is swarming with Royal Guards, but none have followed us.

"That's good news," I said, then turned to the others. "Zephyra thinks we aren't being followed."

"Thank dust," Darion said.

But Zephyra must say something important.

"What is it, Zephyra?" I asked. She normally just got straight to the point, so the statement got my attention.

Zephyra stayed to help little Cas get Elena.

"Yes, and I appreciate that. You've been a great help."

But Zephyra must go now.

"I'm sorry to hear that," I said, stroking her head. "Is everything okay?"

Everything is very *okay. Zephyra is with egg and must nest for many sunrises.*

"Oh. Ohhh! That's *great* news," I said. I envisioned several little Zephyras and couldn't hold back my smile, though it was bittersweet. "She's having chicks," I said for the benefit of the others. Everyone cheered, and she even let the others gather around and pet her, which she had never done before.

"Zephyra, I can't tell you how very much you've helped. I'm forever in your debt for helping me get Elena back."

Remember, little Cas helped Zephyra escape that nasty cage.

"I remember," I said, choking up a little bit at the memory. "I'll miss you."

Zephyra will miss little Cas, too.

With that, she took to the sky and flapped away, heading north. Apparently she wasn't one for long goodbyes. I truly would miss her and hoped I'd see her again soon, perhaps with little birds in tow.

Since Zephyra had assured us that we weren't being followed, we decided to pause for a while. Darion was wrecked after using his Ember for so long, and most of us hadn't had any rest since we'd left the *Wind Runner* many hours ago. We found a well-shaded grove of trees with a stream running through it, and we let the horses drink their fill. They happily grazed on the grass that grew along the bank. I tended to Darion as Jask and Elena scouted the immediate area.

"Ouch!" Darion cried as I dabbed a cold wet cloth on the cut over his eye. It had already started swelling.

"Hold still," I said as Darion squirmed under my *very* gentle cleaning.

It wouldn't be long before Darion's intensive use of his Ember caught up with him, so I only had a bit of time to question him before he was lost to exhaustion.

"What exactly happened with Kael back there?" I asked.

"You saw most of it. He tried to stop us. I didn't let him."

"Do you know *why* he tried to stop us?"

"There was no time to ask."

"I wish we could have talked to him so we could understand why he did what he did."

"He wasn't in a talking mood," Darion said flatly.

"I didn't know he had Chronothene."

Darion nodded. "He and I are among the very few who have it and don't live in the clock tower."

Something wasn't sitting right with me. It didn't seem like Kael had been holding Elena captive. He'd taken the East Road at her request. I *really* wish we could have talked to him. But ultimately, he'd tried to stop us and had attacked Darion, so that was about as definitive as it got.

While we waited for Jask and Elena to return from their scouting trip, I asked Darion to show me how to do the sparrow call he had used back in Grey Spit to attract Jask's attention. It seemed like an excellent tool to add to my skill set.

"The first trick is cupping your hands right," he said as he showed me with his own hands. From there, he showed me the proper blowing technique and how to mimic the pitch and fluttering. Before long, I was singing just like another sparrow.

"It's really not fair how quickly you pick things up," Darion said with a smile.

"I have a good teacher," I said.

Darion taught me a few other calls he had developed to convey basic information to people who knew the code. I learned the signals for danger, safe, fan out, and other tactical maneuvers.

For a moment, as we talked, things felt back to normal. I longed for that feeling to continue, but reflexive mistrust hung over me like a storm cloud.

Soon Jask and Elena returned from their scouting with little to report—there was no sign of anyone as far as they could see. So we all took a well-deserved rest, acting as lookout in shifts, except for Darion, who was sleeping like the dead due to his Ember hangover.

When it was my watch, Elena walked over and sat next to me.

"Thank you for rescuing me, brother," she said as she leaned her head on my shoulder.

"You're the most important thing in the world to me," I replied.

"And you are to me," she said back.

I put my arm around her.

"Can I ask a personal question?" she said.

"Of course."

"What's wrong with you and Darion? You're both acting strange."

This girl was wise beyond her years. In the rush of things, there was so much I hadn't explained. So I told her the entire story of what had happened at Pyrehold, including about Darion and Orlik. She deserved to know.

After I finished, Elena was quiet for a bit. Finally she spoke. "That's...a lot. I'm not sure how to feel."

"Yeah," I said.

"But back at Pyrehold, he didn't give you up. And today he saved us both. That matters."

"It does."

"And I feel like he's the same person he was before. I'm not scared of him," she said.

I nodded, glad to hear that. I wasn't scared of him in the traditional sense, but I *was* scared of what would happen if I let him in again and he betrayed that trust.

By the time we'd all had a good rest, it was midafternoon. Jask stood up. "Well, it's probably time for me to head back. Don't want to get Rook too upset."

I was secretly a bit disappointed. Jask had been invaluable, and I had hoped she might consider staying with us for longer, but I understood that she had her own responsibilities.

"Of course, and thank you," I said. "I'm indebted to you for your help. You can take one of the horses back. We'll make do."

"No need," Jask said. "It's just a couple of hours' walk back to Grey Spit. I should make it before nightfall. Besides, I'd rather not show back up in town on a 'borrowed' horse."

"Hey, I *paid* for these," Darion said with feigned offense.

Jask gave Darion a dubious look.

"And Cas, you're not indebted to me," Jask said. "You paid us for the job. It's cleaner that way. Sometimes jobs just get a little more complicated than you expect. Nature of the business."

"Fair enough," I said. "But I'm grateful nonetheless."

Her response was a tight nod. "If you still plan to head north, this trail continues for the next twenty miles and will keep you away from the main road. Then you'll come to Bitterridge Keep. It's abandoned, isolated, and has a commanding view. It's a good place to camp."

"Where do we go from there?" I asked.

"You can take a trail east, back to the main north-south road. Or, if you're willing to take the risk, this trail continues north through the mountains. It's less traveled, but it's treacherous. Many parts of the path are in disrepair. You'll have to cross Titan's Span, an ancient stone bridge over a chasm. It was standing the last time I was here years ago, but no guarantees."

"Thank you, Jask," I said.

We said our final goodbyes, and Jask strode off down the trail.

"I *like* her," Elena said after Jask was out of sight.

Darion and I shared a glance and a laugh.

"So do we," I said.

"Well, what next?" Elena said.

"Meadowrun is north," I said. "I'd like to go to our old family farm, see what there is to see."

"We still have two horses, so we can go our separate ways if you want," Darion said. "But I'll be going north to get to the Order of Emberlight rendezvous point anyway."

I considered it. Darion stood next to Elena, and for a moment, it was like all the other times the three of us had spent together, when we'd felt like a family. How I longed to get back to that. Only time would tell if it was possible.

"For now, we'll ride north together," I said.

Chapter Forty-One

Bitterridge Keep

We rode single file, with Elena and me up front on the large brown-and-black horse and Darion on the white one with black spots. Elena had named our horse Buttercup, and Darion's she called Snowflake. We kept the pace at a fast trot. It was better to save the horses' energy in case we needed them to run on short notice. The path was sometimes clear and wide and at other times no more than an indentation in the grass. It meandered up and down small hills, through grasslands and patches of trees.

The shadows were long by the time we saw Bitterridge Keep, its stone tower rising above the surrounding trees. As Jask had mentioned, it was long abandoned, likely a relic of the age when Velmorra's north and south regions were two separate kingdoms that were often at war with each other. Despite that, it was in surprisingly good shape, owing to its solid stone construction. Only a few rotted wooden beams and the occasional missing stone indicated that it was a ruin.

We hitched our horses in a small room on the lower level with a fireplace and a few patches of straw that must have served as beds for the occasional traveler. After we tended to the horses, whom Elena had grown quite fond of, we set off to explore the keep.

A staircase rose five stories along the inside walls of the main tower, ending at a lookout with far-reaching views of the surrounding landscape. Rolling tree-covered hills stretched out in all directions. The low sun just peeked over the hills to the west. The faint line of the north-south road made its way through the forests far to the east. We had traveled far enough that the Jagged Coast was no longer visible to the south.

"I hope Jask made it to town and didn't get stopped," Elena said.

I put my arm around her. "If anyone could make it safely, I think it would be her."

She smiled. "You're probably right."

Darion scanned the eastern horizon. "I don't think we should risk making a fire. We're close enough to the main road for the smoke to be seen. It was warm today, and we're far enough from the icy winds of the coast."

He sounded like himself again—always planning, always vigilant. Like the man I'd trusted before things fell apart.

"I guess that's *one* upside to sleeping with the horses," I said with a laugh. "They'll keep us warm."

Elena smiled. "I think that's the first time I've heard you laugh since you rescued me. It's nice."

Darion glanced over and smiled, too.

We all looked to the north, where the mountains rose before us. Beyond that, the land turned to broad plains. That was where our old home was, and a thousand memories with it.

"Tomorrow we head to the farm?" Elena asked, her mood turning pensive.

"That's right," I said. "And maybe we'll find some answers."

As the sun tucked below the horizon and the sky lit up with golds, oranges, and reds, we shared a cold meal. No fire meant no light and no warmth, and since we wanted an early start the next day, we decided to turn in as soon as the daylight disappeared. We all slept in the main room with the horses, making ourselves as comfortable as we could on the straw.

I woke in the middle of the night, a bit chilled. The place where Darion had slept was just an indentation in the straw. The slightest bit of panic tickled my senses, but the spot was still slightly warm from his body heat, so he couldn't be far.

I searched the lower level of the keep for him and found nothing. But thanks to the stillness and quiet of the night, I could make out a faint shuffling of feet far above. I climbed the stairs of the tower, the moonlight just bright enough to guide me.

At the top, Darion leaned against the railing, looking out to the east. His face was angelic in the starlight. As much as I didn't want to feel anything, seeing him like that filled me with warmth.

He saw me approach and smiled. "Sorry if I woke you."

I waved off his concern. "What are you looking at?" I asked.

"See those little flickers of light?" Darion said, pointing eastward.

Sure enough, little orange spots dotted the forest far in the distance. "Campfires?"

Darion nodded. "Along the north-south road. Seems like a sizable group is headed north."

I let my Ember flow the slightest bit. A very faint thrumming was right at the edge of my perception. "Sentinels," I said with a sigh. "I can feel them."

"I don't think we should risk taking that road," Darion said.

"I agree. I guess that leaves the mountain pass."

Darion nodded. "Departing at first light would be best. Hopefully you can make it to your farm by nightfall, and then I can head west to the Order rendezvous point."

"You should take the Emberbane," I said, taking the vial out of my belt. "The Order will need it."

"I'll feel safer if it's with you and Elena. It's already saved you twice," Darion said.

I nodded and put the vial back in my belt, noting that he'd chosen our safety over the Order.

We stood quietly under the moonlight. I looked over at Darion's pensive face, ever thinking, ever planning.

"I have to be honest," I said. "I'm surprised you're willing to go to the farm with us instead of going directly to the rendezvous point."

Darion faced me and looked deep into my eyes. "Maybe I haven't made myself clear. I'd do anything for you and your sister. Anything for *you*, Cas."

I had to look away. The urge to forgive him and run into his arms was nearly overwhelming, but that deeply planted seed of doubt still held me back, gnawing at me like a wild beast.

"I want to believe you," I said. "I *really* do. But I can't get that night at Pyrehold out of my mind. I simply don't understand how you could *ever* treat that monster as family. Even if it was for the greater good."

Darion drew in a long breath, then said quietly, "He murdered my mother."

I stared at him, dumbfounded, speechless, the simple awful truth landing hard.

"When I was young, I never knew who my mother was," he said, still soft and fragile. "I was just a bastard son, sheltered in Orlik's country estate and looked down on by everyone. When I was thirteen, my Embers started to show. I finally did some digging. This was a pattern for Orlik—spread his seed, then clean up the evidence."

His eyes were glossy as he looked to the horizon. "I've had to live with that my whole life. And that night before Pyrehold, when you told me that Orlik killed your mother, it nearly broke me. I wanted to tell you so badly, but I couldn't risk it. Not when our lives were at stake."

The realization hit me fast and fierce. I had said I couldn't understand how Darion could live a double life. But that was no longer true. I understood *exactly* what that kind of trauma could make you do. It was what I had done my whole life.

I had been a fool, blinded by my own rage, unable to see that the man I cared for had the exact same trauma as me. We had simply dealt with it differently. And yet, we ended up in the same spot, together—scarred by the same man.

"Darion," I said, choking back tears. "I'm so sorry."

He looked my way, the pain in his face clear to see. "I'm sorry too," he said.

We came together and held on tight, letting our emotions spill out in the quiet, knowing no one else in this world could ever understand this pain the way we did.

Chapter Forty-Two

Titan's Span

We woke early, hoping to make it over the mountains in a single day. After a quick breakfast and tending to the horses, we set off. The trail rose steadily and twisted into a mountain pass with peaks rising high on either side of us.

The ancient road may have been wide long ago, but disrepair and erosion had narrowed it and made it so rocky in spots that we had to dismount and lead the horses on foot. At points, the trail even cut into the mountainside, and soon we were walking along the edge of a steep slope. The cost of a misstep would be a long tumble down a rocky incline and a broken ankle at the very least.

But possibly the most disturbing thing was how exposed we were on the edge of the mountain. Gone were the trees that had provided cover. Any prying eyes in the area would plainly see us moving along the trail. My thieving instincts hummed with unease.

Although it still felt foreign to me, I had gotten better at suppressing my Ember, and so I'd begun to do it all the time, checking for null fields only every so often. Thus far, I'd felt nothing.

After several hours of steady incline, the trail began to level out. We had reached the top of a mountain pass.

"What's that?" Elena asked, one hand shading her eyes from the sun and the other pointing ahead, where two stone spires rose in the distance.

"That looks like Titan's Span, the bridge Jask told us about," I said. "Let's hope it's in good enough shape to cross, or we'll have to turn back." It was still a ways off, but from here it looked solid.

"Only one way to find out," Darion said.

"Hey, I think there might be somebody following us," Elena said, looking back at the trail.

Sure enough, far down the trail, several dozen figures were heading toward us at great speed. When I let my Ember flow the tiniest bit, I was nearly bowled over by the intense thrumming of the Sentinels' null field. A shot of adrenaline coursed through my veins like fire.

"Sentinels!"

"Dust! We've got to risk riding the horses," Darion said.

He mounted Snowflake, and Elena hopped up behind me on Buttercup. We spurred them into a gallop, heading for Titan's Span as fast as we dared, given the terrain. The path was rough. The horses danced around divots and rocks as we held on for our lives.

Suddenly the thrumming stopped. "Null field's down!" I shouted to Darion, which could mean only one thing: someone was about to use their Ember.

I turned to look at our pursuers. A golden shimmer surrounded one of them. Before my eyes, the figure transformed into a hideous beast.

It was Syra.

She had found us.

She raced along the trail on all fours, taking giant leaps, moving at a speed that rivaled our horses. Her legs were a blur, easily navigating the difficult terrain. If it weren't so horrific, it would have been an amazing sight to behold.

"Syra's here!" I shouted. "She's gaining on us."

Darion peeked back. "She can't keep that up for long," he shouted over the clomping of hooves. "We've just got to outrun her."

The bridge was approaching fast. It spanned a canyon nearly two hundred feet across and was nearly twenty feet wide. On each side stood a stone tower. The bridge itself was a giant arch that had miraculously survived for ages. The closer we got, the more precarious it looked, dotted with holes where stones had once been. It honestly looked like a strong wind could knock it down. With the sheer number of missing stones, there was no way we could ride the horses across it.

I pulled up on my bridle, bringing Buttercup to a halt at the south edge of the bridge, and Darion followed suit. We jumped off our horses and took our first steps onto Titan's Span with the utmost care. Holes peppered the ground, each easily large enough for a person to fall through. I snuck a peek through an opening and immediately wished I hadn't. The valley floor lay hundreds of feet below.

We had made it about a quarter of the way across when Syra reached the edge. I cursed the fact that I had used all my fire vials during our flight out of the cellars. Without pausing, she leapt into the air, flew over us, and landed right in front of us, blocking our path. The entire bridge rumbled from the force of her landing.

The horses bolted, racing to the south side of the bridge.

Darion and Elena drew their swords, and I pulled out my daggers, facing down this horrid beast. Even transformed, grotesque burn marks covered her body. Part of her cheek was missing, revealing her bared teeth. She roared, and hot, foul-smelling breath and spittle flew at us.

Darion shimmered and Elena stood at the ready. My heart dropped into my stomach as I watched the people I loved prepare to battle for our lives.

Darion extended his Chronothene to me. With time frozen around us, we charged toward Syra. Darion was half a step ahead of me with his sword pointed forward, ready for a killing thrust. He lunged, aiming straight for the beast's heart. But the moment his sword made contact, it shattered like glass. The shock of it hit Darion like a punch.

All at once, time sped up.

Darion smacked into the beast and bounced off of her, his sword destroyed. With a swipe of her arm, Syra struck Darion. He went flying toward the north side of the bridge.

My momentum carried me directly into Syra, my dagger bouncing off her hide like it was a toy. She struck me in the chest, knocking all the air out of my lungs and sending me flying. As I flew, I fought desperately for breath. Was this it? Was this how I died? I crashed hard on the bridge's stone surface near the north end, just a few feet from where Darion lay.

I gasped for air, but none came. I tried to rise. My body didn't respond. I had never felt so useless.

Elena shimmered. Even from here, I could smell the ozone and citrus. She charged toward the beast, brandishing her sword.

My brain screamed at me to move, to protect Elena, but all I could do was watch.

Elena's attack was the strongest. Her sword still rattled off Syra's hide, but the force of Elena smashing into the side sent the beast flying toward the edge of the bridge. Teetering off the side, Syra grasped at stones, finding purchase at the last moment. Elena charged again, but the beast was ready this time and smacked her like a rag doll, sending her flying away from us, toward the south side of the bridge. A beast and a chasm separated us.

Rage, terror, and heartbreak ripped through me like wildfire. The air came rushing back into my lungs in a single massive gasp. I forced myself to move because Elena's life depended on it. I jumped to my feet. The beast saw me and started charging.

But beyond Syra, near the south side, Elena was pounding on the bridge with her bare fists. Each blow sent a massive vibration through the structure. She was trying to collapse the structure. But I realized with horror that she was still too far from the southern tower—too far for her to get to safety if the bridge fell.

Syra turned toward Elena, let out a terrifying howl, and started running toward her.

Elena struck the bridge again, and the entire structure began to crumble. She was sacrificing herself for us. She wasn't allowed to do that. That was my job. I had made a vow.

"Elena! No!" I cried.

"Run!" she yelled.

I could feel the stones rumbling beneath my feet. Some were falling away into the abyss.

Darion got to his feet next to me. He could barely stand. He quickly glanced at Elena, then at me. He didn't look afraid. He looked resolved. He mouthed *goodbye* to me as a golden light shimmered around him, then disappeared.

An instant later, he and Elena appeared on solid ground past the south edge of the bridge. Darion crumpled to the ground in a heap. He had pulled Elena off the bridge in the blink of an eye. He had saved her life.

The entire bridge shifted downward, so I turned to run. The north side was impossibly far away. I sprinted as fast as I could. As the stones began to fall, I made one final leap.

I reached out.

The bridge crumbled beneath me.

I hit the side of the cliff, desperately grabbing for any handhold. I slid a long way before my arms wrapped around a tangled root that had been unearthed as the stones around it crumbled. I turned my head to see the entire structure falling into the chasm. After standing for ages, Titan's Span was no more.

Tumbling downward amid the rubble was the woman-beast Syra, her howl muffled by the awesome, terrible sound of the collapse. She bellowed the entire way down, and then her cries stopped abruptly as she hit the jagged rocks hundreds of feet below, huge stones and debris falling on top of her.

For a fleeting moment, the world was deathly silent.

I clung to the side of the cliff, breathing hard, trying to gather my wits.

"Cas?" Elena's voice called out, echoing off the cliffs. "Cas!"

"I'm here!" I yelled back. I twisted around to see her standing on the southern cliff above what used to be the start of the bridge.

"Cas, thank all the gods!" Elena cried out joyfully. "I didn't know if you'd made it. Can you climb up?"

I looked upward. The edge was only about thirty feet away. There were plenty of handholds above me, though I didn't know if they were stable. "I think so." I paused, desperately afraid to ask the next question. But I had to know. "Is Darion okay?"

"I can't wake him up."

Deep breath. Try not to panic, Cas.

"Keep trying," I called out to Elena. "I'm going to try to climb."

"I will."

Slowly, gingerly, I tested each foothold and handhold. Some were stable. Many were not. I had multiple false starts on my way up. I had finally just found a viable path when I was hit quite suddenly with the full force of the thrumming.

"Elena!" I cried. "The null field is back! Watch out for the Sentinels."

Chanting rose from somewhere above me, cold and inhuman. The sound of boots on stone echoed through the valley. My heart stopped. The Sentinels were already here.

Elena screamed—a sound from my nightmares. I twisted my head but could see nothing. And then she went quiet. I could barely contain my terror as I raced to the top of the cliff, scarcely caring if a handhold or foothold gave way. I reached the top at the northern edge of the chasm. Jagged stones poked out where the bridge used to be.

I peered toward the south edge.

Elena and Darion were gone.

Chapter Forty-Three

The Chase

I fell to my knees at the edge of what remained of Titan's Span. My worst nightmare had come true. The people I cared for most had been captured or worse, and I was powerless to stop it. The pain in my chest was a real, physical thing.

But I had to keep going. I had to *try*.

I ran to what remained of the north tower and scaled the structure. Stones shifted as I climbed, but I ignored the danger. At the top, I peered south. Not far down the path, a group of Sentinels marched. In the middle, Darion and Elena rode on horseback, tied up and bound to their horses.

They were alive.

I let out a shout of relief. Now I had something to cling to. One small thread to hold me together.

The chasm was deep, but at least it was climbable. Jagged rocks and long seams in the cliff face made it a tough but not impossible feat. So I started my descent.

Getting down was quick—sometimes too quick. In my haste, I missed a handhold and scrambled to grab a lifesaving seam in the rock. My fingers shifted but held.

Dust, Cas. You can't help them if you're dead.

I paused, took a deep breath, and continued at a pace that was fast but not careless.

Soon I was at the base of the canyon between the two mountains. Rubble from the bridge covered the bottom. Not far away, rocks shifted. Something stirred beneath the debris. Was it possible? Had Syra somehow survived that fall? I couldn't leave anything to chance.

I pulled out my dagger and approached the spot where I had heard the noise. As I approached, the last thing I expected to hear reached my ears: the quiet sound of weeping.

I moved aside a few of the smaller boulders near the source of the noise. There, under a mountain of rubble, Syra's miserable face poked through, her tears forming dark lines through the stone dust and grime on her cheeks.

"I'm—sorry," she said, stuttering out the words.

I was speechless. Frozen from utter shock.

And then a hot rage built in me.

"Sorry?" I said. "*That's* what you have to say?"

She spoke slowly, in fits and starts. "I had...had to...watch. It was horrible." She let out a wretched sound, half groan, half sob. "It...it controlled me. But it's gone. I...felt it leave."

And then I understood. She was an Emberborn slave like all the rest. But the draining of her life force must have freed her. I had this slim window of opportunity.

"Where are the Sentinels taking them?" I said. "Please!"

She puffed out rapid breaths between bared teeth, but her eyes were clear and lucid. "Find Elandra...potion merchant...hurry!"

"Elandra? Where do I find her?"

Her eyes rolled back into her skull. Then she spoke, the words clearer than anything she had said before: "The moon dances with the stars."

She started convulsing as foam escaped her mouth. After one final shudder, her body stilled, and her eyes stared up at me, blank and lifeless.

Despite all the harm she had done, I couldn't help but feel sorrow for this pitiful soul.

The moon dances with the stars? What could she have meant by that? Or was it just the ravings of a mind on the brink of death?

And what was I supposed to do with the single name Elandra? There had to be hundreds of potion merchants across Velmorra. I knew dozens in Analon alone, and as far as I knew, none were named Elandra. Still, it was more information than I'd had before, and it gave me the slightest glimmer of hope.

Climbing up the south cliff was significantly harder than going down the north one. In addition to being more sheer, many of the sections of the cliff were unstable due to the collapse. My arms and legs burned. Halfway up, I found a stable spot to pause and rest my muscles.

It was the first moment since the start of the attack that my mind wasn't completely consumed with survival. The void quickly filled with thoughts of all the things I could have done differently. It was my job to protect Elena, but she had protected me. And Darion had saved her.

He had chosen Elena over himself.

Over me.

And the truth was, I would have done the same.

But that didn't make it hurt less.

I began to sob. I had failed the people I cared for.

Get yourself together, Cas! Those people you care for are still alive and nearby but getting farther away by the minute!

So I buried my hurt deep and continued my ascent.

At the top, I scanned the area. Hundreds of footprints and hoofprints marked the dirt as well as long drag marks—clear signs of a struggle. With the null field up, Elena couldn't have used her Ember. I was certain she had still put up a fight, but she would have been hopelessly outmatched. I ached at the thought of her fighting for her life. Her life and Darion's.

Now it was my job to save them. I raced down the road as fast as my feet would carry me.

I ran for hours, stopping only to drink water from streams or to rest my aching feet for a moment. Only when the trail left the mountains did I catch my first glimpse of the Sentinels far in the distance. A new wave of energy flowed through my weary muscles now that I knew I was on the right path and making progress.

By the time the sun neared the horizon, I was close enough that I had to slow my pace to keep from being detected. I counted twenty-seven guards in total: eight Sentinels, eighteen Sentinel soldiers, and one commander. But most importantly, I could see Elena and Darion. I couldn't tell much about their state from this distance, but at least they appeared to be conscious.

I let my Ember flow the slightest bit and immediately felt the null field slam into me. It made sense that the Sentinels would suppress Elena and Darion's abilities, but it also meant that I needed to be careful not to be detected. I still felt clumsy and forgetful when I suppressed my Ember, but I was at least getting more used to it and better at controlling the flow such that I had just the amount I needed.

With the last light of day dimming, Bitterridge Keep formed a dark silhouette against the glowing sky. It was hard to believe that just this morning, Elena, Darion, and I had left here full of optimism. My heart ached at how much had changed.

I was relieved to see the group slow as they approached the keep. It appeared they were stopping for a rest. I climbed a tree that provided a good view of the area. The soldiers carried Elena and Darion off the horses and into the keep as Sentinels stood guard. A jolt of anger and panic hit me the moment they touched the people I cared for. I burned to run right up to them, brandishing my knives. But that would only get all of us killed.

Through the night, I observed their patterns. Two-thirds of the troops rested while one-third kept watch. Even if I let the full force of my Ember flow, nine guards against one was suicidal.

Deep in the night, I snuck up as close to the keep as I dared. I stood on the edge of their firelight. A typical company of soldiers would be quietly talking, drinking, or playing dice. These simply stood at attention, unmoving, utterly quiet. A twig snapped to the left of me, and all the Sentinels turned their heads in perfect unison in a deeply inhuman way. Just looking at them sent chills running through me.

I remembered Syra's dying moments, how she'd finally been freed from the prison in her mind. I hoped that beneath those steely facades, the real Emberborn still existed and that somehow we could figure out how to free them. Until then, every life I took was the life of a captive held against their will.

At the first signs of dawn, the camp stirred. The Sentinels were on the move again. I shook out my weary muscles and continued pursuing them. The company headed directly east through the forest, presumably to the main north-south road.

The one piece of good news was that Elena and Darion appeared more alert than they had yesterday. They looked from side to side and reacted to the bumps in the trail rather than simply being bounced around. The enormous amount of Ember they'd used during our battle with Syra must have drained them, and a full night of rest had likely done them good.

It was a particularly cruel torture to be so close but completely unable to do anything to help them. My best course of action was simply to continue following them, stay alert, and look for opportunities to act.

One goal I had was to somehow alert Elena or Darion that I was here. If I could get their attention, it might give them hope to know that help wasn't far behind. If they found a chance to escape, they'd know I was there to assist them. But so far, their captors had kept them well guarded. Any attempt to get their attention risked exposing me to the Sentinels. So I continued, watching and waiting.

Within a few hours of leaving Bitterridge Keep, the main north-south road came into view. That presented its own set of problems. On the main road, there'd be fewer places to hide. There'd also be more traffic, increasing the chance of being detected. So before we got there, I decided to take a risk.

Giving the Sentinels a very wide berth, I increased my pace and circled around the group I was following. Once I was sufficiently ahead of them, I climbed a tree that was a stone's throw from the trail, with good coverage for stealth but also a clear view. I could easily hide behind the trunk if I was worried about being detected.

Tucked in my tree, I quietly practiced the sparrow call Darion had taught me. It wasn't perfect, but it would have to be good enough.

Soon I could make out the group heading down the trail in my direction. When they were sufficiently close, I started chirping the tactical signal for "shift left," hoping he'd turn his head and see me. But no such luck. Darion kept facing forward, unaware of my signal. Perhaps I had emulated the bird *too* well. I continued the signal until the group was almost beside me, when it got too risky.

I punched the bark. I had hoped so much that he would see me, that I could give him a sliver of hope.

The company was just passing when Darion dug his heels into Buttercup and leaned hard to the left. The horse bolted so suddenly that the Sentinel soldier holding the bridle lost their grip.

He *had* heard me.

Buttercup charged through the woods in roughly my direction. In the blink of an eye, I was down the tree, shifting my position in the undergrowth so I'd be directly in front of the horse, all while trying to remain invisible. I wasn't sure what I'd do when Darion got to me, but I trusted that he had a plan. I only hoped I'd figure it out in time.

Buttercup was moving fast, but the Sentinel soldiers were in hot pursuit. They were close enough that they would immediately see me if I jumped up from my hiding spot.

Buttercup was upon me, and I still didn't have a plan that wouldn't get me caught. But as she passed, Darion whisper-shouted, "Thornfell," then leaned toward the horse's left again, sending her turning through the forest away from me. The Sentinels in pursuit cut the corner to intercept them, no longer headed in my direction.

From my hiding spot, I watched as the Sentinel soldiers finally caught up to Darion. One of them punched him in the gut. He doubled over and let out a cry. I could almost feel his pain. I gritted my teeth to keep from crying out myself.

Every instinct screamed at me to help him, but if I did, his sacrifice would be for nothing. He hadn't hesitated to risk his life for me.

Soon the Sentinels formed up again and continued east down the path to the north-south road.

Although I'd come up well short of rescue, I'd accomplished two major goals. Darion now knew I had survived and was in pursuit, and more importantly, I knew their destination—the king's private citadel, Thornfell Keep.

Chapter Forty-Four

Thornfell

I kept up as best I could.

But soon the company reached the main road and turned south. There, the sparse trees and flat landscape meant that I had to trail far behind. To make matters worse, anytime a traveler approached from either direction, I had to duck behind a rock or a bush or whatever other cover I could find. I was a wanted man and couldn't risk being noticed.

Soon, however, that became a moot point. A group on horseback intercepted the Sentinels from the south, including a prison wagon similar to the one we had ridden into Pyrehold. My heart ached as Darion and Elena were shoved mercilessly into the back; all I could do was look on, powerless. Then the entire caravan disappeared into the distance.

The good news was that I knew their destination. The bad news was that their destination was Thornfell Keep. Perched on an island and surrounded on all four sides by steep, jagged cliffs, it was unreachable except via a single stone bridge connecting it to the mainland. There was no other way to get in or out unless you managed to sprout wings.

I was struggling to formulate a plan. Ever since I'd begun holding back my Ember, my mind had felt muddy, less sharp. The effect had happened slowly, so I'd barely noticed the cumulative impact. But the time for caution was over, so I let my Ember flow. The effect was immediate. The haze around my brain lifted, and memories and visual details snapped back into place like missing cogs in a finely tuned machine. It was a terrible thing to have to hold back who you were for fear of being caught. How long had Darion lived like that?

First I had to figure out how to catch up with the caravan that held Darion and Elena. I dug into my memories of the maps of Velmorra I had studied in the Order of Emberlight library. The wagon could travel only on main roads, so the caravan would go south to Grey Spit before turning east to Thornfell Keep.

But I could cut the corner.

A path went directly through rough terrain and forest, unsuitable for large caravans and wheeled vehicles. But for a lone determined man on a mission? If I ran hard enough, I might even arrive before them. In any case, I had to try.

With my Ember flowing and a strengthened sense of purpose, I raced into the woods. For the rest of the day and into the night, I rarely stopped. Only when I could no longer see the path and my feet burned like fire did I pause.

Huddled into the hollow of a tree, covered by my cloak, I drifted into a restless sleep, haunted by nightmares of Darion and Elena tied up on racks, lifeless, with tubes of amber liquid flowing into them.

I woke up with a start. The first hints of dawn filtered through the trees, and the morning birds were singing. I had slept longer than I'd intended. Every muscle and bone in my body ached, but the rest had replenished my energy, so I continued down the path.

It was midday when the trees started thinning and the first whiffs of briny sea air hit my nose. Soon the caws of seagulls signaled that my destination was approaching. I had spent my entire trip pondering my options, but I still wasn't sure what I'd do when I arrived. If I beat the caravan, was there any chance I could infiltrate it? If so, I didn't know how.

As I approached enemy territory, I stifled my Ember. The effects were even worse this time, leaving me feeling hollowed out.

Soon the high spire of Thornfell Keep rose above the trees and the last of the forest gave way to grassy seaside cliffs. Before me was the small hamlet of Thornfell, a town that existed solely to accommodate the many servants, craftsmen, and alchemists required to operate Thornfell Keep.

Leading up to the town, the main east-west road extended for miles. Had I beaten the caravan? If they had stopped for a full night's rest, then it was possible. I considered finding a perch and waiting, but if they had beaten me, I'd simply be wasting time.

The town's namesake loomed in the distance, massive, opulent, and grotesque. Its high spires defied nature as they rose from the sea, the foundations of the citadel built right into the sheer cliffs pounded by the relentless surf. Even from here, I could feel the faint thrumming of the null field. But something about it felt worse than normal. Sharper. More wicked. For a heartbeat, my courage faltered. How was I supposed to break into *that*?

I needed some intel. I needed a plan. Not to mention that I could use a real meal and fresh supplies. But I would have to be careful; the town was likely crawling with spies and sympathizers loyal to the Crown. I drew my cloak around me and covered my head with my hood.

The main road into town had a guard station. Rather than test my luck right from the start, I let my Ember flow the slightest bit, scaled the perimeter wall, and slipped into a side alley. The null field was strong and seemed to envelop the entire town, so I quickly muted my Ember.

Despite it being midday, the town felt deserted and unnaturally quiet. Only the soft moaning of the wind through the barren streets broke the silence. I would normally expect to see merchants and people traveling to their destinations. But all the homes and businesses were shut up tight, and only a few lonely souls hurried along the cobblestone road.

The good news was that no one was friendly enough to make eye contact, and I mostly went unnoticed. When the occasional Royal Guard passed by, I ducked into the shadows or hid behind stacked barrels or crates.

Ahead of me was a two-story building with rows of windows. A wooden sign with a picture of a pint of ale hung outside. Perhaps I could get a hot meal and some local gossip. But as I approached, a group of Royal Guard entered, bantering and laughing, likely on the way to their midday meal.

Looked like I'd have to go elsewhere.

As I continued along the street past the inn, something caught my eye down a side alley. The image of a mortar and pestle next to a vial was painted on a wooden sign hanging outside a humble-looking shop.

Syra's words replayed in my mind: *Find Elandra...potion merchant.*

It *couldn't* be that easy. Or could it?

After all, Syra knew where the Sentinels intended to bring us. Could pointing me in the correct direction have been her final act of defiance against those who had enslaved her?

Either way, I desperately needed some new supplies, so I decided to take the risk.

As I pushed through the door, the chime of a bell rang out. The inside of the shop was cramped and dim with a tiny window providing the only light. A wooden counter dominated the room, leaving scarcely enough room to stand. An elderly woman sat at a table with her back to me, her finger running over the words of an open book. She made no effort to acknowledge me.

I stood patiently until the woman licked her finger and turned the page. Only then did I clear my throat.

The woman spoke without looking up from her book. "You're not from Thornfell."

There was something oddly familiar about the voice.

"No, I'm traveling from Analon—"

I hadn't even finished my sentence before she resumed reading.

"I'm in need of—"

"You should try Grey Spit," the woman interrupted, closing her book and getting up. She headed for a door.

"Are you Elandra?" I asked.

The woman froze, her shoulders tensing.

"There's no one here by that name," she said gruffly, then continued toward the door.

"Do you know a Syra?" I asked.

The woman froze again, clenching her fists, still not turning around. "Get out of my shop or I'll call the Royal Guard."

It was clear she knew more than she was telling me. This was my only lead, all I had left. If I couldn't get information here, Elena and Darion would likely be lost.

So I took a deep breath and said Syra's dying words: "The moon dances with the stars."

The woman's shoulders drooped. She spun around, her lips quivering. "Where d-did you hear that?" she stuttered.

The sudden recognition was like a slap to the face. I could scarcely believe it.

"Mrs. Crowe?"

Chapter Forty-Five

Thornfell Keep

"Cassian Nightbrook," she said. "I thought I told you never to seek me out again." Then she drew in a long breath. "The moon dances with the stars. Where—where did you hear that?" Her voice was shaky.

"Those were Syra's dying words."

"That's not possible," she said, her face full of anguish. "My Syra died long ago. There was nothing left of her."

"Just before she died, she was freed," I said. "I saw it myself. Her eyes cleared. She knew who she was. She knew *you*."

"It can't be," she said, looking near a breakdown.

I kept my voice as gentle as I could. "She sent me to you. She said she was sorry."

Mrs. Crowe collapsed on the ground, weeping. "My daughter was in there all along. I could have saved her."

Her *daughter*? I ran to her side and placed a gentle hand on her back as she heaved with sobs. I sat with her for a long while until she had cried herself out.

I felt the weight of her loss. It was something I was all too familiar with. I only hoped that in the end, she'd be able to turn the grief she felt into something other than despair.

I whispered, "You weren't able to save Syra, but she died free and at peace. And you might be able to save others."

She lifted her head, her face still streaked with tears. "What others?"

"People *I* care for. People who might end up like Syra did if I can't help them."

"I wish we could, but it's no use," she said. "The null field around the keep is so strong that any Emberborn trying to pass through the perimeter would collapse in pain and probably pass out."

"Is there no way to counter the null field?"

"There is a potion I could make to get us past the null field, but I'm missing one ingredient, and there's no way we could ever get any."

"You mean this?" I said, pulling out the Emberbane.

Her jaw dropped, and her eyes grew to the size of saucers. "How did you get that?"

"It's complicated."

"Do you realize you could incinerate this whole block if you so much as dropped that?"

"I am aware," I said emphatically. After all, I had almost died in an Emberbane fire twice now.

Mrs. Crowe's expression turned to one of steely resolve. "Let's make those bastards pay."

With the door locked and a pot of water on the fire for tea, Mrs. Crowe and I sat at the table in her back room.

"Syra was my daughter, and I loved her dearly," she told me. "Her father was Emberborn. He died trying to save her. But that bastard in the throne room stole her from us. He corrupted her. I always held out hope that she was still in there, and Tarnasau knew that and used it against me. He's held her life over my head for years, made me do things I'm not proud of."

"But now Syra is at peace at last," I said. "And you're free."

"Her life was the last thing holding me back, hoping I could somehow save her. That's the reason I came back here to our old shop, to see if I could find a way to reverse the corruption. But I failed. And now that she's free, the only thing I want is vengeance. What's your plan?"

I kept the details simple and didn't mention the Order of Emberlight, but I thought she inferred most of what I didn't say. I told her that I needed to rescue Elena and a man who was very special to me and that they would arrive by prison wagon with a company of Sentinels.

"I'm afraid they're already here," she said grimly. "A wagon came in this morning, just as you described. They went directly into the keep."

My heart sank. I couldn't get the image of alchemists experimenting on Elena and Darion out of my mind. But I took a deep breath and gritted my teeth. "Is there any way you can get me into the keep?"

"Yes, I think one of the king's top alchemists *might* be able to gain admittance," she said with a smirk. "With my promising new apprentice in tow, of course."

That caught me off guard. I had known Mrs. Crowe for years. Had she been working directly for the king all this time? If so, she had hidden it well—how much could I truly trust her? Then again, the way she'd reacted to the news of Syra's death had not been an act. I truly believed she had been coerced into helping the Crown. It was a risk, but going into the keep alone would be suicide.

"I'm in."

"Excellent," she said. "Let's make some potions."

"Like old times," I said.

Mrs. Crowe grunted.

We hovered over the fire, ground herbs in the mortar, and mixed reagents. She helped me craft all my usual potions, like my fire and smoke bombs, but she made a few suggestions for additions and changes that improved them significantly.

"Be careful with these," she said as she handed me the vials. "They'll have a bit more kick than you're used to."

With my Emberbane, she crafted several vials of a potion she called Embercloak. "Not only will this get us past the null field, but it will also diminish its effects, making you harder to track. And each vial requires only a drop of your Emberbane."

I stashed two vials in my belt and downed a third in a single swig. The taste was bitter, but I quickly felt its effects rippling through my body. I let my Ember flow. I had never felt quite so connected to it. Everything was more visceral. My mind was sharper than ever, and my limbs begged for something to climb. Also, the oppressive null field that enveloped the entire town felt muted.

According to Mrs. Crowe, the effects would last no more than a couple of hours, and after that I'd have one hell of an Ember hangover, so speed was critical.

Mrs. Crowe also had another use for the Emberbane. She held up two vials, one purple and one green.

"For worst-case scenarios," she said. "Separately, they are inert. But if you mix them, it sets off a delayed chemical reaction. In about fifteen minutes...boom." She made an explosive gesture with her hands. "I call it my time-release bomb. Even this much can knock down an entire building." She let out a long breath, a distant look in her eyes. "Syra helped me come up with this."

Dressed in the robes of an alchemist's apprentice and with my belt stocked to the hilt with potions, I left the shop with Mrs. Crowe at my side. She had donned her finest robes, complete with golden ribbons that signaled her station. As we walked down the street on the way to the keep, people turned to look at us, whispering.

"We seem to be attracting attention," I said under my breath.

"It's been a while since I've been to the keep. It's bound to cause a stir."

"How long has it been?"

"Five years," Mrs. Crowe said flatly. "Had a bit of a falling out with the king."

I stared at her in shock. Mrs. Crowe knew the king? And they'd had a *falling out*? I was frankly surprised she was still alive. "Is that going to be a problem?"

She shrugged. "We'll see."

I suddenly got a lot more nervous about our plan. Was Mrs. Crowe a banished alchemist who was going to attract a lot of attention? But we had come to the entrance of the keep. It was too late to turn back now.

Royal Guards were stationed at the start of the long stone bridge that extended toward the keep. They took one look at Mrs. Crowe and snapped to attention as we passed.

The bridge itself was about ten feet across, and only a short lip at the edge prevented someone from falling to their death on the jagged rocks below.

Thornfell Keep rose before us. Its architecture was unique, to say the least. Many might call it garish, with its absurdly tall towers and overwrought design. Every detail was just a little too much, a reflection of a person who had endless wealth and surrounded himself only with sycophants.

As we approached the ornately carved front gates, they swung open seemingly by themselves. Every instinct told me that this place devoured people like me. I took a deep breath as we walked into the belly of the beast.

A crackle of electricity ran along my skin as we crossed the null field barrier. It was deeply disturbing, and I could only wonder what it would've felt like without the Embercloak potion. I hoped it hadn't caused Darion and Elena any pain as they had crossed it. Once inside the barrier, the feeling disappeared.

We entered a massive entry chamber with marble floors and soaring ceilings. A fountain with a statue of a siren spouting water dominated the middle. Impossibly long banners flowed down from the ceiling. Royal Guards in ceremonial outfits lined the room.

The moment we walked in, a young man with platinum-blond hair and a face that was almost too pretty walked up to us. He wore an impeccable outfit made of lavish silk adorned with peacock feathers.

"As I live and breathe, the legendary Elandra Crowe," he said with a plastered-on smile. "It's been too long. To what do we owe this pleasure?"

"Brannic Yule," Mrs. Crowe said. "It hasn't been long enough."

Brannic's smile faltered for only a moment, and then he turned his eyes to me, assessing my entire body with a look that made me squirm. "And who do we have here?"

"This is my apprentice, Fenwick. He'll be accompanying me."

"And what business do you have in the keep today?" Brannic asked Mrs. Crowe.

"My business is my own. But I am interested in the location of two 'guests' who arrived this morning—a young lady and a man."

"And why, pray tell, would I give you that information?" Brannic said, his voice still sweet but laced with venom.

"Let's just say there's a little detail you may not want the king finding out about, if you understand my meaning," Mrs. Crowe said.

Brannic's face blanched, and his smile disappeared. "You're ready to play that card now? There's no coming back from that."

"I am," Mrs. Crowe said, her voice deadly serious.

Brannic's eyes were like ice. "Very well. The girl is in the lower alchemy lab holding pen. The man is locked in the high spire."

Mrs. Crowe grunted and turned away. "Let's go," she said to me quietly.

"Oh, and Elandra," Brannic said in a frigid tone, "it's fortunate that you're here. We were about to summon you. Orlik Leonom wishes to see you. Now."

Chapter Forty-Six

The Escape

Orlik was here. In this very building. Breathing the same air as me. My skin prickled, and I clenched my fists so tightly that my nails dug into my palms.

I tried to keep my face neutral even as white-hot adrenaline and rage coursed through me. I probably failed, but it hardly mattered, since Brannic and Mrs. Crowe kept their eyes locked on each other. Brannic's mouth twisted into a wickedly smug smile, as if he'd just played the winning move in their game of political coercion. Mrs. Crowe's expression was blank.

She spun around and walked briskly toward a passageway, gesturing for me to follow her. "I'll see Orlik when I've finished my business," she barked as we walked out of the room.

Brannic's face twisted in rage. "Come back here! Guards, stop them!"

Mrs. Crowe ignored him and quickened her pace. She breezed past the guards without attracting so much as a look. They just glanced at each other and shrugged, keeping their eyes away from us. Apparently Mrs. Crowe cast a long shadow in the keep.

When we were down the corridor and out of earshot, Mrs. Crowe whispered, "Well, that complicates things. I didn't even know Orlik was here. We need to hurry."

Complicate was an understatement.

"You should know," I said, barely restraining my fury, "that if Orlik sees me, he'll recognize me, and it won't end well."

Mrs. Crowe shot me a look indicating that my standing with her had just improved. "Noted," she said with a half-smile.

We kept up a brisk pace, but not so fast as to arouse suspicion. At my request, Mrs. Crowe had drawn up a rough sketch of the keep's floor plan when we were back at her shop. We were headed to the east staircase that led to the lower alchemy chambers, where Elena was being held captive. We descended a wide spiral staircase with an open central shaft that seemed to extend upward and downward to infinity. Several levels down, we walked along a corridor lit by the same flameless candles I had seen in the Citadel Library. Soon we approached a door flanked by two Royal Guards holding halberds whose blades glimmered in the light, sharp and deadly. Mrs. Crowe attempted to walk past them, but the guards barred our entry with their weapons.

"Allow me to pass," Mrs. Crowe said, her voice full of authority.

"By order of the king, none may enter," one of the guards said, her voice firm.

"We'll see about that," Mrs. Crowe said. She turned as if to go, then slipped a vial from her belt and flicked it open. She gave me a look of warning, then spun around and placed the vial under the nose of the closest guard before the guard could react. She instantly crumpled into a heap on the ground.

The other guard turned, ready to attack, but I had already flanked him and punched him hard in the kidney. It was just enough of a distraction for Mrs. Crowe to place the vial under his nose.

As the second guard crumpled, I turned to Mrs. Crowe. "You'll have to give me the recipe for that one."

She nodded. "That'll last about twenty minutes. Now we *really* need to hurry."

We entered an alchemy lab that looked very similar to the one I'd seen in Pyrehold, only everything here looked newer and more elaborate. Potions bubbled, and an acrid smell hung in the air. Luckily, only a single alchemist was inside, working on an experiment.

He looked up as we approached. "Elandra! Well, this is a surprise."

Another swipe of the vial, and the alchemist crumpled to the floor.

We ran to a door in the back of the room. Inside was a row of cells. All were vacant except one. Elena lay on the ground, pale and still as the dead.

"Elena!" I cried as I raced to my sister's cell.

I pulled out my lockpicks and had the cell open in record time—the Embercloak potion heightened absolutely everything, down to my fine motor skills. I threw the door open and ran to my sister's side. She was warm to the touch, and the slightest breaths escaped her lips.

"She's likely still impacted by the null field," Mrs. Crowe said. "The Embercloak potion should help."

I gently sat her up and brought the vial of Embercloak to her lips, pouring the slightest bit into her mouth. Her throat bobbed reflexively as I administered the vial's contents. It took a few moments, but soon the blood returned to her cheeks and her eyes fluttered open.

"Cas. Is it really you?" she said, still a bit dreamy.

"It's me."

"How did you find me?"

"It's a very long story," I said as I hugged her.

"Ouch," she cried as I squeezed her tight.

I pulled away in a flash. "Are you hurt?"

"Bruised ribs and a few scrapes. That's about it." Her voice sounded stronger and clearer by the moment. "When we entered the keep, it felt like a sledgehammer hit me. That's the last thing I remember."

"That was the null field," I told her. "The potion I gave you will protect you from it."

"Not to interrupt this touching reunion," Mrs. Crowe said, "but we need to hurry."

"Do you think you can stand?" I asked Elena.

"Yeah, I'm feeling pretty good. My head's clear now. Like the pressure's gone."

I helped her to her feet, but she did most of the work on her own.

We ran out of the lab, pausing only to strip the robes from the alchemist on the floor. They were too big for Elena, but they would have to do. As we approached the staircase, Mrs. Crowe headed for the steps leading down.

"Wait," I said. "We need to get Elena out. Where are we going?"

"A slight change of plans," Mrs. Crowe said as she continued down the stairs. "My entrance was a bit more dramatic than I expected. The guards will never let us just walk out the door as I had hoped. Even now, I'm guessing Brannic is raising the alarm. We need to take an alternate exit."

"I thought there weren't alternate exits," I said.

"There's *always* an alternate exit," Mrs. Crowe said with a sly smile.

"Is it safe?" I asked.

"Perfectly. Only the king and his personal guard know about it. It's not even guarded so as not to attract attention. I found out about it...by accident. It's a longer story than I have time for."

We left the staircase and navigated a literal maze of twisting tunnels. Mrs. Crowe explained that it was a defense mechanism; if an enemy was pursuing the king, the pursuers could easily get lost. Countless doors lined every wall. Occasionally we entered one that led to another tunnel. Finally Mrs. Crowe stopped at a door that looked like every other one we'd passed.

"Through this door is a tunnel that leads under the sea," Mrs. Crowe said. "Inside is a series of doors. As you open each one, seawater will flood the previous corridor. You must go through each door and shut it quickly. Don't stop for anything."

Elena's face paled, eyes wide.

Mrs. Crowe pulled out a key and handed it to Elena. "The tunnel ends in a vacant house in town. Two blocks south, you'll find my potion shop. Here's the key. Wait for us there."

"Us?" Elena looked at me in shock, gripping the key tight enough to make her fingers go white. "Aren't you coming with me, Cas?"

"Darion is still here," I said.

"Then I'm coming with you to find him! I can help!"

I expected this and was ready for it. "You can't," I said. "The guards will recognize you immediately."

Elena's face crumpled. I pulled her into an embrace.

"I have to come," she said, a tear streaking down her face. "I can't lose you."

"I'll be back soon," I said. "I promise." I hated making promises I wasn't sure I could keep, but Elena's safety was more important than anything.

"You'd better," she said.

Horns blared in the distance.

"The alarm," Mrs. Crowe said. "They're on to us. We must hurry."

"Go," I said to Elena. "I'll meet you in the shop in no time."

She gave me one more heartbreaking look, then turned around and ran—it nearly broke me.

When she was out of earshot, Mrs. Crowe said, "This is your last chance to leave with your sister. Your odds of rescuing your friend in the spire are slim."

"I have to try," I said, remembering all the sacrifices he'd made for me.

"He must mean a lot to you."

"More than I can express."

Chapter Forty-Seven

The High Spire

With horns blaring and the guards on high alert, we had to move more cautiously. The pace was *killing* me. We stopped at each intersection, listening for footsteps. All I could think of, all I wanted, was to get to Darion.

"Now that all the guards are crawling around, there's no way we can just go up the central staircase to get to the high spire," Mrs. Crowe said. "But there's another way: the service elevator."

"I've climbed up elevator shafts before."

"You won't be able to climb up this one," Mrs. Crowe said. When I shot her a skeptical look, she said, "You'll just have to see for yourself."

We raced down a long hallway lined with lavish oil paintings. As I ran, one particular painting caught my eye—a scene from over two hundred years ago. Queen Amara stood proudly in front of a sapling that would one day be the Bleeding Oak. Beside her stood her shadowlynx, a massive feline with glossy black fur, large white fangs, and golden eyes. I had never seen the queen depicted in the lush colors of oil paint. Her fire-red hair cascaded over her shoulders.

"We must hurry!" Mrs. Crowe said.

At the end of the hallway was a room that was hard for me to fathom. I had never experienced such an immense indoor space. A massive staircase wound up the middle, climbing more than a dozen stories. Walkways spidered out from the stairs to the far walls, which were lined with a myriad of balconies and doors. How was this building even standing?

And then we reached the service elevator, and I understood. There was no shaft to climb. The entire elevator was just a carriage topped with wire mesh, suspended by a rope. It ran on a track heading up this monstrosity of a room. The rope looked impossibly thin. Could that thing even hold me?

Mrs. Crowe saw my skeptical look. "Braided rope made from Vanara silk. It can carry the weight of a hundred men. No time to waste," she said as she opened the door.

I was more than a bit doubtful, but as Mrs. Crowe had said, we had precious little time. So I swallowed hard and entered the carriage. On one side was a brass control panel with a numbered dial. She set the dial to the number eighteen on the far right and pressed a button. Then she stepped out and shut the carriage door.

"Aren't you coming?" I asked.

She shook her head with the look of a woman facing her fate. "I have unfinished business."

The door made a latching sound, and the carriage started to rise. What powered it, I could not say. I had made it only a few stories up when a sickening voice echoed across the room.

"Elandra Crowe, I've been looking for you." Orlik Leonom walked directly toward her.

The cage hugged the outer wall of the chamber, rising slowly. I tried to open the carriage, but it wouldn't budge and had no visible locking mechanism. I instinctively reached for my dagger, but I soon realized the wire mesh that covered the cage was woven too tightly to fit anything through. Powerless, I shrank into the shadows and watched from above as Orlik approached Mrs. Crowe.

"Orlik, how may I be of assistance?" Mrs. Crowe said, her voice steady and calm.

Several Royal Guards gathered behind Orlik, who now stood face-to-face with Mrs. Crowe.

"A curious thing, you coming back today of all days," Orlik said with cold indifference. "The day after Syra died."

Mrs. Crowe barely moved, but her jaw clenched.

"No reaction?" Orlik said, then nodded. "So you already knew."

The implication went unstated. With Syra dead, they had no power over Mrs. Crowe anymore. She had nothing left to lose. This was why Orlik had summoned her.

In a flash, she pulled out a hidden dagger and lunged toward Orlik. But he was lightning fast and was clearly anticipating this. He grabbed Mrs. Crowe's arm with one hand, and with the other, he slashed her throat with his own dagger.

I had to cover my mouth to keep from crying out.

Mrs. Crowe staggered back, grabbing at her throat as blood poured out.

Orlik simply shook his head and turned away. "A waste of a good mind."

My nails bit into my palms hard enough to draw blood. I would remember this moment for the rest of my life.

Mrs. Crowe fell to her knees. But then she reached for two vials in her belt. They were purple and green.

The time-release bomb.

She made her best effort to throw the vials all the way to where Orlik stood, but her hands were slick with blood, and they fell well short. Even so, the vials shattered, the liquid inside mixing on the floor. The combined contents immediately began to smoke, giving off a particularly acrid odor.

Orlik spun around and took one look at the smoking liquid, and his eyes went wide with recognition and terror. "Sound the alarm! Evacuate the keep! We have only minutes!"

Horns blared. From my steadily rising perch, I witnessed utter chaos as people poured out of doors everywhere and raced for the central staircase.

The elevator rose for what felt like an excruciatingly long time, which left me alone with my thoughts. Memories of Mrs. Crowe flooded my mind. For a heartbeat, I saw her teaching me how to grind herbs, her watchful eye never straying. I couldn't believe the sacrifice she had made, and yet, Orlik had still escaped. I would add hers to the list of lives for which I would hold Orlik accountable.

Finally, the elevator stopped at the top of the keep. The cage door clanked. I tested it, and it opened without effort onto a balcony, one side extending to the central staircase and the other to a hallway. As I hurried down the hallway, I couldn't help but notice how opulent everything was, from the wool rugs covering the floors to the hardwood doors with golden knobs. This looked more like a nobleman's house than a prison.

A door at the end of the hallway was ajar. I made my way to the opening, pressed my body up against the wall, and peeked through the crack. The room was shrouded in shadows, so I slipped inside to get a better look. This didn't look like a prison cell. It looked like a chamber fit for a prince with a stylish wooden dresser, a desk, and an elaborate bed.

Lying on the bed was a figure I recognized instantly. I raced to Darion's side. He was unconscious, looking just like Elena had. Oddly, he wasn't even chained. I took my last vial of Embercloak, gently brought it to his lips, and dribbled it into his mouth. Before long, Darion blinked his eyes open.

"Am I dreaming?" he said with a slight wobble in his voice.

I shut him up with a kiss.

"I guess not," he said with a smile.

"Can you get up?" I asked. "We have to go."

"I think so." Darion sat up and immediately tilted to the side. "Oh, maybe not."

"Here, let me help you," I said as I put his arm around my shoulders.

Together we stood and slowly made our way to the door. I was so distracted that I didn't even see the figure that had entered the room. When I finally looked up, Orlik "The Butcher" Leonom was staring at Darion and me with disgust.

Without a moment's hesitation, I drew my dagger from my tunic and threw it right at The Butcher's head. But halfway to its mark, the blade stopped in midair. Orlik's hand was raised, his fingers spread out toward me. A golden light and a crackling sound came from the ring on his finger, which also began wafting the smell of ozone and citrus.

Before I could react, my body went rigid, locked in place. This seemed to be the same Ember that Caldren had used to stop Syra. But Orlik wasn't Emberborn, and the null field still buzzed around us.

Without my support, Darion wobbled and fell against my side.

"So, this is the mighty Cassian Nightbrook," Orlik said in a wicked, mocking tone. "For some reason, I expected more. I bet you don't even know what you are, do you—or what your sister is?"

What did he mean—what we were? Something burned in my chest, feral and furious. I couldn't say all the profanities I wanted to yell back with my jaw locked in place.

"You like my little creation?" Orlik said, admiring his ring. "All that Ember the null field collects has to be redirected somewhere. Some of it turns to Emberbane. The rest"—he flexed his fingers—"comes to me."

Darion pushed himself upright, swaying once, then steadying. He looked between Orlik and me as if calculating his next move. What in all the hells was he doing?

"Feeling better, son?" Orlik said.

"Yes, Father," Darion said in that cool voice that made my skin crawl.

"What *precisely* was happening here before I arrived?" Orlik asked, his hawklike eyes on Darion.

"This man was trying to kidnap me, I assume," Darion said in such a detached tone that it turned my blood to ice. This couldn't be happening. Not again.

"I see. Do me a favor—take that dagger and stab him in the heart," Orlik said, as simply as if he were ordering a pint of ale.

Without hesitating, Darion took the blade that was hovering in the air.

He turned to me and slowly raised the dagger toward my heart.

But I could see his true nature in his eyes. I trusted this man with my life.

I wasn't scared. Not of him.

Darion spun around and threw the dagger right at Orlik, yelling, "Never call me your *son* again!"

With a simple twist of Orlik's hand, the blade stopped. Another gesture sent it hurtling back, stabbing Darion in the side. Blood soaked his tunic as he cried out—then fell silent, his body locking rigid.

I wanted to scream, but I could do nothing but watch.

"So predictable," Orlik said to Darion. "Bad blood from that bitch mother of yours. You're one of my biggest mistakes."

Orlik turned his gaze to me. He clenched his fist. The dagger ripped out of Darion, dripping with blood. The blade turned, pointing right at my heart.

"Goodbye, Mr. Nightbrook," Orlik said, his eyes as cold as ice.

Somewhere below, a massive explosion suddenly rocked the entire building. Mrs. Crowe's time-release bomb had finally gone off.

The null field wavered.

Darion and I fell to the ground, freed from Orlik's control for the moment. The dagger clattered to the floor in front of me. But I could already feel the null field returning and see the golden light shimmering around his ring.

In a single motion, I grabbed the dagger and flung it toward Orlik, aiming for his head. But he was wickedly fast and deflected the blade with a silver bracer on his wrist.

The moment he did, I drew the dagger strapped to my leg and sent it flying through the air. The knife hit its target, slicing two of Orlik's fingers clean off. The ring clattered to the floor and rolled under the bed, its power gone. Orlik cried out in pain as blood gushed from the wounds.

I drew my last blade to finish him, but just then the entire building shifted, knocking me to the floor. Dust and loose stones rained down from the ceiling. A large rock struck Orlik in the shoulder. His face, normally a monolith of detached cruelty, was now filled with terror. He steadied himself, then raced out of the room, leaving a trail of blood behind him.

When the shaking slowed, I jumped to my feet. I peered down the hallway where Orlik had escaped. I could chase him and finish the job.

But then I turned to Darion, who was lying on the floor, wounded, with an ever-growing pool of blood surrounding him.

In the end, there was no choice at all.

Chapter Forty-Eight

From The Ashes

I raced to Darion's side.

He was no longer the man who had deceived me. He was the man who had stayed and sacrificed everything.

Blood flowed from a gash to the left of his stomach. I ripped off a piece of bed linen and tied it around his waist. "Try to keep pressure on it."

He nodded with a grimace, hissing through his bared teeth.

I paused, wondering if I should look for Orlik's ring. But the shaking building and ever-growing red stain on Darion's side convinced me otherwise.

"C'mon, we have to go," I said, helping him to his feet, his arm around my shoulders. "Can you walk?"

Darion yelped as he shifted his stance. "Not very well."

His legs trembled, and for a moment, I thought he'd collapse. I tightened my grip and took more of his weight.

"We'll have to make do," I said.

We hobbled out of the room and down the hallway.

The building shook under our feet as we made our way across the balcony, heading for the central staircase. Sections of the walls crumbled. The king's banners were ablaze, as was nearly everything else flammable. The last remaining people poured out of the keep.

Darion stumbled, and I barely caught him. His tunic was stained red with far too much blood.

I looked down at the eighteen flights of twisting stairs we'd have to descend. It seemed impossible, but we began to make our way down as fast as we could. Balconies connecting the staircase to the building's sides crumbled before our eyes. The entire massive staircase began to shift.

Darion's breathing was labored. His face was pale. "Cas," he said faintly as his eyelids fluttered.

"Stay with me," I said, hating how desperate my voice sounded.

We still had halfway to go, but I wasn't sure if the staircase would stand for more than a few more seconds. And I wasn't sure if Darion could last, either.

One of the enormous banners on the side of the room farthest from the fire was still intact, billowing in the rising heat. The stairs beneath our feet began to give way. There was nowhere else to run.

I pulled out my dagger and said, "Put your arms around my neck."

Darion shook his head, understanding my desperate plan. "It will never work."

"No time to argue!"

The moment Darion wrapped his arms around me, I kicked off the edge of the staircase with all my strength, leaping toward the banner with my dagger extended. The blade pierced the fabric, and we rode the banner down, clinging to the hilt for dear life as flames danced around us.

But Darion's weight was too much. My hand slipped on the hilt and we dropped like stones. I frantically grabbed at the banner with a raw, unbridled energy I'd never felt before. My nails dug into the fabric as a pain like all the hells combined burned at my fingertips, clawing the banner to shreds in long, parallel gouges. It was just enough to slow our fall. It shouldn't have worked—but somehow it did.

We still hit the stone floor hard, and Darion cried out in pain. His legs buckled beneath him, and he collapsed to the ground.

"We've almost made it," I cried. "Please, just a bit farther."

He nodded through his grimace. I got his arm around my shoulders again and lifted him up, and we continued on our way.

The floor and the surrounding walls where the bomb had gone off were simply gone, as if some giant had carved them out with a knife. Mrs. Crowe's lifeless body lay next to the hole. I choked back a sob.

As Darion and I left the hall, the entire central staircase toppled into the wall. The roof, impossibly far up, collapsed and tumbled toward the floor.

We hobbled through the main foyer that Mrs. Crowe and I had entered less than an hour before. A massive billow of dust and smoke cascaded out of the grand atrium we had just left. Only Darion, a few last survivors, and I made it out of the front gates and down the narrow bridge as the remaining structure crumbled behind us. The oppressive null field wavered, then dissipated completely.

All eyes were on the destruction. No one noticed two stragglers pushing through the crowd.

There was a deafening roar, then utter silence. Thornfell Keep was no more.

As we stumbled through the streets to Mrs. Crowe's shop, the dust and ash billowing around us made us cough. Darion's steps slowed, and his weight on me grew heavier with each passing block. His skin felt cold against my own.

Finally, Mrs. Crowe's shop stood before us. I stared at the door, knowing that if Elena wasn't there, it would break me in a way I couldn't fix. I pushed through, awaiting my fate.

Elena stood just inside. In a flash, my worry for her melted away, replaced with concern for Darion.

Instantly understanding, Elena raced to his side just as his legs gave way.

Darion lay on a bed in the back room, burning with fever and sleeping fitfully. I had cleaned his wound with antiseptic, sewn it up, and bound it as tight as I dared. That was everything I knew how to do. Now all we could do was wait.

I sat next to the bed, lightly clutching Darion's hand, listening to his labored breathing and counting the time between each rise of his chest. Elena hovered nearby, wiping the sweat from his brow and watching with quiet resolve. Her intense love for him was plain to see.

Much later, after my hand had grown numb from gripping his, Darion's breathing steadied. The worst of his bleeding had stopped, and the fever had passed.

Elena looked on, her eyelids heavy with fatigue. The hangover from the Embercloak potion was starting to take hold. It was hitting me too, as I struggled to keep my eyes open.

"Is he going to make it?" she asked.

"I think so," I said, sending her a reassuring smile.

I breathed in deeply, then lightly kissed Darion's forehead, relief flooding through me.

Outside, the sounds of chaos continued. Somewhere out there, The Butcher still drew breath. The Sentinels still hunted. The king's armies wouldn't stop until all Emberborn were dead or enslaved.

But something fundamental had changed within me. For the first time since my parents had died, I didn't feel as if I were standing against the world alone. Elena had grown strong and powerful. And Darion had chosen us—chosen me, even when it had cost him everything.

I leaned down, pressed my forehead to Darion's, and quietly made a promise.

Not to close myself off.

Not to seek vengeance in isolation.

Not to wage my battles alone without trusting others.

Whatever came next, I would both fight and love without letting one destroy the other. And this time, I wouldn't face the future alone.

I felt a warmth growing through me, similar to the feel of Ember, but different somehow. Wild. Primal. A flash of light caught my eye—a sudden shimmer from a dark window across the room. But then I realized I wasn't looking *through* the window. It was a reflection. My eyes were golden and glowing. And something else was off.

For just an instant, so brief I thought I imagined it, my pupils were thin and vertical. I blinked, and they were back to normal.

My heart sped up. I didn't move. I *couldn't* move.

The shredded banner. My burning nails. My *eyes*. Orlik's words replayed in my head. *I bet you don't even know what you are, do you?*

But I had no time to process that as the door to the shop burst open.

Looming in the doorway stood a familiar silhouette. Kael stepped into the shop, brandishing a sword.

Elena was on her feet instantly, blade drawn. I reached for my dagger, ready to strike, but the Embercloak hangover dragged at my limbs, making my moves sluggish.

"For all the gods' sake, stop!" Kael shouted, raising his hand, palm out. "Trust me or don't. But Sentinels are headed this way."

"How could we possibly trust you?" I snapped. "You kidnapped Elena. You attacked Darion. How do we know you're not a spy?"

"I've been trying to *protect* Elena from a spy in the Order," Kael said. "That's why I kept her from the rendezvous. I tried to tell you that before Darion attacked *me*."

"But why do you even care what happens to us?" I asked.

"Because the Crown desperately wants both of you. And I've seen the bounty orders."

Kael fixed his gaze on me. "They want you dead, Cassian."

Then he turned to Elena. "And they want *you* alive."

The sound of boots on stone came from outside, getting closer. There was only a moment to decide.

I had just made a promise to trust others. The first test of that promise had already arrived.

"Help me move Darion," I said. "We go together, or not at all."

To be continued...

The story of the Emberborn is only beginning...

The king still sits on the throne.
The Butcher still hunts.
And the truth hidden in a wishing well still waits to be revealed.

Some destinies are not chosen.
They awaken.

Continue the journey in Book Two of The Emberborn, coming soon.

For release news, bonus scenes, and secrets of the Order of Emberlight, go to https://pmwinters.com.

Appendix

This section contains dangerous secrets. Consider yourself warned.

Primary Characters

- **Cassian 'Cas' Nightbrook:** A twenty-one-year-old talented thief in the City of Analon, sworn to protect his little sister Elena.
- **Mrs. Crowe:** A potion merchant and friend of Cas, who helped him hone his potioncraft.
- **Darion Thorne:** A twenty-four-year-old man with a mysterious past. A member of the Order of Emberlight and a love interest of Cas.
- **Elena Nightbrook**: The fourteen-year-old sister of Cas. Strong and talented with a sword, she helps Cas operate the herb cart.
- **Garrick:** Crime boss and owner of the Charred Snake Tavern in the Wharf District, which operates as a front for Garrick's clandestine business.
- **Orlik 'The Butcher' Leonom**: The top lieutenant for King Tarnasau, known for his hatred of Emberborn.

- **Zephyra:** A whisperhawk and friend of Cas, who can telepathically communicate with him.

Secondary Characters

- **Adela Fenn:** A clock tender in the Citadel Clock Tower.
- **Brannic Yule:** King's assistant and steward of Thornfell Keep.
- **Caldren:** Head of the guard for the Order of Emberlight.
- **Corin Fenn:** Adela Fenn's son, who lives in the clock tower.
- **Master Solcor:** Master of the Citadel aviary.
- **Darrow Elkwright:** Council member for the Order of Emberlight.
- **Edric Fenn:** Adela Fenn's father and master of ledgers.
- **Jask:** First mate of Rook.
- **Kael Marrick:** Order of Emberlight council member and friend to Darion.
- **Mireth Averin:** High Steward of the Order of Emberlight.
- **Rook:** Smuggler and captain of the *Wind Runner*.
- **Sprocket:** Quartermaster for the Order of Emberlight.
- **Syra:** Bodyguard to Orlik. A Marrowbound Emberborn capable of shifting into a beast.
- **King Tarnasau**: The ruthless king of Velmorra who is driven

to eradicate all Emberborn.

- **Teon:** Bouncer for the Charred Snake.
- **Tobias:** Kitchen cook for the Order of Emberlight.
- **Verrin:** A warden of Pyrehold and Kael's contact.
- **Mrs. Yarrow:** Runs an orphanage. Raised Cas and Elena after their parents were killed.

Political Structure

- **The Crown:** The ruling authority of Velmorra under King Tarnasau.
- **The Royal Guard:** Elite soldiers loyal directly to the king.
- **Sentinels**: Specialized anti-Emberborn hunters with Veilsense and able to create null-fields.
- **Order of Emberlight:** A rebel group made up of Emberborn and Unkindled, dedicated to toppling the Tarnasau Dynasty.
- **The Council of Emberlight:** Leadership body governing the Order of Emberlight.
- **Queen Amara:** A beloved former monarch whose legacy symbolizes unity and resistance to tyranny.

Magic

- **Ember:** An energy that flows through Emberborn allowing them to activate their special abilities.

- **Ember (colloquial):** An Emberborn's special ability.
- **Emberbane**: A highly volatile and powerful substance containing distilled Ember. Prolonged exposure is corruptive and dangerous.
- **Emberborn**: A subspecies of humans born with special abilities called Embers that vary from person to person.
- **Embers**: The collective term for Emberborn special abilities.
- **Embersphere**: Ember that flows in the natural environment outside of Emberborn and can be drawn on to activate more powerful Embers.
- **Active Ember**: An Ember that requires drawing on Ember from the Embersphere, although it may have some innate aspects as well.
- **Innate Ember**: An Ember that doesn't require drawing power from the Embersphere. That ability is always active, unless the Emberborn actively suppresses it.
- **Null Field:** A suppressive field generated by Sentinels that weakens or incapacitates Emberborn and allows Ember to be harvested or redirected.
- **Unkindled:** Non-Emberborn humans. The majority population of Velmorra.

Embers (non-exhaustive)

Most Emberborn possess one dominant Ember and some have minor innate ones.

- **Clawsong (innate):** Hear telepathic communications from certain animals.
- **Chronothene (active):** Sense and manipulate time. Can slow time for everyone, for everyone except the user, and in rare cases extend the effect to others.
- **Embermneme (innate):** Retain and recall visual information instantly.
- **Marrowbound (active):** Transform into another form, often with enhanced abilities.
- **Spinescale (innate):** Superior dexterity and climbing ability.
- **Stillbind (active):** Manipulate the physical actions of others.
- **Stryn (active):** Draw on great strength.
- **Veilsense (innate):** Sense Ember flowing through other Emberborn. Often manifests golden shimmering, and the smell of ozone and citrus.
- **Windspirit (active):** Run very fast.

Creatures

- **Bone Rat:** Aggressive subterranean rodent rumored to share a hive-mind awareness.

- **Shadowlynx:** Rare and powerful feline predator, known for its black coat and golden eyes.
- **Vanara Spider:** Large silk-producing arachnid whose threads rival chain mail.
- **Whisperhawk:** Highly intelligent avian capable of telepathic communication with select Emberborn.

Things

- **Bells:** Bells ring six times a day, approximately 4 hours apart, with the sixth bell being in the middle of the night, signaling the new day.
- **Half Bell:** Approximately two hours.
- **Quarter Bell:** Approximately one hour.
- **Goldvein Root:** A key ingredient in many potions, known for its healing properties.
- **Night Willow:** A willow tree that only grows in the light of phosphorescent moss in the Underworld.
- **Vanara Silk:** A silk spun from the Vanara Spiders, rivaling chain mail in puncture resistance.
- **Wildwood Sap:** Extremely sticky sap from the Wildwood tree.
- **Wind Runner:** A fast smuggling ship owned by Rook.

Analon Districts

- **Barracks District:** Brothels, barracks, and bars. Home to soldiers, mercenaries, and the Royal Guard.

- **Garden District**: The wealthiest district in Analon, home to the rich and powerful. Contains many nicer homes and sprawling estates.

- **Industrial District**: Grimy part of the city, containing the city's hard industry, factories, and prisons.

- **Merchant District**: Contains many of the city's permanent shops and is also home to many craftspeople and lesser merchants.

- **Monument District:** Contains the city's tombs and cemeteries and many modest homes.

- **Palace District**: Home to the Gold Palace and many of the supporting buildings. Contains many of the buildings required to run the palace and is home to many of noble birth.

- **Temple District**: Home to temples, clergy, and many of the city's residents who have just enough wealth to move out of the Wharf District.

- **Wharf District**: A largely run-down part of the city, but the hub of all nautical commerce and home to many of the city's poorer residents, as well as sailors and fishermen.

Analon Places of Interest

- **Bleeding Oak**: A 200-year-old oak tree planted to commemorate the birth of Queen Amara. Located in the middle of the Citadel Gardens.
- **Cas's House**: A barn and loft where Cas and his sister Elena live.
- **Catacombs:** Miles of catacombs stretching under Analon, home to bone rats.
- **The Cellars**: Ancient cellars below the Order of Emberlight headquarters, once part of the Ember Chapel.
- **Charred Snake**: A run-down but bustling tavern in the Wharf District, owned by Garrick.
- **Citadel Library/Clock Tower**: A massive library and clock tower, it's the hub of learning and innovation of Analon. The tallest and largest building in Analon.
- **Citadel Market**: A sprawling market housing every imaginable shop. The largest in the city.
- **The Ember Chapel**: Once a grand chapel of the Emberborn, it now lies in ruins.
- **The Gold Palace**: A massive palace backed up to the city walls and the mountain range behind it. The King's seat of power in Analon.
- **King's Grace Temple**: A classic Gothic temple, and the largest in the city of Analon.

- **The Lantern Mile:** The main thoroughfare of the Underworld Market.
- **The Ledger Hall**: Large stone building housing a city bank, records, merchant guilds, and many other commerce-related activities.
- **Old Grove**: One of the last undeveloped spots in the city, a grove of ancient trees.
- **Order of Emberlight Headquarters:** The headquarters for the rebel group, the Order of Emberlight, located within the maze-like Underworld.
- **Pyrehold:** A notorious prison, large and imposing with four smokestacks on top. Rumored to be home to medical experiments on prisoners.
- **Saltworks Row**: A row of shops and businesses catering to the city wharf, including fish processing, warehouses, nautical supplies, and taverns.
- **Queen Amara's Tomb**: Housed at the top of the hill in the King's Rest Cemetery is the elaborate tomb of the beloved Queen Amara.
- **Queen's Causeway**: A wide and grand street that runs from the Gold Palace to the Citadel Gardens.
- **River of Souls:** An underground river connecting the Royal Tomb to Analon Bay.
- **Royal Guard Barracks**: A complex of barracks housing the notorious Royal Guard.

- **The Underworld:** A sprawling under-city formed when the city was rebuilt on top of the ruins of a great fire. Claimed by thieves and home to the Underworld Market and Lantern Mile.
- **The Underworld Market:** A large market in the Underworld, catering to thieves and mercenaries.

Velmorra Places of Interest

- **Analon**: The sprawling capital city of Velmorra. A city of contrasts with many wonders and privileged people, but with a strong class divide and rife with evil and corruption.
- **Analon Bay:** A large bay east of Analon, critical for commerce.
- **Analon River:** A river that runs through the middle of Analon.
- **Bitterridge Keep**: An ancient keep, once a key defensive spot when Velmorra was split into southern and northern regions.
- **Brackmar:** A medium-sized port town, close to Analon. Handles much of the surplus business that Analon cannot handle.
- **Brinewatch:** The third-largest city in Southern Velmorra, it's the hub of nautical trade in the area.
- **Frostbreak**: A town just on the edge of the Everwinter Mountains, and the last stop before the trek to Northern Velmorra.
- **Grey Spit**: A smaller-sized port town.
- **Ironfall**: A city of industry, the second-largest city in Southern

Velmorra. Home to smelters processing the ore from the Rustspire Mountains.

- **Meadowrun:** An idyllic farming community.
- **Redfield/Eastmire**: Farming communities, largely responsible for the food production of Velmorra.
- **Shadowfen**: A small town centered around a keep largely exists for defensive purposes.
- **Titan's Span:** An ancient bridge spanning a chasm, north of Bitterridge Keep.
- **Thornfell:** A town that exists simply to serve Thornfell Keep. Clean, functional, and oppressive.
- **Thornfell Keep:** A tall, lavish, grotesque private citadel to the king. It's built on a small island just off the mainland, with a single bridge connecting it.

Acknowledgements

Since my mother first read *The Hobbit* to me as a child, fantasy has held a special place in my heart. I'll never forget her amazing Gollum impression. "What does he have in his pocketses?" is a line that will always fill me with tremendous nostalgia. It felt only natural, then, to blend my love of queer romantic speculative fiction with one of my greatest passions: fantasy. And so, *Embers of Analon* was born.

Of all my books, this one took the longest to write. I began it *before* I even started writing *The Haunting Between Us.* It went through several iterations, POV shifts, character shifts, and countless revisions until I finally found what resonated with me. I hope the journey was worth it, and that you enjoyed Cas's adventure and will join him again in Book Two of the series.

Of course, I'd like to thank my mom for all the reasons above, as well as for being a wonderful and loving parent who always encouraged my creative side. I love you, Mom. Thanks to Dad for being a big fan and inspiring me to be a writer.

I'd like to thank my early beta readers: my sister Jennifer, my friend Andy, and my author friend Kit Vincent. The book wouldn't be what it is without your thoughtful feedback. I'd also like to thank my entire queer writing group for their insight and encouragement.

Thanks to my editors Chris Barcellona, Alison Cherry, and Arianne Cruz for taking my messy writing and helping to craft it into a coherent, readable book.

Thanks to Cynthia Sheppard for bringing Cas and Darion to life in a stunning illustration.

Thanks to my husband, Peter, for all his love and support, and to my cats, Oreo and Minou, for helping to keep my lap warm during many late-night writing sessions.

Finally, thank you, the reader, for helping to keep my writing dreams alive.

About the author

Paul is a lifelong creative writer whose life is filled with queer joy. His passion is to spread that joy through storytelling, writing books where you might not typically see queer characters. He lives in the Pacific Northwest with his husband and two tuxedo kitties and might have a slight addiction to reading queer fiction. But it's not a problem. He could stop any time he wanted. Honestly.

Email: paul@pmwinters.com
Facebook: www.facebook.com/paulmichaelwinters
Instagram, TikTok, Threads, Bluesky: @pmwintersauthor
Website: pmwinters.com

Also by Paul Michael Winters

The Haunting Between Us — A queer coming-of-age romance and ghost story. Cameron can't believe the boy of his dreams just moved into the house of his nightmares.

Together in a Broken World — A queer post-apocalyptic romance adventure. Two boys fall in love in a deadly world, but it's the secrets they keep that might kill them.

www.ingramcontent.com/pod-product-compliance
Lightning Source LLC
Chambersburg PA
CBHW011658030726
47579CB00043B/480